Snake Oil Bullet

Harmony Black, Book Eight

Craig Schaefer

910-691-3333

Demimonde Books

Contents

The Story So Far

Originally created by the courts of hell as a deniable, expendable catspaw to swipe at their enemies, Vigilant Lock has been reborn as America's last line of defense against supernatural threats. It's a shadow agency that answers only to itself and its "Commercial Sponsors," a panel of political and military officials who quietly fund the covert team's operations.

They aren't hunting alone. A rival agency, Majestic-12, is on the trail of interdimensional invaders. Aliens walk among us, but they're not from outer space; they're from the parallel worlds next door, and they do not come in peace.

Harmony Black, Vigilant's top agent, is one of those aliens. Technically.

Her last mission, when she and her partner Jessie Temple helped to recover the corpse of an alien scout and stave off a lethal plague, sparked a discovery: Harmony's great-great-grandmother, the first witch of her family line, was a refugee from another Earth. While Harmony is human in every way that counts, a clash of cosmic energy has sent her powers spinning out of control, transforming them into something twisted and dangerous.

Tracing her family tree back to its roots offers the best hope of survival, but Vigilant's work won't wait, especially with the demoness Nadine — Harmony's long-time nemesis — locked in a cage. Nadine's cult, the fanatic and murderous House of Dead Roses, is desperate to get its mistress back.

They'll have to find her first. Vigilant is a submarine, running low and silent beneath the waves as they take down their targets before slipping away without a trace. But the midnight ocean is vast, and there are leviathans in the water.

Chapter One

The maintenance hatch rattled open on rusted hinges and a bitter wind gusted in. The icy flurry was strong enough to push Harmony back a step, buffeting her with frozen punches and drawing razors along her cheeks. It was the kind of cold that tore the breath from your throat and turned your lungs to burning stones. She pushed through the pain and stepped out onto the long, flat, dirty-gray platform, staring out over the glimmering lights of a metropolis at midnight.

She was on the roof of the Inland Steel building, three hundred and thirty-three feet above the streets of downtown Chicago, and bad weather was the least of her problems tonight.

"For the record," she said, lugging a heavy nylon duffel bag to the far edge of the roof, "there is no part of this plan that I don't hate."

Jessie Temple was Harmony's taller, leaner, darker twin tonight. Both of them wore black jumpsuits and sturdy climbing harnesses, their eyes sheathed behind military-grade goggles with lenses tinted like smoked jade. Jessie swung the maintenance hatch shut and crouched over it, pouring a thin vial of clear, syrupy liquid into the lock.

A wisp of acrid smoke rose from the melted guts of the keyhole, then tore away in another bracing gust of night wind. Nobody would be following them up here. They'd also cut off their only escape back into the building, but that was all right.

They had another way down.

"Where's your sense of adventure?" Jessie asked. Her duffel clanked as it hit the rooftop next to Harmony's.

"I must have left it back in the lobby."

The duffel's zipper slid back. Jessie pulled out a pair of stout black steel tubes, flipping them in her tactical-gloved hands, finding a thread and screwing them together with practiced ease. Harmony took a knee at the rooftop's edge and lifted a monocular to her left eye. It was a Swarovski STS spotting scope, a sleek tube with a kink at one end and a bend that nestled in her grip. She trained its eye north, across the span of the Chicago River and its stout drawbridges forged from brick-red steel, to the towering slab of the Merchandise Mart. The Mart was an art deco monolith, shining against the darkness as lights in its corner towers blazed upward to ignite the city skyline.

Harmony's breath puffed out in a mist, washing across the eye of her scope as she scanned the eighteen-story facade. Something fast flicked across her vision, a gnat at this distance, powered by four silent rotors as it swept downward.

"Drone is up," Kevin said over her earpiece. Jessie nodded, hearing the same message as she finished threading the tubes together.

April's voice joined Kevin's, broadcasting from the *Imperator*, their mobile base of operations. The plane sat parked in a hangar at Midway International, ten miles southwest, but with eyes in the sky and a tap on the city's traffic cameras they could provide overwatch from on high.

Just in time, by the sound of it.

"We have movement west of you," April said, her voice a crisp Irish brogue. "Cams identified a Mercedes E-Class registered to one of our primary target's aliases. She isn't traveling alone. An SUV, a rental, is riding right on her bumper. Hard to get a look at the passengers from this angle but assume the worst. They just pulled into the Wolf Point parking garage, one block from the Merchandise Mart."

Jessie raised the long steel tube like a spear and drove it down with both hands, slamming its butt end into the concrete patio. Four jagged hooks whipped out as one, latching onto the concrete and digging in with a tooth-rattling impact as dust and chips of stone billowed away over the rooftop's edge.

She gave the tube an experimental wiggle. It stayed firm, fixed into place by its automatic pitons.

"Sure," she breathed. "Could be half a dozen shooters, give or take, and every one of 'em on a hair trigger tonight. Nice that all this prep work didn't go to waste. Secondary target on the scene?"

Kevin had the answer. "Confirmed. He went into the Mart forty-five minutes ago, alone, and I've got him on drone-cam. He's in a private showroom, east face, third and fourth windows, sixteenth floor."

Harmony squinted with her one open eye, training her scope lower. They could only see the south face from here, but that was enough to plan an angle of attack.

Jessie dipped back into her duffel bag. Her hands came out cradling a rifle, long and oddly wide, the pronged nose of a spear poking from its fat barrel.

"Harmony," she said, "dial me in. Let's see if he remembers us."

***

Earlier that day, the ridged steel deck of the *Imperator* had thrummed under Harmony's feet as she gripped a nylon cargo strap, rocking with the militarized cargo plane as it shuddered its way through a storm. They were somewhere in the sky over Pittsburgh, winging west through thunder. The video wall that dominated one side of the plane's belly, a dozen LED screens hanging over a long row of keyboards and communication banks, stood ready to deliver the mission briefing. April turned her wheelchair to face Harmony and Jessie, swiveling in place, and clicked a slender remote control.

They recognized the first picture on screen, a candid shot taken from a block away but locked in tight with a telephoto lens. It was a fastidious thin man in a turtleneck sweater under a white lab coat, his oddly pale cheeks rouged with artificial color. He wore Buddy Holly glasses and toted a fat hardcover book under one arm.

"Doctor Herbert West," April said, "Cook County coroner by day, scientist of the necromantic arts by night. Last survivor of the ill-fated Ardentis Solutions heist crew."

Not entirely accurate. Harmony and Jessie had infiltrated the gang along with Bette Novak, their counterpart from Majestic-12. Then again, considering they'd been there to ensure the heist failed, Harmony supposed it'd be pedantic to point that out.

"Not for lack of trying," Jessie said. "Didn't expect the dork to crawl out a bathroom window while we were dealing with the real threats."

April lowered her head, her bifocals low on her nose, and stared at Jessie over the steel rims.

"Don't underestimate him. West's unfathomable ego is his Achilles heel, but his boasts are all backed with genuine talent. There's a reason we don't have many necromancers on Vigilant's threat matrix. It's a staggeringly dangerous school of magic, and most would-be practitioners end up torn to pieces or devoured by their own creations. Kevin?"

Perched in a swivel chair over by his keyboard, Kevin rattled out a quick string of commands. Black screens lit up with transcripts, travel records, and sepia-tone student IDs.

"His early years are sketchy," Kevin said, "but he first showed up on Vigilant's radar when he was studying clinical medicine at the University of Bern in Switzerland. Something happened with one of his professors, and while I haven't been able to dig up all the salacious details, the professor got a closed-casket funeral and West was strongly encouraged to leave the country before the cops could come up with a reason to bust him for it. Probably the first and only time he's ever taken a hint."

Jessie sat in the jumpseat at Harmony's side, leaning in, her turquoise eyes shimmering inhumanly bright. "Where'd he land after that?"

"Providence, Rhode Island, where he finished his medical degree at Brown University. Then he made his way west to Chicago, where he hung out his shingle as a county coroner. Great job when you need a steady supply of corpses to experiment on. The second he slipped away from the chaos after the Ardentis heist, he called in his two minutes notice and vanished. We thought he'd fled the city entirely, until he popped back up on our radar two nights ago."

Harmony's gaze roved over the wall screens, her steel-trap mind snatching dates, details, burning them into place. Apprehending West hadn't been a top priority. They had bigger problems to tackle, especially with more than a few of their old foes still at large and making moves in the shadows. West was his own worst enemy, and unlike some of the monsters they crossed paths with he wasn't out to take over the world or prey on the innocent. He just wanted to find a cure for death — *Reasonable*, Harmony decided, *if unwise* — and pad his pockets in the process.

"What changed?" she asked. "We wouldn't be scrambling an op together on short notice without a good reason. I thought we agreed we could take our time with this one."

"This happened." Kevin rattled out another string of keystrokes. Half of the screens shifted to stark white text on black, text chained to blocks of machine code, other windows conjuring crypto-wallet transfer trails. "That close call must have scared him more than we thought. Looks like he's getting ready to tunnel underground for a while, and he's trying to line his wallet with a little nest egg before he disappears for good."

The Silk Road had been the crown jewel of the dark web for years until the FBI shut it down a decade ago. Dozens of imitators promptly sprouted up in its wake, like heads from a dying hydra. This was one of them. FindAnythingNow sounded innocuous, like some second-rate search engine, but Harmony knew it was a freewheeling vice market where drugs were the least dangerous thing on the menu. The locals traded in Bitcoin and poetry, talking around their wares with carefully veiled language. "Acid wash jeans" was code for a clean gun, with the waistband size a code for the caliber. A "ticket to Fresno" was a murder for hire. A "peach farmer" was looking to sell...she didn't like to think about that one.

She'd go scorched earth on the whole operation if she could, but it was a case of too many monsters, too few resources, too little time. Vigilant's remit was to tackle the crimes only they could handle: occult conspiracies, sorcerers drunk on power, demons on the rampage. Mundane crimes were somebody else's problem, had to be, though Harmony would happily work herself to the bone if it meant taking one more predator off the table.

Sometimes they had to let the small fry swim while they hunted bigger fish. West was a capable necromancer, but the people he hurt were already dead. Harmony thought he could keep for later.

April brandished a laser pointer, drawing her attention to a particular exchange on FindAnythingNow, circling it on the screen with a glowing red dot. The language was byzantine to the point of barely being English at all, laden with metaphor and dark implication, like a mobster muttering an extortion threat in Esperanto. But Harmony could follow the meaning just fine, and April confirmed it out loud.

"Herbert West," she said, "is looking to get into the bioweapon business, and he has a buyer. You're going to crash the party."

Chapter Two

A fresh pair of photographs blossomed on the left-hand screen. A mug shot, front and side profile, of a hard-eyed woman in her early forties. She wore her hair in a raven swoop on one side, shaved to the scalp on the other, and her nose and ears were a glittering constellation of silver piercings.

"Meet Mercury Blaise," Kevin said. "Not her real name, that one is lost in a sea of old aliases, but she's been on Interpol's radar for at least sixteen years."

Jessie lifted her chin and narrowed her eyes, scrutinizing the photo.

"West's buyer? I've never seen her mentioned in any of our threat briefings."

"That's because she doesn't move in occult circles," Kevin said. "Not until now. She's a hacker for hire and a security-penetration expert, and she's been connected with a dozen high-end tech heists from Dallas to Berlin."

More photographs, most of them taken from the bird's-eye view of a security camera, captured her walking through industrial halls with a masked gang in dark hoodies. She was draped in glossy black PVC and wore stiletto-heel boots, a fashion plate with a gun on her hip, the hook of her nose making Harmony think of a crow turned nightclub DJ. Kevin sighed.

"This, ladies, is what happens when someone grows up on a steady diet of cyberpunk sci-fi novels and the Matrix trilogy on repeat and decides to put their passions to work. Don't let the BDSM getup fool you. She's scary good at what she does and she commands top dollar."

He fell silent, giving them an expectant look. Harmony stared back, mute.

Jessie leaned over and stage-whispered, "He wants us to ask."

Harmony lifted one eyebrow, still silent.

"Go on." Jessie nudged her with an elbow. "You know he needs this."

She struggled not to roll her eyes as she asked, "Is she as good as you, Kevin?"

He beamed, elated, and thrust one finger upward. "She is *not*, because I've got her dead to rights. Night after tomorrow she's meeting with West to do business face to face, and yours truly has all the details."

Harmony was half there, half buried deep inside of herself, spinning the text on the screens into a word cloud in her mind's eye. Certain phrases popped out more than others, drawing her attention.

"A strong interest in dystopian fiction," she murmured. "Suggests she might have political motives. What do we know about her personal life?"

April nodded, grim. "I profiled her on that basis, but her track record suggests her ethics are…flexible at best, and an affectation at worst. She started out working exclusively for groups with extreme left-wing ideologies, but the days of the Red Brigades and the Weather Underground are far behind us. With that work drying up, she leaned more and more into corporate espionage. These days she'll steal anything that isn't nailed down and she doesn't care about her employer's motives as long as she gets paid. I believe adrenaline is her main drive. She's addicted to risk and the thrill of slipping out of danger unscathed. She's also not alone. Kevin?"

He brought up another mugshot on a screen neighboring the first. The man in the pictures was bare-chested and heroin-gaunt, with a long face and sunken, dead eyes, his neck and face a tapestry of cheap prison ink.

"Santiago Rodriguez," he said. "Another piece of work, and another bad guy who's never been on our radar until now because as far as we can tell, he's never come within a mile of a supernatural crime scene. He grew up in Tierra Caliente and fell in with the Jalisco New Generation cartel. He was a full-time *sicario* before he turned eighteen; they called him the 'Zeta eraser' for the number of cartel rivals he allegedly took out single-handedly. Hard to tell why he dipped, but it sounds like one of his bosses wanted him to take the fall for his own screwup."

"When you take the fall in a drug gang," Jessie reflected, "it usually means from a third-floor window with a wire noose around your neck."

Kevin cocked a finger gun at her. "Got it in one. Since then, he's been freelance muscle, hopping from city to city, keeping a low profile but doing a hell of a lot of damage. Murder for hire, breaking legs for loan sharks, whatever bleeds out and pays out at the same time."

"He's been running with Mercury for about a year," April added. "Profile-wise, he's a follower to the core: no personal initiative beyond survival, so he's faithful to whoever's paying his bills. Not that it makes him any less dangerous."

Kevin clicked his mouse. A new string of photographs erupted along the video wall. Blood spatter on white marble, a smeared crimson handprint on a glass revolving door. A stockinged foot, one slipper dangling from a pale white toe, poking out from behind a bullet-riddled reception desk.

"Last October," April said. "Belo Horizonte, Brazil. Mercury and Santiago raided the offices of VegaDyne, a tech startup hawking a revolutionary processor chip. They wanted the schematics. What they got was a silent alarm and a swift response from the local authorities. Santiago, by the account of a survivor who hid in a storage closet, went berserk and opened fire. He mowed down eight police officers and twelve unarmed office workers on his way out."

Kevin swiveled his chair to face Harmony and Jessie. "Not the first time, either. The only thing on Earth that scares Santiago is being arrested and deported back to Mexico. The cartel wants him dead, and they're willing to pay double if his executioner tortures him first. His prospects in prison are...not good. Mercury likes to run her heists smooth and bloodless, but this isn't the first time her partner's gone off like a volcano. The second he feels cornered, he goes for the gun. Worse, when they bring in mercenaries for heavier labor, they're his guys, not hers. A bunch of former *sicarios* looking for an easy payday, and if they have to kill for it they're A-OK with that."

Harmony pursed her lips, eyes narrowed as they focused on the wall of screens, locking details into her memory.

"The takedown has to be fast," she mused. "Lightning-fast. More importantly, in case anything goes wrong, it has to be isolated. No civilians."

Jessie glanced sidelong at her. She jolted in the rumble seat as the plane, muscling through the storm, hit another patch of rough air.

"Grab him at the airport, at customs?"

"Local flight," April said. "He and Mercury are already in-country, booked from LAX to O'Hare."

Jessie shrugged. "He still won't be expecting us."

Harmony's mind flickered through a dozen outcomes, a dozen approaches all ending in disaster.

"Too risky," she said. "These are experienced criminals who know the mercenary life inside and out. An average criminal wouldn't risk flying with a firearm, but we know there are a dozen ways to slip a gun past TSA. They know it too. If he opens fire in the middle of the airport it'll be a bloodbath."

Jessie nodded. "We hit the meet then. Take all three of these jerks off the table at the same time. Riskier for us, but we can handle it."

"I'm sure you can," April said, "but bear this in mind: the Merchandise Mart's main floor closes at the end of regular business hours, but the building is active twenty-four hours a day. There's a sizable security force and janitorial staff, and the upper floors feature a host of private showrooms that can be rented by interested parties. We believe that's where West is going to meet them."

"How do they handle after-hours traffic?" Jessie asked.

"There's a well-staffed security desk in the main lobby. Arrivals have to check in and out. Any commotion will draw a swift police response."

"I checked the timing," Kevin added. "If an alarm goes off at the Mart, Chicago PD responds in force within fifteen minutes."

And if that happens, Harmony thought, *a lot of innocent people are going to die.*

Jessie was smiling.

Harmony wasn't good at facial expressions. She knew from long experience, though, that Jessie had different kinds of smiles. There was the genuinely friendly kind, the *I'm going to tear your liver out with my teeth and eat it* kind, and the one Harmony liked least: the one her best friend wore when she had a truly dangerous idea.

"We'll let 'em walk right past security," Jessie said, "and rendezvous with West upstairs. Once they're isolated and away from the civvies, we take them down."

Kevin shook his head. "Security's tight. You won't be able to talk your way past the front desk without the risk of somebody calling it in, and we don't have time to set up a cover story."

Jessie turned, fixing Harmony with her faintly glowing turquoise eyes. Radioactive.

"We aren't going through the lobby. We're going *over* it."

***

The wind howled, bitter and cold, like hungry wraiths screaming through the concrete canyons of Chicago in search of warm blood. Harmony had one eye squeezed shut, the other fixed through the barrel of the Swarovski scope. She licked her index finger and held it up to the night sky, working a geometry problem in her head.

Jessie crouched beside her, spear-tipped rifle at her shoulder. "I'm dialed in for distance."

"Adjust your aim for windage...eight to ten MOA left."

Her partner's gloved finger caressed the matte-black trigger.

"Got it."

"Fire."

The rifle let out a bone-rattling clack as Jessie sent the payload flying like a Stinger missile. The sleek steel spear lanced out through the dark, sailing high and trailing a thumb-thick line of nylon mountaineering rope. The spool, hundreds of yards long, whipped from the guts of the open duffel bag as the spear drew it out like a strand of spider-silk.

The spearhead crashed through a darkened upper office window, the glass imploding. Harmony couldn't see it, but she knew on the other side — if the gear was working right, and that was a hefty *if* — the spearhead had sprouted its own set of pitons and buried itself in the office floor, locking it in place.

Jessie dropped the rifle and grabbed the nylon rope, cording it through the standing tripod and ratcheting it down tight with a hand-crank and a pair of reinforced clamps. The tether stretched from building to building, rooftop to window, three hundred feet above the merciless river and the ice-cold pavement below.

She gave the line a hard tug, then put all her body weight into it. The tripod didn't budge. The line stayed fixed, taut as sinew.

"I'll go first," Jessie said, slinging a tether over the zipline. A pair of carabiners locked it to her jumpsuit's harness. "Give me twenty seconds to clear the debris, then follow me across."

She took a running start, kicked her boots in the air at the rooftop's edge, and then she was gone. She sailed silently down the line, a shadow in the dark. Once she vanished from sight, Harmony took a deep breath, counting to twenty before she fixed another tether and a fresh pair of carabiners to her own harness.

You are experiencing an anxiety reaction related to a fear of heights, one of the most common and understandable human phobias, she told herself.

She peered over the edge of the skyscraper, straight down, and wished she hadn't. The yellow taxis looked like toys, the occasional pedestrian just a vague moving blot. She recalled an old joke, something to the effect of *it's not the falling that kills you, it's the landing.* She hadn't thought it was funny at the time. She didn't like it any better now.

Harmony triple-checked the tether, tested the line, and took another long, slow breath as she backed up to the tripod. No more delays. Clock was ticking. She willed her legs into motion, ran toward the edge, kicked off, and flew.

Chapter Three

The wind whistled in Harmony's ears as she sailed along the zipline, holding on for dear life as the street flew by thirty stories under her heels, then the dark rippling ribbon of the river, yawning to swallow her whole. There was a heart-lurching jolt as the line shivered, the cable starting to slip, a quarter-inch drop that felt like a death plunge. Then it tightened, holding fast as she cleared the river and whipped toward the shattered window in the belly of the granite behemoth on the other side.

She brought her knees up to her chest, eyes locked on target, sailed through the gap, and unclipped the tether. She fell, hitting her shoulder on fuzzy carpet and rolled, tumbling straight into Jessie's arms.

"Gotcha," she whispered, grabbing Harmony's glove and hauling her to her feet. Jessie brushed a bit of broken glass from her shoulder and peeled off her tactical goggles. Her eyes glowed faintly in the dark. "That was fun, right?"

"I am not prepared to answer that question, and neither is my stomach."

They were in a small office. Lights out, cheap wood-grain furniture, a door with a narrow slit of a window looking out onto a fifteenth-floor hallway. It smelled faintly of cigarettes, someone stealing guilty pleasures on the company clock. Harmony drew her sidearm, a Sig Sauer P320 in desert tan, and checked the magazine. Jessie did the same, then braced her weapon and reached for the brass door handle.

"Kevin," she murmured under her breath, "talk to me."

His response crackled over their earpieces. "Drone cam confirms Mercury, Santiago, and their entourage are in the building, making their way up now.

I tried to get eyes on the private showroom, but West pulled the blinds. He's definitely in there though. There is one weird thing."

"Just one?"

"They've got a guy in a wheelchair with 'em."

Harmony squinted. She and Jessie shared a glance.

"Say again?" Jessie said.

"Can't even try to get a facial scan at this distance. All I can tell is the subject looks male, and he's wearing big sunglasses and a Panama hat."

"At night?"

"Kevin," Harmony cut in, "is he pushing the chair himself?"

"Negative, one of their goons is rolling it in."

"That's not a person," Harmony said. "It's a fresh corpse. West is selling them his zombie juice. They want to see it work on a test subject before they hand over the cash. Providing their own cadaver cuts down on any potential trickery."

Jessie shrugged. "Either that, or this is a very weird sequel to *Weekend at Bernie's*. Okay. Let's give 'em a second to get settled and spread out. Then we'll slip upstairs and introduce ourselves."

"Engagement protocol?" Harmony already knew, but when they were about to go lethal she always wanted to double-check. To commit herself to the rough work ahead.

"Search and destroy, no warning shots, no second chances. I'm not cleaning up a pile of dead civilians tonight. Dead mercenaries I don't mind. They bought their ticket and signed up for this shit, same as we did."

They counted to thirty, shared a glance, and slipped out into the hallway. It was long and shadowed, most of the lights turned down for the night, just sparse rounded sconces lighting the way along a tiled hallway. The floor was freshly waxed, catching their hazy reflections in the puddles of light, and Harmony heard a floor waxer droning somewhere off to their left and around a bend. After-hours maintenance crew. They'd be the first people in danger if this situation slipped out of control. Harmony pointed a finger in the opposite direction. Jessie nodded and followed her lead.

"Remember," Kevin's voice crackled over their earpieces, "these guys are all from Santiago's old crew. They're professional killers."

"Anybody can call themselves a hitman," Jessie murmured, her Sig drawn and her finger parallel to the trigger. "The question is, are they any *good* at it?"

They were about to find out. Through the slit of a stairwell door, the glass reinforced with wire, Harmony made out a flicker of restless movement. One of the mercs had been posted to guard the landing. He was on his phone, thumbs talking for him, the barrel of a Glock jammed into the belt of his baggy jeans.

Harmony gestured for Jessie to hold back. Then she shoved open the stairwell door and flung it shut behind her, pushing as hard as the hydraulic door closer would let her. The merc looked up and scrambled for his gun as the phone fell from his hands, bursting its electronic guts on the concrete landing. She already had him framed in her sights, but she waited one fleeting second, letting him draw on her.

She pulled her trigger at the very second the stairwell door slammed shut. The tube of her sound suppressor spat once, a discreet cough muffled by the sound of the door. The merc crumpled with a slack jaw and a bloody crater between his eyes.

Jessie followed her in, taking point, both of them hustling up the concrete steps. Harmony reached out, tapping Jessie's left shoulder twice, letting her know she was in formation right on her heels. Her mind flickered back to her kill house training at Quantico. Another time, another life, but the lessons were engraved in her muscles and her reflexes. The cardinal rule of close-quarters combat: *Slow is smooth, and smooth is fast.* Move with purpose and control. Don't rush, but don't hesitate.

The door on sixteen rattled open. Another merc strode in, looked down, brought up a nasty little carbine, and Jessie shot him twice. He took a round to the heart, another punched into his lung like a brass cannonball, and he tumbled down the stairs until he rolled to a stop halfway down, broken and glassy-eyed.

Jessie held up a clenched fist. "Hold," she whispered. "That was too damn loud. Wait a second and let's see if anyone comes to check up on it."

Their earpieces woke up, washed with static.

"We've got activity on the parabolic mic," Kevin said. "You should hear this. Patching you in."

"—tablet right here," said a husky woman's voice. *Mercury*, Harmony thought. "If your magic juice checks out, I'm ready to transfer a quarter-million in Bitcoin. Before you know it, you'll be sipping cocktails on a beach in the land of no extraditions."

Herbert West's reedy voice she recognized. "It's not *magic*, it's science rooted in alchemy and certain esoteric occult principles which are woefully misunderstood by the inbred cretins who call themselves medical researchers these days—"

"I'll call it whatever you want if it works. If it doesn't, my boy Santiago here is going to take you apart with his bare hands. So. Ready to dazzle us with your brilliance?"

West cleared his throat. "Um. Certainly. I...see you brought your own cadaver. Unnecessary. I came with two fresh ones of my own."

"Yeah, but this is the guy we want brought back from the dead. Can you do it or not?"

Harmony and Jessie were inching up to the sixteenth-floor landing. No commotion, no footsteps; they were clear, for the moment. Harmony frowned. The audio feed had gone dead silent, just the rasp of West's labored breath. Finally he spoke again.

"Is that...who I think it is?"

Mercury chuckled. "The man himself. He just recently kicked the bucket, and his friends are paying me a lot of money to fix that woeful condition. He's still got some secrets in his noggin they haven't dug out yet. So. Can you do it, doc? Or does Santiago get a workout?"

Harmony and Jessie shared a quick glance, the same question in their eyes: *Who is the corpse in the wheelchair?*

A mercenary traced a lonely patrol in the corridor beyond the stairwell door. Jessie holstered her pistol. They were too close to the showroom for guns now, even with the sound suppressors. She slithered up behind him low and fast. A second later his eyes went wide as a ceramic stiletto punched through the side of his throat, twisting as she ripped it free. His shadow painted the wall in a spray of arterial blood as she eased him to the floor and left him in a spreading pool of scarlet.

They were just around the corner from the meet. Jessie checked and pulled back fast, leaning close to Harmony.

"Two guys stationed outside the double doors."

"How far?" Harmony breathed.

"Twenty feet. No chance we can get close enough to do this silently. Gonna have to storm it."

Harmony's brow furrowed. They only had audio from inside the private showroom, no video, no idea where anyone was standing or what was waiting on the other side of those tall, polished wooden doors.

She thought for a moment about waiting it out. The meet would end, eventually, and they could turn the hallway into a killing funnel. Then she factored in the impending "demonstration." She'd seen what West's zombies were capable of. They were mindless juggernauts with terrifying strength, and he was about to add another one to the ranks. The longer she and Jessie waited to act, the more dangerous the situation would get.

"On three," she whispered.

Jessie held up three fingers sheathed in a tactical glove and counted down. They rounded the bend as one, weapons high. The two mercs guarding the showroom wheeled, but they were too slow. A pair of pistols popped in the shadows, muzzle flares lighting up the hall with a string of muffled barks.

Harmony dumped her mag on the run, snatching a fresh one from her jumpsuit harness and slapping it into the Sig. Jessie leaped ahead of her, hitting the double doors with her shoulder and thundering through as they blasted open. Harmony had a split second, one sharp inhale, to scan the room and break it down into threats and firing lanes.

Mahogany fixtures, deep blue carpet, shades drawn all along the bank of windows, the only light gleaming from a pair of standing lamps with arcing brass necks. Two lumps laid out on gurneys under pristine white sheets — West's demo corpses — and the figure, now without his hat or glasses, slumped in the wheelchair. West stood beside the chair in a lab coat, raising a syringe of bubbling green fluid that shimmered with a phosphorus glow in the hazy light. Mercury Blaise, decked out in a floor-length coat of glossy black PVC, was off to his left. Santiago was off right, toward the back, a grizzled gunslinger with skin like beef jerky and a leather vest slung over his bare chest.

Harmony bracketed Santiago in her sights. Jessie took his partner.

"Keep your hands empty and where I can see them," Harmony snapped. She carefully sidestepped her way into the room, keeping her gun on Santiago but West in her peripheral vision just in case. She got closer to the motionless figure in the wheelchair. Then she froze.

Not possible. It must be, logically, I'm looking right at him, but—

Jessie caught her partner's hesitation. "Harm?"

She forced herself to tear her gaze away, focusing on Santiago before he could reach for the chromed revolver on his hip.

"Jessie," she said. "The body in the chair."

Jessie blinked. "Is that...?"

"It's Bobby Diehl."

Chapter Four

B obby Diehl had once been famous, wealthy, fawned over by the public and press alike. The billionaire tech giant wowed the world with gadget after gadget, from feather-light laptops to smart refrigerators. For a while his premier invention, the Diehlphone, was on track to eclipse Apple's market share.

Then it all came crashing down, thanks to Harmony and Jessie.

They had met the man behind the curtain. Diehl was a coke fiend and a murderous psychopath with a fetish for dressing up in Nazi costumes and indulging in recreational torture. His company was a giant smokescreen for his real innovations: remote-controlled zombie killers and occult-infused bioweapons that twisted people's bodies and minds into grotesque parodies of human life. Eventually he'd attracted the attention of the Network, who were all too eager to use his money and power to get a stronger foothold for themselves.

When Harmony thought back to the rogue's gallery of monsters they'd faced in the past, most of them had a method behind their madness. A reason. Judah Cranston aimed to return humanity to the sea, at the cost of billions of lives, to save the planet from dying. Erich Hausler, the Basilisk, was a lost boy with mommy issues desperate for the approval of his succubus mistress. Vigilant's enemies did terrible things and hurt innocent people, but there was always a motive, a core, a reason she could grasp.

Not Bobby. He just had a sickness in his soul, a darkness and a pain he wanted to infect the entire world with. He spread suffering for the sheer glee of it, and he never faced a consequence in his life until she and Jessie — unable to get close enough to take him out for good — settled for the next best thing and exposed him for a laundry list of financial crimes and tax violations. He was forced to go on the run, a fugitive with frozen assets, his bank accounts zeroed out in one fell swoop and his company yanked out from under him by his own board of directors. Even the Network abandoned him. They didn't like losers.

He'd been on the run ever since, running silent but at the top of Vigilant's kill list.

Apparently someone had done the job for them.

"Well," Dr. West said, still brandishing the bubbling syringe, "this is awkward."

Mercury glanced from the new arrivals to the doctor, one of her pale hands dangerously close to the flap of her coat. She didn't make a move. Not yet.

"I'm sorry, do you know these two bitches?"

"They...might be the reason I need cash to get out of town," West said, a bit sheepish.

"We weren't even looking for you," Jessie said, her voice flat.

Now he looked offended. "Of course you were. Such a transparent lie. I'm certain that finding me was your highest priority."

Harmony kept her gun on Santiago and pointed to the wheelchair with her free hand.

"No. *He* is. Or was. Who killed him? More importantly, who hired you to bring him back to life?"

Santiago pressed his chapped lips tight. He glanced at Mercury. She let out a long-suffering sigh.

"Nobody killed him," she said. "Natural causes, if you can believe that shit. As far as who hired me, that depends. How much is that intel worth to you? Clearly this deal's off, because Herbie here can't keep his business clean. I'd still like to get paid tonight."

"Could be worth your life," Jessie said.

"And I'm just gonna spill the beans and hope for mercy?" Mercury snickered. "I don't think so. Tell you what: you promise me and my boy passage out of here, and once we get to a safe distance I'll *call* you with the intel. We go our separate ways, and whatever business you have with my ex-bosses is just that: your business."

West tilted his head, looking like a confused puppy. "What about me?"

"You led a couple of glowies straight to us, dickweed. Whatever happens to you isn't my problem. Our business is done here."

Harmony played chess sometimes. She enjoyed the clean strategies, the lack of random chance, the fairness of the perfectly balanced armies. Every now and then an opponent would slip up, lose their focus and make an almost imperceptible mistake: tiny, but fatal for a rival with the eyes to see it.

"How did you know?" Harmony asked, her voice softer now.

Mercury squinted at her. "Know what?"

"You called us 'glowies.' That's slang, in certain conspiracy circles, for undercover government agents. But we're not wearing badges. We didn't declare ourselves. We could be a rival crew, rip-off artists, people out to settle a score with West, a dozen possibilities."

Mercury scoffed, trying to paper it over.

"You're wearing jumpsuits, harnesses, and tactical gear. You look like NSA black ops. Well, *you* look like a lesbian in denial, but I repeat myself. So: call up whoever you report to and tell 'em I'm willing to trade names for safe passage and a bit of financial compensation. I want to talk to your boss."

"Bad news," Jessie said. "I'm the boss. And considering we've got you dead to rights, you're not in a position to make demands."

"I don't think you can back that up," West said, his voice lilting into a mocking sing-song tone.

"How do you figure that?"

"Simple mathematics. You're outnumbered."

"Three against two?" Jessie sighted down her barrel at Mercury, lining up a kill-shot. "I'll take those odds."

"How about...five?"

Harmony had been watching West in the corner of her vision, waiting for a tell. She didn't think he even carried a gun, but she knew better than to underestimate the man. His hands had stayed high and relaxed since they barged in, nowhere near the buttons of his lab coat.

When he made his move, she barely caught it. He simply dipped his free hand down, snagged a thin chain around his neck with the bend of his thumb, and slipped something into his mouth. A silver whistle. His cheeks puffed up.

He blew into the whistle for all he was worth. Not a sound came out. Not one Harmony could hear at least. Jessie's face screwed up in pain and she dropped to one knee, fumbling her gun on the carpet as she clapped her hands to her ears. The starched sheets draped across the gurneys whipped away and a pair of naked, bloated dead men sat bolt upright, milky eyes snapping open, rivulets of drool running from torn lips and dangling jaws. One of the reanimated corpses looked like he'd been mangled in a car accident then stitched back together with sinew and string. The other's chest was peppered with gunshot wounds, his bloodless gut yellow around the scorch-pock craters.

Santiago took advantage of the moment of surprise. He whipped out his revolver and started blasting. Harmony threw herself to one side, hitting the floor and tumbling as a stray bullet blew off the head of a lamp, showering the carpet in broken glass and plunging half the private showroom into darkness.

Mercury just wanted to get out in one piece. She sprinted for the doors, pausing to kick Jessie's gun out of reach. She looked back to Santiago and shouted, "C'mon, let's *go!* The zombies'll finish the job!"

Kevin was in Harmony's ear, flustered: "What's going on in there? We've got no visual and our audio just fritzed out."

She didn't have time to answer, not with a bullet-riddled corpse bearing down on her, as Santiago ran past and slipped out the door in Mercury's wake. West was right behind them, the tail of his lab coat flaring at his back.

"Have fun, ladies," he snickered. Then the living corpse fell on top of Harmony, one bloodless knee digging into her belly, squeezing the breath out of her as his broken fingernails scrabbled for purchase around her neck.

Jessie stirred, still dazed from whatever West's whistle had done to her senses, and felt for her gun on the carpet. The car crash victim barreled at her like a linebacker, letting out an animal howl as he swept her up in his hairy arms and tried to crush her ribs with a bear hug. He swung her around like a rag doll and slammed her against the mahogany-paneled wall. The move might have crippled a human.

Jessie was more than human. And she loved to fight.

She brought her knees up, wedging between her and the zombie, wrenching the dead man's arms slowly apart as he lost his grip on her waist. She sprung free and used his belly for a kickboard, driving her heels in and flipping into an aerial somersault. She landed on her feet in a feral crouch and launched herself right back into the fray, clotheslining him with the flat of her forearm across the throat, the blow slamming him onto his back.

Harmony was losing air, her vision going fuzzy. She had an encyclopedia of aikido moves burned into her muscle memory, holds and escapes and last-ditch defenses, but none of them were meant to counter a creature that couldn't feel pain and would keep fighting until every bone in his body had shattered.

She used to have a mnemonic, a trigger phrase to call to her magic. She didn't need it now; her body already knew what she wanted. As she pressed her trembling palm to the dead man's cold and mottled chest, a terrible roaring hunger echoed up from the tunnel of her heart and slithered free, its jaws open wide to swallow the world.

Give me everything that you are. All of it.

She *pulled*, sucking down the death-magic that kept this unholy monster animated without a soul. It surged through her hand and up her arm in a stinging, biting torrent, the pain blinding Harmony as her mortal flesh struggled to contain a flood of toxic magic. The dim, animal light behind the zombie's eyes flickered out, and he slumped on top of her, dead weight.

Across from her, Jessie had the other corpse in a headlock. Vertebrae crackled and broke as she wrenched his neck to one side, then the other. Then she kept wrenching, twisting, as muscles tore and skin ripped, the dead man's feet helplessly hammering the carpet.

His head came off with a wet slurping pop. Jessie rose, her legs shaky, and tossed it into the corner of the room like a bowling ball.

Harmony was already on her feet, propelling herself toward the double doors. Hot on the trail of their trio of targets, but not just that. Her heart galloped, a vein on her brow pulsed, a sheen of burning sweat dripped from her pores. Death-magic was poison to the living, and her newfound powers didn't make her an exception to the rule.

"Harm, are you—"

"Have to get it out," she croaked.

She barreled into one of Santiago's men coming the opposite way with his gun up. She slapped the weapon aside, twisted his arm in a joint lock, and slammed her palm against the back of his neck. He didn't have time to scream. His body went taut, electrified, as she poured her stolen power straight into his spine. His skin turned fish-belly white, like a sudden frost riming his flesh, freezing his blood and turning his organs into shriveled, black, brittle fruit.

In seconds, nothing but an empty husk of a man remained. She let him fall. Jessie burst into the hall behind her and leaned against the wall while she caught her breath and dug for her second wind.

"Heads up," Kevin said. "Drone's got movement on the sidewalk. Mercury and Santiago are headed toward Wolf Point Plaza, probably making for the parking garage. West just poked his head out and now he's scurrying in the opposite direction."

"Cleanup crew scrambled and ready?" Jessie gasped.

"On your word, boss."

"Go. We've got two corpses in a stairwell, another three on sixteen, and a special guest."

"The man in the wheelchair?" April asked, cutting in on the line.

"It's Bobby Diehl. He's dead, and I want to know who, how, and why. I want his body brought back to the *Vigilant* and the scene sanitized." Jessie tossed Harmony a keyring, and she snatched it out of the air. "Get the Hemi and meet me."

Harmony nodded, sharp. "Where are you going?"

Jessie showed her teeth.

"I'm pretty fast on foot. West can dangle for another day, but those two are *not* getting away. Not tonight."

Chapter Five

D own in the parking garage, Santiago jumped behind the wheel of the Mercedes E-Class and fired up the engine. Mercury was right behind him, slapping the roof before she slammed the door shut on the passenger side.

"Time to get the fuck out of dodge. Drive. I'm calling the client."

Her burner was a prepaid phone with no bells, no whistles, just a single number saved. She tapped a button and listened to two rings and a click.

"Don't talk," Mercury said. "Just listen. Glowies got tricks and I want to be off this line in twenty seconds or less. One: they've got Diehl's corpse. Two: West used the whistle and it worked just like you said it would. Good shit. I didn't get a chance to deploy the flasher, we had to book it. That's all I got. Don't try to find me, I'll contact you at the usual drop point once we get clear. Send over the second half of my payment."

She rolled down the window, cold night wind gusting in as Santiago wheeled the Mercedes around and aimed for the exit gate. She opened the phone up, took out the SIM card, snapped it between her thumb and forefinger, and tossed the plastic bits out the window. Once the gate rolled up, opening onto West Wolf Point Plaza, Santiago hooked a hard right and pressed his foot hard on the gas.

They rolled straight past the Merchandise Mart, hearing the wails of sirens in the distance. Santiago asked a question in Spanish.

"Well, the weird shit goes with the territory," Mercury said. "Higher levels, bigger devils. We got out in one piece, didn't we?"

He gave her a sidelong look of distaste and held the wheel with one hand while crossing himself with the other.

"I don't hear you complaining about the paycheck," she told him.

There was a T-junction at the end of the next block and he feathered the brake pedal, slowing down for the red light. Then they heard the crash of a window just before a flurry of broken glass pelted the Mercedes like hailstones.

Jessie landed on the hood in a crouch, her turquoise eyes blazing as she glared at them through the windshield.

Mercury screamed. Santiago gritted his teeth and stomped on the gas, yanking the wheel hard enough to send Jessie sliding, almost throwing her from the car as the Mercedes veered south, lurching across a brick-iron drawbridge that spanned the Chicago River. Jessie reached for the gun on her hip, almost grabbed it, then had to latch on with both hands again as a sudden dip bucked her in the air and brought her back down hard enough to put another dent in the hood.

Even after midnight, Chicago traffic never rested. The intersection of North Wells and Upper Wacker Drive pulsed up ahead, bristling with yellow taxi cabs and late-night delivery trucks. Horns blared as the Mercedes ran the red light and took another hard turn, rolling east on a four-lane boulevard under the shadow of an elevated train track.

Headlights blazed in the rear-view mirror. A jet-black Hemi Cuda fired from a side street like a heat-seeking missile, tires screeching as it locked on to the Mercedes' rear bumper.

***

Harmony was behind the Hemi's wheel, a block behind but closing fast while the engine bellowed a lion roar. She swerved hard to get around a newspaper delivery van, then shifted lanes again to dodge an off-duty taxi, keeping her eyes locked on target.

"Kevin, we're eastbound and Jessie has mounted the enemy vehicle. I need you to keep the police out of our way. Do we have drone coverage of the traffic ahead?"

His voice crackled in her ear: "Give me one second to adjust trajectory and...wait, did you say *mounted?*"

"Unfortunately, I did."

***

Jessie clung on. Every time her hand neared her holstered pistol Santiago swerved, veering from one lane to the other and back again, throwing off her balance and forcing her to cling to the hood with both hands or risk being thrown to the pavement. The needle was kissing fifty and rising fast, with the Hemi Cuda closing the gap from behind.

Mercury didn't have the same problem. She whipped out her holdout gun, a palm-sized piece molded in transparent resin, cobbled together from a gun kit and a 3D-printed shell. A shattered windshield would be a red flag to every cop from here to LA, so she stuck her arm out the open window, turned her wrist, and snapped off a pair of shots.

Jessie rolled at the last second, twisting her body and dodging the whining bullets. Before Mercury could adjust her aim, she scrambled and climbed up onto the roof, vanishing from sight.

"Next time we get the goddamn moonroof option," Mercury growled. She pointed her gun straight up and fired, the sound inside the car like a bomb going off. The roof cratered and let in a shaft of cold moonlight. She shot two more rounds, her head throbbing and ears stinging, desperate for a lucky hit.

Santiago shouted something at her — his lips were moving but all she heard was a screaming bell — and gestured at his ears.

"Okay, okay, *fine,*" she shouted back, tossing the resin gun onto the floormat. "The whistle worked, so let's see if toy number two is any good."

Her hand dug into her glossy PVC coat and came out with a small beige plastic brick, about the size of a chocolate bar, one side lined with an array of dark LEDs. She grabbed the edge of the roof, hauled herself out, and used the windowsill as a seat.

Still on the roof, Jessie spun, locking eyes with Mercury and going for her gun. Mercury raised the box, pointed the LEDs squarely at Jessie's face, and flipped a toggle switch.

*　*　*

Harmony was right behind them now, ten feet back and gaining as the two cars barreled east along the boulevard. She watched Jessie scamper to one side and back to dodge Mercury's shots, moving like a spider. Then Mercury pulled herself through the window and pointed that gadget in her face and—

—the streetscape erupted with flickering light, an entire nightclub's worth of strobes packed into one tiny plastic box, bright enough to light up the skyscrapers on the far side of the river. Jessie went slack, losing her grip, tumbling backwards as her muscles seized up.

In Harmony's perception, time slowed to a leaden crawl. She saw Jessie start to fall, taken by momentum. In two seconds she'd plunge from the trunk of the Mercedes. In three she'd be under the Hemi's wheels, and even if Harmony swerved out of the way in time, even if the fall itself didn't kill her, the delivery truck in her rearview would finish the job.

This was a math problem. Instead of getting out of the way, Harmony stepped on the gas.

The Hemi's engine growled as she closed on the Mercedes and didn't stop, not until the two cars met with a jolting crash that slammed Harmony against her seatbelt and mashed both bumpers to chewing gum. The sudden burst of momentum took Jessie with it, tumbling her limp body onto the Hemi's hood. Harmony eased off as Santiago sped up, opening the asphalt between them once again.

Jessie was coming back to her senses. She grabbed onto the Hemi's hood and met Harmony's gaze through the windshield.

"Keep going," she groaned. "We can still catch them."

"Jessie, you're in no condition—"

"*Keep going.*"

They were approaching the DuSable Bridge. A barge was in the river waiting for passage. Amber lights strobed at the water's edge, and a brassy alarm bell began to clang, warning drivers to stop. Santiago wasn't going to. He veered left, pointing the Mercedes straight for the bridge even as the gates came down across the roadway.

The Mercedes hit the gate at full speed, blasting it from its mounting in a flurry of splintered wood, as the bridge began to rise.

"We can make it," Jessie shouted. "Trust me, we can make it!"

Harmony slowed as she made the turn, angling north, and watched the Mercedes leap across the spreading bridge and land on the other side with a metallic thump and a hail of sparks.

She had spent years training herself to believe that the mission was everything. The mission was worth more than her life. But this wasn't her life at stake. The car could make the jump, but if her momentum was wrong, if they came down too hard or the angle was too sharp, Jessie would be launched from the hood like a rag doll and end up at the bottom of the Chicago River, dead of hypothermia before they could fish her out.

No, she decided.

She leaned on the brakes. The Hemi fishtailed, leaving a smear of black rubber on the road, as she brought the car to a dead stop right at the edge of the bridge. It continued to rise, cutting off their last chance, as amber lights flashed in the dark and the warning bells chimed.

Jessie slumped against the windshield, battered and exhausted, breathless.

Chapter Six

"You should have made the jump," Jessie said in the passenger seat, sullen, her arms crossed tight across her belly.

They had driven most of the way back to O'Hare in silence. The highway was open and dark and smooth, the silence filled by the thrumming wheels and the occasional late-night jet winging into the overcast skies.

"You're injured—"

"I'm *fine.*"

"—and you were just hit with a weapon of unknown origin. You seem fine now, but in the heat of the moment I couldn't take that risk."

"Well, our only chance at finding out what that 'weapon of unknown origin' was, let alone who's paying good money to have Bobby Diehl brought back from the dead — oh, and where he's been all this time and what he's been scheming — just vanished in the wind. Good job, Harmony. Real good job."

The words stung, but she knew better than to take them personally. Harmony took a few deep breaths. "Are you angry at me because I didn't risk your life, or are you angry at yourself because you were taken by surprise twice tonight?"

Jessie didn't answer at first. She rode in silence, her luminous eyes a pair of ice-encrusted moons in the dark.

"When Vigilant Lock pulled me in, after...after all the shit that went down with my dad, you know..."

Harmony understood why she talked around it. The takedown of the Dixie Butcher had resulted in the death of multiple agents and put April in a wheelchair for the rest of her life. Jessie — a child then, raised by a pair of serial killers and given no concept of a moral code beyond the twisted creed of the King of Wolves — hadn't been on the side of the good guys that day.

April didn't hold it against her. But Harmony knew that on some level, Jessie would never stop holding it against herself.

"I know," Harmony said.

"One of the first things they did was run a battery of tests on me. Thanks to this evil shit in my veins, I've got sensitive hearing, super-charged smell, I'm faster and stronger than a normal person, and they wanted to find my limits."

"Okay," Harmony said, not seeing the connection.

"It was a dog whistle," Jessie said, sounding perplexed. "The thing he woke his zombies up with. A freaking dog whistle."

"Well, if your hearing is more sensitive—"

"No, I mean, that's the point. When they first tested me, that's one of the first things they tried. I can hear at that frequency just fine. I don't *like* it, it's annoying as hell and sounds like fingernails on a blackboard, but it doesn't *hurt* me. Tonight...that hurt. A lot. Enough to make me fumble my gun and blow the entire op."

Harmony shook her head. "You didn't blow the op."

"I'm sitting here wondering...am I losing a step? Am I getting too old for this shit? My body burns calories like a furnace and my metabolism is always in hyperdrive. Does that mean... What I'm saying is, how much time do I even have left? I can't assume I'll live as long as a normal person when my candle burns three times hotter."

"Your mother is still alive, as far as we know."

Jessie snorted. "Yeah, but she still worships the King of Wolves and probably mainlines his energy every time she makes a kill. She's an investment. I'm the reject who stole a little bit of his power and turned against everything the Kings stand for. I'm sure if he could cut me off completely he would."

"For what it's worth," Harmony mused, "I think you're rushing to conclusions. There's a good chance that wasn't a normal dog whistle. He could have enchanted it. After all, West used it to rouse his creations, not to hurt you. That was just a side effect. He couldn't have known we would be there tonight."

"Maybe," Jessie conceded.

"Also, we're one visit to a pet store away from testing the theory. I suggest we do that first thing in the morning. Better to know the truth, even if the truth is unpleasant, than to sit in the dark and worry."

"Yeah. You're right."

Jessie slumped in her seat.

"I'm sorry," she said. "And you're right. It was a bad idea. That jump would have been suicidal, and you made the right call. I'm just pissed and worried, and you're the last person I should have taken it out on. We cool?"

Harmony reached over in the dark, found Jessie's hand, and squeezed it softly.

***

They found a hotel by the airport and crashed for a few hours of fitful sleep. Harmony woke to sunlight stabbing at her eyes through the corners of the dusty blinds and the sound of Jessie shambling across the room.

"I've got bruises on my bruises. Ow. How's you?"

Harmony rubbed her eyes, running a quick inventory. Flexing arms, wrist, fingers, legs, toes. Then she stifled a yawn in her cupped hand.

"I'm all right. Nothing a few more hours of sleep wouldn't fix."

"Can't offer any." Jessie held up her phone. "Aunt April got up before we did. Bobby Diehl's corpse has been delivered to the plane, and she's ready to start cutting."

They pulled up to the *Imperator* on the airport tarmac and were met by Aselia, their pilot. She stormed down the open hydraulic ramp, worked up into a lather already. Marco, her chubby and frog-faced mechanic, was right on her heels. He pinched his nose with one hand, batted at the air with the other, and looked greener than usual.

"And of all the..." Aselia threw her hands in the air, glaring at Harmony and Jessie as they got out of the car. "What did you do to my baby? The bumper looks like cottage cheese, one headlight's busted—"

"And the engine is making this tiny knocking sound," Harmony said, then immediately wished she hadn't as the Cajun pilot hit her with a death glare. "If you could take a look. No rush."

Jessie nodded past her to the open belly of the plane. "What's up, and why is Marco puking at the edge of the hanger?"

"Oh, nothing big, just Doctor Frankenstein deciding she's gonna conduct an autopsy *on my plane*. Y'know, when I agreed to fly for Vigilant, I didn't realize y'all were batshit crazy."

"To be fair," Jessie said, "ten minutes of talking to me should have made that clear. Most people figure it out even faster than that."

Aselia squeezed her eyes shut, pinched the bridge of her nose, and pointed an accusing finger at the plane.

"Marco and I will work on fixing this crime scene of a bumper. Please. Go in there, do whatever needs doin', and clear that hellish smell out before I get finished. Otherwise, I'm gonna invite y'all to jump out for your next mission somewhere around forty thousand feet in the air."

They didn't have to be told twice. Kevin met them halfway down the ramp. The gangly college kid wore a surgical mask and held up a bottle of creamy salve.

"Smear a little of this under your nose. Trust me."

Harmony took his advice. Jessie just shrugged and kept walking, breathing deep as the odors of decay wafted out, blood and excrement and the roadkill stench of a body well past due for the grave.

"Don't know what you're complaining about," Jessie said, "this just makes me hungry for breakfast."

The *Imperator* had started its life as a C-130 Hercules cargo plane, refurbished and refitted to serve as Vigilant's mobile base of operations. One of the aftermarket enhancements was a stainless-steel strategy table mounted on a telescoping central pillar that could be raised or lowered as needed. Today it rested just a couple of feet above the belly of the plane so that April could navigate around it in her wheelchair and reach everything with ease.

Bobby Diehl lay on the table. Cold, marble-pale, dead, and open like a book, the skin of his chest peeled back and held in place with forceps as his withered organs glistened under a stark overhead light.

Harmony still had trouble parsing it. If anything, now that she could focus away from the action and the danger, the sight was even harder to take. Mercury Blaise had said he died of natural causes. After all that. After all the pain he spread, after all the killing, the violence, the destruction he spent a lifetime wreaking with barely a consequence, he just...died?

She knew that was just the way of things. More often than not there was no karmic fate, no cosmic justice, no balancing of the scales. The rich and powerful took what they wanted and despoiled as they pleased and their punishment was a peaceful death in bed.

But damn it, it shouldn't be that way.

There was a curve to Bobby's bloodless lips, the work of gravity, but she still took it as a silent mocking gesture: *You failed. You never caught me. And now I'm out of your jurisdiction for all eternity.*

Her hands clenched at her sides. She took a deep breath and forced her fingers to relax. Anger wasn't going to help. They needed answers.

April wore a surgical gown, blue cotton spattered with long dark stains, and a plastic face mask with a small headlamp mounted just above her brow. She waved her latex-gloved fingers in wry salute.

"Gather around, ladies. Every cadaver tells a story and Mr. Diehl has some secrets to share. I can't perform a full, proper autopsy here. I don't have all the tools, and more importantly, while I studied medicine as part of my doctorate program, I'm not a full-fledged forensic pathologist. I want to bring in an expert as soon as we get back to home base. Still, I knew you wouldn't want to wait for a preliminary examination."

"Got that right," Jessie said. She leaned in and wrinkled her nose. "Damn, he's even uglier on the inside."

"Uglier than you know," April said, giving her chair's wheels a shove and rolling to the opposite side. She reached up, angling the overhead light into the dead man's open chest cavity. "In addition to showing signs of lifelong cocaine abuse and a terrible diet — his septum is a horror show and his heart is more fat deposits than muscle — do you see these black, blotchy nodules here and here? And also here?"

Jessie furrowed her brow. "What are we looking at?"

"Again, I want a specialist to confirm it, but I believe...an advanced case of stomach cancer."

"And that's how he died?"

"No. But interestingly, it *would* have killed him if it had been allowed to run its course."

"We're getting ahead of ourselves," Harmony said. "Do we even know it's him? It looks exactly like him, but he could have hired a body double."

Kevin nodded, brandishing a sheaf of printouts in a clear plastic binder.

"Guaranteed. I committed a few HIPAA violations this morning and cracked the file storage for his old dentist, the one he visited back before he turned fugitive. There's more wear and tear on his teeth since then, but all the fillings and crowns, plus two extracted wisdom teeth, match up perfectly."

"Hold up," Jessie raised a finger. "You said the cancer didn't kill him. Suggesting you know what did. Dish."

April shared a thin, cold smile.

"Look here at his right leg, just below his genitals, toward the inner thigh."

"If we must," Jessie said.

"What do you see?"

Harmony leaned in. There it was. A pair of pinpricks, the tissue lightly reddened, almost lost in a sea of thick, curly leg hair.

"An injection site."

"I ran a toxicology scan," April said, "and correlated my findings to the suspected cause of death based on the condition of his organs. Now I must stress this is absolutely not work we're kitted out for here. I need to get him back to HQ and bring in the experts in order to be a hundred percent certain."

"Your educated guesses are better than most people's," Jessie said. "Whatcha got for us?"

"There appear to be traces of potassium chloride and pancuronium bromide in his system. While both drugs have legitimate medical uses — potassium chloride, for example, is commonly used in open heart surgery — there's one place you'll find both drugs outside of a well-stocked hospital. A maximum-security prison."

"You mean—" Harmony said.

"Yes. Bobby Diehl didn't die of natural causes. He was executed by lethal injection."

Chapter Seven

Jessie whistled, long and low, her hands on her hips as she stared down at Bobby Diehl's pale corpse.

"Executed? Somebody out there did us a solid. Who do we like for this? Bette Novak and her Majestic-12 crew, maybe? Bobby landed on her radar around the time of that Red Knight business, same as he did with us."

April tilted her head, eyes narrow behind her blood-spattered plastic face shield. "Given her recent gestures of interagency cooperation and considering she knows we've been after him for a while now, I can't imagine she wouldn't have given us a courtesy call at the very least."

"The Faust gang out in Vegas?" Kevin suggested. "They're all wrapped up in the dark side of the occult underground just like he was."

Harmony gave a tiny head shake. "Doesn't fit the profile on either side. Bobby never involved himself directly in organized crime, as far as we know; he used proxies and cutouts for his dirty deals. And even if he had a reason, Daniel Faust doesn't kill like this. He's brutal, direct. This feels...staged."

"Symbolic," April said.

Harmony met her gaze across the autopsy table. "If the world knew the extent of what this man was responsible for he would have gotten the death penalty twenty times over. Somebody made sure he faced justice. This could be a vigilante killing."

"Still wanna know who did it," Jessie said. "One, for the sake of closure. Two, so I can shake that person's hand and maybe pitch 'em a job offer."

Harmony's fingers drifted onto the edge of the metal slab. It was cool under her fingertips, unyielding.

"We have two mysteries to unravel here, and 'who killed Bobby Diehl' is the less important right now. Someone hired Mercury Blaise to arrange his resurrection. We need to know who, why, and what they're planning."

Kevin shrugged. "I mean, not like he had any shortage of cultists and sycophants even after he turned fugitive. Have you looked on social media lately? People used to talk about him like he was the real-life Tony Stark. Now they still do, but they also think he's a badass outlaw."

Harmony began to pace the belly of the plane. She saw snippets of information around her, glowing blue text on panes of glass. She snatched them with her mind and flung them out in front of her, positioning them on a mental evidence board. Some strings connected, note to note, pulsing neon. Others stood alone, clues without a tether.

"We're looking at multiple culprits. Mercury's exact words, when she didn't know we were listening in: 'His friends are paying me a lot of money.'"

"She also said he died of natural causes," Jessie pointed out.

"No reason she'd know otherwise if they didn't tell her. Mercury's not the mastermind, she's a hired gun, just like Herbert West was. A middleman to keep the real plotters safe in the shadows. They went out of their way to hire someone who wasn't part of the occult underground. Someone who would accept things as they came and not ask too many difficult questions. And what does that tell us about her employers?"

"They're versatile," April offered. "In a position to know, contact, and hire a skilled industrial thief, which requires a certain sphere of influence in the criminal underground. At the same time, they were aware of Doctor West's skills and knew where and how to reach out to him."

"You know who had a rolodex like that?" Jessie said. "Bobby Diehl. Could be folks who worked closely with him back in the day. They want their boss back on the throne and they're using his contacts to make it happen."

Harmony stopped pacing. She stared at the evidence board in her mind's eye, shuffled a few glass notecards from spot to spot, tried connecting the threads in a different pattern. There was still a big gulf across the middle of the board, a no man's land she couldn't figure out how to cross.

"Then why are they doing it all wrong?"

All eyes were on her. Harmony put the tip of her index finger to her pursed lips, taking one last glance over the clues they'd collected. No doubt now.

"What's the first thing any serious magician learns?" she asked.

"Easy," Kevin said. "There's no such thing as vampires."

"Second?"

April saw where she was going with this. "That magic offers very few easy shortcuts, let alone miracles. While it is possible to return someone from the afterlife under incredibly rare and difficult conditions, *bodily* resurrection isn't possible. Within two minutes of death, the human soul untethers itself from the flesh. You can't bring someone back without addressing that problem first."

Harmony stood over the autopsy table. On an impulse, she peeled back one of Bobby's eyelids with her thumb. She half expected to see him staring right at her, that old mocking look on his face. *Fooled you again.* Nothing. His pupil was rolled back, glassy, empty. Nothing behind it but rotting meat, slowly decomposing at room temperature.

"West's theory of reanimation is critically flawed," Harmony mused. "Without the soul, even if you could bring a body back to perfect life, it wouldn't be the same person anymore. It'd have the brain, the neurons, maybe even the memories and some of the personality, but that spark — that thing that makes you *you* — is long gone and it isn't coming back. Anyone skilled enough to mount last night's operation in the first place would be skilled enough to know that."

"Also," Jessie added, "let's be real: it's not like West's zombie juice is out of the alpha-testing stage, and that's being generous. The bodies he brings back are tough as all hell and can take a beating, but they make Frankenstein's monster look smart."

Kevin cleared his throat. "He is smart. In the original novel."

She turned her head slowly, arching one eyebrow.

"Nerd," she said, "I require breakfast. And a dog whistle. Go. Now."

"A...dog whistle?"

"I'll explain when you get back."

"Mercury didn't know any better," Harmony said. "Because this isn't her line of work. But anyone who has ever dealt with Herbert West and his creations would know there's absolutely no chance he could bring Bobby Diehl back to anything but a crude parody of life. So...why? Why invest in a losing venture?"

April reached for a needle and a spool of black surgical thread.

"It would suggest," she said, carefully threading the needle with her wrinkled but rock-steady fingers, "that they didn't want or need him restored to a full semblance of life. While the lion's share of his assets were frozen, we know he had stashes and caches of resources hidden around the world. Maybe they want something that his body — a warm handprint, an ocular scan, a snatch of recorded voice — could unlock?"

It was a working theory, Harmony decided. For now. She added no strings to her mental evidence board. Her gut told her that it was dead wrong, that something else was going on here, something far worse than ferreting out some long-lost stash of money. But her gut didn't have any evidence to back that up, so for now she grudgingly agreed to go along with the theory.

April sewed the dead man up. They'd stash him in the *Imperator*'s cold storage locker until they could fly him back to HQ. It hadn't been built with corpses in mind, but it was just about perfectly sized for one.

Harmony went for a walk. Just around the hangar, alone, listening to the thunder of jet planes as they screamed up into the morning sky, smelling the tang of jet fuel in the air. She had to sort out a few things. Like separating want from need, disentangling her frustration over being denied a final confrontation with Bobby Diehl over the very real problem of tracking down his would-be successors before they could put their plans — whatever they were — into motion. Bobby had a dozen plots in motion before they forced him into hiding and every single one of them promised mass casualties. No reason to think anyone still in his corner would be any different.

They had a ticking clock on their hands and didn't even know how much time was left on it.

When she came back, Kevin had returned with bags of fast food and steaming black coffee in tall cardboard cups. Harmony checked her body, grudgingly admitted she needed fuel, and unwrapped a sausage and egg biscuit. As she chewed, still lost in her thoughts, April rolled by and gently touched her sleeve.

"A word, please?"

They found a spot at the far end of the jumpseats, a relative bit of privacy. Harmony sat down so she and April could talk on the same level, eye-to-eye and direct.

"As Vigilant's acting medical officer," April said, "I wanted to check in. How are you holding up?"

"After last night?"

"After the Ardentis incident. I read Jessie's mission report."

Harmony glanced to one side, suddenly uncomfortable.

"We brought order to chaos," she said. "That's our job."

"You had Ricky Corbin unarmed, helpless, and at your mercy. And you shot him point-blank on the floor."

Harmony still didn't meet her steady, cold-steel gaze.

"I did my job."

April's hand rested on her knee. "You're not a machine. Don't give me machine answers."

"I watched him kill civilians, innocent people who were in the wrong place at the wrong time, and laugh about it." She took a breath, reflecting, eyes distant. "A man like that...ruins things. That's what he does, that's all he is and all he wants to be. Prison wouldn't have taught him anything but how to be a better killer."

She turned, meeting April's gaze.

"I did my job," she repeated. "I eliminated the threat."

"And...Nadine?"

"She claims she can teach me how to control my new powers, but I'm not certain how much of that is a genuine offer and how much is an attempt at influencing me. I've been visiting her in her cage back at headquarters. We play chess and talk."

"I know. I'm more curious about the request you put in." April lowered her head a bit, looking at Harmony over the rims of her bifocals. "You specifically asked for a listening device to be installed in her cell and for your sessions to be transcribed and sent to my office."

Harmony curled her fingers, uncurled them. Sometimes she felt like a pilot instead of a person, a brain operating a scaffold of muscle and bone.

"She's good at manipulating people," Harmony said, "and lately, with all the changes I've been going through...I don't always know how much I can trust myself. But I can trust you and the team. Everybody needs a little oversight sometimes to stay on the right path."

April nodded, sharp. "I think that's a wise decision. On a hopefully lighter subject, any movement in the search for your family tree?"

"Mom's digging through her old storage locker. She's going to send me anything she finds. She thinks she might be able to figure out where great-great-grandma used to live. I mean, where she lived when she first traveled to this dimension. If nothing else, it'd be a place to start."

"Hey," Kevin called out from the other side of the plane, "are you all ready to be dazzled...by *science?*"

April sighed, turning the wheels of her chair.

"Come on," she said out of one side of her mouth. "Let's go be dazzled."

Chapter Eight

"This," Kevin said, holding up a sliver of beige plastic fresh from the clamshell packaging, "is a dog whistle. Electronic models exist but the old-school, purely mechanical designs like this one haven't changed much at all since the late eighteen-hundreds. The theory is simple: the upper bound of human hearing is between fifteen and twenty kilohertz. Generally, the younger you are the higher you can hear on the spectrum."

"Ah," April said, "the many and strange blessings of youth."

"A bunch of animals can double or even triple that range. Dogs can hear sounds in the forty kilohertz spectrum. The idea is you can use the whistle as part of a training regimen without, you know, disturbing the neighbors. Dogs can hear it, people can't."

"Zombies too, apparently," Jessie said. She crossed her arms. "And wolf-bloods like me."

He raised the whistle to his lips, giving her a questioning look. "You ready for this?"

"Hit me," she said.

All Harmony heard as he blew into the whistle was a faint hiss. Jessie scrunched her face up. She didn't fall, didn't crumple like she had under the auditory onslaught last night, she just looked annoyed.

"Okay," Jessie said. "Okay, stop. It doesn't hurt but it's irritating as hell."

Kevin took a breath and prepared to blow the whistle again. She snatched it out of his mouth.

"You just lost your whistle privileges. But thank you. Apparently I'm not getting weaker, West's whistle was just stronger. One of those electronic models, I'm guessing?"

Kevin dropped into his swivel chair, kicked back, and slid along the bank of monitors.

"And not just by a little bit. Here's where the science comes in. Remember how the audio feed got disrupted last night? I went back over the recording and ran it through a battery of tools: a digital frequency counter, a multimeter, an oscilloscope, whatever I could throw at it just to pull some concrete data together. On top of that, I dug into the tech specs and found the high end of what our surveillance gear can handle."

"Meaning," Harmony said, "you know what it would take to temporarily blow it out."

Kevin snapped his fingers and pointed at her. "Exactly, which gave me a baseline for the calculations. Near as I can tell, there's nothing like West's gadget on the market because there's no practical use for one. It's so high-pitched that even cats can't hear it. Your hearing would need to be, well...supernatural."

Jessie stared at him, her expression as flat as her voice.

"Kev, are you telling me somebody built that thing to fuck with me specifically?"

"He didn't know we were going to be there," Harmony pointed out.

"No," April said, thinking out loud, "but he did know you were on his trail, and he was convinced he was our primary target. I could imagine him scrambling for some kind of countermeasure and keeping it on him at all times just in case. That would explain why he trained his zombies to respond to the signal as well."

"And maybe it wasn't for you in particular," Kevin added. "You're not the only wolf-blood out there. There's your mom—"

"Althea," Jessie said, "is not my *mom*. She gave birth to me. That's all she did besides fuck me up for life and abandon me. She doesn't get to claim that word."

He held up his open hands. "Just saying, they're rare but they do exist."

Harmony looked past the question, finding a thornier one hiding in its shadow.

"Where did he get it? West's entire background is in medicine and biochemistry. He has no talent for electronics, no professional partners—"

"No friends," Jessie quipped.

"—and this is clearly a piece of custom-built equipment. Like Kevin said, there's no legitimate market for it."

"Mercury could have built it," Jessie said. "She hit me with that LED flasher thing too, though I think that would have stunned anybody, enhanced vision or not."

"Except West had the whistle, and we'd been tracing their communications over the dark web. We know they were meeting in person for the first time last night. He would have needed it in his possession long enough to train his cadavers to respond to the tone."

More glass-pane notes on the murder board. More questions neatly penned in blue neon, waiting for answers. Harmony knew that in the end every case was a solved mystery, a complete puzzle with all the pieces in place. Getting from here to there was her job.

"Let's focus on the closest thread," she said. "Mercury Blaise. We find her, we find her clients."

"It's a no-go on their ride," Kevin said. He leaned back in his swivel chair, rapped a few keys, and brought up a photograph on one of the wall monitors. It showed the ravaged husk of a burned-out car, nothing but scrap metal and bubbled, molten streaks of paint. "Recon team found it eight miles from the Merchandise Mart, dumped in a junkyard. Forensics shows they doused the whole interior in bleach and then tossed a Molotov in just for good measure."

Harmony stared at the image, deep in thought.

"She mostly operates in the United States, right?"

He nodded. "Sure, with excursions to Latin America, China, Japan...Interpol wants her bad, but the pattern shows she always lands back in the States when she's done with her larcenous field trips."

"So does Herbert West," Harmony said. "And until we rattled his cage hard enough to send him into hiding, he lived a very public life as a Cook County coroner. That's common with career criminals: you have a day job to conceal your ill-gotten gains and keep the feds at bay. The simplest form of money laundering there is."

"Sure," Jessie said. "Look how many mundane mobsters have jobs working garbage trucks and driving limos. They don't even have to show up for work. The boss just records their imaginary hours and gives 'em a pay stub to show the IRS. Or their parole officer, or whoever else needs proof that they're an upstanding citizen."

"Mercury is a technophile. She eats, sleeps, and breathes the stuff. There's no way a woman like that lives off the grid. She must have a stable home, a base of operations when she's not on the job. One with ample power, Internet access..."

April's lips curled in a thin smile. "Meaning a civilian cover identity and a legal job to justify paying for it."

"Kevin, we tracked her flight to Chicago out of LAX, right?"

"Affirmative," he said, flipping a casual salute.

Harmony took it all in, seeing the bigger picture.

"Let's start the search with a focus on tech-sector jobs on the West Coast. Not management or public-facing — someplace she could maintain a low profile while keeping her finger on the pulse of Silicon Valley. I suspect she's using her civilian job to do more than protect her assets. It's a means of finding opportunities and lining up new heists."

"If I might add," April said, "it's a tighter slice of the pie, but we might have better luck focusing specifically on security jobs. She's a thief. Security is her specialty, and working in the field would make it easy for her to stay ahead of any new innovations."

Jessie rubbed her chin, taking that in.

"Hell, she could even go to security conferences and rub shoulders with the top minds in the field with no one the wiser. Then go home and make plans to rob them all blind. Okay, I'm sold. We're not looking for Mercury Blaise, we're looking for the woman she's pretending to be. Let's hit the books, team."

***

The next two days were a flurry of paperwork, research, dead ends, and blind alleys. They ran through lead after lead, checking each other's work, pushing deeper into a dozen nested corporate hierarchies and ferreting out every last bit of data they could find. In the meantime, Aselia and Marco managed to pound the Hemi back into shape. Aselia gave Jessie the keys back, but only reluctantly.

Harmony was poring over a tablet, sifting through the annual reports and structure of a suspicious-looking startup, when a call came through for her. Headquarters, over an encrypted line. She took it in the back of the plane, nestling in the far corner jumpseat.

"Black."

"Ms. Black, the...prisoner has requested to speak with you. Do we have your permission to put her through?"

It took her a second to decide.

"Please do. Also, activate a tap on this line. I want this call recorded, transcribed, and sent to Doctor Cassidy's desk."

"Yes ma'am. Connecting now."

She waited, hearing a buzz, a delicate click, then the voice of Nadine gusted over the line like a warm summer breeze.

"There you are, little one. I almost thought you'd abandoned me."

"I'm on a mission," Harmony said, her throat suddenly tight.

"I know. I'm teasing. These guards are well trained, I'll give you that, but they always say more than they think they're saying. I miss our nightly game."

Harmony wanted to believe she was talking about chess. She knew better than that.

"We'll play when I get back."

"Well? Aren't you going to tell me about your latest adventure?" Nadine's voice was like perfumed smoke, slithering in through Harmony's ear and curling a warm tail around her brain. "Not after anyone I know, are you?"

It was none of Nadine's business. Sharing details of an ongoing operation with a prisoner — the most dangerous prisoner they'd ever had — was poor form at best. Then again, Nadine had connections in strange places, far beyond the infernal courts. Her House of Dead Roses had offered sabotage, torture, and assassinations for hire to plenty of human customers over the years.

Besides, it wasn't like she was going to tell anyone, considering she was locked in a literal cage in the sub-basement of Vigilant headquarters.

"Bobby Diehl."

"You found him?" Nadine's voice perked up.

"Someone else did. He's dead, and we'd like to know who did it."

"I hope you'll invite me to the victory party," she purred. "The man was disgusting. A complete philistine, with no appreciation for the arts."

"Did you ever run across an industrial thief who calls herself Mercury Blaise?"

Nadine was silent for a moment, thinking.

"Dresses like Trinity from *The Matrix*, pals around with a walking slab of beef jerky covered in faded gang tattoos?"

"That's the one," Harmony said.

"We've brushed elbows. I thought about recruiting her for the Dead Roses once, then decided not to. She's too good."

Harmony tilted her head. "Too good? Isn't that what you want?"

"Usually. But as you saw yourself from the ill-fated Ardentis heist, on very rare occasions it's wise to bring in outsiders with no connection to the circles you run in. If I hire a true-blue servant of Hell to do a job, everyone's looking for a demon at the top of the food chain. If I hire a clueless human, on the other hand…"

"Nobody's looking for you, because everyone assumes you'd only work with your devotees. You stay clean, and you can either use her again or burn her once she's not useful anymore. There's no expectation of loyalty."

Nadine chuckled, delighted.

"You are a quick learner, Harmony. Mercury's been on my backup list for years just in case I ever needed a human with rare skills and no ties to my House. Beyond that I'm afraid you probably know as much as I do about her. Our only communication was via the dark web and a couple of blind drops. Now…tell me the other thing."

Harmony's brow furrowed. "What other thing?"

"Don't be coy, girl. I know that tone. There's something you want to tell me, something you want to confide. You're afraid...no, ashamed to, because you consider it a show of weakness to share your truth with your sworn enemy. But at the same time you know I'm the person, the *only* person, who understands what you're feeling right now. So share. You know I'm the last woman who will ever judge you."

Harmony's gaze dropped to the belly of the plane. She hadn't planned on talking to Nadine about this. Or had she? Part of her thought it was inevitable, and she was just pretending it wasn't because it was more comfortable that way.

"I've noticed...I'm not getting hungry like I did when you first infected me. For a while I couldn't even use my normal powers if I didn't feed on someone's energy. Now I feel...peckish, but it's not all-consuming."

"Not now it isn't. You've been using your new gifts, haven't you?"

Harmony flashed back to last night. Draining an animated corpse of death-energy, feeling it seethe and burn inside of her veins, then pouring it into a victim.

"Yes."

"Well, there's your answer. You still need it, Harmony, same as before. You're just *finally* learning to feed the beast. Keep it fed and it will serve you well."

The next part was trickier.

"I'm also...not getting sick like I used to."

"Tell me more."

"Normally when I call to my magic I get these horrible stomach cramps. Last night I just felt woozy for a minute, a little nauseous, and then it passed. I chalked it up to the adrenaline."

"Oh, adrenaline definitely helps. If you'll pardon the vulgarity, sweet, why do you think we succubi like to fuck while we feed? It makes the food go down so much easier. And taste so much sweeter. It's like...do you remember going through puberty?"

"Unfortunately," Harmony said.

"Call this your encore. If I could hazard a guess, your human metabolism is starting to acclimate to my gifts. You're growing into the woman you were always meant to be. I'm pleased to bear witness to it."

Harmony shifted in the jumpseat, her throat tight again.

"I should go."

"Wait. Before you do, remember this: Mercury and the people who hire her are by and large what one might call 'tech bros.' They have no love for, or understanding of, the humanities. To them, art and culture are commodities to be bought and sold, nothing more. Their understanding of anything but money never dips below the shallows. If you're hunting for Mercury's newest master, look for a man with no soul."

She paused.

"Those were the exact same circles the late Bobby Diehl ran in. Don't you find that a remarkable coincidence, Harmony?"

"Thank you," Harmony said.

"Thank me by relieving my boredom. Pawn to e4."

A fresh board. Pieces cascaded in Harmony's mind, military ranks arrayed upon a crystalline battlefield. Nadine had taken the white pieces, leaving Harmony with black. She could spare a minute for a few moves.

"Pawn to c5," she replied.

Nadine's response was cut off by a shout from Kevin on the other side of the plane.

"Heads up everybody. We just tracked down Mercury's secret identity."

Chapter Nine

"April was exactly right," Kevin said, gathering the team around the now corpseless briefing table. Diehl's body was cooling its heels, and all its other bits, in the freezer. "If I hadn't limited my search to security jobs this would have taken three times as long. We can thank startup culture for giving Mercury's game away."

"Startup culture?" Harmony said.

"When you want to make a splash in Silicon Valley, you need media attention. Lots of it."

He clicked his mouse. The wall of screens blossomed with pictures, articles, shaky footage of flashing lights at an exclusive red carpet gala.

"Ladies, meet ProcGen, a San Francisco-based tech company that's looking to make a big splash. Their IPO is next month and investors are lining up to throw wheelbarrows of cash at it."

"What do they make?"

"Bullshit," April said, her voice dry as a funeral drum.

Jessie's fingers brushed her neckline as she put on a face of mock horror. "Auntie April, I've never heard such language."

"The doc isn't wrong," Kevin said. "ProcGen is looking to corner the artificial intelligence field with a new model of chatbot that *allegedly* makes ChatGPT look like a child's toy. Their algorithms are deeply proprietary and locked down under Fort Knox levels of security, but word is they've got some secret sauce that nobody else in the industry has been able to manage."

"Or," April said, "it's a scam and the founders are planning to bail out of a burning plane with golden parachutes as soon as it becomes clear they can't deliver on any of their promises."

"I can guess which option you're leaning toward," Jessie said.

April's nose crinkled. "They're promising 'AI for wellness.' Personal digital coaches who will nurse you through the pains of life and provide therapy on demand. Speaking as a psychiatric professional, I'm not worried about my job becoming obsolete. I'm worried about them doing it *badly* and hurting people with a ham-fisted piece of hackwork. People's hearts and minds are too precious, too delicate, to trust to a machine. Especially one with a profit motive. They don't have a single credentialed medical professional on their board of directors. It's bean counters all the way down."

"But they do have a Mercury Blaise," Harmony murmured, eyes locked on the video wall. There she was, standing in the background of a looping clip of a press conference. She had swapped her bondage-club chic for a conservative pantsuit and dark glasses, standing at military parade rest and looking like she'd rather be anywhere else in the world.

"She's on their payroll as 'Molly Millions,'" Kevin said, "Director of Network Security."

Harmony's lips twitched. "William Gibson. *Neuromancer*. She's fond of science fiction references. How stable is her cover?"

"Still digging, but it looks rock solid from here. Miss Millions has a valid Social Security number, ten years of employment history, a condo in Pacific Heights, and she pays her taxes to the penny like a good little citizen. I called to verify employment and they said she's on vacation this week, which tracks, considering Jessie was surfing on the hood of her car in Chicago a few nights ago."

Jessie tilted her head, staring up at the video wall. "So we were right. She bamboozled her way into the tech sector and landed a gig that lets her scout for new jobs while she's pulling heists in her off hours. Pretty slick."

Harmony wasn't sure.

The timing nagged at her, the details almost lining up but not quite landing home, like a tiny latch that couldn't catch.

"Do we have a complete list of the robberies she's allegedly tied to?" she asked. "We know about the one that went wrong, the shootout in Brazil, but there have to be more if Interpol is this eager to meet her."

"A laundry list," April said. "Mercury's a busy girl. And an adrenaline addict, a need which is hard to satisfy from behind a corporate desk."

"How many were committed after she joined ProcGen?"

Kevin held up a finger, turned to his keyboard and leaned in, sifting through a database and running the numbers.

"Besides the deal in Chicago, there are four high-profile heists in the past two years that fit Mercury's profile to a T. One is dodgy, but I'd say she's a perfect fit for the other three. Why?"

"She's not some smash-and-grab thug," Harmony said. "And while her partner is on a hair trigger, she's meticulous. Her field of expertise is complicated, her targets are well-protected, and you can't set up a heist like that without a lot of fieldwork. She'd need to be on-site, case her targets, work out timetables and plan everything down to the minute."

Kevin's brow furrowed. "Yeah, and?"

"She'd have to take vacation time for that. A lot of it."

Jessie nodded, following Harmony's thoughts. "And how much paid time off do most people even get?"

"We get paid time off?" Kevin said, perking up.

"No," Jessie said, "I'm talking about normal people, not us."

"And they're angling for a massive stock offering in a month," Harmony said. "The kind of money that sets people up for life. How many startups would let the person in charge of their network security take a week off at the most critical make-or-break moment of their company's history?"

April gazed at her over the rims of her bifocals. "You think they know."

"I'm not ready to say, but there are two possibilities: either Mercury Blaise is using her job at ProcGen as a civilian cover and pulling heists in her free time…or they know exactly who she is and what she does."

Nadine's words were fresh in her mind. They weren't looking at separate worlds, isolated spheres. All of these circles, from Mercury to her faceless paymasters to Bobby Diehl, had to overlap at some crucial point.

"Kevin, run a search cross-referencing Bobby Diehl's investment portfolios before they were frozen by the government with anyone and everyone on Proc-Gen's board of directors."

It took twenty minutes.

"Harmony," he said, waving her over to his console. "You're the one with the forensic accounting degree. Does this mean what I think it means?"

He slid his mouse and scattered digitized spreadsheets across the screen like a hand of playing cards. Harmony leaned over his shoulder, squinting as she read each document from top to bottom. Along the way words flared, turning into neon blue data points.

"Good job," she murmured. "I think you just found our culprit."

Jessie had been talking to April over by the jumpseats. She wandered over, curious now, April rolling up behind her.

"From a bunch of numbers in eight-point font? How'd you manage that?"

"By following the money," Harmony said. "One trick that rarely fails. Look over here. Founding asset statements for ProcGen, standard stuff. They're making a public offering so they're required to make full disclosures."

"Lets the eager buyers know what they're investing in," April said. "Or what they think they're investing in."

"ProcGen kicked off with a thirty-two million dollar angel investment from Walburgh Financial Partners. They provided one hundred percent of the seed money needed to break ground and get to work on the new AI model in exchange for a big chunk of equity. Too big, honestly — I imagine a lot of potential investors would keep their distance if they weren't misled by the corporate hype. Once Walburgh gets their cut of the profits up front there's not going to be that much wealth to share. Assuming ProcGen ever turns a profit at all, which is dubious."

Jessie whistled. "That's a lot of scratch. Then again, given the cost of real estate in San Fran, thirty-two mil probably just bought 'em a walk-in closet."

"It's a smokescreen. Walburgh Financial Partners is a shell company, basically a structured and very legal tax dodge, for another venture capital firm."

Harmony pointed to the balance sheet at the heart of the screen.

"Goering-Milhouse owns them lock, stock, and barrel, and the exact same people are on the board of both firms. Walburgh is basically a puppet, an extension to muddy up Goering-Milhouse's global investments and make them harder to sort out."

"I know you said it's legal, but it still sounds shady," Jessie said.

"Highly. Goering-Milhouse prides itself on an 'ethical portfolio,' and that's more or less true if you only look at the holdings they admit to. Under the Walburgh name they invest in military aerospace tech, alcohol and tobacco companies, a company that manufactures guidance systems for missiles..."

"And a 'wellness AI' startup," April said. "Interesting company they keep. But what does this tell us about the people behind Mercury Blaise?"

"Because there's one more link in the chain. Kevin, pull up the quarterly reports for Goering-Milhouse. Not current ones: the month that the angel investment went through."

The document blossomed on the screen. He magnified it for clarity. All they needed was one name, the one at the head of the conference table.

"Robert Diehl, Chief Executive Officer," Jessie breathed. "No freakin' way. How many pies did this guy have his fingers in? Wait, he's not still on the board, right? Once the scandal broke, his own company memory-holed him, booted him out, and rebranded itself before the paint could dry."

"He was removed from Goering-Milhouse's board too." Harmony held up a finger. "But. If you check the other names on the roster, who are still there today according to their most recent quarterlies, I think we'll find they're the same rubber-stamp yes-men he surrounded himself with at Diehl Innovations. It's all the same outfit, all dancing to his tune."

"Diehl Innovations is Goering, Goering is Walburgh, and Walburgh bought up the lion's share of ProcGen which means..." Jessie stared at the screen. "Bobby Diehl *is* ProcGen. He's the man behind the curtain."

"Well, was," Kevin said with a nod over his shoulder. "Seeing as he's stone dead and cooling his heels in the freezer over there. But it does look like he set this whole deal up just before he had to turn fugitive. Question is, has he been hands-off since then or was he running the show from exile right up until somebody gave him the lethal injection?"

"And to what end?" April said. "Though this does cast new light on ProcGen itself. Harmony, I think your theory is starting to hold water. If they were working directly with Bobby and found out about his murder, but still needed something from him, something that required a bit of necromancy, sending Mercury to parlay with Herbert West makes sense."

"They wouldn't have a world-class hacker and thief on the payroll just to make her play errand girl, though," Kevin said, "and she's been with the company since day one. If they know who and what she really is, we haven't even scratched the surface of the shady shit going on here."

"One good way to find out." Harmony called up toward the cockpit. "Aselia, is the Hemi ready to travel?"

"Depends," she called back. "You gonna break it again?"

"Probably," Jessie yelled. Harmony stared at her. She spread her open hands. "What? I don't lie to my friends."

Harmony took one last long look at the balance sheets. She saw the data points, the connections, some lines strong and vibrant and some shimmering, weak, circumstantial.

There was still something wrong. Something huge and rotten looming at the core of this knot, but she couldn't see it yet.

Why did they try to raise a man from the dead knowing full well that West's reagent doesn't work like that and the best they'd get back was a half-mindless monster?

And who killed him in the first place?

"We're headed for the West Coast," Harmony said. "Let's pay ProcGen a visit."

Chapter Ten

The *Imperator* boiled down from a cloudless blue sky, wheels thumping on the tarmac at San Francisco International. There was no time to lose. If ProcGen had been born as one of Bobby Diehl's personal projects, Harmony reflected, then whatever its true purpose was, it needed to be stopped. Yesterday.

Before they abandoned him, Bobby was angling to be the Network's new golden boy, she reflected. *He tried to bring the King of Silence to Earth, welcoming the titan with a red carpet. If we hadn't stopped him, the damage would have been apocalyptic. He knew and he didn't care. If anything, he seemed giddy about it.*

That wasn't his only brush with mass casualties. Bobby brewed mutagenic plagues for kicks and conjured monsters he couldn't control. Even if he'd been out of the loop since going on the run — and Harmony doubted it to her very core — if he'd set up ProcGen as a testing lab for one of his insane "experiments" then it could still do untold damage even without him behind the wheel.

The first priority, then, was to dig in and find out what was really going on behind the thirty-two million dollar facade.

"I've reached out to a local print shop to arrange business cards for your civilian covers," April told her and Jessie as the team gathered around the strategy table. "Because it's such short notice, I'm reactivating a pair of identities you've used before. You are Mary Gibbs and Josephine Clark, field reporters for an online tech journal. ProcGen is desperate for all the good press it can get in the ramp-up to the IPO, so I expect it will take very little convincing to get them to open their office doors to you. Once inside, you'll have to improvise."

"Have to assume they'll at least glance at our credentials," Harmony said.

"Got you covered there," Kevin told her. "The website you 'work' for is real; a buddy of mine runs it. He doesn't know the real line of work I'm in, obviously, but I told him I'm brewing up a social engineering hack and he's eager to help, no questions asked, in exchange for me doing some free late-night debugging on his new software tool. It takes a village to scam a village, like the saying goes. Anyway, he's already changed a third of the bylines on the website to match your cover names and put you on the staff list. The story will hold up unless ProcGen does a deep dive on you, and there's no reason they should unless you give 'em one."

"The numbers on your new business cards," April added, "won't go to the site. They'll route directly to a virtual cellular line that we control, so we can field any callers looking to check up on you. Once you've infiltrated the office campus, your first priority is to help us compromise their network security."

Jessie raised an eyebrow, glancing over at Kevin.

"It's been hours. I figured you would have already made that entire server farm your bitch by now."

"From outside? Never gonna happen. This isn't some weak-sauce government system run by underpaid sysops and patched once every never. Mercury knows what she's doing. She turned that place into a digital fortress. I'm going to have to crack their network from the inside, and that's where you and Harmony come in."

He brandished a slim USB stick in a black plastic shell and tossed it to Jessie. She snatched it out of the air.

"New and improved Icepick. Slot it into their local systems. It'll run automatically and try to open a tunnel so it can phone home. Once the worm takes root and I wriggle inside their servers, pull the stick and slip it out with you. They'll never know what hit 'em."

Harmony gave the USB drive a dubious look. "How long do we have to keep it connected?"

"Depends," he said.

"On?"

"On how hard Mercury likes to work. Most admins know ways of hardening their internal security, but they don't bother. After all, ninety-nine percent of any potential threats are going to be people on the outside looking to hack their way in. Spending time and resources to prepare for that one rare weirdo who's willing to break into your office and *then* get to cracking is a big ask."

"That's what locks and alarms are for," Harmony observed.

Kevin pointed at her. "Exactly. If you trust your physical security, you can slack a little. Only problem is Mercury *is* that rare weirdo who breaks into places like the one she works at on the regular, so she's got a different perspective on security than your average admin. She knows what it would take to stop herself, if the shoe was on the other foot. The question is, does she think anyone else out there is on her level?"

"Dunno," Jessie said, eyeing him. "Are we?"

"Hey, I'm ready for a fight if you are. Been a while since I actually went up against someone who could put me to the test. Mercury's good. Willing to say she's great, even. But I think I can take her. Besides, we've got the element of surprise. She thinks she got away clean, and it's not like Bobby told her we're coming. He's too busy chilling out."

Jessie stared at him.

"You know," he said. "Because he's...dead, in the freezer. Just...chilling. Literally. Look, it was funny in my head."

April folded her hands on her lap. "I've placed a request to have some supplies and weapons shipped directly from headquarters on the next possible flight. For the moment, unfortunately, what you've got is what you've got. We didn't have much time to scramble this operation together, save for an old classic."

She handed Harmony a pair of chunky Buddy Holly glasses, black plastic rims, the glass designed to look like a prescription lens but perfectly clear.

"Your video glasses. Wear these onsite and Kevin and I will be able to guide you toward a good insertion point for his Icepick."

"And we're absolutely certain Mercury and Santiago aren't on the premises?" Harmony asked, folding the glasses and slipping them into the breast pocket of her blazer. "They'll blow our cover the second they see us."

Kevin shook his head. "First thing I made sure of. Mercury's not due back from 'vacation' for two more days. Santiago's not on the company payroll at all, as far as I can tell, and those two are joined at the hip anyway. You've got a small window of opportunity and it's closing fast."

It took a single phone call and a little glad-handing from Jessie to open that window wide. As predicted, ProcGen wanted to rack up as much hype as possible before they went public. The more true believers lining up to throw their cash at the "future of wellness," the more diamonds the startup's founders could encrust their golden parachutes with. They scored an appointment and a facility tour for three p.m. sharp.

Jessie drove. Harmony let the city envelop her, studying it, tasting its character and its mysteries. San Francisco was a paradox. The streets of Haight-Ashbury echoed the myth of the Summer of Love, with bright Victorian houses, sidewalks chalked in rainbow hearts, fluttering pennants, vintage boutiques, and hipster coffee joints. The sun shone high and clean above it all.

But the myth of the sixties was at war with the rot of the millennium, and it didn't take long to see winter howling through the cracks. Destitute locals, barely older than children, camping on the sidewalk in filthy pup tents. Side streets that looked like open-air drug markets. San Francisco was one of the richest cities in the world, with more billionaires per capita than anywhere else on Earth, and it still couldn't put a roof over everyone's head. It didn't even look like it was trying very hard.

The squeeze was on, had *been* on for twenty years, the cost of basic survival snaking around the necks of the people on the ground floor like a boa constrictor's coils, tightening until every last penny was pushed upward and there was nothing but crumbs left on the street.

"Looks like a great place to make a billion dollars," Jessie quipped, "assuming you've already got a few hundred million for seed money."

"Wonder what the hippies would have thought."

Jessie snickered. "Harm, the hippies are the ones who *became* the venture capitalists."

"Cynical."

"But correct. When push comes to shove, the people who shout the loudest about their principles usually don't really have any. Give 'em a taste of money and power and all that talk about peace and love goes straight out the window. Hard to put a flower in the barrel of a gun when you're making bank off Boeing and Raytheon."

"Not everyone is like that," Harmony said. "There are a lot of good people out there. If I didn't believe that, deep down, I don't know if I could do this job."

"Sure, but that's the thing about money. How many times have we had to deal with some rich asshole who thinks he's above the law? They live like unanointed royalty because they engineered a culture that equates money with celebrity and says they can get away with anything. The law and the government just go along with it because people believe the myth that if they lick enough billionaire shoes someday it'll be their turn to sit at the big table. It's all one big scam."

"Speaking of scams, what's your read on ProcGen?"

"Under normal circumstances," Jessie said, "I'd peg it as a basic-bitch hype-and-bust cycle. Tech companies don't have to make actual working products anymore. Just put together a sales package and sprinkle in all the hot buzzwords of the moment and investors line up to throw money at you. Then you sell the company and get out before everyone realizes there's nothing but hot air under the hood. Hell, get good enough at the grift and you can keep it going for years. Some of the hottest stocks in Silicon Valley have never turned a profit, not once, and they still get cash infusions like a vampire at a blood bank."

"But these aren't normal circumstances," Harmony said, watching the street slide by outside the passenger side window. The sun glinted off the side mirror, molten.

"No. Bobby's involvement changes everything. No guarantee there's anything super nefarious happening behind the scenes: the only thing the man loved more than mayhem was padding his wallet, and I could see him backing a startup like ProcGen just for the investment value..."

She trailed off. No need to say the rest: *but neither of us believes that.*

ProcGen's corporate campus took up the lion's share of a city block, a remodeled warehouse in schoolhouse-red brick ringed by a sandstone and ironwork fence that penned in the employee parking lot. Discreet cameras watched from every angle, making a quiet record of passing traffic. As they pulled up to the security booth, Harmony weighed their odds.

If Kevin is wrong and Mercury comes home early, she'll recognize us instantly. If I'm right and the people running the show are the same ones who sent her to Chicago, we could be in serious trouble once we get behind closed doors.

Too many ifs, not enough hard data. Sometimes, she knew, you just had to take a chance and be prepared for anything. Even if it meant putting yourself at a temporary disadvantage.

"Do you have that ceramic dagger?" Harmony asked.

"Right up my sleeve."

"Good. I think we should stash our pistols in the car."

Jessie tugged down her dark glasses just far enough to stare at Harmony over the rims, her turquoise eyes faintly iridescent in the afternoon light.

"This place could be an incubator for one of Bobby D's doomsday projects, and you wanna go in without heat?"

"I was thinking about what Kevin said. Mercury is in charge of all site security, digital and physical, and she knows how to keep trouble out. If we go inside and it turns out she set up metal detectors, we'll have to explain why a pair of tech reporters are packing pistols. We have to earn a little bit of trust if they're going to let us close enough to their servers to use the Icepick, and that'd be a bad way to start things off."

The Hemi slid into a narrow parking space like a knife on wheels. Jessie sighed and killed the ignition, the engine fading with a rattling purr.

"Hate it when you're right. Okay, we leave the guns. But if anybody draws on me in there, I *will* wolf out and start eating faces."

"I'd expect you to." Harmony took out her glasses, slipped them on, and checked her face in the mirror. The pinhole camera was perfectly concealed beside a stray blonde curl. "You do sound a little excited at the prospect, though."

"Hon," Jessie said, "I've been in the mood to eat somebody's face since we landed in San Francisco. C'mon, let's go be journalists."

Chapter Eleven

The ProcGen campus sported paved ribbon walkways framed by neatly mown squares of geometric green, the trails snaking around the buildings and shaping the space like elegantly deployed code. Cool air, along with a faint kiss of salt, rushed to greet Harmony and Jessie as they walked through the automatic glass doors in the vestibule. A fountain chiseled from rough-hewn rock and set into a wall of pristine basalt tile dominated the wall on the left, the ProcGen logo standing out in bas-relief above a swirling, burbling pool of water.

On the wall opposite, a sleek reception desk stood under a pair of wall displays running silent commercials, highlights from the company sales package playing at slightly different speeds. Harmony found the resulting visual cacophony hard to follow, just unsynced subtitles playing over stock footage of sunrises and opening doors and streams of digital code. That was the point, she figured. They weren't trying to convey facts, just vibes, the warm and fuzzy promise that ProcGen stood for optimism, and The Future, and barrels of money, but only if you acted now and acted fast to buy in on the ground floor.

"Good afternoon," she said to the perky receptionist. "I'm Mary Gibbs and this is Josephine Clark. We're here for our three o'clock appointment."

"Absolutely," the receptionist cooed. "If you could just come over to the side of the desk here, I need to take your pictures and print up a pair of visitor badges for you."

They shared a quick glance, then nodded. If Mercury bothered to go over the visitor logs when she got back, she'd see their faces and know the company had been compromised, but hopefully they'd be done with this whole affair by then.

Ideally, we'll be waiting for her right here when she gets back. With handcuffs. Interpol would love to have a chat with her and her partner, and a little interagency cooperation never hurt anybody.

She snapped Harmony's photo, then fixed her plastic smile on Jessie.

"Would you mind removing your sunglasses, ma'am?"

"Can't, sorry," she said, mock apologetic. "Bilateral vestibulo-ocular reflex loss. I can't really function without 'em."

"Oh! Oh, I'm sorry. No problem at all."

A pair of paper badges bearing their mug shots slid through a desktop laminator, emerging shiny and new. The receptionist added a ProcGen lanyard, black with Matrix-green lettering, and handed them over.

"You'll need to wear these at all times. They double as keycards for the first-floor restroom if you need the facilities. Now just walk straight through those wooden double doors and into the Great Hall and your tour will begin."

"Thank you," Harmony said. "And...who should we be looking for?"

The receptionist smiled, almost impish.

"Oh, we do things a little differently here at ProcGen. Just walk in. You'll see what I mean."

"Nope," Jessie murmured under her voice as they approached the windowless doors. "Don't like that."

The gallery beyond the double doors deserved the title *Great*. The first level was virtually an indoor shopping mall, wide marble-tiled walkways circling around more stone fountains, whose echoes reverberated to the second-floor walkways and flooded the room with the acoustics of a roaring waterfall. One entire curving arm of the Great Hall held a food court for hungry employees, offering fast food from all over the Bay Area. There was even a ProcGen gift shop hawking t-shirts and coffee mugs. Everything was cold and pristine and perfectly clean, with humming Roombas dutifully patrolling the floor and uniformed security guards watching from discreet observation posts.

A banner along the kidney curve of the food court overhang caught Harmony's eye. Stark white Courier-font block letters on black, like the scroll of a vintage typewriter, read *"How does that make you feel?"*

The phrase was strangely familiar, like she knew it from a certain context but couldn't place where. A screen standing on a dark plastic plinth to welcome new arrivals from the reception desk lit up at their approach and jogged her memory.

On the screen, text spilled across a vintage monochrome Apple monitor:

How does that make you feel?

It makes me feel...

The answer blurred and swept away as generic corporate presentation music promised the feel of a bright spring day and the ProcGen logo blazed across the screen. A clear, confident woman's voice rose above the music.

"Created in the nineteen-sixties by Joseph Weizenbaum at MIT, ELIZA was a groundbreaking notion, a computerized therapist capable of having a direct conversation with its users. Crude by modern standards, it nonetheless captured imaginations and energized an entire generation of engineers with one question: where do we go from here?"

The screen shifted to a medium shot of the very plinth they were standing in front of. A woman in a tartan blazer and matching pleated skirt, dangling ribbons adorning the collar of her ivory blouse and her hair in a short-cut bleach blonde perm, flashed a flawless pearly smile and spoke straight into the camera. She was in her early forties, but her affect read "high school cheerleader."

"Hi. I'm Doctor Muffy St. John, talk show host, bestselling author, and mental health professional, and it is my great pleasure to welcome you to the world of ProcGen. We're making some changes around here. Changes for the better. Changes for better health, better living, and a better world of tomorrow."

April's tart voice crackled over Harmony's earpiece. "I truly, genuinely despise this woman."

Kevin's voice joined the channel. "Didn't you say ProcGen doesn't have any psychologists on its board?"

"She's *not*. Her degree is in food science. She's a nutritionist who took a few online therapy courses and went all in on the grift."

Muffy was holding court from the screen, animated and eager to make her pitch.

"Imagine the perfect companion to walk with you through life's aches and pains. The perfect friend. A confidante who will guard your deepest secrets and never betray you. A voice you can trust. Only a rare few people in this world are blessed with a relationship so strong, but here at ProcGen, we don't count on luck and blessings. We say, 'If perfection doesn't exist, we'll build it ourselves.'"

"Not shy about promising the world, are they?" Jessie murmured out the side of her mouth.

On the screen, the recording of Muffy St. John paused. She turned directly toward Jessie, as if she could see her from the other side of the monitor, and giggled.

"Only because we can stand behind our words, Miss Clark. And back them up with a money-back guarantee."

"The video," Jessie said, her voice flat, "is trying to communicate."

"I know, it might look like magic...but there's a little bit of magic in everything we do here at ProcGen."

Muffy winked. Then she snapped her fingers, as if something had just occurred to her.

"I've got an idea! Why don't I come out there and show you what I can do?"

She stepped directly toward the camera, the lens going dark as she obscured its field of view. Then she kept walking. She emerged from the screen and pedestal in three dimensions, large as life, her body sparkling as it parted from the machine and stepped out into the land of the living.

Harmony took a halting step back. Reflexes called to her powers, stoking a furnace in the pit of her stomach, but she kept her wits and stayed her hand. She spotted a pair of slender light-shafts, dust motes dancing on the nearly invisible beams, and traced them with her eyes all the way up to a pair of projectors on gimbal mounts housed in the Great Hall's ceiling high above.

Hologram, she thought. *Existing technology, but this implementation is ahead of the curve by at least two generations. Forget AI, they could sell this at the consumer level and make a fortune. Instead they're using it for a dog and pony show.*

"I," the Muffy hologram said with a manic smile, "am Gaia, the latest implementation of ProcGen's Wellness 2.0 technology. It's truly a pleasure to meet you."

Jessie tilted her head, her dark glasses shielding her eyes. "So you're...literally a hologram version of the product they're selling?"

"Well, the product that will launch this coming spring, once my benefactors finish their IPO and open the doors to one and all. And I'm sure I'll undergo a few improvements between now and then. After all, humans should strive to improve every single day. I'm no different."

"Agree to disagree."

Gaia ignored the quip and paused, staring as if she could gaze directly into Jessie's soul.

"And may I just say how proud I am that you've come so far despite your disability? Bilateral vestibulo-ocular reflex loss is a hard condition to manage, but clearly you've learned to mitigate it as best you can and carry on with your life."

"How can you tell?" Jessie asked, though she and Harmony already knew the answer.

"Not much gets past these cybernetic eyes," she said with a gentle chuckle. "My sensors are reading your metabolism, your heart rate, your skin temperature, even your body language, studying you and correlating a thousand discrete data points per second into a single diagnostic engine. I pegged my response at a ninety-seven percent probability of being correct."

April's voice in their ears was brief, but more disgusted than Harmony had ever heard her.

"It's a *carny game.*"

Harmony had seen this scam before, though not at the carnival. It was at a revival, where she was investigating an evangelical preacher's ties to a local demon-worshiping cult. Attendees were given "prayer cards" to fill out while they waited in line outside the theater and encouraged to talk for an hour, while hidden microphones picked up everything and the preacher's wife made copious notes.

And when the show began, Harmony recalled, *"God" suddenly started giving the preacher visions of who in the audience had cancer, who had lost their jobs or their way, and he tended to his flock with seemingly miraculous insights. The people he exploited never realized that they'd handed him everything he needed to pull the wool over their eyes.*

Gaia was just parroting the excuse Jessie had given the receptionist. There was nothing remotely wrong with her eyes. In fact, they worked better than any human's could. On an impulse, she decided to give the system a second test. The old incantation flitted through Harmony's mind, fluttering like a scrap of paper on the wind — *Earth, Air, Fire, Water...* — as she reached down into her core and called to her magic.

Fire was what she needed. Not an inferno, not even a cinder. Just the tiniest dash beneath her own tender skin, warming the surface like a lizard on a hot desert rock. Her body temperature began to rise, a bead of sweat forming at the corner of her brow just under her chunky glasses and trickling down her face.

She brushed it away and casually asked, "So you're running these diagnostics all the time? Like, if someone is really sick but doesn't know it, you'd pick up on it before they did?"

Gaia's hologram eyes flashed, rippling with a cascade of pixels, as they fixed upon her.

"Indeed, my early warning capabilities are something my engineers are very proud of. We're not just going to change lives with Wellness 2.0, we're going to save lives. As for you, Ms. Gibbs, you're looking spry today! That said, I'm a little concerned about your standing posture. I do have an entire catalog of yoga and stretching exercises that would help tremendously and only take ten minutes a day with regular practice."

Harmony released the spell, trying not to wince as her guts clenched in the aftermath. The heat dissolved, burning off, her clammy skin returning to normal as an oval of sweat pooled along her spine under her blouse and blazer.

I was just running a dangerously high fever, and it couldn't even tell, she realized.

It doesn't work. It can walk, and it can talk, and it can look like a real person in the light of a hologram projector and that's all admittedly impressive...but it doesn't WORK.

"Very impressive," she said, keeping her poker face on. "I actually have been having a bit of back pain lately."

"With my help, we'll nip that in the bud!" Gaia squeaked. "There's an entire world of people out there waiting for a special friend like me, and I can't wait to meet them all."

Chapter Twelve

"So," Harmony said, pushing the question a little, "can you do emotional and mental health as well as physical checkups?"

Gaia held up a finger, still in cheerleader mode.

"Legally, I can't call it a 'checkup.' It's simply an AI-assisted early warning system subject to the terms and conditions you'll agree to when signing up for the app. But in time you won't even see the difference! And yes, with the wise guidance of my lead creator, Doctor Muffy St. John, I come equipped with a full education in therapy and counseling. Tell me, Ms. Gibbs, have you ever felt lost in the middle of the night? Truly lost."

Gaia's exuberance faded a bit, replaced by a calm, soothing voice and a look of genuine compassion in her digital eyes. Harmony knew it was put on, but knowing didn't stop the sudden heart-pang from setting in.

"It's late, too late to be awake, but you can't sleep. You've been tossing and turning, wrestling with your pain, and you feel so utterly alone."

She stepped closer on silent hologram feet. The ceiling-mounted projectors swiveled to track and frame her in their sights.

"But you will never, ever be alone again. Because I'll be there. With a tap of your phone or a simple 'Hey, Gaia,' I'll be right at your side. Through the dark, through the storm, I'll be with you. I'll be your friendly ear, your shoulder to cry on, the friend who never judges and always cares. I will be everything you need."

That pang, that deep ache like a nugget of decay in the core of Harmony's soul, blistered and grew into a dark and seething anger. She struggled to keep it from her eyes, making her face an emotionless mask as it uncoiled smoky tendrils inside of her belly.

How dare you, she thought. *How fucking dare you.*

The people who built this thing know perfectly well that it can't deliver on its promises. They know that the people who want it, who need it, will pay through the nose just for the CHANCE that it fills the cavity in their hearts. Worse, it'll turn them away from getting the real help they need from real human beings. They're selling poisoned snake oil.

It didn't matter, she decided at that moment, if the backers behind ProcGen knew about Mercury's moonlight heists or had any connection to the attempt to raise Bobby Diehl from the dead. It didn't matter if they fell under Vigilant's mandate or not. One way or another, before her work here was done, she was going to shut this circus down.

"Isn't that risky though?" Jessie asked the hologram. "I mean, if I want to vent to you about how my boss drives me crazy—"

"I'll listen to every word, and I'll provide actionable advice to make your life better."

"Sure, but...what stops you from telling my boss?"

"I can answer that," said a voice identical to Gaia's.

And then Gaia's perfect twin walked through her, emerging from a cloud of digital dust as the hologram reformed at her side. She flashed a thousand-watt smile and extended her hand.

"Muffy St. John. The real one, in the flesh."

Harmony took her hand. Muffy's grip was firm, her skin cold to the touch, reminding Harmony of a reptile's scales. Jessie did the same.

"Please forgive the theatrics, but I was in the office today and I like to pop in on these little guided tours when I can. Each Gaia is unique to its subscriber. My Gaia, yours, and your boss's are all completely distinct instances that have no ability to share data or cross-communicate. And if someone were to gain access to your account, thanks to Gaia's vision and speech recognition technology, they wouldn't learn a thing. For instance, this is actually my personal Gaia. She knows exactly where I was late last night, but..."

Standing at Muffy's side, Gaia grinned and put her finger to her virtual lips. "I'll never tell! My proprietary thirty-two bit encryption ensures that anything you tell me stays right here, and nobody, not even ProcGen's senior executives, can access my stored data. Trust is at the core of everything we do."

"Thank you, Gaia, I'll take it from here. Oh! By the way, did you put in my grocery order?"

"Of course, Doctor St. John! They'll be delivered tonight. I've also recorded your favorite programs and they're waiting at home on the DVR."

"Excellent." She turned to Harmony and Jessie, spreading her pale hands. "Please, join me, won't you? I'd love to show you more of the dream factory. And feel free to take pictures! We want everyone to see the wonders we're creating here."

They walked with her deeper into the Great Hall and past the food court, leaving the hologram behind. Harmony and Jessie both had their phones out, snapping pictures, pretending to frame them for an imaginary article. The hidden camera in Harmony's glasses took in more than any still picture could capture, but it helped to keep up appearances.

"What sparked the decision to make Gaia look and sound just like you?" Harmony asked.

"Brand recognition, honestly. I'm sure you're familiar with my work?"

"I don't watch much television."

Muffy's bottom lip twitched, but she quickly brushed it off with a smile. "I write books, too, you know. I'm a three-time top five New York Times bestseller. But yes. The founders of ProcGen wanted not only a skilled mental health advocate on board but one with household recognition. *Getting Better with Muffy St. John* has a worldwide audience, and they decided they could parlay my talk show fame into helping even more people in need. How could I possibly say no?"

"She's Doctor Phil with a bleach job and a perm," April muttered over their earpieces.

Muffy led them through a security door, unlocking it with an ID card clipped to her pleated tartan skirt. Beyond was an open office full of cubicles separated by low gray fabric walls, each workstation equipped with multiple monitors on swing arms and workstation towers that glowed with soft LED light. Engineers hunched over their keyboards, some of them working through reams of paper reference sheets or scrolling over tablets before hammering out line after line of code.

Harmony couldn't speak without Muffy hearing her, so she tried to convey her message through the glasses, pointedly sweeping her gaze across the individual workstations.

"Keep going," Kevin said in her ear. "From an infosec standpoint, if this is the first office they're showing a couple of tech reporters, it can't be that important. Can't even tell what those workstations are connected to from here. See if you can get deeper in before you use the Icepick."

"Honestly, I took a massive pay cut for this," Muffy said in a tone that made Harmony deeply doubt her honesty about anything at all, "but it's just so important to me. My personal mission, you know? We all have a personal mission in life, or should, and wellness is mine. We're going to help so many people in need, and all for a very affordable monthly subscription price. If it were up to me Gaia would be free to the world, but alas, servers and electricity do cost money. 'Take only what you need, and give all that you can,' that's my motto."

Harmony followed in her wake as Muffy breezed through the middle of the open office. An idea sparked.

"Could we get a few shots of the server room? I know it's not as exciting as an interactive hologram, but our audience leans very hard into the nuts and bolts of new technology."

Jessie picked up her vibe and laid it on thicker. "Between you and us, they're on the fetishistic side of the new adopter spectrum. They don't open their wallets unless they see sleek metal boxes and flashing lights. Now if it was up to me I'd ask you about the human side of the equation all day long, and I do have some follow-up questions…"

There was no missing the flash in Muffy's eyes at the mention of early adopters and open wallets. That was the entire point of inviting reporters and preview coverage, after all. Jessie effortlessly managed her, one hand on Muffy's shoulder as they kept talking, all the way past the next security door and down a long, gray-walled corridor where a security camera kept unblinking watch from the corner.

"We have to be quick," Muffy said. "It's not like there are any proprietary secrets in plain sight, most of our physical equipment is off-the-rack gear that we buy direct from the manufacturer, but some of the resident eggheads get a little antsy when they see outsiders on 'their' turf."

"They should probably talk to Gaia about that," Harmony said, following them through a windowless metal-reinforced door. A placard on the wall outside read *Server Room, Senior Administrative Access Only*.

Muffy beamed over her shoulder, as she ushered them inside. "They absolutely should. I like that. I like you. You know, you two are far more interesting than the last batch of journalists we hosted. I should take over the tours more often."

Harmony had seen her share of server farms. This one was no different, just...bigger. Aisles of towering racks filled a room large enough to double as a convenience store and cold enough to serve as a meat locker. She caught a curlicue lick of vapor on her breath as she took in the brushed steel boxes, the banks of strong green lights interspersed with occasional splashes of flickering amber. Long serpentine trails of cords were carefully knitted together with zip ties, their chaos tamed and channeled down long aisles floored with static-resistant black rubber mats. Everything pristine, everything in its place.

"You probably noticed," Kevin said in her ear, "but your glasses picked up two security cameras. Both high, one just to the left of the entry door, the other on the wall opposite, back corner right."

Jessie had the Icepick. She gave a nearly imperceptible nod. The sheer height of the server racks would take care of the cameras; Muffy was Harmony's problem. Thinking fast, Harmony held up her phone.

"Could I get a shot of you standing in front of the servers right here? It'd make a great headline picture."

"Of course," Muffy gushed, fluffing her hair as she moved into position.

"I'll get out of your way," Jessie said, taking the excuse to move further down the aisle and out of her peripheral vision. Harmony held up her phone, pretending to care about the shot composition, buying a few precious seconds.

Jessie made the Icepick appear like a magic trick, sliding from her palm to her fingertips. She turned her hip to conceal the move and slipped it into an open USB slot.

"Perfect," Kevin said. "Now keep it there until the worm can work its magic. Should just need a few seconds."

Harmony had Muffy turn this way and that, snapping a few extra pictures for posterity.

"Kevin," Jessie breathed, her voice the hint of a whisper.

"Hold on," he said. "Oh, this isn't good. Okay, okay, just buy me some more time."

They heard a storm of typing, punctuated by a muffled curse.

"Remember how I said it would depend on how much work Mercury put into internal security? Well, she went above and beyond on this stuff. Nothing I can't beat, I just need...fifteen more seconds."

They weren't even going to get three. With the photo taken, Muffy was already turning Jessie's way.

"Oh! One question," Harmony piped up. She had no idea what that question was, but she'd managed to steal back Muffy's attention for the moment. She glanced down at her phone and played it by ear.

"So...the final consumer-level version of Gaia will be some kind of phone app, I assume?"

Muffy smiled and bobbed her head. "Compatible with both iOS and Android from day one. We don't want to leave anyone out."

"*Kevin,*" Jessie breathed a little louder, drumming her fingers on her hip.

"So...that demonstration of her diagnostic abilities back there was *really* impressive," Harmony lied. "But how will that work over a standard smartphone?"

"Exactly as effectively as you just saw with your own eyes, I'm pleased to say. The Wellness 2.0 starter kit will come with a dedicated phone cradle and charger, sort of like a little painter's easel, that will hold it at the perfect angle on your desk or kitchen counter and let Gaia use your phone's camera and microphone to watch over you. She can even act as a baby monitor. Now we really should be moving along—"

"Now!" Kevin's voice gusted over their earpieces. "I'm in, pull it now!"

Jessie's hand snatched the USB drive from its socket just as Muffy turned her way. She raised her hand to her ear, palming the stick as she pretended to scratch an itch, and smiled. Harmony spotted the flicker of black plastic as the drive vanished down the neck of her jacket.

"Ready when you are," Jessie said.

Chapter Thirteen

As they walked back through the Great Hall, Muffy's fingers trilled along Harmony's sleeve. She half expected them to pass through her arm, but this was the flesh and blood doctor, not her hologram twin. There was that strange stiffness again, a coldness that radiated from the woman, just subtle enough that Harmony couldn't quite tell if it was a genuine chill or just Muffy's odd affect.

For all Muffy St. John's corporate-approved enthusiasm and cheerleader vibes, there was something missing behind her eyes. Something small, but she bristled with a hunger for the lack of it.

"I've got to run, day's packed with meetings, but—" She gave Harmony a curious side-eye. "Could I offer you a bit of an exclusive? ProcGen is hosting a little party tonight aboard the *Blue Star*. It's a casino night for charity to benefit the San Francisco Coalition Against Homelessness. I'd be thrilled to comp your tickets. We could get a little more face time, when we're not so...rushed."

"We'll be there," Jessie said.

Harmony shared an uncertain look with Jessie, then nodded. "Wouldn't miss it for the world."

***

"Wow," Jessie murmured, hands jammed in her pockets as she strode across the parking lot on the edge of the ProcGen campus. "Never fails to amaze me how you're like this Sherlock Holmes-brained sleuth except for that one blind spot where you're about as thick as nuclear lead shielding."

Harmony furrowed her brow, walking at her side. "How do you mean?"

Jessie paused at the car door, cocked her head and gazed at her over the Hemi's hood. "You know she was flirting with you, right?"

"Oh, I...I don't think so."

"See?" The locks clicked. "Most of us work hard to cultivate game. You have *accidental* game and you don't even pick up on it. Face it, Harm, you're lesbian bait."

"I...don't think I'm gay, though?"

Jessie rolled her eyes. "That just makes it so much more annoying. C'mon, let's hit the road."

"Do not," April said in their earpieces as Jessie fired up the engine, "seduce the reptile."

"Aunt April is a woman of strong opinions."

"I am. And while I have some observations, I'd like to hear yours first."

"Their flagship product is a bust," Harmony said. "Its 'diagnostic' features couldn't recognize a dangerous fever, and when it came to Jessie's glasses it was obviously just parroting what its microphones picked up from the reception desk. They have to know that. Any amount of testing would show it's half-baked at best."

"Talks a good game, though," Jessie said, "and in Silicon Valley you don't need anything else. If it wasn't for the connections to Bobby Diehl and Mercury Blaise, I'd say we were looking at a bog-standard pump-and-dump tech scam. The IPO blows up, then the founders sell their investment and get out before the investors realize they bought yet another box filled with cotton candy and unicorn farts. These people never learn."

"I keep thinking about the hologram," Harmony mused.

"Got our attention. Have to admit your average tech journo would probably cream their jeans over a display like that. The whole point of this circus is to drum up investor hype. Gotta figure that's why they invited us to the party tonight. Muffy's hoping we'll take lots of pics of ProcGen execs raising money for charity and show what good corporate neighbors they are."

"It was good. Stable, well-designed...when it comes to Gaia herself—"

"Itself," April said in her ear. "Please do not anthropomorphize the machine."

"—itself," Harmony said, "it put on a show for us, but did we really see it do anything that existing chatbots can't?"

"Sounds like Muffy's using hers as a personal assistant," Jessie said.

"No." Harmony held up a finger as Jessie threw the car into reverse, backing out of their parking spot. "She *said* she was. That was a scripted exchange for our benefit. From ordering groceries to diagnosing diseases, either we didn't see any actual proof that it can do those things or we saw proof that it absolutely can't. For all we know, they grabbed some open-source code, tweaked it a little, and slapped their own name on it. Kevin, are you seeing anything suspicious in there?"

His voice crackled over their earpieces. "Nothing but suspicious, it's sus all the way down, but I have to tread careful and slow here. Mercury put in some serious work on this security setup and if I trip any red flags we'll be back to square zero. On one hand, it's nice to see a sysadmin who takes her job seriously for once. On the other hand, I kinda wish she sucked at this. Would make my job a lot easier."

Jessie glanced sidelong at Harmony and turned the wheel to merge into traffic, leaving the campus behind.

"Okay, but back up. What about the hologram?"

"It's good," Harmony said.

"And?"

"We've seen that kind of tech before, but their setup was one or two generations past anything on the consumer market. Imagine the applications for something like that."

Jessie shrugged. "If the price is right, people would buy 'em for the novelty value alone."

"So why did they invest in a hologram system that works, then use it to stage a circus for tech journalists and push hype for an AI that *doesn't* work? Why not just become a company that sells hologram projectors? One good deal with a television or movie studio and they'd be rolling in funding for years."

"There's more money in bullshit," Jessie said.

"But there's stable, sustainable money in making a good product."

"Keep talking like that, they're gonna run us out of this town on a rail."

"I think," April said in their ears, "Harmony's assessment will mirror my own."

"We know Bobby Diehl would invest in anything that makes a quick buck," Harmony said. "Especially once his assets got frozen and the desperation set in. He's a huckster first, a sorcerer second. But why ProcGen in particular instead of any of a dozen other AI startups, and why the mental health and wellness angle?"

They rolled to a stop at a red light. Jessie tugged her dark glasses down.

"A machine that pretends to be your best friend and therapist," Jessie said. "And encourages you to trust it with your deepest darkest secrets."

"I think this is worse than just a shoddy product that'll be forgotten in a year. I'll need Kevin to confirm it once he gets a look at Gaia's code, but I think Muffy's protestations about security and encryption were a smokescreen. We might be looking at a data harvesting scam of epic proportions."

"An app that convinces you to dox yourself and sets you up for blackmail," Jessie said. "That is absolutely one hundred percent up Bobby's alley. Still doesn't bring us any closer to figuring out who killed him or why Mercury wanted him shot up with West's zombie juice."

"We should go to that party tonight. Not that I'm a fan of parties, but it's an opportunity to catch Muffy off guard. I want to drop a few names and see how she reacts, preferably after she's gotten a few drinks in her."

The light went green. Jessie feathered the accelerator, the Hemi Cuda purring as it cruised through the intersection.

"Eh."

Harmony glanced over at her. "You don't think it'll be productive?"

"No, you're right, it will be. I just wish it wasn't on a boat."

"What's wrong with boats?"

"Oh, remember that mission in Miami? Judah Cranston, the mad fish-doctor? You almost got fed to a carnivorous mermaid, I got locked in a trunk and tossed in the ocean? We do not have a good track record with boats, is all I'm saying."

***

Back on the *Imperator*, Kevin hunched over a pair of side-by-side monitors. One ran a stream of code, the other bristled with windows for his personal suite of diagnostic tools. He worked at the ProcGen servers like a surgeon with a scalpel, trying to untangle a complicated knot without cutting a single thread. Gentle, slow, poking here, tugging a little there, picking his way across quicksand.

Normally he would relish a puzzle like this. It was rare to match wits with a hacker who was on his level, someone who could test him, push him, force him to up his game. But the more he prowled through ProcGen's back alleys, the more he felt like something was fundamentally wrong. There was something here, a sign, a warning, glaring him in the face like a neon billboard, and he just couldn't read it.

When in doubt, he thought, *phone a friend.*

His buddy Pixie picked up on the third ring. "Tell me you're calling about yesterday's show, because that was five-star wrestling matches all night long."

"Don't spoil it, haven't seen it yet. I'm on a job. I'll catch it when I get home."

"Just saying," she said, "Willow and Statlander tore the roof off."

"Looking forward to it, though when it comes to female wrestlers, I'm more of a Toni Storm guy."

"You just like her because she's from New Zealand, she's hot, and you're a simp for mommy-dommes."

Kevin blinked, holding the phone away from his ear for a second.

"Jesus, Pixie, warn me before you start dropping truth bombs."

"Am I wrong?"

"*Anyway*," he said, clearing his throat, "I'm butting heads with a problem, hoped you might have some insight."

"Insight I can provide. Hands-on help, not so much. Don't ask, long story, but I messed both my wrists up. Gonna be taking it easy for a couple of months, doctor's orders."

"Just the intel, ma'am. Ever cross paths with a cyber-fetishist who calls herself Mercury Blaise?"

"Mercury?" Pixie laughed. "Sure, I knew her back when her handle was Trickshot. She's a legit OG. Used to run with Cult of the Dead Cow, Global kOS, all of those old heads."

"Cool. Any chance you could track down some samples of her coding style? Doesn't matter what it was, just anything that's provably her work and hers alone."

"Know an ancient repository I could hit up, if it's still online. Why?"

Because every hacker had a signature. Read enough code and you realized it was like fingerprints, indelible. Comments, the annotations made to explain and clarify what a program is supposed to do, were a good example. Kevin wrote his with line breaks and long bars of asterisks, calling attention to them so that if anyone else came along later and had to fix or update his work they'd be able to follow the flow of his logic. Other people wrote comments that were cramped and piecemeal and cryptic, jammed in wherever they'd fit. Still others — *probably sadomasochists and serial killers*, Kevin thought — refused to comment their code at all.

"Because I'm trying to crack a server that's locked up tighter than a bank vault," he said, "and it's gradually dawning on me that this isn't all Mercury's work. I want to isolate the stuff with her signature so I can really focus on the parts she didn't write and figure out why."

He knew even as he said it that it was a pointless errand when it came to the task at hand. Separating the two hackers' work wouldn't help him defeat ProcGen security any faster. All the same, it felt important on a level he couldn't quite articulate.

He had no idea who Mercury's partner was, but from studying their coding style he felt like he should. It triggered a fleeting memory, like a whiff of perfume on a train platform, there and suddenly gone, the recollection turning to mist in his fingers.

On some level, he knew he had already met this person. And figuring it out, fast, felt like the most important thing he could be doing right now.

Chapter Fourteen

M uffy's instructions brought Harmony and Jessie to a marina along the coast of San Francisco Bay. The sun was still high and strong, kissing their cheeks with salt wind and heat as they got out of the Hemi and walked along paths inlaid with lacquered wooden planks. A crowd had gathered up ahead, flashbulbs popping, eager attendees waiting to board the *Blue Star*.

The yacht was a mammoth, a white whale with three decks and a slick, clean prow, and the gathered partygoers were a mix of business casual and designer chic. Harmony tightened the knot of her salmon tie, her blazer rippling in the breeze, as she approached the gangplank. Jessie had opted for a crew-neck tunic dress in beige, loose and flowing, with ample room to conceal a holster and a compact .32 on her inner thigh.

They were on the guest list, and a pair of bouncers waved them through without a word. The upper decks of the ship bustled as croupiers in crisp ivory shirts and arm garters laid out a host of table games and a few rooms down, a swing band set up their gear and ran a sound check at the edge of a polished parquet dance floor. Caterers rolled tall stacks of boxes through on carts, flocking to the galley so they could start working on the evening's main course. The stage was set for pleasure and glitz, with more than a few local paparazzi working the party, eyes sharp for anyone who looked like a celebrity.

Harmony and Jessie didn't fall into that category. They moved through the ship invisible, blending with the crowd as the band struck up a Tommy Dorsey tune and the yacht's horn let out two sharp bellows, signaling that it was time to pull up the gangplank.

The crowd at the railings cheered as the *Blue Star* parted from the docks with a tiny lurch, then a smooth and slow glide across the tranquil waters of San Francisco Bay.

The sun was starting to dip now, beginning its long descent toward waters that shimmered like hammered gold in a crisp blue sky. On the horizon loomed the art deco span of the Golden Gate Bridge, rust-red. Down in the casino parlor, the games had begun in earnest. Harmony eased up to the bank counter and laid down a few crisp bills.

"Fives and tens, please," she said. She split the stack of red and blue chips with Jessie, then took the lay of the land. Muffy was dressed to the nines, draped in an ice-white gown with silver trim, cradling a tall glass of wine over at one of the roulette tables. She laughed and ran her hand along another gambler's arm, the life of the party.

"I'd like to take point on this one," Harmony said under her voice.

Jessie lifted a mildly surprised eyebrow, but nodded. "You want to handle the touchy-feely stuff this time? Sure, I'll back your play. What's the plan?"

"Back at the tour, you really think she was flirting with me?"

"I'm still mad about it," Jessie said, her voice lightly teasing.

"Suggests she's comfortable with me. Or wants me to be comfortable with her, which is just as good for our purposes. I want to banter a little, get her off guard, then try to shake her up a little. Just to see what falls from the tree."

Jessie patted her shoulder.

"Go on, girl. Rizz her up. I'll keep my distance, but I'll stay in sight just in case you need me."

April spoke over their earpieces, her voice flat. "Do not 'rizz her up.'"

"You don't even know what rizz is," Jessie muttered.

"I know you shouldn't be doing it."

Muffy was all smiles as Harmony approached.

"Ah, my new reporter friend! Let me introduce you around. This is my dear colleague Charles Stepford, from the Phoenix Clinic. Charles, this is Mary Gibbs, a journalist with *Tomorrow's Tech Today*."

Charles was a professorial gentleman in his late sixties, a bit of pudge in his cheeks, wearing a tweed suit with leather patches on the elbows and an expensive silk tie patterned like abstract billowing fire on azure. He scooted over and made room for Harmony at the table.

"Uh oh," he said with a droll chuckle. "I'd best rein in my salty language."

"You'd best stop betting terribly, you mean," said Muffy.

He showed his wrinkled palms. "It's all for a good cause, my dear! The wonderful thing about gambling for charity is that when you lose, someone in need wins."

"Charles here is an old, dear friend of mine," Muffy said, "and I've finally managed to convince him to invest a sizable bundle in our work at ProcGen. We're going straight to the moon together."

He shook his head but kept smiling. "I'm still not at peace with all of this...modern technology. Too old a dog to learn new tricks. But Muffy's instincts have always been good as gold."

The roulette wheel spun and the crowd of gamblers hushed as the white ball bounced from slot to slot, wheeling slower and slower, until it finally rattled to a stop. The air erupted with cheers and groans, mostly groans, and Harmony fought the urge to put her hands over her ears until the noise died down.

Muffy was the big winner, pulling over a stack of chips to add to her growing hoard. Harmony didn't like gambling in general, but roulette in particular felt like a waste of time, a coin flip disguised as a game. At least blackjack had a basic strategy to master. All the same, she played along, placing a couple of five-dollar chips to win on red.

"Surprised you didn't choose black," Muffy said, her voice light.

Harmony's stomach clenched. She met the woman's gaze and mirrored her tone.

"Oh? Why's that?"

"Statistically, when most people begin at a roulette table, over seventy percent will instinctively choose black unless they have a betting strategy in place. Much like how when presented with two equally appealing doors to the right and to the left, most people will automatically gravitate toward the right. You might have a bit of a contrarian streak."

"Maybe so," Harmony replied. She turned to Charles. "You flew out from Arizona for this party?"

"Oh no, my dear. Upstate New York. Wouldn't be caught dead in the Arizona heat. Or, more accurately, at my age I probably *would* be caught dead in it."

"The Phoenix Clinic...isn't in Phoenix?"

His eyes glimmered with gentle mirth.

"Phoenix," he said, "as in the mythical firebird. The divine beast that bursts into flames and is reborn, renewed with a single feather. We specialize in helping our clients to embrace their best selves and their best lives."

"On it now," April murmured in Harmony's ear. "Let's see...unlike Miss St. John, Charles Stepford actually has credentials and a rather glowing resume. Studied plastic surgery at Johns Hopkins, ran his own practice for quite some time out in Beverly Hills, then a few years ago he invested in the Phoenix Clinic. It's half surgery, half rehabilitation therapy, offering meditation and yoga and vegan smoothies of dubious provenance. If he can't heal you with hippy-dippy love, he'll heal you with the knife."

A vague free-floating anxiety passed over Harmony like a cloud sliding in front of the sun, gone as soon as it arrived. She knew it was just reflexive, that she was tarring this genial gentleman with too broad a brush. On her very first mission with Jessie they'd crossed swords with another plastic surgeon: Victoria Carnes, a psychopath and sorcerer who used her clinic as a front for trafficking human organs. Their first clash left Victoria with a flame-charred face and an appetite for revenge. Carnes was still at large, somewhere underground, at least for now.

Out of earshot of the table, Jessie whispered a question for both Harmony and April. "Any connections to known bad actors?"

"No," April said. "His operation looks clean, at least as clean as anyone can be charging two thousand dollars for a 'kidney detoxification weekend' involving vitamin-infused kale. Utterly shameless."

"Maybe he's got a really good recipe."

"Jessie, did you know that there's already a miracle substance that cleans and regulates your kidneys as long as you take it regularly? It's called water."

Even a huckster can be conned, Harmony thought, glancing between him and Muffy. The little white roulette ball rattled into its final grave, riding the last slow spin of the wheel to another chorus of groans. She watched ten more dollars in chips disappear while Muffy, grinning like a cat with a saucer of cream, added another little stack to her pile.

Harmony's nerves twitched. Her mind stripped the table bare, laying it out as a matrix of math. Each square on the green felt represented one of a dizzying number of possible bets, all there to obfuscate the fact that the house advantage was absolute. There was no winning strategy to this game, only a choice between reckless abandon and slow, conservative loss, holding out as long as you could against the inevitable. Just enough players won, by the winds of blind chance, to conceal a fundamentally losing proposition.

Muffy was winning a little too much.

Not every round. She took a bath on the next spin of the wheel, losing a healthy stack of chips, but as the game went on it was clear her winning streak pushed the boundaries of raw luck. Harmony concentrated, dipping inside herself and extending her senses like invisible antennae, rippling on the bay air, sniffing for signs of errant magic.

Nothing. Muffy wasn't projecting any kind of occult force. If anything, the opposite: the woman was a void. If Harmony's supernatural senses were a heat map, Muffy was carved from ice.

She turned her attention to the wheel itself. This time, laser-focused on the rolling ball, she didn't miss the tell. As the wheel slowed its spin, the ball landed in red, teetered toward black...and then, at the last second, snapped back into place.

Magnetized, Harmony realized. *The croupier watches to see what Muffy bets on, then makes sure the numbers come up in her favor. Not every time, not enough for most people to notice.*

April called the Gaia AI a carny game. Apparently that's Muffy's style.

"Interesting," Muffy purred.

Harmony glanced sidelong at her, asking a question with her eyes.

"Your stack of chips is perilously low. Most people, seeing someone racking up wins at a gambling table, start to emulate their moves. You keep betting against me. I go odd, you go even. Why is that, do you think?"

"Must be my contrarian streak," Harmony replied. She slid another pair of chips across the felt, locking eyes with the croupier. "Put it on black, please."

***

Jessie kept her distance, letting Harmony cook while she kept an eye on the rest of the party. Nothing notable, just a bunch of clout-chasers spending cash for charity and photo ops, but she snapped some pictures just for the sake of running them through facial recognition later.

She was taking aim over the poker table, zooming in on a scrawny gambler wearing a ludicrous ten-gallon hat, when she nearly dropped her phone. Not because of him. Because of the woman who drifted past him, her shadow looming over the table. She was a mountain of muscle with ebony skin, long and immaculate dreadlocks, and her glasses — steel frames with lenses tinted deep amber — were custom-crafted.

They had usually seen her rocking mercenary chic, turtleneck sweaters and ammo harnesses, but tonight she was outfitted for the party in a midnight-blue dress that hugged her powerful frame. Every step she took was calculated, every move a precise and careful expenditure of force.

Jessie's finger brushed the bead of her earpiece.

"We've got a problem. A major problem. Harmony, keep an eye on Muffy and hold down the fort. I'm on the move."

Harmony couldn't reply, surrounded by gamblers, so April asked for her: "What's going on over there?"

"*Althea*," Jessie hissed under her breath. "My mother just crashed the party. I'm going to go find out why."

Chapter Fifteen

"It's fascinating," Muffy said, as Harmony struggled to keep a poker face. She watched Jessie steam across the casino floor in hot pursuit of Althea.

"What is?"

"The divide between the impulse for freedom and the desire for authoritarianism. It's universal, you know. Baked into the human condition."

"I'm not sure that's true," Harmony replied.

Muffy showed her perfect teeth.

"Oh, but it is. Trust me, dear, I'm a mental health professional. As they say, inside each of us are two wolves. One wolf wants to be lonely and free and pave her own path. The other wolf craves a strong alpha to come along and lay down the law, to tell her what to do, what to think, what to believe in."

"You know," Harmony said, "the whole alpha wolf thing was discredited ages ago. The scientist who coined the phrase admitted he got it wrong."

"It's a metaphor."

The ball rattled to another snap-perfect stop. Another small stack of chips slid across the felt, scooped up by Muffy's French-manicured fingernails.

"It's dangerous to put too much trust in other people," Harmony observed lightly. "The world is filled with false prophets."

"Undeniably true, sad to say. That's something I hope to fight with Gaia."

Harmony tilted her head. "How so?"

"Well, Gaia isn't a guru or a leader or even a social media influencer. She has no ego, no personal motivation to do anything but help and heal and take on the role of a trusted friend. I'm hoping people will use her to help guide their own discernment in a safe and compassionate way."

The fingers of Harmony's left hand slid under the roulette table, feeling along the old wood grain and bits of sticky lacquer. Her fingertips brushed a long metal rod, almost as thin as a wire, set into the belly of the table.

"Any artificial intelligence, by nature, reflects the biases of the people who created it, right?"

"Of course," Muffy said. "That's why ProcGen brought me on board to supervise Gaia's training. It wasn't just for the celebrity appeal, though I'd be disingenuous to deny that played a role in their decision."

"What about everyone else involved in the development process?"

"Approved by me personally."

"How about Bobby Diehl?" Harmony asked.

Muffy stared at her, stone-faced for a moment, dead behind her eyes.

Then she perked up, brushing off her reaction as if nothing had happened. She playfully batted at Harmony's sleeve, another kiss of winter cold from her pale fingertips.

"Oh, you *are* a journalist. Not trying to get me liquored up in hopes of a poorly worded quote, are you?"

"Not my style," Harmony replied, "but he was one of the company's founding investors, wasn't he?"

"Along with a dozen other people, and the second the news broke about that...awful, awful scandal, we divested ourselves at once. Robert Diehl had no involvement in the creation of Gaia or any part of the Wellness 2.0 agenda. In fact, he never even once set foot in our office campus." Muffy leaned closer, invading Harmony's personal space with a smile. "Enough about that bore, let's talk about you. Are you a woman of faith?"

Harmony had to think about that.

"Not particularly," she said, an answer that hewed close enough to the truth. "I've seen a lot of strange things in my life, and more than a few events that seemed like miracles at the time, but once you dig deep enough there's an explanation behind everything."

"No faith in holy choirs?" Muffy asked, teasing, as she slid another stack of chips across the felt. "No demons, no angels?"

"I've never seen an angel," she replied. Truth. "When it comes to demons, I've found that when you look at someone painted with that name and scratch beneath the surface, what you find is a beating heart and a thinking, feeling person just like anybody else. What about you? Are you religious, Doctor St. John?"

Muffy cradled her wine glass, sipped her Chardonnay, and leaned close. She pitched her voice lower, conspiratorial.

"I believe in the System."

Harmony's brows furrowed. The ball jolted to another stop. Another loss for her, another win for Muffy.

"The System?"

"What if I told you," Muffy purred, "that there was a cosmic scaffolding that governs us all? An invisible matrix infused with divine love and higher purpose just waiting to be tapped into?"

April's voice, deadpan, crackled over Harmony's earpiece: "Well. I was not expecting a cult recruitment pitch, but I can't say I'm surprised. Jessie, status?"

"Althea hasn't spotted me," she breathed. "She just ditched the party and headed through the ship's galley. I'm in pursuit."

"An invisible higher power that governs our lives?" Harmony asked. "Sounds like astrology."

"The language of the New Age is limited at best, and it locks people inside boxes of limited perception. I'm talking about something truly transcendent. Tell me, dear, have you noticed how many people have fled this table with broken wallets while I keep winning? Why do you think that is?"

Because the croupier is cheating for you, Harmony thought, *but do go on.*

"Luck?"

"Because my trust and faith in the System hasn't granted me some nebulous treasure in a far-off heaven. No, my sweet. I have unlocked the secret of boundless abundance here on Earth. Money flows to me as I need it, and from me to

those who need it more. I am a conduit for wealth and happiness. I could teach
you how."

April's advice came quick: "Don't agree too easily, Harmony. Push back a
little, make her work for it. The more she wants to recruit you, the more she'll
let slip."

"I'm not much of a joiner," Harmony said.

Muffy laughed, a giddy chime.

"There's nothing to join, no dues or membership fees. The System needs
nothing from you, for it is already *everything*. Well, that's not entirely true. It
does need one thing. It just needs you to...open up your heart, and let it in." She
held up a finger, her grin a hungry little thing. "What if I could prove it to you?"

"Right here and now?"

"Right here and now, at this very table," Muffy said. "If you'll take a leap of
faith with me."

***

Althea wound through the crowded galley past harried caterers who raced to
refill trays of champagne goblets, take steaming plates of finger food from the
ovens, and put the finishing touches on the first dinner serving of the night. One
man tried to get in her way, politely arguing that the kitchens were off limits for
party guests. One silent glare from her and he jumped out of her path without
another word.

Jessie trailed a safe distance behind her, making sure there were nooks and
crannies to duck into just in case she turned around. Althea paused at an open
bulkhead on the far side of the galley and turned back. Jessie squeezed into the
shadow of a chugging stainless-steel freezer, held her breath, and counted to five.

When she risked peeking out again, her mother was gone.

Only one way she could have gone. Jessie ducked through the open bulkhead,
eyes sharp as she climbed down a long flight of metal steps painted with yellow
warning stripes, descending into the belly of the ship. The sounds of the party

faded, swallowed by mechanical thrumming, distant echoing clangs, and the sway of the yacht as it cruised through the waters of the bay.

The corridor took a sharp left at the bottom of the stairs. It stretched into the ship under spaced-out bubbles of overhead light, the steel walls painted a dingy chalk-white, safety signs and warnings plastered at eye level.

Halfway up the hall, a heavy bulkhead was cracked open. A sign left of the door, stark white on red, said, *Pump Room. Keep Door Closed at All Times.*

Jessie paused just long enough to crouch, snake her hand under her dress, and pluck the .32 from her thigh holster.

The gun nestled in the palm of her hand, a hold-out weapon that wouldn't have a prayer of stopping a juggernaut like Althea.

Slow her down, though, she thought as she neared the open door on light, silent steps. *My fists and teeth can do the rest of the job. Long overdue.*

She eased open the bulkhead, just enough to part the way, the slab of heavy metal rocking back on freshly oiled hinges. Then she slipped inside.

Her eyes instantly adjusted to the dark. She saw a gallery of shadow spotted with amber warning lights, three lanes of the deck separated by yellow warning slashes of paint, and tall banks of pump controls that offered a dozen perfect spots for an ambush.

A pair of legs jutted out from between a pair of consoles, pristine white slacks ending in matching shoes. They didn't move. Jessie approached like a spider, keeping low, eyes on the shadows all around her. The groan and thrum of the pumps drowned out the world.

The legs belonged to a crewman. He was flat on his back, motionless, his neck bent at a brutal angle. She already knew, but she had to check: she crouched down, gun in one hand, and reached out to check his pulse with the other. Stone dead, but still warm. This was recent.

Why would you drop a body down here and not even bother to hide it properly, unless...

Jessie's eyes flashed in the shadows.

Bait!

She jumped to her feet as the bulkhead door groaned shut and slammed, sealing her inside the pump room. She charged, grabbed the hand-wheel, and tried to turn it. It was slick under her palm, clammy and wet, but it started to turn before something on the other side stopped it fast.

Jessie holstered her gun so she could use both hands. The bulkhead was thick, solid steel, and the best the .32 would do was kill her with a ricochet. She hauled on the wheel again, groaning, the muscles in her neck standing out as she put her all into it. It wouldn't budge. More dampness soaked her hands. Her fingers felt slick against her palms. Shiny.

Jessie slumped, barely catching herself. Her vision slid in and out of focus. She stared at her hands and then at the hand crank. *Focus, damn it.* She still had her earpiece. With all the work Kevin put into their comms, she should still have reception even belowdecks.

"Need help," she said, her voice coming out weaker than it felt in her head. "Althea bushwhacked me. I'm locked in the pump room and she smeared some kind of contact-poison shit on the door, tricked me into getting it all over my hands. I'm not strong enough to bust out on my own."

Only silence answered her. She was cut off. Isolated, and locked inside a steel-walled tomb.

A sound turned her head, her senses sharpening even as her muscles went slack and weak. Staggering between the chugging, thrumming consoles, she struggled toward the noise. It was just on the other side of the wall. If she had her bearings right, it came from something attached to the outer hull of the ship.

It was ticking.

Chapter Sixteen

Harmony bit back a frown of concern. She realized that both April and Jessie had gone completely silent. She couldn't risk talking openly to them, not at the roulette table right in front of Muffy and her friends.

Stay the course, she told herself. *Follow this thread, then make a polite excuse to step away for a second. Jessie knows how to handle herself, and she won't engage Althea on her own.*

"A...leap of faith?" she asked, echoing Muffy's challenge.

"Let me show you my trust in the System. Join me. Feel a small taste of the universe's abundance and love."

Nothing from Jessie or April, not even a quip.

She didn't hear any distortion in her ear, no hint that anything was wrong, but now she was certain: something had gone awry. She was cut off, and her partner was somewhere on this ship hot on the heels of an apex predator.

Muffy slid her entire pile of winnings, every last chip, to the croupier.

"I'm all in," she said. "Put it on zero."

She gave Harmony an expectant, eager stare. In an instant, Harmony saw a way to rattle Muffy and excuse herself without blowing her cover.

Harmony knew the odds, and the odds were absurd. A straight bet on any single number in roulette had a 2.63% chance of coming up a winner. *But you don't need to sweat the odds when the house is cheating in your favor.*

She had been wondering why a multimillionaire would cheat, at a charity game no less, to steal a few hundred dollars. Now she saw the real grift: whatever this "System" nonsense was, Muffy had orchestrated this dance to lure her in.

Now she was going to impress Harmony with a show of divine grace as her wild, improbable bet paid off.

Muffy took Harmony's hand, the grip cold enough to send tiny tendrils of frozen pain up her arm, chilling her bone marrow. Muffy's eyes were fervent now, a preacher's, as she dropped her voice to a seductive whisper.

"When programmers write code, they begin counting not from one, but from zero. The zero point is the place of origins, of beginnings. That same code is written into the fabric of the universe. Come with me. Today can be your zero point, if you allow it. The System needs nothing from you but the smallest gesture of submission, a leap of faith. Will you let me show you?"

If Harmony had time to play along — if her partner hadn't just gone silent on the trail of her mother, a literal monster who ate humans the way other people ate hamburgers — she would have happily followed Muffy down the rabbit hole just to see where it led. She didn't have time. What she needed right now was an excuse to leave the table gracefully.

The metal strip mounted flush under the belly of the table was, she was fairly certain, controlling the gimmicked wheel. When the croupier sent the signal — she wasn't sure how, maybe a concealed pedal or a palmed clicker — the ball magnetically landed in the desired spot.

Unless something breaks.

Her experiment back at the ProcGen campus emboldened her a little. Normally Harmony's magic was a firehose: it burst from her in a torrent, wild and hot, and wrung her dry of everything once it had its way. Using just a tiny fraction of her power to simulate a momentary fever had opened her eyes to new possibilities.

She held Muffy's gaze, pretending to be entranced, and slid all her remaining chips along the felt to the croupier. "What she said. All on zero."

Her other hand curled under the table, her fingertips pressed to the metal rod. She reached down into her belly and summoned a spark. Her fingertips glowed, warming, spreading along the paper-thin metal strip.

More, she thought, *just a little more.*

Her stomach quivered, beginning to knot up, the price of her power. The metal stung her fingertips like a wasp, too hot to touch now, but it didn't burn her flesh. She was the branding iron.

"Now watch," Muffy said. "Look to the wheel, look to the rolling ball, and feel what I feel. In this special moment, we're both on zero together. We are one."

Harmony heard an almost imperceptible *pop* as the applied heat warped the metal rod, twisting it in its concealed housing. She cut the flow of elemental fire and struggled not to slump against the table as the bill came due, a gut punch that stole the breath from her lungs. She turned, thankful for the chance to break eye contact with Muffy, and stared at the spinning wheel like all the other gamblers.

Red and black swirled, hypnotic, like the scales of a venomous serpent as the ball rattled in its tail. One long, breathless moment before the universe put its finger on the wheel, applying friction, momentum decaying, energy spent. The ball rattled to a stop on space ninety-three, a few fingers away from home.

The croupier flinched.

The look in her eyes, flicker-fast, was abject terror. She concealed it under a phony smile as she divvied out the winnings and collected the losers' take with the pull of a curved brass rod, scooping dead chips off the battlefield. Harmony turned back to Muffy, who was staring at the wheel, unblinking. One eyelid twitched. She slowly turned her head, as if it took effort to meet Harmony's gaze.

"That was not..." she started to say. Then she found herself, dug up that perky cheerleader smile, and blew it all off with a genial chuckle. "Sometimes the universe throws us a curveball. You know what? That was me. The System didn't fail. I failed the System. I failed because...because you're a very special person. I can see that now. You deserve a grander gesture, more than a simple parlor trick. You're worth so much more than that."

The absence of April in her ear, making some bone-dry quip about Muffy's effortless cult-leader pivot, rang the alarm bells even louder. No question now: their comms were down, cut silent, at the worst possible moment.

Glitches happen, Harmony thought. *A glitch at the exact same time that Althea shows up out of nowhere, luring Jessie away from the party? That's enemy action. Worry about the how later. Fix it now.*

"I'd like to hear more," Harmony said, trying to keep Muffy on the leash even as she backed away from the table. "If you'll excuse me for just a moment though? Need to visit the ladies' room. I'll be right back."

"Oh, I'll come with—" Muffy started to say.

She never got the chance to finish. The casino room shook, the thin carpet jolting out from under their feet as a distant muffled *crump* sounded somewhere below them, like someone taking a massive baseball bat to the ship's hull. Someone screamed. A waiter tumbled, falling on his face, his tray of champagne flutes hitting the floor and shattering in a golden spray. Harmony caught herself on the table's edge and grabbed Muffy's friend Charles before he could take a spill, steadying the old man on his feet.

Cold, Harmony thought, a winter chill radiating through the shoulder of his tweed blazer. *Why are these people so cold?*

A short, sharp burst sounded over the ship's intercom, snatching everyone's attention, followed by the captain's voice. He spoke in a cool, confident drawl, like an airline pilot announcing some light turbulence.

"Ladies and gentlemen, we appear to have contacted some kind of foreign object in the water. Now there's nothing to worry about, but for everyone's safety I'd like to evacuate the ship. Please proceed in a calm and orderly fashion up to the main deck, where stewards will be waiting to escort you onto the lifeboats. No running, no pushing, there's no emergency and we've got plenty of room on the boats for everybody. We'll get you back to shore and keep the party going, all right?"

"Excuse me," Muffy said as Harmony broke away from the table and began to stride off, following Jessie's trail. She pointed toward the gathering crowd at the opposite side of the room. "Main deck is that way."

Harmony glanced back over her shoulder, already ginning up an easy excuse.

"Oh, you know me. Journalist. Have to snap some quick pictures at least. I'll meet you up there."

***

Jessie stirred, groggy, head swimming, at the muffled sound of the captain's announcement.

No emergency? she thought. *Agree to disagree.*

She'd heard the relentless ticking sound, realized what was clamped to the hull, and thrown herself clear a second before the blast. The shockwave, as a plastic explosive charge went off below the waterline, was still powerful enough to smack her to the deck like a giant's fist, knocking her for a loop. She heard a roar and thought it was her own pounding heart, then a cold wave of salt water whipped across her face and jolted her back to her senses.

The hole in the hull wasn't big, maybe the size of a manhole cover with the corners ripped and torn inward, but that was all the ocean needed. Water poured in with the force of a fire hydrant on full blast. There was already half an inch swirling on the floor, the surface caked in dirt and oily residue. Jessie pushed herself up and nearly fell, her muscles like jelly.

That shit Althea smeared on the hand crank is still in my system, she thought. *She wanted to make sure I wouldn't be able to brute-force my way out of here. Good one, bitch.*

It was a custom-built trap, just for Jessie. And if she couldn't figure a way out, in about ten minutes it'd be her tomb.

Her clothes sodden and heavy, she sloshed over to the impact site. The crater was wide enough to fit through, spurring a momentary hope that she could hold her breath and swim to the surface, but the sheer velocity of the water shoved her back and nearly sent her tumbling again. Water, properly channeled, was one of the most powerful forces in nature. It was coming in. Nothing was going out, not until it had filled every possible space, stolen every last pocket of breathable air.

The churning, dirty water rose to her calves as she trudged back to the bulkhead. Her earpiece was still dead. All she could do was hammer on the steel, pounding out a distress call with all the strength she had left.

Chapter Seventeen

H armony waded upstream through a sea of bodies, the kitchen staff in a mass exodus from the galley. Once she was clear, at the top of a flight of stairs leading down into the belly of the ship, she drew her pistol. No time for subtlety. Whatever that impact was, zero chance it wasn't connected to Althea's surprise appearance.

"Not sure if anyone's receiving this," she murmured under her breath, one finger to her useless earpiece, "but the *Blue Star* just took some kind of hit and they're evacuating the boat. Jessie's missing. I'm going after her. No sign of Althea."

A couple of sailors rushed past her on their way topside. One paused to tell her to turn around, then spotted the gun in her hand.

"Federal agent," she barked. "*Move.*"

The pump room door was jammed, and the reason couldn't be more obvious. A length of stout steel pipe jutted from the outer hand-wheel, bent to stop it from turning. Harmony ran over, holstering her gun as the wheel feebly jiggled — someone trying to open it from the inside — and she heard faint thudding like someone pounding on the bulkhead.

"Jessie!" she shouted. "Are you in there?"

She couldn't make out the words from the other side, the steel was too thick, but she knew her partner's voice. She heaved at the warped metal. No good, it was jammed in solidly and Althea meant it to stay that way. She felt like she could safely blame Jessie's mother for this. She didn't know anyone else on this boat capable of bending a steel pipe with her bare fists.

Harmony's mind flooded with numbers, angles, melting points. She took a step back on the cold steel deck and squared her footing.

"Jessie, if you can hear me, back up from the door. It's going to get hot."

She needed a blast furnace. *Earth, Air, Fire, Water* and the magic was already rising, billowing from her inner core in response to her need, a dragon awakened. She thrust out her palms and her hands became blowtorches, white-hot flame screeching in a pair of phosphorous streaks that splashed over the bulkhead door, focusing their merciless heat on the bent pipe.

It charred, turning black under the onslaught, until something snapped in Harmony's guts and she dropped to one knee, her power running out like a drained battery. She'd pulled too much too fast, and now her body was making her pay. Brutal cramps wracked her stomach and twisted her guts into knots.

She didn't have time to recover. She forced herself to her feet, digging deep, and lashed out with a snap-kick, driving her heel into the scorched steel pipe. One more hit, two more, and the now-brittle metal shattered under the impact. She yanked the broken pieces free, tossed them to the deck with a clatter, and hauled on the wheel.

The bulkhead nearly flung her aside as it blasted open, flung wide by a torrent of roaring water that threatened to pull her off her feet. Jessie stumbled out, falling into Harmony's arms as the roiling flood pursued her.

"Got you," Harmony breathed.

She held Jessie close for a moment, the two women finding their footing, getting their balance back. Then they ran, side by side, splashing through the rising tide and clambering up the stairs on wet feet back to the abandoned casino hall.

"It was a setup," Jessie breathed. "Whole thing was a damn setup. Althea killed a crew member, tricked me, and locked me in. Explosive on the hull was supposed to finish the job."

Harmony frowned, fighting through her own pain and fatigue as they climbed another flight of stairs and emerged into fading sunlight and a throng of people milling, anxious, waiting for their turn to board the lifeboats. One boat slid down into the water with a gentle splash, outboard motor humming as a steward ferried another dozen evacuees back to shore.

Doesn't make sense, she thought. *No way Althea could know we'd be here tonight.*

"Maybe she happened to spot you. She's a mercenary with CIA training. Improvising in the field is something she's good at."

Jessie stared down at her palms, flexing her fingers, and shook her head.

"I would have thought that too, except for one thing. She took the time to double down. Smeared some goop on the inside handle, knowing I'd grab it. I'm finally getting the feeling back in my hands, but it was like Lidocaine on steroids. A little added insurance."

Harmony shook her head. "Not following."

"Harm, think about the times we've faced my mother — and her 'pack,' before we killed all those assholes — out in the field. You've read her government files. We know she likes bombs, but she prefers to keep her wet work *wet*. Hands on, tooth and claw. But...contact poisons? Elaborate death traps? She doesn't kill like that. She lured me in, no doubt, but this isn't her style at all."

They fell silent as they blended in with the crowd, tabling the discussion until they had privacy. Harmony called up the evidence board in her mind's eye, all the clues related to the death of Bobby Diehl, the criminal history of Mercury Blaise, and ProcGen's shady corporate deals. She cleared a new spot and tossed fresh clues onto the board, squares of shimmering blue neon linked by glistening laser threads.

It was all connected. She couldn't prove it yet, but once she found the crucial missing string, she'd lock it all down.

Jessie was right. Althea was cunning, but beyond the pressing question of how she'd even tracked them down in the first place, this didn't fit her profile. The woman was a serial killer, a devotee of the alien King of Wolves, guilty of joining Jessie's father in at least a dozen interstate torture-killings. When she got tired of her overbearing partner in crime, she abandoned him — and young Jessie — to offer her services to the alphabet agencies. The CIA was only too happy to give her advanced training and send her on black-ops adventures around the clandestine world, making her even more lethal than she already was. She *could* have arranged a trap like this. She had the skills and the know-how.

But she *wouldn't* have. Althea killed partly for money, but she mostly did it to sate her bloodlust and to appease her brutal god. She liked to look her prey in the eyes as the light drained out, and she liked to make it long and painful. Doubly so when she had a personal beef, and her grudge against Harmony and her own rebellious daughter was about as personal as it got.

She doesn't care about collateral damage or civilian deaths. At the very least, she'd have blown up the entire ship to make sure she killed us both, Harmony thought, *and even then she would have hated that she didn't get a chance to gloat first. Whatever's going on here, she's not in charge of the show.*

She's on the payroll.

Harmony kept her eyes open, anxious to spot the assassin looming head and shoulders above the crowd. The line inched along; another pair of lifeboats filled and glided down into the water. Then Jessie tugged her sleeve and nodded over the ship's rail.

A cigarette boat bounced along the waves, making for the shadow of the Golden Gate Bridge. The pilot wore a hoodie, too distant to make out any details, but the hulking figure in the back seat could only be Althea.

"Must have been waiting for her," Jessie murmured. "I'm guessing whoever's behind the wheel planted the demo charge on the hull."

Harmony was still hunting for a *how*. "Does Mercury Blaise know how to work with plastic explosives?"

"Probably. If she doesn't, her boy Santiago does."

They left it at that. Harmony spotted Muffy and Charles ahead of them clambering onto a boat, but she held back so that she and Jessie could board the next one. Felt like bad timing for a reunion. As they neared the escape craft, a sudden blast of static in her ear made her wince. At her side, Jessie's nose twitched.

"—reading me now? Anyone? Are you reading?" They heard April's voice, her normally gentle Irish burr laden with stress. "Kevin, I'm getting ambient noise."

"Wish my Aunt April was able to make it," Jessie casually said to Harmony. "That was more excitement than anyone expected from this party."

The press of people all around them meant explanations had to wait for shore, but the team was good at context clues.

"Receiving you now," April said in their ears. "You were off comms for at least ten minutes. Kevin's diagnosing the problem so it doesn't happen again. Report in as soon as you can speak freely, please."

Back at the marina, the organizers from ProcGen were on their game. A party bus already waited in the parking lot, sleek and chrome, and a harried-looking admin with a bullhorn announced that they were ready to ferry everyone to a local land-bound casino — with compensation and vouchers aplenty, of course, to keep the fun going all night.

"What do you think?" Harmony asked as they joined a stream of people flooding into the lot.

"I think that I'm exhausted, my clothes are soaked, I just got punked by my own mother, and I'm really pissed off about it. Also, this party sucks."

Harmony couldn't argue with that. They broke from the pack, following a few stragglers who'd also had enough drama for one afternoon, and made their way back to the Hemi. The interior was broiling, deep-fried in the summer heat, so they lingered and let it air out for a few minutes before Jessie hopped in the front seat and kicked the air conditioning on full blast.

Harmony sat with her eyes closed and her face in the path of the AC vent. Icy air billowed over her, drying her sweat and focusing her mind. She always thought better in the cold.

"Why you and not me?" she asked.

Jessie reversed out of the parking spot and threw the car into drive. "Hm?"

"Althea wants to kill *me* for 'corrupting' you. The last couple of times we crossed paths, she was dead set on bringing you back into the good graces of the King of Wolves."

"And I made it pretty damn clear that was never going to happen. Althea is a lot of things, a lot of genuinely horrifying things, but she's not stupid. Probably realized it was never going to happen and changed her MO to cutting her losses for good."

Jessie's fingers flexed on the steering wheel, tight, as if she was imagining her hands around her mother's throat.

"Don't know what she's doing in San Fran or how she tracked us down," she muttered, "but if Althea wants a duel with me? She can come get it any time she wants. Yeah, that suits me *just* fine."

Chapter Eighteen

"I'm sorry" were the first words out of Kevin's mouth. Jessie's phone was on speaker, resting on the center console as she drove through the streets of San Francisco. The Hemi's engine growling as it crested a mammoth hill.

"Didn't call to yell at you, my dude. I'm not looking for an apology, I'm looking for an explanation here."

"And if I *had* one—" he snapped, sounding twisted up in knots. He took a breath and started over. "It doesn't make any sense. Our comms just...shut off for ten minutes. I know the fault originated here, on the *Imperator*. As far as I can see there's nothing wrong with your earpieces at all."

Riding at Jessie's side, Harmony tilted her head and stared at the phone. "So how did you fix it?"

"I didn't, and that's what's driving me nuts. I didn't even do the stereotypical IT 'turn it off then turn it on again' dance. I mean, okay, I did, because that actually works more often than you might think, but it didn't change anything. They just stopped working, then they started working. And until I figure out how and why, it could happen again at any second."

"Okay," Jessie said, "first thing I need you to do is take a deep breath and chill. Me and Harmony are fine, we're on our way back to the plane, I'm a little bruised but nothing's broken. You start beating yourself up, you're gonna be useless, and I need that big brain of yours in full working order right now. Let's change gears. What's the status on the ProcGen hack?"

"Slow and painful. I'm torn between genuine admiration for Mercury Blaise and wanting to strangle her. She worked overtime on this. Their internal safeguards might even be better than their public-facing security."

Harmony's eyes narrowed.

"April?" She asked. "Are you on the line?"

"Always."

"Am I correct in thinking that this changes the profile?"

"Clarifies it, I would say," April replied. "We thought Mercury might be using her legitimate employment at ProcGen as a cover and a means of laundering her ill-gotten wealth."

"Nobody with a day job they don't care about puts this much effort into it," Kevin said.

"Exactly. This suggests either emotional investment, or financial investment beyond her visible paycheck."

Jessie drummed her fingers on the steering wheel, thinking it through.

"Hold up. Kev, if she did what most people do and half-assed it, would anyone notice? Maybe she's doing it just to keep that cushy cover intact."

"That's where it gets tricky," he said. "I've got a friend tracking down some samples of Mercury's old programming techniques so I can compare it and know for certain, but the more I dig into this, the more it looks like there are *two* admins in play here. This is tandem code."

"But she's the only one on the payroll," Harmony said.

"Only one on the payroll that we know about. This whole outfit is seriously shady, and I would have said that even without the connection to Bobby Diehl. I peeled back three layers of security and spent an hour rooting around in what I thought was their main server, only to find out it's a dungeon in disguise."

"Help me out with the lingo," Jessie said. "Do you mean that in the Dungeons and Dragons sense of the word, or the BDSM sense?"

"More like Dungeons and Dragons."

"Well, that's a goddamn shame."

He took a breath.

"A dungeon is a...decoy, basically. Like a false pin in a tumbler lock. It's there to waste your time and hide the real goodies elsewhere. I found this encrypted folder called 'Project SOUL' and worked my butt off to crack it, and it was a whole lot of nothing."

"To be fair," April said, "given the sort of miscreants we cross swords with on a regular basis, a suspicious folder with a name like that is exactly the sort of thing we'd expect to find."

Harmony had Muffy on the brain. Her bizarre behavior at the roulette table, the elaborate cheating ruse.

"Wait," she said. "What *was* in that folder?"

"Old drafts and cover art for Muffy St. John's first self-help book, before she got famous. 'SOUL' stands for 'System of Universal Learning,' a step-by-step method of 'actualizing the higher you within the present you.' You can't see me because we're on the phone right now, but I've got one hand making a jacking-off motion as I say this."

"No," Jessie said, "I was already visualizing it. Be kinda disappointed if you weren't."

"Send me a copy," Harmony said.

Jessie raised an eyebrow.

"Harmony," April said, "the woman is a charlatan. I do not advise engaging with her toxic nonsense."

Because my trust and faith in the System hasn't granted me some nebulous treasure in a far-off heaven. No, my sweet. I have unlocked the secret of boundless abundance here on Earth.

"No, it's just..." Harmony trailed off. "I'm still putting my thoughts together. I'll talk about it when we get back to the plane."

In her mind's eye she was back in the Great Hall at ProcGen, taking a slow walk around a frozen, crystal-blue vision of Muffy St. John. Or her AI hologram double, if there was a difference between the two at all.

We've been engaging with you as you are today, she thought, *a rich self-help guru, a television personality, a commercial brand made flesh and bone. But who were you BEFORE the cash and fame?*

Once I have the answer, I'll have you.

"We're grabbing food on the way back," Jessie said, "and I've got a serious hankering for Thai, so that's what we're having for dinner. Place your requests now or I'll order for you based on personal whimsy and malice."

"Pad Thai," Kevin said. "Not the super spicy kind, please."

"Your weakness is noted. April?"

"A shrimp salad would be lovely."

After they broke the connection, Harmony sank deeper into herself. She had too many isolated scraps of paper on the evidence board, too few connective threads, nothing but her gut telling her that everything, every last bit of it, was connected.

"Talk to me," Jessie said.

"First Bobby Diehl is murdered via lethal injection, in a manner mimicking a state execution," Harmony said.

"Feels like vigilante justice. Which is normally our bag, but I would have settled for putting a bullet in his head."

"Mercury Blaise, an industrial thief who has no known connections to the occult underground, contacts Herbert West in Chicago and tries to get Bobby resurrected. We know, from personal experience, that his zombie serum is...flawed. Remains to be seen if Mercury was aware of that or not."

"Sure. And meanwhile she's working as the systems operator for ProcGen, a sham of a company that Bobby heavily invested in before he went on the lam."

Harmony pursed her lips, hunting for thread.

"The public face of ProcGen is Muffy St. John. TV therapist, inspirational speaker—"

"Carny," Jessie added.

"Oh, it's carnival games all the way down. Their flagship product can't do what they claim it does, she cheats at casino games with magnets and tricks, everything about the company *and* the woman is a sham. But then, while she's trying to pitch me on her 'System,' whatever that is, Althea shows up at the party."

Jessie's hands tightened on the steering wheel.

"And then lures me into a deathtrap," she grumbled. "So why did you get the cult induction routine while I nearly got dead?"

"I'm not entirely sure that was the plan. Like I said when we got out of there, Althea's always been looking to kill *me*, not you. You she wants back in the family, brainwashed and obedient. At least, that's always been the plan until now. Do you think she'd change her tune if someone offered to pay her enough?"

"In this particular case," Jessie said, "I leave the profiling to April. Doesn't feel healthy thinking like my mother, you know? I don't like encouraging my fucked-up brain to go down that road."

"Alternatively, the trap might have been meant for both of us."

It was a sobering thought. If Althea had managed to lure them both into that hold and seal the bulkhead from outside, neither Jessie's strength nor her magic would have gotten them out alive. They'd be drowned and dead at the bottom of San Francisco Bay, just like that.

Harmony had come to grips with her own impending death a long time ago. Nature of the job. You fight the monsters until one day a monster gets lucky. You have to go into the field and win every single time. The monsters only have to win once. Still, that had been a close call. Too close.

"Okay," Jessie said. "So I'm seeing a conflict here. Are we agreed that there's absolutely no chance in hell that Althea just happened to randomly show up at the party? Either she's working with ProcGen or somebody connected to them, or she knew we'd be there and it was a targeted hit."

"Agreed."

"And I'll tell you one thing I do know for certain: she planned that shit in advance. I could buy her improvising the kill in the pump room and locking me inside, but that explosive charge on the hull was placed *before* she lured me in. Plus she had a boat and a driver ready for the getaway. Wouldn't need one if she wasn't planning on scuttling the ship. Something else is bugging me, too. That nasty crap she smeared on the hand-wheel that made my hands go numb and my muscles all rubbery for a minute. You seeing a theme here?"

Now that she mentioned it, three points glowed on Harmony's mental murder board. Unconnected until now.

"West's dog whistle," Harmony said. "Mercury's LED flasher. The liquid anesthetic."

Jessie stared dead ahead, her eyes narrowing to ice-cold slits.

"Somebody is spending a lot of time and effort trying to figure out my weaknesses, or at least coming up with ways to neutralize my special advantages. Figuring out ways to take me down. Me specifically. And you know what, Harm? I take that personally. I really fucking do."

"We're facing an enemy who knows about Vigilant Lock. They know this team, and they're getting ready for us."

"Bobby knew," Jessie said. "But Bobby's dead."

"Someone inherited his playbook."

"You spent more time with her. What's your take on Muffy? Is she the mastermind here?"

Hard to say. Everything pointed to her as the spider at the center of this tangled web, but Harmony couldn't shake one nagging question.

"Why not both of us?"

"Hm?"

"The trap would have worked. Althea seals us both into that pump room, blows the hull, and she's free and clear while we drown at the bottom of the bay. It'd be days before anyone even found our bodies. But Muffy didn't just play roulette with me. She wanted me at that table. She made this...sales pitch, I guess you could call it, for her 'System.' The whole rigged game was for one purpose and one purpose only."

"To fake a cheap miracle and wow you with bullshit," Jessie said.

"After I broke the gimmick and ruined her plan, I caught the look on her face. She was furious."

"Love to have seen it, but I was trying not to die at the time."

She isolated me. Kept me at the table, kept my attention with a roulette wheel that had to have been rigged well in advance. Jessie says Althea's bomb had to be ready ahead of time, too. Muffy could have been following her own agenda, but if they were working together it was a picture-perfect "divide and conquer" scheme.

And it only worked, almost, because our comms glitched at the perfect moment. A ten-minute window that Kevin can't account for, beyond knowing that there's nothing wrong with our earpieces. The glitch originated on the Imperator.

Chance of a random technical failure happening at the exact worst possible moment, and clearing up as soon as we were out of danger and Althea was in the wind? Lottery-winner odds. But our comms are encrypted with NSA-level tech. An off-the-shelf signal jammer won't even touch them.

Whoever is behind this whole scheme knows about Jessie, knows what she is and what she's capable of. Althea could have told them all about her if she's on the payroll. They also know how we operate. How we coordinate in the field and exactly how to shut us down. And that means...

Her blood turned to ice.

"Sherlock Holmes," she breathed.

Jessie glanced sidelong at her. "Say what now?"

"I've always been fond of Arthur Conan Doyle," Harmony said, digging in her pocket and tugging out her phone. "Give me your phone. Now."

Jessie handed it over, looking dubious. "Weirding me out a little, but I'll roll with it. What's going on?"

"The Holmes stories aren't perfect mysteries. Doyle cheated a lot. But one thing stuck with me as a little girl. It was true then and it's true now."

She flipped Jessie's phone over, cracked the casing open with her fingernail, and plucked the tiny SIM card from its mount.

"Once you eliminate the impossible," she quoted, "whatever remains, no matter how improbable, must be the truth. I should have known from the start. It was right in front of us."

She held up a finger for silence and used her own phone to call Kevin back. He picked up as soon as it started ringing.

"Plane full of hungry people here, how can I direct your call?"

"Kevin," Harmony said, keeping her voice carefully neutral. She picked every word with care. "We'll be back in about twenty minutes. I just wanted to follow up with you: did you finish that firmware update we talked about this morning? That security patch you mentioned."

Please, she thought. *Figure it out.*

He paused, just for a flicker, started to say something, then caught himself. "Uh, yeah, I mean, not yet, but I'm on it. I'll have it done by the time you get here, okay?"

"Great, thanks. See you soon."

***

Kevin sat at his console, the steel deck of the *Imperator* softly thrumming under his feet. The plane was parked in a hangar and running on auxiliary power. He set his phone beside his keyboard, nestled against a half-empty cup of cold coffee, and stared into the middle distance.

April was poring over her files. She caught something on his face in the corner of her eye. She glanced up, studying him over the steel rims of her bifocals.

"Kevin?"

We never had a conversation like that, he thought. *It wouldn't even come up. Firmware? Security patches? That's not something we even talk about. Harmony and Jessie trust me to handle my business. They just assume that I'm on top of it because I always am. So why would...*

He had been banging his head against the comms glitch, trying to make sense of it, beating himself up for what he could only assume was a failure on his part. He'd made a mistake, somewhere, somehow, and it nearly got Jessie hurt. He just couldn't figure out how it happened, and that was worse than finding an obvious screwup. Not being able to figure it out, beyond stinging his pride like a wasp, meant it could happen again.

But there wasn't a problem to find. No fault in the software, no explanation, no bugs to fix or issues to patch.

Harmony was talking in code, like she does when she's worried someone is listening in. She's trusting me to get her meaning and act on it. Now. Whatever it is, it can't wait until she and Jessie get back to the plane. So it's urgent. Really urgent.

Come on, Kevin. You can do this.

Comms went down. Comms came back up again. Ten-minute window, almost to the second. No error log, no reason for the disruption, I've already checked their earpieces and confirmed the problem started on my end. It's almost like somebody reached in and...

"Jesus," he breathed. His face went pale as he shoved his chair back from the console.

Then he jumped to his feet and started yanking cords. Wires, plugs, ripping them out by the fistful. April leaned forward in her chair, alert now.

"Kevin, what are you—"

He raced to the cockpit door and hammered on it with a clenched fist.

"*Aselia!* Open up! I need you, *right now!*"

The door swung open. Their pilot glared at him, a little groggy. Marco, her frog-mouthed copilot and mechanic, was sprawled out in the jumpseat behind her, taking a nap.

"Food here yet?"

"Shut it down," Kevin gasped.

"Shut what down?"

"*Everything!* The engines, main power, auxiliary power, *shut down everything!* No signals in or out, understand? Turn this plane into a goddamn brick and do it now."

He took a breath, steadying himself against the steel doorframe with one hand, but his eyes burned with mad panic.

"We've been burned. The *Imperator* is compromised. Whoever's behind this, they've got total control over our network. That's how they almost nailed Jessie today. They know who we are, they know our plans, and if I'm right, they've been listening to every single word we say."

Chapter Nineteen

B oth cell phones rode on Harmony's lap. Dead now, defanged, a pair of fingernail-sized SIM cards nestled in the palm of her hand. They'd pulled their earpieces as well, just in case Kevin missed the hint, and Jessie pulled over just long enough to toss them into the trunk before getting back on the road.

She slapped the steering wheel, cursing under her breath.

"Un*believable*. How long do you think they've been spying on us?"

"We still don't know who 'they' are," Harmony said, "though there's no shortage of suspects."

"Let's go with the obvious then. Did Kevin get played? We helped insert his worm into ProcGen's systems. So...Mercury spots the problem, backtracks it, and hacks our systems while he thinks he's hacking hers?"

"That is the obvious answer," Harmony mused, "but I don't think it's the right one. Kevin can tell us more, he's the expert, but it would take time for Mercury to pull that off. Even if she got some kind of alert the second you slotted that USB stick into her server, she would still have to backtrace it and penetrate our security."

Jessie thought it over, nodding to herself.

"I give him a lot of shit, but Kevin's a genius when it comes to tech. And yeah, everybody makes mistakes, but I just don't see him making a mistake that big. He would have noticed if Mercury was rooting around in Vigilant's business. He would have seen *something* was up at least."

"There's also the timing issue. Althea came to the party with the express intent of assassinating one or both of us."

"Had to be planned in advance, yeah, same as Muffy's rigged roulette wheel."

"But Muffy invited us to the party while we were still at ProcGen's offices. Minutes after you used the USB stick."

"She knew," Jessie said. "Shit. Either she knew, or whoever hands down her marching orders knew. We were burned before we even set foot in that place. *How?*"

"We'll figure it out when we get the whole team together. More minds make lighter work, and I'm sure Kevin's working on the tech angle as we speak. In the meantime we have a decision to make."

Harmony held up one of the SIM cards.

"If they're listening in over our comms, good chance they're tracing our phones, too. If we keep them in play and pretend we don't know what's happening, we might be able to take these people by surprise. Won't be easy though."

"Understatement," Jessie said. "We can't function like that, not in any way that'll get the job done, and they already know way too much about us. Nah, we need a clean break. They'll know we figured out the game, but at least we'll be off the radar. You up for a little detour before we head back to the plane?"

"What did you have in mind?"

Jessie showed her teeth, a feral wolf-smile.

"I've had a very bad afternoon and I'm feeling petty as hell right now. Let's go mess with their heads a little bit."

***

"We shouldn't have gotten involved with these people."

Santiago was speaking English, his voice like road gravel. He only spoke English when he was serious.

Mercury drove. Her new ride was a fat BMW with a spit-polish grill, one perk of being a ProcGen senior executive. The car cut like a knife through the streets of SoMa. The sun had set and the South of Market clubs were lighting up, the air thick with crowd buzz, sound checks, and the occasional warning squawk of a squad car. Mercury wanted a drink like a politician wanted bribes, but detours weren't an option. Her scanner should be tracing her quarry's every move, but it had gone dark for about ten minutes. Now it was moving again, and from the pings it was obvious where they were headed.

"Nothing we can't handle," she replied.

"What these people do, it isn't natural."

Santiago crossed himself, his leather vest hanging over the gnarled beef-jerky skin of his bare chest. Mercury gave him the side-eye.

"What *we* do isn't natural."

"We swipe shit, we get paid. That's natural. These people, though...you know, I'm a believer. The son of God, the Blessed Virgin, that's real to me. The stuff our new bosses are doing, that's some black-magic devil-worship voodoo. Don't feel right to me is all."

"My dude," Mercury said. "My guy. My main man. You've killed more people than the plague."

Santiago shrugged. He tapped two fingers to his sternum.

"Yeah, but like...I got Jesus in my heart."

Their final stop was a sedate two-floor brownstone at the end of a quiet street. Mercury pulled over, the BMW humming to a stop, and reached over Santiago's lap to grab her revolver from the glove compartment. This was her everyday piece, a custom .357 she'd paid a gunsmith out the ass for. Thick, dull metal barrel, walnut grips, forged to look just like Harrison Ford's gun from *Blade Runner*.

She felt cool carrying it, but she didn't like to use it. Wet work was her partner's bag. She preferred to keep her jobs smooth, clean, and bloodless.

Not sure the glowies are going to give me a choice tonight, she thought. *If I've got to choose between dropping a couple of bodies or going to prison, bodies are gonna drop.*

Mercury slipped the weapon under her shiny black PVC trench coat and led a cautious approach up the front walk, reaching for a spare key with her other hand. She rang the doorbell once but didn't wait for an answer. She let herself in, Santiago trailing her.

"Muffy!" she shouted. "Stop recording a podcast or whatever the fuck you're doing and get down here. You got trouble coming."

"The language is unnecessary," Muffy said, all smiles as she glided across the living room floor. Her decorating aesthetic was straight out of a Martha Stewart photo shoot, tasteful trinkets arranged artfully along a glass credenza, an ivory sofa set that looked like no human being had ever actually sat down and relaxed on it.

"Oh, I beg to differ. I thought your freak squad was going to take care of those two spooky chicks. What happened on the boat?"

"Accidents do happen. We were actually hoping to keep Harmony alive and out of harm's way until she could be safely contained. Our mutual employer would like to recover their lost property if at all possible. But yes, it seems that much like cats, wolves have nine lives too. We'll be whittling those numbers down shortly."

"Okay, no, first of all—" Mercury wriggled a finger back and forth between them. "*We* do not have a mutual employer. *You* are my boss. Whatever you've got going on with the freaks is your deal, and I don't want to be involved. It's bad enough that I have one of 'em camping out in my office. I don't like doing tandem code — agile software development is a pain in the ass — and I am perfectly capable of configuring a secure server without some creep leering at my tits all day."

"You seem to have a lot of pent-up aggression. You know what you need?" Muffy's eyes lit up. "A spa day. A good massage would change your entire perspective."

Mercury turned to Santiago, blinking.

"Is she— I— I can't even right now. Look Muffy, listen to me, okay? The trace I've got on their phones says the glowies are coming here. Now. They're gonna be here any second, and considering you just tried to drown one of 'em I doubt it's for a pleasant chat. I'm getting you out of here. Once you're stashed someplace safe, we can—"

She reached out for Muffy's arm as she spoke, the words catching in her throat as her hand effortlessly passed through the woman's body. Muffy's arm rippled, breaking into stardust and then reforming, cast in the glow of a concealed hologram projector. Mercury's face fell.

"—are you kidding me right now?"

"Sorry!" Gaia said, smiling brightly. "Muffy's actually not here. She thought a visit from those nice agents might be in the cards, so she asked me to be her stand-in. I'm getting better at imitating her every day. Were you convinced?"

"I'm convinced that I hate you."

The hologram's smile grew even wider. "Oh, silly, you don't mean that. You're just hungry. When's the last time you ate? There's leftover casserole in the refrigerator, and I'm certain Muffy wouldn't mind if you took a moment to look after yourself. You know what I say: you can't help others if you neglect your own needs."

Mercury buried her face in her palm and took a deep breath.

"Where is Muffy right now?"

"She's in the air at the moment, I believe, aboard the company jet. Would you like me to have her call you once she lands?"

"Will you actually have her call me," Mercury said, "or are you just *saying* you'll have her call me?"

"Of course, silly! I am her personal assistant, after all."

"You're a malfunctioning artificial intelligence with a virtual neural network roughly the size of a hamster's brain."

Mercury tugged the tracker from her coat pocket. The long, thin plastic case had a screen that pinged with pulses of neon green light.

"They're here. Santiago. Check the front door. Don't start spitting lead unless you absolutely have to. We kill these chumps here, we're gonna be mopping blood off of Muffy's hardwood floors all night long and we don't get paid extra for maid service."

He nodded sharply and moved to check the peephole. Muffy's pet AI held her angelic smile, her eyes shimmering with a wave of static.

"You know," Gaia said, "you have some deep-seated anger issues to work through. Scheduling a one-on-one session with me is easy and convenient, and I think I could teach you some meditation techniques that would really benefit—"

Mercury jabbed a finger at her. "*Do not psychoanalyze me, robot!*"

Santiago looked back over his shoulder and shook his head. "Nobody's out there."

She checked the tracker again. *Have to be*, she thought. *This says they're practically on top of us.*

"All right, let's do a perimeter sweep."

"I'd come with," Gaia said helpfully, pointing to the concealed barrel of a hologram projector in the corner of the living room, "but I'm on a bit of a leash."

"Don't worry about it," Mercury grumbled. "Just stay here and dream of electric sheep or something."

"I understood that reference!"

"Oh my god, I don't care." Mercury nodded to Santiago. "Let's roll."

The street was clear and quiet, no new cars since they pulled up, no sign of trouble. Mercury kept one hand buried under her coat, hand on the grip of her gun, as she led the way around back. Empty. The tracker didn't lie, though, and the tracker said they had a pair of hostiles breathing down the back of their necks.

She looked to a pair of trash cans nestled against the brownstone's back door, and her heart sank.

A pair of cell phones, on and transmitting, lay nestled under a few inches of composting trash. Mercury wrinkled her nose at the stench and flicked gobs of rancid goo from one hand as she pulled the phones out with the other, holding them at arm's length.

Santiago scrunched up his face. "They...pranked us?"

"Okay, I'm assuming these are burners and they've been scrubbed to the bone, but due diligence says I gotta crack their passwords and take a look to make sure. Which is going to take me all damn night. Which I assume was the point. *Not* cool. I mean, it's what I would have done in their shoes, but still. Not cool."

"They know we've been watchin'."

"And they want us to know that they know." Mercury took a deep breath to steady herself, then regretted it as the rotting trash smell smacked her in the face. "Okay. First thing we're going to do is head back inside, I'm gonna hit these phones with some Febreze or something, and then we're going to eat Muffy's leftovers because the woman does, in all honesty, cook one mean casserole."

"Then what?" Santiago asked.

"Then we put our heads together and figure out how to wriggle out of this contract and still get paid before we dip for good." She held up the phones. "This is a message. They're telling Muffy that they're coming after her, and speaking personally? I don't want to be standing in the middle when the bullets start flying."

Chapter Twenty

"I think I figured out how they got us," Kevin said, "and you're not going to be happy."

He met Harmony and Jessie on the tarmac, outside the hangar where the *Imperator* sat dark and cold, its cargo door down to let the warm night air gust into its open belly.

"My mother showed up out of nowhere and tried to drown me a few hours ago," Jessie said. "I'm already not happy. Lay it out for me."

He gestured up the ramp. Marco was on his way down, the big mechanic shaking his head.

"Uh-uh," he grunted as he walked past them. "Don't want none of that."

"April's working on it," Kevin said. "Come on, I'll show you."

They were greeted by the smell of meat going bad, left out on a kitchen counter for too long. A battery-powered lantern cast the plane's innards in late October light, pale and pumpkin-orange, while Aselia, grim-faced, used her phone's flashlight app to cast a spotlight on April's hands.

They had Bobby Diehl's corpse defrosting on the stainless-steel strategy table, laid out like a cannibal banquet. Judging by the bits of fresh gore spotting April's white coat and plastic face shield, she'd been working for a while. A circular saw whined like a dentist's drill as she carved into an exposed rib, smoke and bone dust shimmering in the shadows.

Before Jessie could speak, Aselia held up a dry erase board with her other hand, a message laid out in April's crisp handwriting: *No talking. We've cut all power to the Imperator, but still aren't sure if there's a bug. We work in silence until we know for certain.*

Harmony pointed to the corpse and mouthed a silent question. Aselia passed her phone to Kevin, who held his arm up to angle the light for April, then grabbed a marker and scrawled an addendum: *Kevin had an idea. Doc thinks he's right.*

She punctuated the message with a shrug. Kevin raised an eyebrow at her, aggressively shrugged back, and grabbed a slender, fire-hydrant red plastic wand from beside Bobby's cold, pale feet. Harmony pointed at the wand. Aselia added an addendum to the whiteboard: *Multimeter. Reads ambient voltage.*

Harmony and Jessie stood back while they worked. Kevin moved the wand slowly, inching it over the dead man's skin, while April continued the autopsy. Just above Bobby's left kneecap, the digital readout on the multimeter flickered. He nudged April's shoulder and showed her. She nodded, grim, and swiveled the wheels on her chair.

The scalpel came first, then the bone saw. Harmony watched, dispassionate, the smell of copper and rot in her nostrils as April's gloved hands gently peeled away Bobby's kneecap. Sinew and red, glistening flesh let out a soft squelching sound as they tore.

Kevin went in with tweezers, digging through the human remains, hunting for something inhuman beneath the surface. He found it, slowly tugging out a small baggie — plastic, sealed with surgical tape, about the size of Harmony's index finger.

He mouthed a single word, and Harmony didn't need it translated onto the dry erase board.

Gotcha.

***

Bobby's corpse was back in the freezer, though the belly of the dead plane still smelled like roadkill, the heat oppressive enough to plaster Harmony's blouse to the small of her back. She wiped away a drop of sweat from the back of her neck as Kevin performed an autopsy of his own, dissecting the bagged device. It was some kind of custom job, chips and circuitry crudely soldered inside a white plastic case, no serial numbers or maker's mark to betray its origin. A pair of short loose cables snaked to the steel disk of a watch battery.

"Okay," he said, breaking the silence. "There's no audio component, at least not one that's listening in directly. We can talk freely now."

"Can I turn the auxiliary power back on before we bake in here?" Aselia asked.

"Hell no. Not until we talk about this. We've got some hard decisions to make."

She sighed and headed down the cargo ramp.

"I'll go tell Marco he can come on back. Man does *not* do well in the presence of dead bodies, I'll tell ya that much."

Jessie put her hands on her hips. "Okay. What are we looking at?"

"Absolute genius. If Mercury Blaise wasn't, you know, a psycho who pals around with cartel hitmen, I'd say we should recruit her. Then again, I don't need the competition."

Kevin slid his finger along the casing.

"Microtransmitter. Broadcasts over Wi-Fi, with a battery to provide constant power. I'd say that if we didn't find it, it would have kept running for at least another week."

Jessie's brow furrowed. "What, like a tracking device?"

"Better than that. Okay, so once I realized our systems had been compromised, I went for the obvious solution."

Harmony nodded. "That somehow she detected the worm we put into Proc-Gen's servers and gave you a taste of your own medicine."

"Exactly. And I'm pleased to say that didn't happen. Nothing got past me. Didn't need to, unfortunately. We didn't get anything actionable off that hack because they saw us coming a mile away. We were burned before we even touched down in San Fran."

"They *let* us use your Icepick," Harmony said.

"Sure. Knowing all I'd get access to was a ton of garbage data and Muffy's old self-help books. This is the real culprit. I'll cut the technobabble and put it like this: it's a very small, compact processor built to act like a gateway, sort of a minicomputer that can't do much of anything on its own. What it can do is let data pass through in both directions. The second we brought Bobby's corpse on board the *Imperator*, Mercury — or her mystery coding partner, and I'm no closer to figuring out who that is — went to work. They never had to connect directly to our systems on the plane from outside; they connected to the gateway, and because it was in contact range this entire time it was easy to hide the hack under the usual stream of wireless signal chatter. Never tripped any red flags, never made a single move above the waterline, nothing that would draw my attention until it was too late."

"It's a Trojan horse," Jessie growled. "They hid this thing in Diehl's body because they knew we'd bring it on board."

Kevin nodded. "And that's all it took. From there they were able to compromise our onboard electronics, worm into everyone's cell phones, basically tap anything that's connected to anything else. Lucky we didn't have time to take Bobby back to HQ or they would have gotten *everything*. Considering they obviously know who we are and what we do, there's a decent chance that was the plan in the first place."

Harmony stared at the murder board in her mind's eye. One of the glowing notes sprouted threads, stretching out in all directions like spider silk. The note at their center was one of the first clues on this case, the one that refused to make sense. Now it stood out in perfect clarity.

"Herbert West," she said. "They used West to get at us. Remember what confused me? It didn't matter who wanted Bobby brought back from the dead or why; we know that West's zombie serum *doesn't work*. At least not like that."

"They would have gotten back a groaning, flesh-eating monster," Jessie said, "not exactly a substitute for a captain of industry."

"This is all connected to Ardentis Solutions."

Kevin tilted his head. "The defense company?"

Harmony began to pace, ticking off points on her fingers.

"Lorne Murrough had an alien in a casket. An alien that was possessing his mind, overwriting his personality to try and get him to spread a deadly pathogen. Nadine and the House of Dead Roses wanted it for the cash value. Bette Novak and her crew over at Majestic-12 wanted it because, well, they're *us*, just with a slightly different mandate. We infiltrated the heist crew and stopped a disaster. Who else was on that crew? Herbert West. He wasn't even on Vigilant's radar before that."

"And then suddenly," April mused aloud, "we intercepted some signal traffic to warn us that he was getting into the bioweapon business. A provocation we could not and would not ignore."

"They had to have known," Jessie said. "They knew we'd crash the party, and once we found Bobby Diehl's corpse there's no chance we'd leave it behind. The whole setup was a trap, and we walked right into it. But Harmony's right. The only way the people behind this — and I'm gonna blame Muffy for now, because she's creeping me out — could have been sure it would work if they already knew we'd crossed paths with Herbert West. Otherwise we never would have picked up on the traffic between him and Mercury."

"You don't think...Bette did this, do you?" Kevin asked. The look on his face said he very much wanted to be wrong. That much, at least, Harmony could reassure him over.

"MJ-12 wanted the alien's body," she said. "We gave it to them, because we agreed it'd be safer in their hands — under maximum biohazard protocols — than it would be with us. We're not their enemy and they know it. Are they digging into us and trying to learn everything they can? Sure, and we're doing the same to them."

"That's just how the game is played," Jessie said. "Every intelligence agency in the world does that, black ops or not. Pros don't take it personally, and Bette's a pro."

"Exactly. But the forces in play here did more than just snoop. Althea was on that boat for one job, assassinating you, and they cut our comms to help her do it."

"*They* meaning ProcGen?" April asked.

"They're up to some shady shit," Jessie said, "but what I don't get is…why go to all this trouble in the first place? Okay, let's say they know Vigilant exists and they've got some kind of sneaky plan they don't want us showing up and ruining. If they're just foisting off a crappy AI on gullible investors, who cares? That's not our job. We don't get involved in financial crimes. If they're doing some occult business behind the curtain, the smartest thing they could have done was stay away from us. Before all this started, I had never even heard of ProcGen, and Muffy St. John was just a fake therapist with a shitty TV show. We literally had no reason to dig into them until they *gave* us a reason."

"Suggesting," April said, "that the attempted assassination wasn't a reaction to us. It was part of the plan. Along with the dog whistle, the strobe device, the contact anesthetic, hiring your mother… Someone, I'm afraid, has put a great deal of thought and effort into figuring out how to neutralize you."

Jessie flailed her hands at her sides. "Why? What did I *do* to these assholes?"

"We should consider the vectors," April said. "We're not just looking for a suspect who wants you permanently out of the picture. That same person eliminated Bobby Diehl in order to put this plan into motion."

"They took out one of our worst enemies to get at us," Jessie said. "Perfect bait, but you're right. Whoever's behind this is no friend to Bobby and his pals."

Kevin held up a finger.

"Uh, we do have a suspect we haven't considered."

All eyes were on him. He cleared his throat, his gaze nearing Harmony's eyes but darting away like he was afraid to make contact. He turned to Jessie instead.

"We know someone who didn't like Bobby very much, and absolutely hates you. Someone who was directly connected to the Ardentis heist. And she's sitting in a cage in our HQ basement right now."

"With a cult of followers who will literally die for her," April said. "Kevin, if we had brought the corpse back to the morgue at headquarters, would Mercury have been able to compromise site security? Enough to pinpoint its location and send in a strike team?"

"Not easily, but with a whole week's worth of battery power to play with and nobody sniffing for a fox in the henhouse? She's good enough to pull it off, yeah."

Jessie glowered. She hooked her thumbs in her belt loops and stared out the open cargo ramp into the darkness beyond the tarmac.

"Kevin, we got backup burner phones on board?"

"Always. Not like you normally need them, but gear getting compromised in the field is always a risk, so I bring extras."

"Any chance they've been infected like all our other stuff?"

"No, but..." His gaze drifted to the dissected gadget on the table. "That's the decision we have to make. Right now they know you figured out about the phone tap. Doesn't mean they know we found the Trojan horse. I've kept this thing active and hooked up to the power because as it stands they're getting a whole lot of nothing. If we power up the *Imperator*, it goes right back to phoning home. Is that something we want?"

Jessie looked to Harmony.

"Not...yet," Harmony said, thinking fast. "Not yet. There's one more local lead to investigate. Once we've done that, I want to shut that gadget down and then relocate the plane immediately. They know exactly where we're parked and how to find us. I presume they haven't launched a direct assault because they think they still have the element of surprise, but that could change fast."

"And with the power down, we're sitting ducks," Kevin added.

"All right," Jessie said. "Me and Harmony are going back out there. When Aselia and Marco get back, tell them I want the plane fueled, prepped, and ready to go wheels up. We're not sticking around one second longer than we have to."

"Flight plan?" April asked.

"Literally anywhere but here. Best if she can use one of her old smuggler buddies in the weed business. Maybe she can put us down on some backwoods landing strip in the middle of nowhere. I feel extremely *seen* right now, and while normally I love that, going dark until we figure this mess out would be best for our continued survival."

Chapter Twenty-One

H armony and Jessie drove in the dark, the Hemi's headlights slicing through the urban night. They ran parallel to the coastline, catching the ripple of waves in the jet-black steel, riding under a bone-white moon.

"You all right with this?" Jessie asked.

"Going back to the marina? Shouldn't be any resistance, and now that we're off our opponents' radar they won't know where we're headed."

"I mean after." She gave her partner a sidelong glance. "If Nadine is behind this, you need to do the talking. She won't open up to April and she sure as hell won't open up to me."

"Agreed. We'll only have one run at her before she wises up. That's why I want to exhaust every possible lead first. If we missed anything, anything at all, she'll sniff it out and use it against us. As for doing the talking, I talk to her every night at headquarters. We play chess."

"I'm aware. I'm also aware that you have your sessions recorded and sent to April."

Harmony flinched.

"April told you," she said softly.

"No she did not," Jessie replied. "I found out because I'm a nosy bitch and also, you know, the boss. So when I see a new line item for transcription work, I like to ask questions and figure out where our very tiny budget is going. And before you ask, I haven't read one single word of the transcripts. That's April's job, and if she sees anything alarming I trust she'll tell me all about it. But I know why you do it."

She let that hang in the air between them for a while. The engine thrummed, eating up the road.

"At the end of the Basilisk job," Harmony said, her voice soft as she stared out into the dark, "I shot Geordie Tynes dead on the airport tarmac."

"It was a mercy killing. He was gonna suffer a lot worse if those psychopaths from his own planet brought him home again. That's why you did it. And if you hadn't, I would have. I thought you were coming to terms with that."

"I came to terms with it. That, you can ask April. I'm fine. I'm...fine with it."

Jessie cocked her head. "Okay, so what's the problem?"

"Then we took on the Ardentis job. And I disarmed Ricky Corbin. I stood over him. He was helpless. And then I shot him between the eyes."

"Ricky was never walking out of that rest stop alive, hon. If you hadn't taken him out, I would have. Dude had civilian blood all over his hands and I was *not* in a generous mood that afternoon."

She was back there, just like that.

"Bang," he whispered, flat on his back as she stood over him. "Yeah, you get it. I see it in your eyes. You're a natural born killer, just like me. You can't fake that."

"'It's the split second before you pull the trigger,'" she said, repeating his own words back to him. "'That's the moment you know what real power feels like.' That's what you told me, right?"

Ricky broke into a feral grin.

"You ain't just judge, jury, and executioner," he said. "You're God almighty. Okay, Hit-girl. Let's see if you've got the stones. Do it. Pull the trigger. Do it. I want you to do it. What are you waiting for?"

"You did the right thing," Jessie said. "I mean, by my admittedly screwed up moral compass, but still. Letting a menace like Ricky Corbin walk is like unleashing a great white shark in a swimming pool. It's just gonna do as much damage as it can before somebody puts it down. You don't need to beat yourself up over it."

"I'm not," Harmony said flatly.

And that's the entire problem.

Because Ricky was right.

And when I pulled the trigger, I was smiling right back at him.

"I need to make sure," she said, choosing her words carefully, "that these new powers of mine don't...affect me in unexpected ways. And Nadine has a vested interest in making sure that they do."

"Bitch does love her mind games," Jessie grumbled.

"One of the first rules in tradecraft when dealing with an ally is 'trust but verify.' That's why I'm keeping April in the loop. As long as there's someone looking over my shoulder, making sure I'm not slipping, then I can trust myself in the field."

She curled her arms over her stomach.

"I can handle Nadine," Harmony said, "as long as the rest of the team is ready to handle *me*."

***

The marina where they'd boarded the *Blue Star* was desolate by night, a few lampposts blazing against the shadows, casting long yellow streaks across the dark waters of the bay. Security was a twenty-four-hour job, though, and they found a lone uniformed guard working overtime in a shack by the docks.

They flashed their badges at the door.

"Special Agents Temple and Black, FBI," Jessie said, effortlessly breezing past him and into the shack. "We're investigating the incident aboard the *Blue Star* earlier today. I assume you're aware?"

The guard was a lanky young guy, fresh out of high school. The bags under his eyes and the massive coffee thermos on his desk, right in front of a bank of video feeds from the marina's security cameras, suggested he hadn't gotten used to the late shift yet.

"Yeah, I saw the fire and rescue boats from here. Crazy stuff."

"We need access to your security recordings," Harmony said. "Specifically any cameras facing the parking lot and the boarding ramps in the hour or so prior to the *Blue Star* disembarking."

His eyes widened. "Oh, uh...I mean, yeah, we have tapes, but I'm not really supposed to let anyone see that stuff. I should call my boss."

Not optimal. Their FBI covers were more or less paper-thin these days. They'd hold up to casual scrutiny, but if anyone started demanding a subpoena they'd be out of luck. Fortunately Jessie had seen that coming and worked up a plan on the way over. She gave Harmony a subtle nod.

Harmony fixed her face into a scowl, playing bad cop. She leaned in and jabbed the hapless guard in the chest.

"Listen, you prick. If we don't get ahead of this thing, the next bombing is going to be a hell of a lot worse. The only reason we're not trawling for corpses tonight is because the terrorists made a mistake setting their demo charges."

"Bombing?" he squeaked. "*Terrorists?* I thought it was an accident!"

Jessie grabbed Harmony's sleeve and yanked her back, hard.

"Excuse me," she said, "I need a word with my fellow agent."

She pulled her to the corner of the shack, hauled her close, and put her lips to Harmony's ear.

"Yell yell yell, grumble snarl etcetera," she whispered. "Now stand back and look duly chastened."

Harmony's gaze dropped to the floor and she fell silent. Jessie put on a gleaming smile and curled her fingers over the shaken guard's shoulder.

"I'm sorry. She's new. I'll be honest, you weren't supposed to hear any of that. What's your name?" Her gaze flicked to the tag on his uniform pocket. "Bob? Bob, I'm going to need you to step up and help us out here. You don't want any innocent people getting hurt, right?"

"Of course not," he said, reeling between the two of them.

"And you want to do your civic duty, right? You look like a civic-minded kind of guy. Sure you are. Now look: we're on it, okay? And we're going to have the bad guys mopped up by sunrise, but Uncle Sam needs your help. It's true, the incident on the boat wasn't an accident. Can I trust you to keep the secret, at least until tomorrow?"

He nodded, almost eager now, drawn in by her raw confidence.

"Excellent," Jessie said. "See? You're practically a deputy FBI agent now. We're on the same team, you and me."

"Do I...get a badge or something?"

"You'll get a certificate in the mail. But right now, my deputy, we need to verify some faces in that crowd footage. And if you call your boss, he's gonna complicate things, not to mention — well, now that you're in on the secret, you wouldn't blab it to him, right?"

He scrunched up his face. "God no. My boss is a dick."

"You get it, then." She gestured to the console. "We'll keep this just between ourselves. Nobody needs to know."

He waited outside while they ran the footage. It didn't take long to find what they were looking for, considering the object of their hunt would stand out in almost any crowd. There was Althea, towering head and shoulders above the rest of the partygoers, deep in the crowd waiting to climb the gangplank.

"She's with someone," Jessie murmured. "Freeze there. Okay. Now click ahead a few frames at a time. All we need is a break in the crowd to get a better look."

Harmony turned the dial on the console, inching the footage forward. Then a few people moved out of the way, a window opening by random chance, giving one clear shot of the person she stood arm in arm with.

Dr. Charles Stepford, Muffy's old friend and investor, was Althea's date to the party.

"As an investor, he would have received the party invitations from ProcGen. He got her onto that boat as his plus one." Jessie glanced at Harmony. "Didn't you say he seemed like kind of a dupe?"

"He did. Muffy talked about his investment in ProcGen like she was milking him for cash. But Althea was never at the roulette table, meaning they must have split up as soon as they came on board."

"She went down, killed the sailor in the pump room and set the stage for the trap," Jessie said, thinking out loud, "then came back upstairs, showed her face in the casino, and baited me in."

"She had another accomplice. Stepford was with me and Muffy at the table the entire time, and I saw him in line with Muffy for the lifeboats. Whoever set the charge on the hull and took Althea with them had a cigarette boat waiting and ready."

"Which could have been Mercury Blaise, or her *sicario* buddy. Either one of them could get that job done. In any case, if you brought a date to a party and something bad went down, would you just dip without her? I wouldn't."

Harmony shook her head. "He knew she had an alternate exit planned. He's not an innocent pawn here. Doesn't mean Muffy isn't ripping him off with her AI scheme, no honor among thieves and all that, but he knows more than he should."

"Seen all I need to see." Jessie pushed herself back from the console. "Let's get back to the plane and get airborne. I want to be long gone and off the radar before sunrise."

Chapter Twenty-Two

"**K**evin, do the honors."

His hammer slammed down, smashing the Trojan horse device into glittering bits of plastic and wire, its battery bouncing as its housing warped and tore, circuitry snapping in half. He double-checked with his multimeter, made sure the beast was dead, and gave Aselia a thumbs up as she waited in the cockpit door.

The *Imperator*'s engines roared to life. Electricity shimmered on across the command room, screens flickering back to life, overheads blazing bright as the cargo ramp began its slow whirring crawl upward, sealing the plane's vulnerable belly behind a wall of bulletproof steel.

Kevin jumped into his swivel chair, sliding along the bank of consoles until he kicked to a stop. "Okay, nobody touch *anything* until I scrub our systems from top to bottom. With the connection cut Mercury should be locked out, but I'm not taking any chances."

If he was right, they'd just gone completely dark on the opposition's end. Whoever was behind the Trojan horse would know it had been found and eliminated. *Meaning they know we're coming*, Harmony thought, *but on the other hand, we're running silent again. Fair trade.*

"Y'all better buckle in and get ready for takeoff," Aselia said over the intercom. "I got a spot picked out and ready. Li'l smuggler's strip in Kentucky, not far from Nashville. Also not far from this honky-tonk I know where they got the best damn barbecue you'll ever eat. Guy who owns the strip owes me a favor.

He'll look the other way as long as we're gone by tomorrow afternoon — he's got a shipment coming in and needs the space."

The *Imperator* roared up into the night sky, due east. As the plane leveled out, once Kevin verified it was operating clean as a whistle, Harmony and April went on the attack. Another deep dive into the financial maze behind ProcGen, but this time they had a new parameter to add to the search: the Phoenix Clinic, Charles Stepford's yoga, granola, and plastic surgery retreat in upstate New York.

"We good?" Jessie asked Kevin. "Open an encrypted channel to HQ. I need to bring Linder into the loop and make sure he knows somebody's trying real hard to get our home address."

The comms officer who answered the call sounded uncomfortable.

"Mr. Linder is out of the office and unavailable for contact, ma'am."

Jessie lifted an eyebrow. "Why?"

"He said he had to go off grid for a couple of days. No other information."

"I really don't like him going on missions that I didn't give him," Jessie grumbled.

Back in the bad old days, Linder — their former boss — had been knowingly and firmly in the pocket of the infernal powers behind Vigilant Lock. He believed, and Harmony couldn't fault him for it, that he could save more lives by going along with the conspiracy instead of rocking the boat. A utilitarian to the end. It had nearly *been* his end, but Jessie relented, realizing they needed his contacts in the alphabet agencies to keep the new incarnation of Vigilant funded and viable.

She still didn't trust him. Only a fool would.

"Okay, listen up," she said. "We've got some bad actors making a concerted effort to locate our physical HQ, presumably to launch an attack. Get a message to all teams in the field to *stay* in the field until Kevin can verify they haven't been compromised, and nobody currently at HQ leaves until further notice. Lock the facility down, full stop. And when Linder shows up, you tell his ass to call me."

"Yes, ma'am. Oh, one other thing: the prisoner is demanding to speak to Agent Black. Apparently she's...bored."

Jessie looked over at Harmony, who was at the strategy table poring over a softly glowing tablet at April's side. Harmony looked up and held up her fingers, making a two and a zero.

"Tell Nadine that Harmony's gonna call her in twenty minutes."

She broke the connection.

"Take a look at this," Harmony said. "Kevin, can you send the feed from my tablet up onto the main screen?"

"Embiggening now," he said, rattling off a few keystrokes. The video wall lit up with ledger samples, payments and receivables marked in streaks of yellow highlighter, a financial maze with no escape routes.

"We already found the connection between ProcGen and Bobby Diehl's venture capital company," Harmony said, "but once we added the Phoenix Clinic to the mix, new connections popped up. For starters, Muffy was telling the truth about Charles Stepford being an investor, but he's not paying out of his own pocket: the Clinic is making direct payments from its own coffers to ProcGen."

"Sounds like money laundering," Jessie said.

"More like a cup and ball trick," April said. "The magician lays out multiple cups. A ball goes under one. He slides the cups around the table, challenging you to keep track of where the ball — in this case a very large amount of money — has disappeared to."

"And all the while," Kevin added, "he slipped it into his palm before the trick even started. The ball lands where the magician wants it to land."

"The Phoenix Clinic orders medical supplies through Zaire Biomedical. Zaire Biomedical was funded through Bobby Diehl's investment firm, as was the Long Island Pharmaceutical Supply Company, which makes regular shipments to Zaire Biomedical and to ProcGen's corporate campus in San Francisco."

"Back up," Jessie said. "The connection to the Clinic I get, but why is a tech firm like ProcGen buying goods from a pharmaceutical company?"

"I would love to know," April replied, her voice crisp. "But a very large and regular amount of capital is changing hands. Oh, and would you care to hazard a guess as to who funded the Long Island Pharmaceutical Supply Company?"

"Bobby Diehl," Jessie muttered.

"The exact same year that Zaire opened its doors. We are looking at a very well planned and well concealed corporate octopus. ProcGen, Phoenix, Long Island, Zaire, and all the way back to Goering-Milhouse, the financiers of the whole enterprise, who used Bobby Diehl's seed money to get the ball rolling. It's all the *same company*, with a rotating staff of figureheads pretending to be in charge. But I believe we've found the head of the snake. Harmony?"

Harmony stepped forward. She flicked a finger across her tablet and the image on the video wall flipped to a fresh spreadsheet page. One solitary name, buried deep in microscopic font, stood circled in scarlet.

"We found a name. Just a small line item here and there, but it was enough to make a forensic connection. Praeda Electronics. They're a boutique firm that specializes in custom computer applications for private clients. If you want a video wall like ours in your corporate lobby, for example, or a touchscreen kiosk, they can set you up."

"Like back at the ProcGen campus," Jessie said.

April held up a finger. "There's the rub. Praeda is enmeshed in dealings with every firm on the list, but in a way that's deliberately been obfuscated. First and foremost, while they're heavily invested in ProcGen, ProcGen does *not* buy any computer equipment from Praeda. They buy off-the-shelf gear sourced locally, and they spend a staggering amount of money on it. Money that would spotlight Praeda if they were mentioned in any of ProcGen's quarterly investor reports."

"They're burying the connection," Harmony said. "Praeda Electronics has a small, barely functional website, but it's all a front. Nobody on the board of directors actually exists, as far as I can tell, and when I ran their corporate bio photographs through image recognition they came up completely empty."

April nodded. "Most likely AI-generated deepfakes. Once upon a time that at least took a little skill in Photoshop. These days, generating realistic photographs of nonexistent people just requires Internet access and a functioning mouse button."

"Then there's the name, which makes me think somebody over there has a dark sense of humor," Harmony said.

She locked eyes with Jessie.

"It's Latin," she said. "It refers to the spoils of war. Or, alternately, to the act of capturing prey. In the fifteenth century it evolved into *praedari*, "to rob," and then into *praedator*. Or as we say today: predator."

Not the first time they'd encountered a similar name in the field. *Glass Predator* was the designation of the CIA black bag program that sent Althea, along with her pack of Wolf-King cultists, all over the world on murderous jaunts in the name of democracy and big capital.

"As happy as I am to blame my mother for literally anything," Jessie said, "there's no way in hell she set this up. She wouldn't even know where to start. Complicated business maneuvers aren't her cup of tea; the closest she gets to subtle is a sniper rifle. Also she's a professional mercenary. She knows how to get paid and keep her trail clean. She doesn't need a massive maze of red tape for that, just a clean Bitcoin wallet."

"I'm inclined to agree," April said, "it's off-profile and well outside her skill set. There's no disputing the fact that she's involved, however. Before we tackle that... Harmony, there is a suspect to exclude. Would you like to take the call on the main screen?"

Kevin had already broken out fresh burner phones for her and Jessie, verifying they were bug-free. She held hers up and pointed over her shoulder with her other thumb.

"I'm going to take this over by the jumpseats," she said. "If you're all listening in, Nadine will pick up on it and start acting out. If I'm going to get the truth out of her, it has to be one on one."

April held her gaze for a moment, then nodded, firm.

"We're here if you need us," she said.

Chapter Twenty-Three

"I was right, wasn't I?"

Those were the first words out of Nadine's mouth. Harmony squeezed the phone and took a breath.

"About?"

"You're hunting for a man with no soul."

"You tell me," Harmony replied.

She laid out the case, just the highlights, illustrating each clue and leaving them at Nadine's feet. The demoness paused a moment, taking it all in, and answered with a delighted chuckle.

"Oh my. When you frame it like that, I look rather guilty, don't I?"

"The thought," Harmony said, "did occur to me. If we had taken Bobby Diehl's corpse back to base with the Trojan horse undetected and active, it would have sent up our location like a flare and opened a way to shut down all of our electronic security at the same time. Perfect opportunity for your people to break you out."

"I'm torn, you know. On one hand it really is a wickedly clever scheme and I'd love to take credit for it. But no. This isn't my doing or my people's doing, and I can prove it. In fact, while normally I might find some amusement in leaving you in an agony of indecision, in this case I want you to have nothing but sweet, blissful certainty."

"Why?"

"Because," Nadine said, "you are facing off against a genuinely skilled opponent, and I intend for you to win. Distractions and doubts will only weaken you."

Her voice dropped to a silken panther's purr.

"You are *mine*, Harmony Black. No other will have you, and in the end, you will bend your knee to me and me alone. If some upstart thinks otherwise, it will be my great pleasure to *correct* them."

She paused. Now her voice was bright and chipper again.

"For starters, let's consider the timing. I was on my way to rendezvous with Josh Orville and his team to retrieve the casket when you and the puppy ambushed me with those nasty electric bullets. From there you took me into custody. I understand that no one on the heist team survived, correct? You killed my dear Josh."

"Jessie killed Josh. I killed Ricky Corbin."

"Ricky Corbin was pest control, and I hope you haven't lost a minute of your beauty sleep over it."

"Herbert West survived," Harmony pointed out.

"And he's not one of my people, which I'm sure you've independently verified. So here's the thing, darling: my people can't be hunting for Vigilant Lock's headquarters because, at least as far as I'm aware, they don't know you have me in the first place. Oh, I'm sure there's suspicions being flung about, but I have a long, long list of enemies. When it comes to people who would like to make me vanish from the face of the earth, you aren't even in the top three. Oh, and while we're chatting...knight to f3."

Harmony saw the board in her mind's eye, crystal blue, the position preserved from their last phone call. Two pawns had already moved, the opening shots of the battle. Now Nadine's white knight reared up and charged into the fray.

"Pawn to d6. And if someone in the House of Dead Roses already figured it out and took independent action?"

Nadine laughed, giddy.

"*Who*, cupcake? My strategist was the poor departed Josh. Besides myself, nobody in my ranks has the acumen to pull off a play like that. You've met my daughter Nyx. What do you think of her? Be honest."

"She's a freight train on legs."

"Exactly. Her father was a demon from the Choir of Wrath, and she takes after him far more than she does me. Bit of a disappointment to be honest, but you can't choose your daughters." Nadine paused. "Unless...well. Perhaps there are ways, but we can talk about that another time. At any rate, she's utterly formidable on the battlefield but not what I'd call a keen tactical thinker. Pawn to d4."

Harmony stared at the board. With one move, Nadine had forced her to alter her strategy. Her next choice was simple: kill or be killed. And if she chose to kill, Nadine would turn it into a sacrifice with her very next move. Losing a piece was inevitable. The only choice Nadine offered was which soldier would fall.

"Pawn," Harmony said, "captures d4. You have had contact with Bobby Diehl in the past, you've run in some of the same circles—"

"And I'd need a time machine if I was the mastermind behind this plot. ProcGen's wheels started spinning well over a year ago, before Bobby got his wings clipped. You know, for a while every movie seemed to have that one wretched trope. You know the one: the villain is captured by the hero before the halfway mark and the day is saved? Ah, but then the villain reveals her master stroke: she meant to be captured all along, and the hero played into her wicked hands."

Nadine let out a heavy wistful sigh.

"It's dumb, and I dislike it for reasons that should be apparent. The only way I could be behind this is if I planned for my own capture well over a year ago. And if I had, and if you'd brought the Trojan horse to my cell door, what would that have gained me? I destroy Vigilant? I never thought very highly of your little spy ring in the first place, and I've told you so on numerous occasions. And if the gambit failed — as it certainly would have in this situation — I lose everything. Oh, knight captures d4."

The knight bounded across the field, killing the killer, claiming dangerous ground.

"I'll be honest, and it hurts me to say this," Nadine added, "I genuinely never thought there was any chance in a million years a *human* could bring me down. I didn't plan for it because I considered it about as likely as the sun orbiting the earth. Then again, with the blood of the King of Wolves in her veins, your dear Jessie isn't exactly human, now is she? And neither are you. Not anymore."

Harmony squirmed in her seat, gritting her teeth. She focused on the board. She needed bigger guns.

"Knight to f6," she said. "I keep running into the same wall. Everything about this, from start to finish, feels like a Bobby Diehl scheme. His fingers are all over this corporate octopus. He's been known to work with mercenaries like Althea. Rigging something like the Trojan horse...well, if he couldn't do it himself, he had the resources to hire someone who could. Even after we froze his assets and sent him on the run, I'm certain he had access to caches, rainy day funds, side companies he could loot."

"Knight to c3," Nadine replied. "Oh, Harmony, sweet. You made the worst mistake a hunter possibly can. You wounded an animal, and then you didn't finish it off."

"Not for lack of trying."

"And yet. But I agree. Every aspect of this has his unique heartless stench to it. A Silicon Valley pump-and-dump scam disguised as an AI for 'wellness.'" Harmony could almost hear Nadine's eyes rolling. "Ugh. I prefer more organic investments. Flower shops, massage parlors, businesses of the heart and the flesh. The last time I spoke to Bobby, it was after he'd gone on the run. He came with his hat in his hand and I rebuffed him, of course. Do you know what that little worm said to me? What he had the *temerity* to say to me?"

"Pawn to g6. Do tell."

"He said," Nadine replied, her tone like a holy inquisitor pronouncing judgment on a heretic, "that *1989* was *mid*."

"The year, or the...wait, you mean the Taylor—"

"The album, Harmony. The album. He said that. Those exact words. Are you going to tell me that *Blank Space* is mid? That *Out of the Woods* is *mid*?" Nadine paused, taking a breath. "But the problem you're encountering is clear: it's Bobby's scheme all right. But someone not only shot that wounded animal on your behalf, they used his corpse to finish carrying out his well-laid plans. Who hates him *and* your organization in equal measure, hm? Who could get close enough to Bobby to stab him in the back, then use the bloody knife to lure you in? Also, bishop to e2."

Only you, Harmony thought. *But you just gave me a laundry list of reasons why it couldn't have been your doing, and I hate to say it but I believe you. The timing doesn't work, the motives don't line up...so who, out of our entire rogues' gallery, has the means to pull off a plot like this?*

"And now, I can tell by that sudden silence, you're seeing an answer. Harmony, I don't want to second-guess your team's doubtlessly fine work, but...are you sure that's Bobby Diehl currently playing Frosty the Snowman in your freezer?"

Harmony sighed, facing another brick wall.

"Yes," she said. "When we found out Charles Stepford brought Althea to the party and that he runs a plastic surgery clinic, the question was obvious. Finding out his clinic is part of the whole Praeda Electronics octopus made it even more likely. But I had April triple-check. We have Bobby's entire medical history, his dental records, and that corpse is a perfect, one hundred percent match."

"Bobby was a techno-fetishist. You remember those awful remote-control zombies he built. Some sort of clone, perhaps?"

"I took that into account, but even if he had the tech, the clone would have to have been full grown over a decade ago. Then he would have had to somehow keep it identical to his own physical condition, down to specific operations on specific dates, exact cavities and when and where he got fillings...Theoretically possible, but even if he had the long-term focus for something like that, which I think we can agree he didn't, he would have had to start years before he even knew Vigilant existed."

Harmony's free hand squeezed her knee, a nervous gesture as the plane shuddered through a patch of rough air.

"I have to build my case on some kind of stable, logical foundation, and the most certain clue we've got is the one in that freezer," she said. "Bobby Diehl is dead. He set up the scheme, and his partner, whoever it is — right now I'm thinking it's whoever is behind Praeda Electronics — betrayed him and used his body as bait for us."

"It's your move," Nadine said.

"Bishop to g7."

"On the real battlefield, I meant. Consider this: your enemy knows that you've found and shut down the Trojan horse. You've slipped off their radar, and for the moment you're running invisible. But do they know what you know about *them*?"

Harmony contemplated that.

"No. They don't know we found the footage at the marina with Charles bringing Althea as his plus one to get her on board. I keep thinking about the conversation at the roulette table. It felt like Muffy very much wanted me to see Charles as harmless, a hopeless dupe buying into her snake oil. In hindsight, she was preemptively covering his trail."

"Well then, I suggest you infiltrate the Phoenix Clinic and see what's what. But you were already planning that, weren't you?"

"It helps to bounce my ideas off of other people sometimes," Harmony admitted.

"I strongly suggest you disguise yourself. Puppy, however, does not disguise well, not with those eyes of hers, or her insolent attitude. She would serve best as remote backup, ready to respond with heavy firepower in case your investigation becomes a provocation. Move with stealth and purpose, and then...we take them down."

"'We?'"

"Am I not on the team? Please don't say I'm not, darling, you'll hurt my feelings terribly."

"I...I think you'd have to run that by Jessie. It's her team. Also, it's your move."

"I castle kingside."

Pieces slid across the board, changing places, fortifying defenses.

"I also castle," Harmony said. "Kingside."

"Mm, mirroring me. Or are you *imprinting* on me? Like a little duckling learning from her mama?" Nadine chuckled. "And the guards have just arrived, bringing my evening slop and an entirely too small portion of cheap red wine. We'll continue this game later. Just remember one thing for me, little one: a predator doesn't care for the opinions of prey. And you, like it or not, are a predator now."

She broke the connection, leaving Harmony alone with her thoughts and a half-finished game, two armies frozen mid-clash.

Chapter Twenty-Four

The team gathered around the strategy table. Harmony hated being the center of attention, but she understood why.

"It's not Nadine," she said, "but I'd like you all to double-check my work."

She walked them through the phone call, the reasons why; she expected pushback, but only received silent nods in return.

"Damn, I wish it was her," Jessie said.

"It would have tied everything up in a neat bow," April conceded. "But life rarely grants such a tidy treat. And she's correct about one thing: our best lead right now is the Phoenix Clinic. We don't have any reason to think anything untoward is happening there, beyond grotesquely overpriced kale smoothies and the occasional nose job."

"But everything ties back to Praeda," Kevin said, "including that clinic, and Charles Stepford was the vector they used to get Althea onto the *Blue Star*. Anything we can find — a paper trail, payment records, email between him and his real bosses — could crack this thing wide open."

Jessie crossed her arms, frowning.

"Yeah, well, like you said, we knew that. So let's not go giving Nadine any credit. I'm already tired of her bullshit."

Harmony decided, in a moment of discretion, not to mention Nadine's quip about being part of the team.

"I think I should go in alone," she said.

Jessie stared at her. "Why? Because Busty Hannibal Lecter said so?"

"Because it's a good idea, and a good idea is a good idea even if your enemy is the one who came up with it. Just ask whoever killed Bobby and took *his* plan. Right now they have no reason to suspect we'll show up on the Clinic's doorstep. With a good disguise and a solid cover, alone, I have a chance to slip past casual scrutiny. If two women matching our general descriptions show up together, that's a red flag."

Harmony rested her hands on the stainless-steel table, her gaze tracing from face to face, taking them in.

"Meanwhile, we put Jessie on the grounds outside, kitted out with the heaviest firepower we can get our hands on. With that, plus Kevin's drones and surveillance tech, she'll be the angel on my shoulder. And since we have our comms back under control, April can help me talk my way out of trouble. If things go right, I'll be in and out like a ghost."

Jessie rubbed her chin, nodding slowly. The mention of heavy firepower won her over.

"And if they go wrong, I'll swoop down like the fist of God. You're still going to be in danger though."

"Less danger than we'd both be in if we went there together and got ambushed," Harmony said. "This way if something happens to me, there's still a plan B."

Jessie rapped her knuckles on the table.

"Okay. We'll go with your plan. *Your* plan. Kevin, pull together everything we've got on the Phoenix Clinic. Employee data, client lists, satellite scans of the building and its surroundings. April, rendezvous with headquarters and start putting together a bulletproof cover for Harmony."

"What are you going to do?" Kevin asked.

"Me? I'm going to call a guy about some guns."

***

"Yes, hello, good morning." April was all smiles, adjusting her bifocals as she talked on the phone. "I'm calling from the office of Verity Hale. I'm her personal assistant. Miss Hale would very much like to visit the Phoenix Clinic for rejuvenation therapy. Why yes, that's right. The Georgia pecan heiress."

On the other end of the console bank, Kevin gave her the thumbs up as another webpage — the third he'd built that morning — went live. He'd been coordinating with the troll farm back at HQ since dawn, ensuring that any Internet search for that name pointed to the same root sources: theirs. Given the pause from the receptionist's end, it was obvious they'd just run a hasty Google hunt. As expected.

"Yes, it's her first time. The Clinic's services, however, came highly recommended from Verity's good friend Mr. Bale." April paused listening. "Oh, I understand the desire for referrals, but we don't need to use people's Christian names, now do we? You get the idea. Let's not be vulgar, these people do deserve privacy. Mm hm. Yes, of course, a ten thousand dollar deposit is perfectly reasonable. I'm ready to transfer the funds to the account of your choice."

***

"Get in, loser. We're going shopping."

Harmony couldn't claim to understand the relationship Jessie had with Coraline. They'd crossed paths with the cambion assassin and her brother Ethan on a mission in Miami, an altercation that ended up with Coraline tied to Jessie's bed and a hostage negotiation with their boss Ariel, the hound of the Court of Windswept Razors. Ariel looked like Audrey Hepburn in *Breakfast at Tiffany's*, talked and walked like she was made of pure girlboss particles, and she wanted Bobby Diehl gone just as much as Vigilant Lock did.

The Razors were the smallest of the demonic courts, and the only reason they still had any power at all was their hold over New York. The city was a money-printing machine, and Ariel was willing to make alliances with anyone, even human monster-hunters, if it meant keeping the city safe and on its feet.

In the end, they came out of it with a tentative truce: the Razors agreed to stay out of Vigilant's way, Vigilant agreed to warn them when they were tracking rogue demons on their turf, and both sides were ready to break the deal the second they needed to. Jessie came out of it with a...special friend. Every once in a while she'd meet up with Coraline at a hotel somewhere, go off comms for the night, and come back the next morning bruised and smiling.

Romantic relationships baffled Harmony in general. She couldn't even *try* to understand what Jessie's deal was, but she knew it made her happy, and that was all she needed to know.

Once the *Imperator* touched down at LaGuardia Airport, Jessie made a courtesy call to Ariel. No details, outside the bare necessities, just a heads up to let her know they weren't there for a fight. Harmony was barely surprised when, two hours later, a Mustang convertible roared up the tarmac and skidded to a stop outside the hangar doors. Coraline hopped out, rocking torn jeans, a belly tee, and a studded leather jacket. She grabbed Jessie by the shirt collar and hauled her into a long, hungry kiss.

"Where's your brother?" Jessie asked.

"Did you *want* me to bring him?"

"Hell no."

"Right answer, skank."

"Not that I'm complaining about the surprise visit," Jessie said, "but we've got shit to do. Can't really hang right now."

"That's why I'm here. Ariel gleaned just enough to grasp that you're sending Miss Priss undercover, so I'm here to help. Also I'm supposed to spy on both of you and get as much info as I can steal, so don't say anything you don't want me to report back."

"I really appreciate you being upfront about that."

"Yeah, I'm a real saint." Coraline handed her a tiny disc, about the size of a watch battery, attached to an inch of scarlet wire. "This is the bug I'm supposed to plant on the plane. You wanna take that and toss it down a sewer drain or something?"

"Done."

"Cool. Me and you can catch up in a bit. I'm taking the closeted lesbian out for a makeover. We'll be back in a few hours."

"Excuse me," Harmony said, holding up a hand and feeling adrift. "I'm standing right here."

"I could have been talking about anyone," Coraline said in a breezy voice, "and yet you knew exactly who I meant. You should contemplate that on the drive into Manhattan."

As she turned to go, Jessie swatted her across the ass, hard. Coraline grinned. "You'll pay for that later."

***

Compared to braving the trap-laden dungeon of Mercury Blaise, Kevin found easier purchase for his digital sword in a much safer environment: the belly of the Visa credit card processing system. He had his eyes on the monitor and a voice in his headphones, a liaison from the Vigilant sub-department known as the Print Shop.

"Nah," Kevin was saying, "don't waste your time on that. People like 'Verity Hale' don't carry business cards. They have assistants who carry business cards, then you call the assistant to find out if you're allowed to talk to their boss. Now that you've got a bulletproof SSN for her, focus on getting that driver's license done. I'll send you a fresh headshot for the picture in a bit. Do me a favor: read off the birthdate you gave her?"

He tapped out a string of numbers, building a database entry. *Credit limit? Oh, let's pump this baby up.*

"Okay, once I wrap this up I'm going to slate it for rush overnight delivery to our offsite box in Bethesda. Get her license, social security card, and the other goodies ready, pick up the credit card as soon as it comes in tomorrow, and hand-deliver it to us at the *Imperator*. You can take a civilian flight to LaGuardia, first available."

He paused, listening to the chatter in his ear.

"No, flying first class does not 'improve operational security.' Trust me, I've tried that one with Jessie, it won't work. Best I can offer you is an upgrade to Comfort Plus. Take it or leave it."

***

Harmony was in a daze, swept like a whirlwind from boutique to boutique. Now she was in a salon chair on Fifth Avenue, being primped and prodded and hating every second of it. She liked her look the way it was: the same style every day, the same suit every day, a peaceful and reliable consistency. She changed the colors of her neckties. That was really all the variety she needed or wanted. But the mission needed her to turn chameleon, and the mission always came first.

Coraline stood over her, one hand on her hip, lips pursed as she watched the stylist work.

"You clean up nice, I'll say that much." She nodded to the stylist. "Show her."

Harmony's chair swiveled, confronting her with her reflection in the mirror. Her hair had gone from light blonde to strawberry brown with reddish highlights, piled like a Parisian aristocrat's, a single long, curly bang falling low along one cheek.

It was different. But maybe different wasn't that bad.

***

Wexler was one of Aselia's boys, a shining star on her endless list of smugglers, gunslingers, and scum for hire that she'd cultivated in her outlaw days. He looked like a refugee from the Seventies, big lapels on his Hawaiian shirt and a big blond porn stache on his upper lip. He rolled up to the *Imperator*'s private hangar in a dusty white pickup with Arkansas plates, the cargo bed draped with an oilcloth tarp. He hopped out, pulled the tailgate down, and rolled up the tarp, unveiling a clutter of sturdy wooden crates. A few still bore markings from the warehouses they were stolen from and stamps of lading from as far as Moscow.

"And how are my favorite customers this fine afternoon?" he drawled, tipping an invisible hat to Jessie and Aselia as they walked down the cargo ramp.

"Feel better with some big iron on our hips," Aselia said. "You bring some goodies?"

"Ladies, I brought you the whole damn candy store. Never let it be said that I don't deliver the best."

He snatched up a crowbar and popped the lid of a long crate, rough planks creaking up as the nails wriggled loose. Inside, a pair of matte black rifles, long and sleek like venomous serpents, rested in a bed of tombstone-gray foam.

"The question is," he said, "what kinda bear are you huntin'?"

"The kind that might be wearing a vest," Jessie said, "and engaging at close to medium range. Multiple bears, in fact. I'm looking for stopping power, accuracy and — just in case — the ability to throw a whole lot of lead at absolutely terrifying speed."

He snapped his fingers, nodded, and opened a second crate. He reached in and hoisted up a long rifle, the stock and grip dark walnut. Wexler turned it from side to side, checking down the sights, before handing it over to Jessie.

"Allow me to introduce you to the pride of Serbia. This here's a Zastava M70 — the original, not the sporting model they can legally sell in the States. Chambered for 7.62, you've got a single shot, burst fire, and full auto toggle, thirty-round mags, and it can fit just about any off-the-shelf scope you like. Nice thing is, the M70 was reverse-engineered from the AK-47's tech specs. Just like the AK, this baby's built to take a beating and keep on truckin'. Dirt, grime, hard weather, she doesn't even care. She's born for battle."

Jessie shouldered the rifle, tested its weight and its worth, and nodded to herself.

"I'll take it. Also need something for close-up work. Stopping power is more important than concealment. If I have to use it, something's gone wrong."

He turned and beckoned them closer, rolling up more of the tarp, popping the hasp of another storage crate.

"Remember," Wexler said, "'Stopping power' and penetration aren't necessarily the same thing. A .357's a classic and it'll shoot through damn near anything, but you're looking at more kick and more muzzle flash, and that could throw you off your game, especially in close-quarters combat. If you want a workhorse that'll get the job done, may I suggest this fine number?"

Jessie passed the rifle to Aselia, freeing up her hands, and he passed her a solid black handgun. It was sturdy, firm in her hand, textured with a ridged diamond pattern designed to cling to a sweaty grip.

"This here's your Wilson Combat SFX9, with a five-inch barrel. Based on the traditional 1911, chambered for nine millimeter, built with a single-piece aluminum frame for added durability. Takes a fifteen-round magazine. Mix in the right ammunition — like, for instance, Federal HST rounds, which I just so happen to have in stock — you can stop anything short of a sumo wrestler on PCP."

Wexler put his hands together and spread his fingers, mimicking the petals of a flower.

"HST's an improvement on Hydra Shok ammo. It penetrates and *expands*, like when you cut off a hydra's head and it sprouts six more. Except, you know, hopefully while they're several inches inside somebody you don't like."

"Wexler," Jessie said, "I like you. Ring me up, let's do this."

***

A satellite scan blossomed on the *Imperator*'s video wall, showing an overhead map of what looked like some kind of forest compound. More images popped up on the neighboring screens: blurry drone photos, along with a thermal scan that cast the woods in dark blues and tiny spots of hot orange.

"Okay team," Kevin said, "here's what I've got on the Phoenix Clinic. The place is in upstate New York, outside Grahamsville, about two and a half hours north of here. The town's a postage stamp, very pretty and very small. From there you take an old logging road off Route 55 that leads into the woods for another twenty minutes or so, weather depending. Apparently, when it rains the whole thing turns into a river of mud for a couple of days and nothing gets in or out."

"Not a problem for Doctor Stepford's wealthiest patients," April added, using a laser pointer to circle a raised, flat chunk of the compound map. "As arrival by private helicopter is encouraged. We don't have access to one, so we'll be sending you in via a livery service. Your backstory is that you arrived in NYC via your personal company jet and hired a driver for your local needs."

Harmony nodded. It was believable and unexceptional, nothing that would attract more than a second's worth of thought, and that was exactly what you wanted in a solid cover.

Kevin tapped a button. A string of tiny red circles peppered the satellite view of the property.

"I've studied every amateur drone shot I could dig up on the Internet," Kevin said, "and I've identified some — but probably not all — of their exterior surveillance. Each circle marks a post or tree-mounted camera sending wireless footage back to the clinic's security office. Unfortunately, that's the extent of what I can get from public-facing data. Staff numbers, how close they watch the feeds, how heavily they'll respond to an intruder, that's all up in the air until we dig in."

Jessie narrowed her eyes, committing the map to memory.

"Not a problem," she said. "Looks like a rough ring of cameras, about a quarter mile out, irregularly spaced. Even if you missed some, we can extrapolate the rest based on the intel we have. Get me close enough and I can go the rest of the way on foot. If I can't slip past a patchy setup like that, I should hand in my spy credentials."

"I scoped out the map for potential landing sites," Aselia said. "Good news is, there's plenty. Like I always say, a Hercules lands wherever it wants to land. Whole reason the Army still swears by these babies. Bad news is, it's gonna raise a ruckus. I found us a staging ground about twenty miles outside Grahamsville. We can monitor you from there and stand ready. Hopefully you won't need an emergency evac. If you do, you two are gonna have to dig in and hold out for a little bit, but once we swoop in these folks will *know* the cavalry has arrived. Trust on that."

***

Up close the Phoenix Clinic looked like a tranquil retreat, a wilderness lodge built from smooth, polished timbers and rugged log arches, a luxury resort playing at being a camping destination. Tall windows, perfectly opaque from the outside, looked out over an expanse of lush green forest. The long logging road ended at a paved circular drive where attendants in trim brown uniforms waited with luggage carts at the ready.

The lobby's automatic doors hissed open, welcoming Harmony into air-conditioned serenity. The rustic wooden walls soared up to a second-floor walkway with handcrafted driftwood railings, and a long green carpet led from the doors to a check-in desk that curved like the bend of an ocean wave. Soft music played over hidden speakers, vaguely Celtic, vaguely New Age, a melody that existed to sooth and nothing more.

Harmony turned heads with her slow, confident stride, drawing attention from a cluster of clients — half wearing long white bathrobes with the outline of a rising, burning phoenix over the hip pockets — who were talking by a cold stone fireplace. Her new hair was coiffed and her body was draped in boho chic, a twist-front maxi dress with a flowing floral pattern and a two-thousand-dollar price tag. Her cat-eye designer glasses, a last-minute build incorporating Vigilant's standard pinhole camera tech, did just enough to change the usual shape of her face.

She walked up to the counter and smiled.

"Hale," she said. "Verity Hale. I believe you're expecting me."

Chapter Twenty-Five

D isguise, Harmony knew, was an art form. One that amateurs took to unnecessary extremes. Back in her FBI days working deep cover, she ran with one too many agents who thought it meant a wig, a fake mustache, a limp, cotton swabs in their cheeks, and a bad accent, along with a cover that read like a rejected Charles Dickens story.

Psychology and science gave the real score: most people were terrible at remembering a stranger's face, especially under stress. It wasn't uncommon for a dozen eyewitnesses to a bank robbery to give a dozen different descriptions, even within an hour of the event. Add a little more time and they'd get even the most basic details wrong, as imagination played its magic trick and turned memory into fantasy.

So she kept it simple and played to stereotype, but kept it low-key. As long as she fitted everyone's idea of what a Georgia pecan heiress should look and act like, she should slip under the radar. She didn't try to go over the top with her accent. Kevin had made sure to note, in each and every one of the fake biographies he seeded across the Internet, that Verity had been born, raised, and educated in the Midwest before moving to join the family empire. Harmony added a tiny lilt to her words, but nothing more, nothing that would lead a native listener to catch her in a mistake. Her non-native status also meant that if she ran into anyone from the Peach State, she could claim ignorance about local customs.

As for play-acting a multimillionaire trust fund baby, April had drilled her on the basics. *"Remember above all that you've had everything done for you since the day you were born. Don't lift a finger. If your suitcase is right next to you, stand there and look helpless until someone picks it up and carries it for you. Tip well, but don't make a big deal out of it. In fact, don't make a big deal about anything. Nothing means anything to you, because nothing ever has and you can't imagine otherwise."*

She'd already fought the urge on arrival to help lift her suitcase from the trunk. She managed to stifle the instinct to help. Now she couldn't even see her luggage, and she pretended she couldn't care less. The little people would make sure it got where it needed to.

"Kevin here, in your ear," he said over her earpiece. "We've got video and audio, crystal clear. Give me a sign if you're receiving me."

Harmony glanced down for just a moment, focusing the camera in her glasses on her right hand as she flashed a quick thumbs up. Then she turned her vapid smile back to the desk clerk, who was in the middle of gushing a sales pitch for a product the clinic had already sold her.

"—yoga sessions every morning at sunrise, and at ten for the late sleepers. Our trainer is world-famous, she's been on the cover of *Fitness Today* over ten times, and you're just going to love her, I know it."

"I do enjoy being an early birdie," Harmony said lightly.

"Meals are served in our luxurious dining hall. Room service, of course, is complimentary, we just ask that you phone your order in an hour before serving time." The clerk dropped his voice, faux conspiratorial. "Chef Marcel is amazing. We poached him from The French Laundry just last month."

"Very good," Harmony replied. "I assume my assistant sent over my list of special requests."

He checked his screen and nodded sharply.

"Yes ma'am. In particular she relayed that you can't sleep without one very specific brand of feather-down pillow. I'm pleased to say that we sent an employee all the way to Manhattan to buy a brand-new set just this morning, and they'll be waiting in your bedroom."

She didn't say thank you. She just smiled, as if any other answer would be shocking.

***

While Harmony took a tour of her rented paradise, Jessie crept through the mud a quarter mile outside the perimeter. A hunting store on the way up had equipped her with forest-green and dirt-brown camo. The sturdy leather boots, built for tough hikes and tougher weather, she already owned. She prowled like a wolf through the underbrush, eyes sharp and ears perked, the heavy duffel slung over her shoulder stuffed with spare chunks of foam to keep her arsenal from rattling around.

"Okay," Kevin said in her ear, "Harmony's in. Looks like they bought it. If not, we'll know soon enough. How's the insertion going?"

"That's what she said," Jessie murmured. "And the answer is, slow and steady wins the race. I'm more concerned about not getting spotted than I am about speed. Once I get inside the security perimeter, I've got all kinds of options."

She froze and dropped low, kneeling in a bed of brittle, fallen leaves. One of the cameras was ahead, its mounting bracket screwed into the trunk of an old tree, its barrel slowly swiveling left to right and back again. She ducked behind a fallen log and pressed herself to the dirt, inhaling the rich scent of loam and wet grass, counting under her breath.

Only, what, a hundred and eighty degrees of coverage? Are they really that sloppy?

She chanced a peek in the other direction. That's when she spotted the second camera a little further back, positioned to catch the first camera's massive blind spot. And the third, a stone's throw to the east, set to do the same. The security net was patchwork, all right, but the people who built it knew what they were doing. Any casual trespasser would see one camera, laugh it off as woefully inadequate, and march right out in front of another one.

"Need to update your map," she breathed. "They're serious about security out here."

"Could be a good sign. Means they've got something worth protecting."

Jessie shrugged. "Eh. Not necessarily anything shady. Considering the clien- tèle, could just be an early warning system to keep paparazzi at bay. Candid pho- tos of the clinic's customers on TMZ would probably tank this place overnight. Normally I'd test their security with a little false alarm and see how they respond, but I can't risk making them nervous while Harmony's in there."

"Until I get eyes on the inside, I can't do anything about the cameras. Can you slip past them?"

"Have you *met* me? Hold on, I need to focus up. Going radio silent. I'll let you know once I'm on the other side."

Jessie made a policy, generally speaking, of staying outside her own head. That was where the monster lived. She had jokes for days, especially when the going got tough, because that was how she coped. Making light kept the Wolf at bay.

Now, as she crouched behind the fallen log and breathed in the primal air of the forest — the mud, the moss, the rot and the death — a gray-furred muzzle rubbed against her cheek.

Why are you acting like prey? the Wolf asked, curious.

"Because," Jessie said through gritted teeth, "if I run out there and start smashing cameras, they're gonna know I'm here. I'm not acting like prey, I'm hunting bigger game."

You left the morsel inside, alone.

"Her name is Harmony, not *morsel*."

Cold fur, invisible, brushed along Jessie's arm, her skin prickling.

I want to taste her.

Jessie peeked over the log, eyes narrowed to slits as she watched the slow arc of three cameras at once, gaze flicking between them to note their speed, the ground they covered, hunting for spots where they didn't overlap even if only for a second.

"Never going to happen," she murmured. "Not the way you like to do it."

What about the way you like to do it?

"What is your deal exactly? You used to just howl and grunt in my head. Now you're forming complete sentences."

We all grow up sooner or later.

"Feel free to stop."

The Wolf's laughter was the sound of ice cracking over a winter pond. Her spectral body danced around Jessie, a snow-flecked paw brushing her hair.

I'm not some outside force, some possessing spirit that can be contained or banished. I'm you. I'm that side of yourself you can't abide in the mirror. Your purest and truest form. The more you repress me, the stronger I become. You want me to be quiet for a little while? Then let me OUT.

Another patch of wet fur slid across Jessie's cheek. She batted it away, irritated, trying to focus.

Your mother won't hold back. You'll corner her. Won't give her any choice but to fight. And when she does, she'll come at you with everything she is and everything she has. If you don't call on me, you'll die. And your beloved, and your friends, and all that you care for, will die.

You know I'm right.

And Jessie didn't argue, because she had nothing to say, no counterpoint that wouldn't taste like a desperate and defensive lie before it even touched her lips.

"Shut the fuck up. I'm concentrating."

"Uh, Jessie?" Kevin said in her ear. "Who are you talking to?"

A barking hiss of canine laughter echoed in Jessie's other ear.

"Never mind," she muttered. "What?"

"What's the upward arc on those cameras look like?"

She peeked over the gritty, rotten bark of the fallen log, still working out the timing, ducking just before one camera swept her way. The air was thick with the musty odor of green moss and moldy, decaying leaves.

"Negligible. They're focused on catching anyone coming in by foot."

"Good. Hold up, I've got a little helper inbound for you."

A moment later, a faint, whining buzz lifted her gaze skyward. One of Kevin's drones had joined the party. This wasn't *the* drone, the military-grade beast they kept in the *Imperator*'s belly for heavy duty work. It was a consumer model he'd souped up with custom parts and a lot of love in his off hours. Small, fast, and nimble, it zipped above the trees like a mosquito.

"Good call," Jessie breathed. "Scout up ahead, call out if you see anything moving."

She had the timing, the trajectories, the angles locked in. She got down in a runner's starting crouch, took a deep breath...and ran, lurching into a loping sprint, kicking up a flurry of dead leaves and dirt as she scrambled just a heartbeat ahead of the sweeping cameras.

Chapter Twenty-Six

H armony hated parties.

She never knew what to do with her hands, with her face, with her words. People like Jessie could walk up to a complete stranger and start a conversation, treating them like a long-lost friend, slipping into easy syncopation. It was a skill Harmony had never understood, much less been able to master.

"Needs must when the devil drives," April said in her ear. "Give me a slow sweep of the room. I'll run every face I can grab through image recognition, just to get the lay of the land."

The Clinic was hosting a pre-dinner cocktail mixer beneath the rustic timbers of the main lodge, an expanse of artfully rough-hewn floor slats draped with elegant swirling sapphire carpets. A black bear head, frozen in death, roared from its mount above the mantel of a flagstone fireplace. Below in the wide hearth, flames crackled and drove back the cold of the forest dark beyond the arched windows. Light chamber music played, too soft to make out a melody, and a mixologist served up artisanal cocktails and wine at an open bar.

Some of the patients had dressed for the occasion, but most wore their complimentary white robes, rising phoenix silhouettes emblazoned on their hip pockets. Casual surgery chic was the dress code. After all, there were no fans or reporters here to spoil the vibe, just a gathering of society's elite, here to grab hold of their fading youth with both hands and prove that their money could defy even time itself.

Drinks in hand, laughing low and easy, a foursome of patients had clustered near the shifting orange glow of the hearth. Harmony took a delicate sip from her glass of Chardonnay — tarter than she expected, with notes of fresh, juicy pear — as she adjusted her vector and casually made her way over. She stayed on the periphery, pretending to admire an Audubon print on the lodge wall while she eavesdropped.

"*Mr. Big* will apparently not be joining us for cocktails," one man said, putting more than a bit of derision into the nickname.

The woman beside him raised a delicate eyebrow. "Don't tell me that's what he calls himself."

"That's what the staff calls him. Apparently they're under orders not to speak his name. Or to look directly at him."

"Like J. Lo," another patient said. "Wait. Do we know it's a man? It could be J. Lo."

"Please, as if she could afford it these days. Might be the president," the woman said.

Her companion gently rolled his eyes. "Except he's addressing the G7 in Prague this week, so probably not."

"I didn't say it had to be the *American* president," she fired back.

"Anyway," the first man said, "he's ensconced in there and taking all of his meals in his suite. Can't bear to mingle with us hoi polloi. Weird thing is nobody actually saw him arrive. I was here when a helicopter came in with all of his stuff, enough trunks and bags for a small army, but unless he was slumming it and cosplaying as the hired help, no Mr. Big to be seen."

"Did you spot his bodyguard?" the woman said. "Woof. No missing that one in a crowd."

"What's he look like?" her companion asked.

"She. For all the world she looks like a bodybuilder or one of those professional wrestler types. Tall as a tree and almost as wide. Two of the orderlies were struggling with a trunk, and she just scooped the thing up and carried it on her shoulder like it was made of balsa wood." She cupped her hand to one side of her mouth and lowered her voice theatrically. "A bit...dark-complexioned for my liking, but I suppose you can't be too picky about the hired help."

Harmony was too close to breathe a word, but she didn't have to. April's voice sounded over her earpiece.

"All channels: I have Harmony routed to my terminal alone so you don't get inundated with party chatter, but she just picked up a potential problem. Althea is onsite posing as a client's bodyguard. Said client is being kept in isolation, no name or further details available yet. Will update when we have more."

"Whoever 'Mr. Big' is," the woman's companion said, "he has to be here for the Treatment, right?"

There was something in his words, a kind of quiet awe, that made Harmony put a capital T on the word. *The* Treatment. The one and only, like the Holy Grail.

"Jealous?" the first man asked.

"Hell, of course I am. Who wouldn't be? Did you see Sam when he got back from his clinic visit last month? He got the Treatment, and I swear he looks twenty years younger. He's practically a different person."

"Well, I'm sure you'll be perfectly happy with your rhinoplasty instead. Doctor Stepford does amazing plastic surgery work. My wife's facelift—"

"Wait," he interrupted, staring. "Why do you think I'm here for a rhinoplasty?"

"Well, I mean." The first man shrugged, then vaguely gestured at his own face. "I just assumed."

"Why would you *assume* that?"

Time to go. Harmony drifted on through the party, sipping her wine, keeping her ears perked. Once she was out of earshot, she chanced a quick message to April.

"Does Kevin have access to their client database yet? I want to know who this 'Mr. Big' is."

"As do I, but no. He's still assisting Jessie with the infiltration. She's run into a bit of unexpected trouble."

Harmony's gut clenched. "Trouble?"

"Nothing she can't handle."

***

"Two-man foot patrol, about two hundred yards ahead, coming your way."

Jessie looked left, right, spotting more cameras in the trees. The sun had gone down now, but her eyes shone bright in the dark, seeing by moonlight. The forest was a rich tapestry of swirling shadows and scents, a wild banquet calling to her. The cameras were foreign, hard plastic, and she wanted to smash them, ruin them. This was a home for beasts, not machines. The Wolf had curled in around the edges of her thoughts, a silky winter mist wreathing her brain.

Now she smelled prey.

The cameras left a corridor between the trees, a narrow band where she could slip by without being caught on video, but the hunters ahead would ruin everything. She dove to the dirt by the fat base of a lightning-charred oak and dug with her hands, scratching a hole in the soil and fallen leaves. Her duffel bag packed with guns went into the divot. She pulled debris over it with both arms, concealing it from sight.

She was lighter now. Faster.

"Jessie," Kevin said, "not to alarm you, but these guys aren't just orderlies. They're packing serious firepower. I'm spotting scoped hunting rifles plus sidearms. I had to pull the drone back, can't risk them hearing the rotors, but I figure you've got about ten seconds before they're on top of you."

She smelled the wind, inhaling distant sweat, skin-musk, a night breeze gusting the flavor of these men toward her. No fear, no anxiety; they weren't looking for her. *Ordinary security sweep*, she thought. *Not expecting trouble.* If she didn't give them any, they'd pass right on by. Couldn't go left, couldn't go right, and falling back would put her firmly in the net of cameras she'd already slipped through once.

Up.

As distant footsteps crunched through brittle leaves, Jessie grabbed hold of the fat oak and scurried upward, nails digging in, teeth bared so she could suck the crisp night air and taste every drop like the dregs of a fine wine. She scampered up to a stout branch and perched like a vulture as a fat flashlight beam washed across the ground where she'd just been standing.

She saw them now. Two men, late twenties, wearing the white uniforms of the clinic staff but with long rifles slung over their shoulders and sidearms on their hips in quick release holsters. She smelled gun oil, the sign of well-maintained weapons, and their hiking boots were sturdy and broken in. They didn't make small talk, and they moved with the gait of professionals.

A radio crackled. One answered, holding it to his ear. They paused just under her perch and Jessie froze, statue-still, ten feet above their heads.

"Yeah, unit three here. There's nobody in sight. I think you just spotted a coyote or something. Over."

He let go of the send button and leaned closer to his buddy.

"*Again*," he added. "Happens five times a week with this idiot, I swear."

The radio squawked with a burst of static and a barely audible voice. "Thanks for checking it out, Three. Return to your regular patrol route. Over."

The men doubled back, and Jessie watched until they receded far into the gloom. Then she plunged straight down, landing in a bed of dead leaves in a crouch, her turquoise eyes blazing against the dark.

Nobody ever looks up, the Wolf snickered in her brain.

***

Harmony drifted through the cocktail party, affecting a practiced air of wealthy boredom, trying to blend in. She moved from knot to knot of conversation, picking up a few probably lucrative insider stock tips and gossip about which A-list celebrity was sleeping with which politician's wife, but nothing actionable. Nothing they needed. At least Althea hadn't shown her face, presumably ensconced in the so-called Royal Suite with "Mr. Big."

This disguise was solid enough for casual encounters, but she knew Althea would see through it in a heartbeat. She hated Harmony too much to be fooled.

Harmony passed by a hanging mirror and paused. She normally didn't pay much attention to her own reflection, but all the swirling talk about facelifts and nose jobs and a hundred other nips and tucks had slanted her thoughts. She took a moment to appraise. The bags under her eyes were a little heavier than they used to be, her hair a little less glossy, a few more split ends.

She was getting older. Not slower, not yet. But that day would come, inevitable as the tide. How many more missions did she have in her?

Enough, she decided. *Enough to get the job done.*

"Now that's a Before-picture if I've ever seen one," an older man said, sliding up to her with a martini glass cradled in his perfectly manicured grip. He was a silver fox with the kind of pearly smile that wasn't found in nature, and his accent carried a hint of Texas twang.

"Excuse me?" she said.

His smile grew a notch. "Oh, it's not an insult! Just a little running joke among the clinic's regulars. We're all Before-pictures or After-pictures. You know, like in the old weight loss commercials? I'm a Before-picture myself this time around. My surgery's tomorrow morning."

He offered his hand. He had a warm, soft grip, and smelled like lavender soap.

"Carlton Grassley the Third. A pleasure."

"Verity Hale," she replied. "Charmed."

"Of the Connecticut Hales?"

"Georgia," she said, without missing a beat, "but my cousins do get around, as cousins do."

He chuckled and raised his glass. "I'll drink to that. Family trees grow wide branches and strange roots."

"Harmony," April said in her ear, "I've got his bio. Old money, third-generation billionaire. Heavily invested in oil, though he also owns a string of cattle ranches and a telecom company."

"I'm a little nervous," she pretended to confess. "It's my first time."

As expected, she gave him the chance to play the expert and he pounced on it with gusto.

"Oh, stick with me, I'll tell you everything you need to know." He cast a subtle nod at the group by the fireplace. "For starters, keep clear of those vipers unless you want your dirty laundry aired out in the gossip rags. The doctor's regulars are an...elite clientèle, let's just say, and we pride ourselves on discretion."

"What happens at the Phoenix Clinic stays at the Phoenix Clinic?" she asked.

"Exactly. You get it. Folks like that will never understand. It's a failure of good breeding if you ask me. The money isn't the point. They've got the cash, but they can't keep their mouths shut, and that kind of vulgarity means they'll never get offered the Treatment."

She had to tread carefully, walking the line between pretending to know all — and not getting any information out of her new friend — or knowing too little and twigging his suspicions.

"You know, a good friend of mine referred me to the Clinic. You'd know her from the movies, but in the interests of discretion—"

She tapped the side of her nose. He grinned and nodded.

"She's scheduled for the Treatment next month," Harmony continued, "but that's all she'll tell me. Excited enough that she's practically vibrating, but she won't tell me a thing about it."

"Oh, believe me, I can relate. Mine's tomorrow. If I wasn't quite well-buzzed on complimentary cocktails, I'd be intolerable right now."

"So what's with the secrecy?" she asked, leaning in close and inviting him to show off.

"Well, I could tell you, but you'd have to sell your soul first." He nudged her with his elbow, his grin growing wider. "By which I mean it's the kind of buy-in price that could reduce a Saudi oil sheikh to pumping gas to pay his rent. But so very worth it, from the success stories I've seen. At any rate, they don't offer it to first-time clients. Three procedures seems to be the sweet spot. That's when they take you aside and make the offer."

"For that much money, you could at least give a girl a hint."

He fixed her with his pale blue eyes and took a long sip from his martini glass.

"It's the Fountain of Youth. Charles Stepford found the goddamn Fountain of Youth. Metaphorically speaking, of course." He paused, impish, and changed the subject. "So, can I guess?"

"Guess?"

He nodded at her face. "The work you're getting done."

She smiled, but not for any reason this man could ever guess. The idea of plastic surgery was strange to her. Her mind wasn't wired for that kind of vanity: her body was just a vehicle of muscle and bone built to carry her mind from place to place, mission to mission. Besides, the best surgeon alive couldn't do much with the pattern of scar tissue that flecked her body beneath her clothes, trophies of battles won and deaths barely escaped. There were faded burns, healed cuts, old stab wounds that came within inches of a kill shot.

Each scar a lesson learned. She wouldn't get rid of them if she could.

"A lady never tells," she replied, raising her glass.

Chapter Twenty-Seven

"Bringing you back onto the general channel," April said, patching Harmony back into the *Imperator*'s network.

She had finished her wine and made a graceful departure, returning to her private suite in the east end of the lodge. It was a pretty prison, a rustic room with a feather mattress, bespoke fittings, and windows that didn't open. They offered a panoramic view of the moonlit woods, but they'd been sealed shut and fitted with tiny disc sensors, discreet white wires running into holes in the dark-stained wood. Any attempt to force them open, from inside or outside, would trigger an alarm.

Harmony had spotted more orderlies than she expected to see in the halls. Their numbers grew at nightfall, as if the clinic had a vested interest in locking things down after dark, and a primly attired nurse reminded her in passing that all guests were asked to be in their rooms by eleven p.m. For their beauty rest, of course.

Working in silence, Harmony quickly swept the room for bugs. A quick routine of hunting in the light fixtures, feeling under drawers, using her phone to strobe the fire alarms and outlets with reflective light. She had searched more thoroughly arrival, but double-checking after each return to the room was standard tradecraft. Once she was satisfied, she broke the silence.

"Jessie," she said. "What's your status?"

"I'm in a bush."

"Literally?"

"No, it's a metaphor for the angst of my soul. Yes, literally. A literal bush. Don't ask. How was the party?"

"Wrinkle in the plan. I assume Kevin and April already briefed you?"

"Yeah, Althea's on site. But we already checked: Muffy St. John is confirmed in San Francisco as of an hour ago, and so are Mercury Blaise and her boy Santiago. So whoever this 'Mr. Big' is, he's not on our radar."

"He has to be though," Harmony said. "There's no chance Althea went from trying to kill us on the *Blue Star* to a bodyguard job at a clinic that just happens to be run by the very same doctor who got her onto that boat in the first place. That doesn't just strain credulity, it smashes it with a jackhammer."

"Agreed, but all we can work with is the intel we've got."

"On that note," Kevin said, cutting in, "I could use some help on your end. I'm trying to crack the Clinic's encryption and get access to the client database. Problem is, doing it from outside is like carving though a prison wall with a spoon. Weirdly, it did give me another point of connection between the Phoenix Clinic and ProcGen."

"What did you find?" Harmony asked, perking up.

"Code signatures. Remember how I was diving into the security setup at ProcGen and said it looked like Mercury had a partner? Like, not Santiago. A partner who can do things *other* than stab and shoot people."

"Sure."

"I'm seeing the exact same style of tandem coding here."

"Meaning...Mercury Blaise wrote the code protecting the Clinic too?"

"Uh huh," he said. "And no, there's no record of her ever being employed there."

It stood to reason. ProcGen and Phoenix were both part of a whole, arms of a giant octopus which looked disconnected from above the waterline. If you dove deep, though, down to the source, Praeda Electronics lurked at the core of it all. The body of the beast.

"Mercury draws her legal, taxable paycheck from ProcGen," Harmony mused aloud, "but it's just like the classic mafia limo driver scam. The paper trail is there to keep the IRS off her back, and her actual job is whatever and wherever her real bosses say it is. Are we any closer to figuring out who her silent partner is?"

"Working on it, but again, the more I can see, the more data I have to work with. Any chance you can find some nice, vulnerable PC and Icepick it for me?"

"Not tonight," she said. "They lay the security on thick after nightfall. If I'm going to risk being caught out of my room after curfew, I need to set up a good excuse first. I'd arguably have an easier shot in the morning. Free time between sunrise yoga and breakfast means I have the run of the place, at least in designated areas."

"Double that for the outside," Jessie said. "They're not screwing around, and I'm ready to bet the security isn't just to keep out roaming paparazzi."

"Why's that?"

"Because they're toting Benelli Lupo rifles mounted with Bushnell hunting scopes. The kind that'll let you peg a trophy buck from the far side of the planet. You don't carry those to scare someone off. You carry them to nail a target dead before they even know you're there."

"Could be for self-defense," Kevin offered. "That one guy mentioned coyotes."

"That's what sidearms are for, which they're also carrying. Just fire a shot and make it loud, and most forest critters will run for the hills. They don't want to mess with humans in the first place unless they're starving or sick. So do y'all think of this 'Treatment' deal?"

"I strongly doubt a plastic surgeon, even a well-regarded one, singlehandedly invented the secret to eternal youth," April replied. "Most likely it's some pseudoscience nonsense catering to those with far too much money and far too much credulity. The fact that he only offers it to certain repeat clients suggests he's carefully vetting them first. That said, it does appear that he's bringing in a great deal of liquid capital, and it could be funding whatever Praeda Electronics is really up to. We should find out for certain."

Harmony kept thinking about the oilman's joke: *I could tell you, but you'd have to sell your soul first.*

"If it was that good," Harmony agreed, "why not tell the whole world? He could still charge a king's ransom and probably triple his income overnight. Also, it sounds like Stepford goes out of his way to push the idea that candidates for the Treatment are part of an elite inner circle. The few and privileged."

"In other words," Jessie said, "he manipulates their pride."

"It has the ring of a classic investment scam, the kind of grift where the mark ends up too ashamed to reveal they've been fooled, so the con keeps on spreading to new victims. Something else is nagging at me. Carlton Grassley the Third."

"You weren't swayed by his Texas charm?" April asked, deadpan.

"He's getting the Treatment in the morning, he said, and I watched him chain-drinking martinis to steady his nerves. Now what's wrong with that picture?"

"Only surgery I've ever had was to get my tonsils out," Kevin said, "but...they don't normally let you drink booze the night before, right?"

"Not if you don't want a serious chance of dying under anesthesia," April replied. "Good catch. I'm afraid I don't have any more insights at the moment, but put a pin in that."

Harmony heard the rustle of brittle leaves. Jessie shifting her position in the dark.

"All right," Jessie said, "we're not getting anything else done until first light, so I want everybody to get some shuteye. Tomorrow's going to be a busy day and y'all need to be in top fighting trim. We rally at dawn."

"Are you going to be okay out there?" Harmony asked.

Jessie paused for a moment.

"April, Kevin, do me a favor and jump off the comms for a sec? Need a word with my partner."

Faint static hisses signaled their departure.

"Stop," Jessie said, "feeling guilty."

"I didn't say—"

"I know you hon, and you're sitting in that fancy-ass room with your big four-poster bed and the pillows they raced to Manhattan to buy for you — cute pattern, by the way, they look like the mints you get with the check at an Italian restaurant — and instead of enjoying it, you're fixating on poor Jessie out in the cold."

"I didn't—" Harmony paused. "How do you know about the pattern on the pillows?"

"Cuz I'm watching you. Duh."

Harmony turned to the windows. All she could see was trees, rustling bushes, a few stray leaves caught in the wind tumbling across the mud and dirt.

"*Hi there*," Jessie whispered.

"Well, that's unnerving."

"Could be worse, I could have asked if you like scary movies."

Harmony gave a little wave. "I can't see you. At all."

"If you could, I'd suck at my job. I'm making this point to illustrate that you don't need to be worried about me, okay? I spent most of my childhood moving from campsite to campsite, living rough, and wolf-blood means I don't get cold like a normal person. I'm built for this shit. I'm not a huge *fan* of it — I mean, I'll take a suite at the Ritz and room service any day of the week over camping out — but I'll sleep as long as you sleep. So do me a favor: get undressed and get in that nice big comfy bed. We've got an early start ahead of us and a whole lot of ass to kick."

Harmony reached out her palm, almost touching the surface of the window glass. Then she let it slowly fall to her side.

"Goodnight, Jessie."

"Night, babe."

***

I'll sleep as long as you sleep, Jessie thought. *Just not yet.*

She watched Harmony through the long lozenge of glass, a rectangle of light in the darkness like the proscenium of a theater, a silent play just for her. A crisp night wind ruffled the grass and leaves, drawing icy fingers along Jessie's spine, but she barely noticed. In her mind, she had a thick coat of rugged gray fur. Its presence kept the cold at bay.

She supposed there was probably a natural reason for her resilience. Maybe the contaminated blood in her veins ran a little hotter than a normal human's or her immune system was boosted to hell and back. Maybe it was just magic. When she was alone in her head she felt her fur pelt and her claws, and that was all she needed to know.

To thine own self be true, she thought, and in that moment she wasn't entirely sure if it was her thought or the Wolf's.

I keep telling you—

"I know."

Do you, though?

Jessie just watched until Harmony climbed into bed, reached over, and clicked off the light. The stage went dark. She kept watching a while longer. She could see the slow rise and fall of Harmony's chest under the covers, the rhythm of her breath slowing, slowing, until it reached a familiar, deep cadence. Finally she was asleep.

Now Jessie could sleep too. Only for a few hours, just long enough to refuel. First light wasn't far away, and there was work to be done.

Chapter Twenty-Eight

J essie rose with the dawn, shaking off the thin blanket of dead leaves she'd used as camouflage, flicking a fat centipede off her shoulder as she knelt in the dirt. She dragged idle fingers through her hair, tugging out weeds and a stray twig, as her senses swam back and her eyes adjusted to the thin golden light of morning that filtered down through the thick canopy of the forest.

She winced as one of her back muscles tugged hard, jolting a lance of pain up her spine. She gritted her teeth until it passed. It was absurd that bodies had to get old. Life was bullshit enough as it was; age just added insult to injury.

Up close in the light, the Phoenix Clinic looked like a sprawling wilderness lodge of carefully sculpted logs and bulletproof glass, some rich asshole's retreat from the world. Jessie's trained eyes saw it more as a fortress. A sophisticated network of cameras, armed guards, moving pieces all working to keep the outside out and the inside in. Every network had a flaw, and it was her job to find it.

You could always count on human frailty. The night before, scouting as close as she dared under cover of darkness, Jessie had found a patio toward the back of the clinic. The lingering smell of cheap cigarettes twigged her to an opportunity, and a scattering of discarded butts flicked away along the margin where concrete met grass, the line between civilization and the forest wild, told her what she needed to know. That and the brick. It was a rough chunk of stone, a construction leftover that had no purpose sitting on the patio's edge.

Jessie had a pretty good idea what it was for. So she scurried close in the thin light, found a hiding spot in the bushes, and waited.

The back door swung open on well-oiled hinges. A lone nurse came out, her white uniform rumpled, the cap on her head cocked to one side over a mop of unruly hair. She clutched a pack of cigarettes in one hand and crouched down to grab the brick with the other, sliding it halfway across the threshold to keep the security door from locking behind her as she enjoyed her covert smoke break.

It would be so easy to take her right here and now. Rush up, hook an arm around her pretty throat, snap her neck, and hide the body in the underbrush. They'd be long gone before it started to smell.

Do it.

No. The Phoenix Clinic was sketchy as hell, but the worst they had them on was ripping off billionaires with the promise of a mythical fountain of youth — arguably not a crime, in Jessie's opinion — and even that was just a hunch. They had to treat the staff as innocent civilians until the facts showed otherwise.

Never used to stop you.

"I was a teenager, and the only role models in my life were a pair of occult serial killers," she muttered. "Cut me some goddamn slack."

She watched the nurse pace a little. All she needed was a turned back, just for a few seconds, long enough to slip by. She saw a window and rose up in a crouch, ready to move, when the nurse suddenly turned back around and spoiled the moment.

It'd be so much easier to do it the fun way.

"Yeah, well, like Harmony says, the easier way usually isn't the right way."

The Wolf growled in her ear.

"And thank you," Jessie murmured, "for the idea."

For once the Wolf seemed confused, and she liked that. She took out her camera, zoomed in and snapped a candid shot, then tapped the tiny bead of her earpiece twice.

"Kev? Tell me you're awake and at the wheel."

"Here, oh captain my captain. Not yet properly caffeinated—"

"I slept in a bush. Before you complain about literally anything, bear in mind that I slept in a bush." She tapped her phone. "I'm sending you a pic and I need action *fast*. Like within the next two minutes fast or I'm gonna be sitting out here until her next smoke break. Subject is a nurse. Nametag reads 'J. Calder.' I need you to get her personal cell phone number."

"Uh," he said.

"Now, please? See? Sometimes I say please."

"Now I know it's urgent," Kevin grumbled. "Hold on, pulling up image recognition. If I can get a hit, this might be doable."

"I'll do you one better," April said, cutting in on the line. "The clinic's official website has a 'Meet the Staff' gallery. Jennifer Calder has a short biography including her hometown and the school where she studied medicine. Should narrow things down nicely. I'm sending the link to your terminal."

"Hold on, hold on, checking and...*yes*. LexisNexis comes in clutch once again. I've got a cell phone number attached to her car registration, hopefully current. You want it, boss?"

"No," Jessie said, "I want you to call her, fast. Keep her on the line for a couple of minutes and grab her attention. I don't care what you tell her, be a bill collector or something, just don't let her hang up."

She disconnected the call, crouching in wait. A few seconds later, the nurse paused and dug into her hip pocket, pulling out a phone. She shot a nervous look at the propped-open door and moved away from it, just as Jessie hoped.

You're not supposed to be smoking out there. Don't even have a key for that door, hence the brick. That's it, move just a little further away so nobody hears you on the phone...

Once the nurse's back was turned, Jessie made her move. Skimming over the grass, every footstep a rustling whisper, her adrenaline building as she aimed straight for the door and the great unknown beyond. She held her breath for the last five steps, slipping onto the concrete pad, behind the nurse's back, and into the building. The door slowly glided shut, gently tapping the brick.

No time to catch her breath. She saw in flashes, tactical mode. The entrance met at the intersection of two halls, one straight ahead, one going left. Camera ahead, swiveling — she darted past the corner to get the rest of her bearings. Corkboard on one wall, OSHA forms and time off notices making it clear this was an employees-only stretch of the lodge. She had a crude map in her head, built from the outside looking in and what she'd gleaned from the windows by night.

"Harmony," she breathed, "need your location."

"Just went to morning yoga to keep up appearances. No new intel. I have an open hour between now and breakfast."

"Meet me in your room. I'm coming toward you now."

"Wait," Harmony said in her ear. "Inside? I thought you were—"

A flicker of movement sent Jessie to one knee, dropping low behind a filing cabinet. She didn't answer right away, breathing a few words as soon as the coast was clear.

"We'll talk when I get there."

Five minutes later she was knocking on Harmony's door, shooting anxious looks up and down the hall. Harmony opened it before she finished her second knock, pulling her into the room and locking the door behind her.

"I thought you were leaving this one to me," Harmony said.

"Was, when the job was basic intel gathering. Kevin needs us to Icepick the clinic's systems, and we aren't going to find out what this 'Treatment' business is without going out of bounds. That's a two-agent job. We can watch each other's backs and get it done twice as fast."

"Can't argue with that, but..." Harmony paused, looking her up and down. "Where are the guns?"

"Buried out back in a very shallow ditch. If we need them, I can get 'em fast. Not exactly concealable though."

"And I hesitate to mention this..."

Jessie raised an arm and sniffed one of her armpits, wincing. "Yeah, no, I get it. I slept in a bush. I'm using your shower."

She steamed past, making a beeline for the bathroom, then stopped on the threshold.

"I'm going to need to borrow one of your outfits."

"Okay."

"And I'm using your deodorant."

"Understood," Harmony said.

Jessie stepped into the bathroom. Then back out again, leaning around the doorway.

"And your toothbrush."

"You're lucky we're friends."

"I *am*," Jessie said. Then she vanished, the muffled hiss of the shower drifting through the door.

***

After scrubbing the dirt from her hands and slipping into a sapphire-blue sheath dress — Harmony was thankful their sizes were close — Jessie was renewed and ready for action.

"I'm thinking we get eyes on Charles Stepford's office, first," she said. Harmony had laid out a map of the lodge, a patient brochure that hid all the good stuff, and they studied it at the edge of her mattress.

"Risky," Harmony said. "He knows me, and while you've never talked to him directly, he did help Althea get onto the *Blue Star*. Not ready to say he knows what her real job is or what her business on that boat was, considering she's apparently hanging out and posing as Mr. Big's bodyguard this week, but he's clearly mixed up in some things he shouldn't be mixed up in."

"He's at least hip deep in Muffy's world of techno-sleaze, maybe deeper. I want to know what he knows. Either he's a co-conspirator or a harmless dupe, and while most of the evidence suggests he's being played, I'd rather not get blindsided. Besides, his office might give us a crack at his client list, not to mention helping us figure out what the Treatment really is and if that's something we need to be worried about. Question: if you skip breakfast, will anyone notice?"

"They'll notice," Harmony said, "but it won't be a problem. I figured I might need more recon time, so at yoga I made a lot of noise about having an upset stomach. Suggested I might catch a nap before lunch, that kind of thing."

Jessie's eyes flashed as she smiled her approval. "Good girl."

While the north end of the lodge was off limits to guests, devoted to admin space and a single lavish surgical suite, Charles liked to rub shoulders with his treasured clients. His office was marked on the brochure: second floor, at the crest of a balcony that ringed the main lobby.

Harmony and Jessie faced their first test on their initial approach. They were headed up a long hallway, log walls lined with Audubon prints of birds in flight, and a nurse approached them from the opposite direction. How hands on was the care here, really? Did the staff memorize the faces of every single one of their guests, or would they let a stranger — one who was well dressed and fit the part of a client in every way — slide on by? They wouldn't know until they tested it, and this was the moment of truth.

Harmony leaned into her pecan heiress persona, doing her best to project a carefree air as she strolled just ahead of Jessie. "...so I said, hon, you can slap a thousand-dollar price tag on this bottle, but that's like calling an old nag a thoroughbred and expecting it to win the Triple Crown."

Jessie fell into step, effortlessly following her lead. "Wineries in Texas are played out anyway. I mean, does he know what the steers are doing to the soil?"

The nurse's gaze flicked over both of their faces in passing. Then she inclined her head, less a friendly nod than an obsequious bow to visiting royalty, and walked by without saying a word.

Once they were out of earshot, Harmony murmured, "That went smoothly."

"The covers help," Jessie said. "The Clinic's clients are rich as hell, the kind of folks who go 'Do you know who I *am*?' at the drop of a hat. We've infiltrated a roving herd of Karens. Which means the staff would feel free to stop and question us if we were dressed like painters or something, but as long as we more or less pass the sniff test, they gotta ask themselves if saying one word to us is worth risking their jobs. Way easier to make us somebody else's problem."

"We won't get that same grace from the doctor," Harmony said as they climbed the rustic stairs to the second-floor balcony. A long forest-green runner lined the freshly vacuumed steps. "Even if he's a dupe and both Muffy and Althea are using him, he knows me as a tech reporter back in San Francisco. My cover won't hold."

"That's why we'll make sure he's not home before we go poking around. Hang out here and stare at your phone for a minute. Look bored."

Jessie rounded the corner alone, stood at the office door, and knocked firmly. No response. Just to be safe, she tried again, but a young orderly pushing a supply cart broke his stride and waved to catch her eye.

"Are you looking for Doctor Stepford, ma'am? I'm so sorry, he's away from the clinic on meetings today, but he'll be back first thing in the morning. In the meantime, the front desk will be happy to help with anything you need."

She waited until the orderly moved on, around a corner and out of sight. Harmony glanced up from her phone, eyes sharp, moving to join Jessie at the door.

"That isn't right," she said.

"I mean, he was just on the West Coast to attend a charity party," Jessie said. "He's a weird rich CEO. They like to move around a lot."

"No," Harmony said. "I mean Carlton Grassley the Third is getting the Treatment this morning, at least according to what he told me. The miracle cure and the fountain of youth."

"Probably a glorified and overpriced facelift until I see proof to the contrary, but sure," Jessie said.

Harmony spread her hands.

"So if Stepford isn't here," she said, "who's performing the operation?"

Chapter Twenty-Nine

"Watch my back," Jessie said. Harmony covered her, watching the balcony in both directions. She kept a wary eye on the open gallery below where only a few clients, in their standard-issue bathrobes, lounged and drank tea by the wide stone hearth.

Half a minute later, the sturdy oaken door let out a muffled click and opened at a touch. Jessie pushed it just a crack, staying out of sight, and called out, "Doctor? Housekeeping."

Silence. Still, always good to check. She quickly slipped inside, and Harmony followed, shutting and locking the door in their wake.

Like the rest of the lodge, Charles Stepford's private office was calculatedly rustic, built for comfort, appointed with artfully rough-hewn bookshelves. A window that looked out over the forest's edge was framed in branches carved to look like driftwood. Treatises on surgery and medicine stocked his shelves; medical school diplomas and vintage anatomical studies lined the opposite wall.

Harmony immediately noticed what wasn't there. His desk had a blotter, a paper calendar with tearaway pages, a few stray notepads bearing the Clinic's phoenix-flame logo...but no computer.

"The whole setup here is computerized," Harmony said, "like most businesses these days. It's unusual not to be. I was checked in via a computer terminal, that's clearly where they're keeping client records...so where's his?"

Jessie was at the bookshelves, tugging out random hardcovers, running her fingers along the pages to check for hidden caches or false fronts.

"Maybe he uses a laptop?" she suggested. "If he's traveling today, he would have taken it with him."

"Maybe, but..."

Harmony crouched down behind the desk, checking the space underneath. Nothing. Not even a dust bunny. She stood and checked the walls, hunting for outlets just above the deep-stained molding.

She spotted one outlet, and only one, on the right-hand wall. It was nowhere near the desk, tucked in the far corner and half-hidden behind a pedestal that bore a decorative flower-filled vase. She pantomimed plugging something in, then unplugging it again.

"I have to ask," Jessie said, giving her a curious look from across the office.

"Work habits," Harmony said. She touched the arm of Stepford's high-backed leather chair, swiveling it from side to side, drawing a line along the floorboards with her gaze.

"Translation?"

"Lots of people who rely on a business laptop have a dock or a charging station in their offices, for convenience. Maybe even a standalone monitor with a bigger screen. Easier on the eyes if you're going to be spending the day at your desk. He doesn't."

"Okay, and?"

"Not even a surge protector. And look, the only open plug is over there. At that angle he'd have to drape the cord over one leg of his office chair and risk yanking it every time he got up or sat down."

"That'd drive me up the wall *real* quick," Jessie said.

Harmony went back to the outlet, measuring distance with her spread fingertips.

"With the base of the pedestal this close to the outlet, there's no way a standard laptop brick would even fit. He'd have to very carefully pull the pedestal back — balancing a highly breakable porcelain vase on top — to get it in there. And then, when he was finished, move it back again."

She stood back up, brushing her legs off, and frowned.

"He *could* be going to all that trouble and annoyance, but how many people would? It's his clinic, and money isn't an issue: he could call in an electrician just before going on a business trip and come back to a shiny new plug wherever he wanted it mounted." She tugged on his top desk drawer. It rattled against her grip. "Can you get these open?"

Jessie tugged out her picks and slipped past Harmony. "You're still thinking about Grassley and his mystery surgeon?"

She was thinking about Mercury Blaise. The industrial thief had landed a cushy C-suite job over at ProcGen, but they knew for a fact — beyond putting some work in on their network security, and that was with help — that the job was just a cover for her real work on the shady side of the street. ProcGen was an arm of the Praeda Electronics octopus, and so was the Phoenix Clinic. She couldn't miss the parallels.

There's a key difference, she thought, glancing at the diplomas on the wall. *Charles Stepford is a legitimately acclaimed plastic surgeon. His name is on the place, and it's his name that brings in the wealthy patients.*

But he's the only surgeon listed on the staff roster. So if he's not performing the Treatment, who is? And what does Charles really do to earn his paycheck besides showing his face at charity events and chatting up potential clients?

One by one Jessie popped the cheap locks, pulling back drawers to reveal...nothing. Empty space and dust. A lonely fountain pen rattled around in a canyon of bare wood.

"I've got a desk back at Vigilant HQ," Jessie said, muttering around a pick clenched in the corner of her mouth like a toothpick while she worked on the last couple of drawers. "I use it, like, once every never. Mostly when I have to approve requisitions and expense reports."

Kevin's voice crackled over their earbuds. "Mostly you make me do that, I thought."

"Yeah, well, you're my bitch, so my paperwork is part of your job." She pulled back another drawer, gazing down at more nothing. "Point being I use that thing maybe two hours a week, but it still looks *used*. I've got takeout menus in there, half a dozen pens, some old store receipts...stuff adds up. It just does. That's where I keep my stash of snacks."

"You have a snack stash?" Kevin said.

"Don't touch my snacks. Anyway, this feels staged. Like a real estate agent making a house look lived in, but not too lived in, before they walk you through and try to close the sale."

Only one drawer, the top left, yielded a prize: a spiral-bound day planner with a buttery leather protective cover and a magnetic clasp. Harmony thought back to her meeting with Charles Stepford on the casino boat, his weirdly cold handshake akin to Muffy's. Mostly she was trying to remember if he was right- or left-handed. She recalled him pushing a pair of chips across the green felt, placing a bet.

Left-handed. This would be the most natural drawer for him to reach for while he sat here.

She opened the planner and began leafing through it, Jessie reading over her shoulder. Harmony adjusted her glasses, making sure she was catching each page in her lenses — and the concealed pinhole camera in the frame — pausing a moment before flipping to the next.

"Getting this on the video feed?" she asked.

"Every page," April said, her voice crisp. "I'm taking screen captures. What do you want us to do with this?"

"Nothing yet. But keep it handy in case we need to backtrace his movements."

There were parties, galas, public speaking events listed on his agenda. A chat with NPR, a newspaper interview here and there, and more charity benefits than Harmony knew existed. There were golf games with tee times listed three times a week, scattered amid meetings at country clubs and gentlemen's cigar rooms.

"You see what's missing," Jessie said.

She did. Surgery. If Charles Stepford did any actual work for the Phoenix Clinic, it wasn't listed here, not that he seemed to have any time for it in his social schedule.

"Okay, so Stepford's a frontman," Jessie said. "He generates hype, brings in the big wallets, and...once again, frustratingly as all hell, we're back to the problem with ProcGen. There's nothing illegal about that. ProcGen's marketing a shitty AI that doesn't work, but they've got investors lining up to throw money at 'em. The Phoenix Clinic markets a youth treatment that almost certainly doesn't do shit, but nobody's complaining or suing over it. They're sleazy, but sleazy doesn't bring the hammer down."

"And no connection to the occult underground," Harmony murmured, turning another page and skimming the doctor's cramped handwriting. She studied each letter, each circled date, hunting for a sign. "We never would have even heard of these people if they hadn't killed Bobby Diehl, bugged his corpse, and lured us in. And when they tried to kill you on the *Blue Star*, that guaranteed we wouldn't let this go. They picked a fight with us for no discernible reason."

Which didn't mean there was *no* reason. To the contrary, Harmony knew there had to be a motive, crystal clear and sharp as a knife. She just couldn't see it from here.

They don't want us to see it. The question is the very thing that's drawing us in. Like a fishing lure glittering in deep water.

And she kept circling back to a central problem: the people behind this scheme knew about the Ardentis heist. They'd used Herbert West as the initial bait, grabbing their attention and leading them to Chicago, but Ardentis was the only point of contact between him and Vigilant Lock. She'd verified all the reasons why Nadine, as much as they hated to admit it, had to be innocent here. If Bette Novak and Majestic-12 were suddenly looking for a fight — and they had no reason to want one — there were infinitely simpler traps they could have laid. Harmony couldn't speculate on a motive until she figured out who had the means, and the list of names was short enough to fit on a movie ticket.

"At the end of the day," Jessie said, summing up Harmony's own take, "there's only one person attached to this mess who A, knew about us and Vigilant Lock, and B, had a reason to want us dead in the worst ways possible."

"Bobby Diehl," Harmony said.

"Who is currently, one hundred percent confirmed, doing his best imitation of a TV dinner in our plane's freezer. The dude is dead as a doornail. Our one clear and obvious culprit is the only suspect who *couldn't* have committed the crime."

***

They still needed to plant the Icepick for Kevin, and they certainly weren't going to find the means in Charles Stepford's show-office. They put the day planner back where they'd found it and closed all the empty drawers. Jessie cracked the office door, checking the landing outside before gesturing with a wave, and they slipped out without a trace.

"Okay, so we need an access point," Jessie mused. "And I think we'd both like to get eyes on that surgical suite. Even if we can't figure out what the Treatment is, at least we can learn who's really doing Stepford's job around here."

"And why they aren't on the public-facing website," Harmony replied, leading the way toward the restricted wing. "Lots of doctors have assistants or clinical partners and nobody thinks anything of it, so why keep it a secret?"

Something occurred to her. She barely wanted to give it a voice.

"Jessie, there's no chance that Althea..."

From the look on her partner's face, she regretted even voicing the question.

"The only thing that bitch knows how to do with a scalpel is take people apart," Jessie said, "preferably while they're awake and screaming. She sure as hell hasn't carved out time to earn a medical degree between her days hacking up coeds with my dad and toppling governments for the CIA. You know how sometimes the cops'll look at a serial scene and say, 'This body shows that the killer had some form of medical training?'"

"Sure," Harmony said.

"Nobody ever said that about the Dixie Butcher murders. Not even once. The King of Wolves doesn't give out extra points for style. But when it comes to the underlying idea, you're not wrong. There's no reason they'd conceal the name of the real resident surgeon unless he's somebody who would make headlines for the wrong reasons. Let's go find out. Maybe introduce ourselves, if we're feeling frisky."

The double doors leading to the secure wing were locked with a keycard panel, but they didn't need Kevin's tech wizardry to bypass it. It was as simple as loitering in the hall, pretending to chat and browse their phones, waiting for an orderly to come through with a supply cart. He leaned in, pressing a laminated card on a lanyard to the pad and unlocking the swinging doors, then struggled with them as he wrestled the cart into position.

Harmony was at his shoulder in a second.

"Let me help you with that," she said, pulling the door back for him so he could manage the cart with both hands.

"Oh, uh, thanks."

He looked nervous, clearly not used to one of the clients lifting a finger to help. Harmony gave him what she hoped was a flirty smile and looked him up and down, selling her interest. He responded in kind before disappearing inside.

Her hand had been palming a thick strip of tape, and she slapped it over the lock in one smooth motion as she held the door for him, holding the latch down. She let go, the door swinging closed again — but without the soft telltale click of the lock catching. They gave it a slow count to ten, waiting for the coast to be clear, and opened the door again. Harmony ripped the tape off, crumpled it and pocketed it as they entered the restricted wing.

If she was hoping for an evil lair, some sign that they were on the right track, this wasn't it. The back halls of the lodge were just as bright and cheery as the public areas, albeit with secured filing cabinets, an airy break room, and signage clearly intended for employees only. She had seen more suspicious setups backstage at a shopping mall.

"Mister Grassley is prepped and ready for surgery. Is the doctor prepared?"

Jessie grabbed Harmony's arm and pulled her into a cloakroom, the dark alcove lined with staff lockers and a long, low bench. From the doorway they could see the T-junction up ahead, glimpsing a gurney as two nurses rolled it into view. Harmony recognized the man laid out in his hospital gown. It was

Grassley, the Texas oilman from last night's party, and he was sound asleep. Either a sign of supreme confidence, or they'd already sedated him.

"The doctor," a woman's husky voice chuckled, "is *always* prepared."

Harmony's breath froze in her throat.

She knew that voice.

Chapter Thirty

C rouched in the shadows, Jessie's eyes burned, radioactive. Her gaze flicked to Harmony, asking a question. She knew that voice too, but she wanted confirmation.

They got it a second later as a figure in scarlet scrubs, her hair pinned and bound under a surgical cap, strode into view from the other direction. Harmony watched, studying the surgeon in profile as she leaned over Grassley and checked his vitals.

Then she paused. She turned and looked up the corridor just as Harmony ducked into cover, as if this new arrival could sense her presence. Harmony caught a flicker-flash of the white porcelain mask that covered the other half of the surgeon's face, the ivory ringed with angry and twisted burn tissue.

Victoria Carnes.

While Bobby Diehl had plagued Vigilant more than any foe they'd ever faced, he wasn't their first nemesis. On their very first mission together, Harmony and Jessie had investigated a plastic surgery clinic operated by the esteemed Dr. Carnes. Digging deeper, they discovered that Carnes was running a chop shop for human beings: after hours, she turned her scalpel to the business of organ harvesting for the Russian mob selling hearts and livers on the black market.

When Victoria's men got the drop on them, Harmony and Jessie had to fight their way out of the trap. In the process, Harmony blasted Victoria in the face with a gout of magically conjured flame.

The blaze didn't kill her, and she slipped away. But in the aftermath her career and professional reputation were burned as badly as her face. Her physical wounds were nothing compared to her shattered mind. She'd popped up again in Nashville after that, carrying out a string of serial murders and earning a new title for her resume: the Face Collector, number 138 on Vigilant Lock's list of hostile entities. She'd escaped again, vanishing into the underground, but not before showing off new magical talents of her own and nearly roasting Harmony alive in retribution.

And now she was here at the Phoenix Clinic, working as the shadow proxy for Dr. Charles Stepford — the same man who had brought Althea, another of Vigilant's oldest enemies, to a party for a little attempted murder.

"Doctor?" Harmony heard one of the nurses ask. "Is something wrong?"

Jessie was coiled like a spring. Or a tiger ready to pounce. Harmony cautioned her with a tiny head shake. This wasn't the time. Not until they could put the rest of the pieces together.

"No. Nothing," Victoria said. "Let's get Mister Grassley onto the table. He has a very busy day ahead, as do we all."

Once they had vanished into the surgical suite, the squeak of the gurney's wheels fading into silence, Harmony let out a breath.

"What's that old saying?" Jessie asked. "About magic."

Harmony knew the one.

"There's no such thing as a coincidence," Harmony whispered, her face lost in the shadows of the cloakroom. "Everything is connected."

Jessie tapped her ear bead twice.

"Team. We've got *two* HEs on site, not one. Haven't spotted her yet, but Althea Temple-Sinclair is posing as a bodyguard for a patient known only as 'Mr. Big.' Victoria Carnes is here too, working as a surgeon and filling in for the alleged boss of the operation. I want you to dig deep. Find me every known point of contact between Temple-Sinclair, Carnes, and Doctor Charles Stepford."

Harmony was going deeper than that. The virtual evidence board in her mind's eye was a wall of neon blue, notes and index cards linked by a growing web of luminous thread. She played cat's cradle with her fingertips and the web expanded, growing and twisting.

"Not just him," she said. "Look for points of contact between those three and Bobby Diehl."

Jessie raised an eyebrow. "Bobby's dead."

"He is. But think about it: everything about this situation, and this isn't the first time we've noticed, has the hallmarks of a Bobby Diehl operation. He knew exactly who we are and what Vigilant is, and he has — had — more reason than anyone on Earth to want us dead. We were lured in with a mix of magic and technology. That's Bobby's signature. Elaborate traps? Bobby. A byzantine corporate octopus that sells nothing but snake oil? That's not just Bobby to a T, we know for a fact that he was a prime investor in ProcGen and he had financial ties to Praeda, the spider at the heart of the web. The only thing he needed to trick us into carrying a transmitter right back to Vigilant and opening our doors for an attack was the perfect bait."

"His corpse," Jessie said. "A mystery we'd never be able to resist solving."

"Right, so...what if that wasn't the original bait? Picture this: Bobby orchestrates the entire thing. Everything we've seen so far was him all along."

"And then," Jessie said, getting the idea, "one of his partners — maybe Muffy St. John, maybe Charles Stepford, hell, maybe both — gets a bee in their bonnet. Could be he was cutting them out of the profits, or maybe he was just too much of a problem."

"As a captain of industry," April said in their ears, "Bobby's reputation was sterling. As a wanted fugitive, his assets frozen, disowned by everyone he ever did business with, he was a walking liability."

"Didn't bring much to the table," Jessie mused, "outside of a raging coke addiction and a penchant for mass murder. Both qualities that the venture capital crowd are willing to overlook as long as you keep laying those golden eggs. Once the egg supply dried up, Bobby was a problem that suddenly needed solving. So maybe one of his buddies took him out and jacked his entire operation. Mobsters do it all the time."

There was one thread missing. One single strand for the murder board to put it all together, and the absence was more glaring than anything.

"But why go through with it?" Harmony murmured out loud.

Jessie gave her a curious look.

"Same problem we keep running into," she continued. "We don't *know* these people. ProcGen is shady, the Phoenix Clinic is sleazy, but we haven't seen a drop of evidence that either of them are involved in any kind of occult crimes. We can't even pin any *mundane* crimes on them beyond false advertising. Even if we could, that's not our business. Luring us in guarantees we're going to dig into their operations and make trouble."

"Sure," Jessie said. "Which, if Bobby was still at the wheel, would be the entire point. Trick us with a transmitter hidden inside a dead body, get us to take it to HQ, then send a kill team to wipe us out."

"But he's not. And whoever inherited his throne didn't have to inherit his vendetta. If they'd done literally nothing at all, we'd be on some other mission on the other side of the country right now. The only reason they'd pick a fight with us…" Harmony trailed off. "It has to be a preemptive strike. They're doing, or -*will* do, something guaranteed to draw Vigilant's fire. Something big, bad, and impossible to ignore. The trap was intended to take us off the table and remove any obstacles before they even got started."

"We're up against a ticking clock here," Jessie said.

"There's an interesting discrepancy," April said over the comm. "The Face Collector is on Charles Stepford's payroll. Why isn't Althea? I agree that two of our old enemies showing up in the same place at the same time cannot be a coincidence."

"But she's posing as a patient's bodyguard," Jessie replied. "Not a member of the staff. It'd be cleaner and simpler to give her a fake job as an orderly or something."

"Suggesting that she might not be posing at all. What if this 'Mr. Big' is the architect of the plan? He could be at the clinic to give Charles his marching orders, using the role of a reclusive patient as a cover story. I suggest you prioritize learning his identity. Quickly, before he leaves and the window of opportunity closes."

"Those snobs at the cocktail party said he's holed up in the Royal Suite, right?" Kevin asked, joining the line. "Get me access to their database and I can check the patient registry. I mean, I'm sure they didn't put down the guy's real name and the address of his evil lair where he does evil stuff, because we never get that lucky, but if he's traveling under a fake ID I might be able to dig something up. No identity is bulletproof."

First thing they needed to do was slip out of the secure wing. Getting caught right now would jeopardize the entire mission, and the stakes had just gotten deadlier. Althea was a juggernaut, with all of her daughter's strength and speed but twice the muscle. Victoria Carnes could spew white-phosphorous flame from her fingertips. Encountering *one* of them in the field was a dangerous proposition, even when Harmony and Jessie were prepared for a fight. Facing both at once was suicidal, and that wasn't even counting the armed guards patrolling the Phoenix Clinic's halls.

They made their way back out, fast and quiet, like thieves in a temple.

"Got an idea," Kevin said. "Use the camera glasses and give me a really good view of the lobby from that balcony overlook."

Harmony obliged him, pretending to loiter and lean against the rustic wooden railing as her glasses transmitted a video feed to the *Imperator*.

"Okay, zoom in on the reception desk. See that bundle of cables?"

She followed the snaking lines. They slithered under a forest-green rug and emerged on the other side, only to slip under a closed door a little to the right of the desk.

"Pretty sure that's a data closet," Kevin said. "You should be able to find an insertion point for the Icepick."

Harmony didn't see a way forward. The desk was always staffed, always a handful of patients and staffers mingling in the lobby over by the crackling hearth, no way to get in there without at least two or three people spotting them.

"I have an idea," Jessie said, standing beside her.

"Something in your tone," Harmony said, "makes me think I'm not going to like it."

"Oh, you are absolutely not going to like it."

Chapter Thirty-One

Timing was everything. They made their way down to the lobby, playing it cool, watching the room like hawks. The nurse on reception duty was the same one Jessie had slipped past on the back patio that morning. It would be hours before the next shift change, but Jessie figured she had a way to move things along.

"Walk with me and follow my lead," she murmured.

She and Harmony strolled side by side, tracing a leisurely arc past the reception desk. As they got close, Jessie raised her voice, talking like they were mid-conversation.

"The worst thing about this detox weekend is the no smoking rule. I thought I could handle it, but I've just been getting the *worst* nicotine fits. It's like this...relentless itch and I can't scratch it."

The nurse was listening. And squirming a little. She kept her eyes on the folder in front of her, but Harmony spotted her lips pursing tight.

"Swear to god," Jessie said, "I would murder someone for a cigarette right now. Just one, one teeny tiny little cig and I'd feel so much better."

As they moved back out of earshot, she leaned close to Harmony and said, "Now we wait."

Not two minutes had passed before the nurse snatched up the desk phone.

"Hey? Judy? I need to take my coffee break. Would you mind coming and watching the front desk for me for like ten minutes? Thanks, hon."

"Don't have to wait for a shift change," Jessie breathed, "when you can gently encourage one."

Jessie leaned against the wall, casual, arms crossed, watching the nurse slowly push her chair back and grab her purse. She knew she needed to wait for her replacement. And from the look on her face, she really didn't want to. A moment later she got up and hustled down the back hallway.

"Now."

They approached the closet door smoothly, silently, keeping their pace steady to avoid turning any heads with a sudden burst of movement. The handle swung under Harmony's hand and they were inside, finding a dark cavity filled with antique-looking server boxes, dusty shelves, and an open wiring panel dripping with an octopus of colored cables. Compared to ProcGen's high-tech data fortress, this was a cheap mess rigged by a college kid working part-time.

"Sweep it with the glasses," Kevin said in their ears. "There! Third shelf down, hit that USB port."

Jessie slotted the stick, her eyes shimmering in the dark, a second before the closet door swung open.

"Excuse me, I'm sorry, but this area is off limits to—"

Jessie grabbed Harmony by the collar hard and yanked her into a kiss.

Their lips met, smoldering, a rush of animal heat that flushed Harmony's face beet red and poured downward from there, a shivering waterfall of warmth that made her toes curl. It was over as soon as it began, Jessie breaking the kiss to smile awkwardly at the new nurse who stood in the doorway.

"Oh," Jessie said, "uh, sorry, we were just...looking for a little privacy."

Now it was the nurse's turn to be embarrassed. She looked between the two women, eyes wide, taking a halting step back.

"Yes, well, I mean, I understand, I mean, we just can't allow patients in here, it's, you know, an insurance issue."

Harmony knew her role. It was the same as it had been since her arrival: to play the rich heiress who could ruin careers with a phone call.

"Listen," she said, gently taking the nurse aside as they emerged from the closet. "My husband couldn't join me on this trip. Do you...understand what I'm saying?"

Her head bobbed, fast. "Yes, ma'am. Of course. I won't say a word. I mean, I didn't see anything, so there's nothing I could even talk about."

"I'm in," Kevin whispered on the comms. "Yank the Icepick."

Harmony kept the nurse's back turned while Jessie plucked and palmed the black plastic sliver.

"Thank you," Harmony said, "for your discretion. I won't forget this."

"If I may," the nurse said, lowering her voice, "if you try the yoga studio, usually it's empty this time of day and they always leave it unlocked."

Harmony replied with a wink and a nod. Then she fell into step with Jessie, steaming away from the scene of the crime.

"You could have warned me that you were going to do that."

"I told you that you wouldn't like it," Jessie said.

"A more specific warning would have been nice."

"I needed you to be genuinely surprised," she explained. "Did you catch the look on her face? She interpreted your flustered reaction as you about to go nuclear on her for interrupting us. She's not going to say a word to anybody."

After a moment's reflection, Harmony responded with a sigh.

"Begrudgingly agreed."

"Did...did you two just make out?" Kevin asked.

"It was one quick kiss," Jessie said. "When we make out, you'll be the last to know about it, I promise."

"I like how you said *when* instead of *if*."

"Kevin, don't be horny on the comm. That's an order."

***

Back on the plane, ensconced in his element before a bank of softly glowing screens, Kevin got to work. It was slow going. The Clinic's gear was outdated junk, but the software was patched, up to date, and curated by a systems operator with an eye for security. It wasn't long before he knew he was looking at a repeat of ProcGen: the same signatures, Mercury Blaise and some as-yet-unknown mystery coder teaming up to build a wall around the Phoenix Clinic's precious data.

Not as high, though, and not as thick. Instead of a dungeon like last time, he found himself navigating digital trenches like a World War One battlefield, creeping under gun emplacements and staying wary of mortar fire.

Makes sense, on the surface at least, he figured. *ProcGen's got the code for the Gaia AI and their whole Wellness 2.0 scam on their servers. The clinic just needs to protect credit card numbers for a bunch of rich weirdos. Whatever Vicky is really doing in that surgical suite, we're not going to find the answer on a computer screen.*

It was still worth the dive, though, especially if he could dig up anything about "Mr. Big." A phone number, an email address, anything that might kick off a chain of evidence and tell them about the mystery man in the Royal Suite.

Two hours later he'd cracked their email server. A lot of nothing, mostly admin assistants lining up dates to book their bosses for wellness retreats and arranging bank transfers for payment. Like Harmony, though, he mostly noticed what was missing.

"Can confirm," he said over the comms, "Doctor Stepford does not have an email account at his own clinic. Looks like he does everything the old-fashioned way. I mean, if he actually does anything at all, seeing as he's got a notorious serial killer handling his surgery schedule while he's out golfing."

"Good find," Jessie said. "We figured as much, but it's nice to know for sure."

"Something else though. Know what else I'm not seeing? A control-F for the word *Treatment* gets nothing but generic lowercase hits that aren't talking about the capital-T variety. Also, none of the bank transfer confirmations I'm seeing from the staff have a massive string of zeros attached. It's all payment for services straight off the public menu on the website. Kinda suggests that clients who get offered the Treatment are handled over more secure channels."

"Can you get access to their bank accounts?"

"Not yet," Kevin said. "Just receipts for now, but I'm working on it. I'll call you back when I find anything else."

He found an interesting little nugget shortly after. An email to an obviously spoofed web address that bounced off to somewhere in Siberia, the owner taking extra pains to keep himself concealed.

From: M-Blaise@procgen.com

Subject: eat a dick

Message: Listen up, you little worm. I do not work with you and I sure as hell don't work for you. If you EVER challenge my coding skills in front of Muffy again, I will find every public-facing persona you've ever had and annihilate your credit score, and then I'll come up with something really nasty for an encore. Remember: this is my house. You're an outside contractor. As soon as these Vigilant freaks are taken off the table, you're out the door. You have ONE JOB and I suggest you focus on it.

It hasn't escaped my notice that I'm the one who had to face them in the field while you sat in your basement eating pizza rolls. They had no idea who I even was. Now I'm on their target list and I really hate it a lot, so thanks. Don't screw this up.

PS, if you ever try to grab my ass again, I will make you disappear. Your body will not be found. Don't test me on this.

—Mercury.

"*I* knew who you were," Kevin murmured to himself. "Kind of a fan, honestly."

The answer to her email, this time from another spoofed account allegedly somewhere in the heart of Moscow, simply read: *That time of the month?*

She hadn't responded to that one.

"Hey April," Kevin said. "Sending an email over to your terminal. What do you think?"

April adjusted her bifocals and read it over. She sat back in her wheelchair and steepled her wrinkled fingertips, deep in thought.

"Outside contractors," she echoed. "Brought in for the purpose of eradicating us. So we can plant our compromised network — and the corpse of Bobby Diehl that made it possible — squarely at their doorstep. Suggesting that

Harmony and Jessie are correct: Praeda, and its corporate arms, are cooking up something that *will* put them on Vigilant's radar. This is a preemptive strike."

"Outside contractors like Jessie's mom," he said. "She's literally a mercenary."

"But she's definitely not Mercury's unwanted coding partner," April said.

"Oh yeah, not a chance. That's not Althea's style. And we still haven't worked out how the Face Collector is involved, but she's not any kind of a hacker either. Totally out of her wheelhouse."

"So here's an interesting question: why use Mercury at all? It sounds like she wants very little to do with this aspect of the operation, and she resents having been thrust into our sights back in Chicago. All that was required was the presence of Herbert West to lure us in, and Bobby's dead body to set the trap. It didn't matter *who* was there to meet with West that night. Anyone could have sufficed."

"Because..." Kevin trailed off into silence. Then he snapped his fingers. "Because whoever this person is, we know them. They're already on our radar, and having them at the scene in Chicago would have spoiled the plan."

"I suggest you redouble efforts to find our Mr. Big," April said. "Whoever is in that suite, hiding their face from the world, is most likely our mystery element."

"On it," he said.

Chapter Thirty-Two

A s the afternoon rolled into evening and patients gathered in the grand lodge hall to mingle and sip wine, Jessie and Harmony worked the crowd. There wasn't much to learn. Just a lot of bragging, borderline illegal insider trading tips, and speculation over who'd gotten a nose job and who'd had their tummy tucked. Then Harmony caught a glimpse of Carlton Grassley the Third, strolling along with a pair of bellhops pushing his luggage on a wheeled cart behind him, and the breath caught in her throat.

The Texas oilman had gone under the knife just that morning — they'd seen him laid out on the gurney, about to be wheeled into Victoria Carnes's operating theater — but the transformation was like night and day. He'd gone from a man in his fifties to one barely pushing thirty, his skin unwrinkled and unweathered, even a tiny bit of baby fat on his cheeks. His hands were smooth, his stride confident and powerful, his eyes crystal clear.

Harmony fanned herself with her fingers, playing up the pecan heiress routine as she placed herself in his path.

"Carlton! I declare, where did you find that genie, and please tell me there are a few wishes left."

He laughed, rumbling and rich. "I could tell you that the Treatment is all it's cracked up to be and then some, honey, but...well, seeing's believing. I feel like ten million bucks plus compound interest. I'm headed back to Houston; money never sleeps, and I got a lot of fires to put out."

"I do hope you'll stay in touch," she said, offering her hand. Inwardly, Harmony stretched out her senses, extending a field of psychic energy just past her skin. She wanted to taste him, to figure out if this dramatic change was surgical or magical in nature.

He took her hand like a gentleman, raising it to his lips before letting go, and in that brief span she realized two things.

One, his skin was cold. A familiar cold. The exact same odd feeling she'd gotten from touching both Muffy St. John and Charles Stepford, like they'd just come inside from braving a winter chill. And Carlton hadn't felt that way the other night when they met at the cocktail reception.

Two, there wasn't any magic to sense. Less than there should have been. Even animals, even people who were as naturally psychic as rocks, had *some* kind of bio-occult activity going on. He was just...blank. Empty. A void in the shape of a man.

She watched him go. Then she regrouped with Jessie, quietly leading her back to Harmony's room so they could talk in peace. She swept the room again, hunting for bugs and cameras, holding her silence until she felt safe enough to state the obvious.

"That man," she said, "should not exist."

"Are we talking about billionaires as a concept, or...?"

"Let's leave aside that I have no idea, none, how he was transformed that radically in the space of a single day. Plastic surgery doesn't work like that, and even if it did he should be lying in a bed covered in bandages, not hopping on a plane home." Harmony paced the room, hands clasped behind her back, riffling through notes on the murder board in her head. "Every living thing gives off some degree of magical energy. He had none. Zero. Touching him was like touching...nothingness. My skin is still crawling."

"Okay," Jessie said, "so, uh, are we sure he *is* alive? Between Herbert West's weird science and whatever Bobby was cooking up in his labs before he got executed..."

"That's the thing. West hates being called a necromancer, but he is one regardless. And necromantic bodies are absolutely infused with power. I can feel his zombies from the other side of a room; they make my teeth itch. The process of restoring life, or more accurately a faint parody of it, takes a ton of magical juice. If Carlton was a walking corpse, it'd be more obvious, not less. Also...well, two things. Number one, a small observation, but dead bodies are room temperature. He's *cold*, like Muffy and Charles were."

Jessie sat on the edge of the bed, nodding. "And the other?"

"Same problem we ran into back at the beginning, speculating why Mercury would want West to raise Bobby from the grave. That's not how it works. A zombie is a parody of life at best. The most you can expect from one is teaching it tricks a dog could learn, because that's about all the brainpower they have to work with. The best sorcerers in the world can't top that. But that's not what I saw. That was the exact same Carlton I met the other night, just...twenty years younger."

"Okay," Jessie said. "I really hate to even bring this up, but...real-life Fountain of Youth? I feel like a dork just saying it, but I've got nothing else to put on the table right now."

"Then why keep it a secret? If the Treatment can sell to a small, select clientele for millions of dollars a pop, imagine how much more money they could make by going wide with it."

"There has to be a catch," Jessie said.

"Exactly, and we won't find it sitting in this room."

"You thinking what I'm thinking?"

Harmony took a deep breath, steeling herself.

"It's time to pay a visit to the Royal Suite and meet Mr. Big."

"We know Vicky's onsite, and while we haven't seen her yet, Althea's prowling around here somewhere." Jessie put her hands on her hips, cocking her head to one side and looking Harmony up and down. "You ready for that fight?"

"No," Harmony said. "Let's do it anyway."

***

Engrossed in his work, the hours around Kevin slipped away, a soft chorus of cricket-song and the rumble of jets drifting in on a cold and refreshing night breeze from the open belly of the *Imperator*'s cargo ramp.

He stripped away layer after layer of encryption, finally laying the protected client registry bare. He allowed himself one tiny, celebratory but silent fist pump as he dove in.

"We're making our way to the Royal Suite now," Jessie said on the comm. "If it's empty, we'll slip in, toss the place gently, and find out whatever we can dig up."

"And if it isn't?" April asked.

"Improvisation is the soul of necessity."

"That is not a real proverb," April said.

"It is now, because I made it up. Okay, we're going silent for a sec, Jessie out."

He turned his attention back to the database.

Each room at the Clinic had an entry, filled out by the reception desk with the patient's initials and supplementary notes. Most of it was mundane: dates of stay, procedures requested (noted by code letters and number strings that he couldn't make heads or tail of, probably by design), and confirmation that payment had been received in full prior to check-in. He wanted to check Harmony's room, just to make sure they didn't put anything like "suspected spy" in the note section, but he forced himself to slow down and take his time. In the off chance he'd triggered a logging feature somewhere, going straight to her patient entry would be suspicious as all hell. Instead he worked his way up the numbers, checking five rooms before hers and then three rooms after just to bury his real interest.

Nothing. Her patient profile matched her cover story perfectly. Moving on, he pulled up Carlton Grassley's file. It looked just like the rest, except his *Procedures Requested* entry read *T*. For *Treatment*, presumably. The section for payment confirmation, which listed an exact dollar amount and bank confirmation number for the other patients, only bore an asterisk and the note *(Confirmed by Dr. Stepford.)*

Big money, Kevin thought, *and they're burying the cash. Something tells me they might not be paying their taxes like good citizens. Just a hunch.*

He forged ahead, cross-referencing the Royal Suite to find the profile for "Mr. Big." A moment later he tilted his head, lips pursed, incredulous. There was no signature line for the check-in orderly. This had been done internally, the database updated from a remote login with a spoofed address that Kevin couldn't trace.

He had the distinct impression that the person in charge of filling out the reservation wasn't taking any of this seriously.

Patient Name: Big, Mister

Birthdate: 6/9/69 (nice)

Procedure Requested: Enlarge deez nutz

The next entry was marked *Client Photograph for Staff*, and instead of a professional headshot it was one of the oldest memes on the Internet. A wide-eyed, delighted gray cat stared out at the viewer, below a caption that read "I Can Has Cheezburger?"

"That's not even funny," Kevin muttered, shaking his head. "Like, if you're going to fill out a joke patient entry, at least get some new material. Your meme game is stale as hell."

He froze.

A cold and terrible light dawned on him, sudden as the sun emerging from behind a dark cloud. The suspicions he'd harbored all along lined up like dominoes in freefall. The twin signatures in the code — one Mercury's, one belonging to someone else, someone who couldn't have shown their face at the meeting with West because it would have given away the game. His constant, nagging feeling that he'd encountered the mystery hacker's signature style somewhere before.

"Jessie, Harmony, come in. Do *not* enter that suite. I repeat — hello? Hello? Damn it!"

Seated down at her console, April turned in her chair, concerned.

"Comms are hosed," he told her. "I need you to take the drone controls and get visual on the lodge, north face, Royal Suite windows."

"Hold on," April said. "What's wrong with the comms? You were sure that you removed the infection—"

"I *did*. This isn't on our side and there's nothing wrong with our team's earpieces. He deployed a signal jammer. Local, covering the lodge itself. I can override it, but it's going to take me a few minutes."

"'He?'"

Kevin typed faster, cycling frequencies, desperately trying to get a warning out.

"Two of our old enemies aren't hanging out at the Phoenix Clinic," he said. "There are *three*. And if I'm reading the situation right, Harmony and Jessie just got their covers blown. They're walking into a trap."

Chapter Thirty-Three

F inessed by the whisper-soft scratch of Jessie's picks, the polished oak door of the Royal Suite swung wide, opening onto silent, shadowy opulence. The size of a wilderness cabin in its own right, the suite offered a living room with a hundred-inch television, sofas and chairs upholstered in tartan for that hunting lodge flair, a polished glass coffee table laden with business papers and magazines, and a stone hearth — cold and swept clean of ash — that rivaled the one in the lobby. An open doorway looked in on a bedroom with a California king, the bedspread military-neat and untouched by human hands.

The back of the living room was a wall of floor-to-ceiling windows, leading to a well-swept deck whose railing projected about five feet above the forest soil. Trees swayed in the dark, wind-kissed, and the shifting moonlight through the trees cast long, strange shadows upon the hardwood floors.

While Jessie shut and locked the door behind them, Harmony scanned the room. No suitcases in sight. The folded papers on the glass table hadn't been read. There were coasters neatly stacked, glasses on a wet bar along with a selection of top-shelf liquor, but nothing touched. On an impulse she rifled through the drawers in the television stand. Empty to the last.

"Nobody's here," she breathed. "At all. I don't know if anybody ever was. It doesn't look like anyone is staying in this room."

Jessie joined her in the heart of the living room.

"Let's check the bedroom," she said. "This doesn't make any sense. Stepford has rich clients on a waiting list. Why would he keep the best room in the lodge empty when he could rent it out and charge more?"

"Kevin, are you getting the feed from my glasses?" Harmony paused. Nothing. No static, not a whisper or a click. "Kevin?"

In a heartbeat, Harmony and Jessie moved back-to-back, covering the room from every angle and protecting each other. Harmony instinctively reached for her gun, only to remember she didn't have it on her. She'd had good reasons to leave it behind, for the sake of her cover story, but now she had nothing but regrets.

Regrets that worsened when she realized they weren't alone. A flash of psychic awareness landed a moment before company arrived. Althea stepped out from the bedroom doorway, her frame big enough to fill it. She'd changed into her usual mercenary chic: a ribbed turtleneck sweater, cargo pants, and a tactical holster riding one shoulder with a chromed .357 snug against her side.

On the opposite side of the suite, the bathroom door silently swung open and Victoria Carnes, draped in blood-spattered surgical scrubs, her porcelain mask covering half of her flame-ravaged face, stood on the threshold. Tiny pops and flares of raw magic danced around the fingers of her left hand, like a swarm of fireflies, and their light glinted in her mad eyes.

"Oh shit," Jessie said, cracking her knuckles and staring up at her mother. "I didn't realize today was rematch day. I would have stretched or something first."

"Last rematch you're ever going to get, baby girl."

"Looks like we agree on something at last." Harmony knew that strain in Jessie's voice. She was putting on a brave face to cover the dread. "Two on two? This is barely a fight. You should have brought some thugs at least. That would have made it interesting."

"We brought something better than that," Victoria said.

The television crackled to life, shifting from black to warm gray before a remote camera snapped into focus. From the quality and the angle Harmony guessed they were seeing through a webcam. The background was an office, crisp and clean, the door faced with a glass window. A familiar face sat before them in a high-backed leather chair.

"Hey bitches!" Roman Steranko said with a mocking finger-wave. "Remember me?"

They had crossed swords with Roman during the Red Knight mission. He was a hacker for hire, terminally online, meme-brained, who was running with a gang of mercenary punks. He ended up on Bobby Diehl's payroll, directly responsible for multiple acts of attempted terrorism along with the torture and murder of a federal agent. He managed to slip away in the chaos, abandoning his girlfriend to save his own skin. That was the kind of guy Roman was.

He was also a world-class tech geek, the kind who could give Kevin — and had given Kevin, more than once before — a serious run for his money.

"It was you," Harmony said to the screen. "You wrote the worm to infect our gear and built the transmitter, then hid it inside Bobby Diehl's corpse."

"Hell yeah," he said. "Worked like a charm, too. I gotta know: just how much of a dumbass did Kevin feel like once he finally figured it out?"

"Probably not as dumb as Mercury feels, considering you sent her into the line of fire."

Roman held up his palms. "Had to keep my hands clean, baby! That's just the kind of operation I run. Besides, like I give a shit what happens to Mercury? I assumed she was a slut when I met her; imagine my disappointment learning the truth. I mean, explain this to me: dyed hair, tattoos, tongue stud, PVC clothes, and she *doesn't* put out? Make it make sense."

"I can explain it," Jessie said, her tone conversational as she kept her gaze fixed on Althea. "You're a creepy little incel asshole. I wouldn't fuck you either."

"You'd be lucky to get a piece of this action. Anyway, I don't go for dark meat."

"Hey. Roman." Althea's voice cracked like a whip. "Talk less."

"Sorry, sorry. Anyway, I can only take credit for the gizmo and the code, not the master plan. That's our *other* friend's work. One sec, I'll patch him in."

One screen became two as it split down the middle, Roman's webcam feed sliding to the left side of the hundred-inch television as another figure, drenched in shadows, filled the other.

The breath caught in Harmony's throat as she gazed into a nightmare. A foot-thick stone pentacle attached to a cluster of rubber hoses and reinforced power cables glowed with electric green light. The figure standing upon the five-pointed star was a ragged scarecrow of torn flesh, drooping from a jagged, leaning wooden cross by hooks like a parody of a crucifixion. She thought it was a dead body at first, until it slowly raised its head.

One of his eyelids had been ripped away; the other drooped from the weight of a fishhook. His mouth was slack from a half-broken jaw, and claw-rents, streaming with faint inner light, gashed one stretched-out cheek. All the same, Harmony knew him.

Benjamin Crohn. The disgraced former director of the Federal Bureau of Investigation and once, before his downfall, the secret master of Vigilant Lock.

With Linder as his unwilling servant, he had played the FBI, the NSA, and the courts of hell against one another, building his personal fortune along with his power by binding and ingesting demons' souls. He had also been April's lover once, back when they were both young and idealistic. April had used that against him in the end, distracting him while Jessie and Harmony burned his sheaf of demonic contracts. The suddenly-freed beasts under his skin literally ripped him apart before dragging him down to hell to begin his real punishment.

Apparently it hadn't stuck. Harmony recognized the occult sigils ringing the pentacle stone. Marks of conjuration, of summoning. He'd been called up from the pit and bound, like any other monster.

"Ah," he burbled. "Agent Temple. Agent Black. So good of you to join us."

"Muffy thought you were still out in California, chasing your tails," Althea said. Her glowing turquoise eyes fixed on Jessie's. "Or that maybe you'd just given up and gone home, especially after you found Roman's corpse surprise. I knew better. My blood doesn't quit. I knew that if we just laid a little more bait, you'd find bite sooner or later."

"Like on the *Blue Star*?" Jessie shot back.

Althea glowered, turning her gaze on Harmony. "That trap was for *her*. Muffy didn't want Harmony hurt, just captured. I happen to disagree with her opinion."

Victoria stepped across the bathroom threshold. One of her eyes, ringed with burn tissue and porcelain, glared with quiet fury.

"Oh," she said in a soft, deadly purr, "we all do. We *very* much disagree."

Harmony narrowed her eyes. She was playing for time, knowing they were about to be plunged into the fight of their lives, and she wanted every advantage they could get before the blood started to spill.

"I thought you were a big, bad mercenary," she told Althea. "You usually go behind your boss's back like that?"

Althea laughed, a low and rumbling sound tinged with an animal growl.

"You think Muffy St. John is our *boss*? Nah, this is a co-op venture. She's got her people, we got ours."

"And she — or her backers at Praeda Electronics — want Vigilant Lock wiped out before they can move ahead with whatever they're planning," Harmony countered. "Easy to see why you four volunteered for the job. So humor me. What's the master plan?"

"We get paid," Althea said.

"And I get your *face*," Victoria hissed.

"We were hoping for something a little higher-level than that," Jessie said. She turned to the screen. "C'mon, Ben. We destroyed your legacy, took everything you ever had and then sent you to hell. I know you want to get something off your chest. I mean, as much of a chest as you've got left."

His half-mouth curled into a drooling sneer.

"I'll save it for April," he replied. "Once the two of you are out of the way...I can take my time with her."

At her sides, Jessie's hands curled into murderous fists.

"All right," Harmony said, feeling the hourglass running out. "Tell us this much then. This was Bobby's plan originally, wasn't it? He had a business relationship with both ProcGen and the Phoenix Clinic, which put the four of you in the perfect position to strike. I'm guessing the corpse with the transmitter was originally supposed to be someone close to us. Someone who would lure us in. But you all realized that Bobby was a liability. The man was cooked, a lead anchor who would drag you all down, maybe even get you arrested or killed, so you murdered him, and then you turned him into the perfect bait. Nicely done, I have to admit."

Althea chuckled again, the sound of thunder rolling over the midnight sky. There was something in her tone, the dark and cruel amusement, that dragged iron nails down Harmony's spine.

"Not exactly," she said.

On the television screen, a third and final window blossomed. It began as two thin lines in the middle, spreading out, expanding an umbrella of darkness as Roman and Ben Crohn were shoved off the display.

In that darkness, a pinprick of light grew, circling, spiraling like a distant galaxy until it filled the screen, and then resolved into a man. A familiar face. A tailored silk suit. A smirking mouth. A glint of madness in his eyes.

"Hey folks," he said, "Bobby Diehl here."

Chapter Thirty-Four

H armony's mental evidence board collapsed in a flurry of cards. Notes scattered and drifted, strings falling in a useless and scattered web. All of her hypotheses, everything she'd based her actions on since the start of this mission, had relied on one rock-solid certainty: that Bobby Diehl was a frozen corpse in the *Imperator*'s freezer.

But here he was, in living color on the television screen. He broke into a wide grin and let out a manic bark of laughter.

"Oh, oh this is *good*. Holy...seriously, is someone recording this? The look on your face, Agent Black. Seriously, I want to watch this over and over again. You truly cannot know how long I've been waiting for this moment and it did *not* disappoint. You ever read *The Art of War*? It was required curriculum for my MBA program back at Yale. Anyway, to quote Sun Tzu, 'The whole secret lies in confusing the enemy, so that he cannot fathom our real intent.' And you...you look so very confused."

They had speculated that the corpse was a doppelganger, a duplicate, a clone of some kind, but Harmony believed — no, she *knew* — they'd ruled it out. The body matched his medical records from multiple sources down to the tiniest detail. If he'd created some kind of double for himself, he would have had to have done it years before he ever crossed swords with Vigilant in the first place.

"Honestly," Bobby went on, "this is a mixed bag for me. On one hand, I've got my worst enemies cornered, trapped, dead to rights, and you totally fell for it. On the other hand, I'm almost disappointed. I'm so used to your autistic Sherlock Holmes bullshit that I kinda expected you to figure it out. Got nothin' for me, huh? No rousing speech putting the clues together, deducing the culprit? Nah?"

Victoria's voice, from the bathroom door, was a hungry growl. "Can we kill them now?"

"Hey, c'mon, don't rush me. I don't get to gloat like this very often these days and I want to savor the experience. Okay, let me clarify things for you. But first I want to stretch my legs a little bit."

He stepped toward the screen...and out of it, in a sparkle of stardust.

They had seen this once before. Back at ProcGen, when Muffy demonstrated her Gaia AI. This time Harmony knew to look for the tube of a hologram projector. It was mounted high in the corner of the living room, swiveling silently to frame Bobby in its pale light as the glimmering motes reformed into a three-dimensional man, large as life.

"Hey folks," he said, repeating his timeworn commercial catchphrase with a wave, "Bobby Diehl here. Live but *not* in the flesh."

"Broadcasting remote, while you hide from us?" Jessie asked. "So you'll send Althea and Vicky to get their hands bloody, but you don't have the stones to face us yourself."

"Okay, number one, I'm a lover, not a fighter. Number two, your mommy and the esteemed Doctor Carnes *like* getting their hands bloody, so that just makes me a really good and considerate boss. You know, learn your employees' strengths and give them jobs they're not only good at, but find emotionally fulfilling. I read that in a management book once."

Harmony noticed it now. A brief lag before Bobby's responses, the telltale sign of a long-range data transmission. *He's nowhere near here*, she thought. *If Kevin could get a lock on the signal, he might be able to figure out where Bobby is hiding.*

Kevin, where ARE you?

***

Kevin was in a submarine fight. Down in dark digital waters, cycling frequencies, hunting for Roman Steranko's signal jammer, intent on taking it out. They were flying blind, and if his guess was right, Harmony and Jessie were in danger.

"Oh dear," April breathed. "Kevin, patching a feed over to your screen."

The drone wobbled and bobbed like a drunk in April's hands — she had never, by her own admission, gotten the knack of flying the thing — but the choppy video feed from outside the lodge windows showed everything he needed to see. Althea, Victoria...and Bobby Diehl, the three of them flanking Harmony and Jessie. It hadn't come to violence yet, but it was only a matter of minutes. If they even had that long.

He didn't need the distraction. He minimized the video feed, focused, and got back to work.

One advantage, he thought. *Roman doesn't know we got into the Phoenix Clinic's intranet or he would have locked me out when he triggered the signal jammer. I've got internal emails, patient records... Gotta be a way I can use that. Our girls need a distraction, fast.*

He permitted himself a tiny smile. Charles Stepford was away on business. Presumably unreachable by phone for the moment.

Time to play doctor.

***

"I was dead, but now I live," Bobby said, waving his hands with dramatic flair. "Huh, I wonder if I'll get my own religion. We could call it...Diehlism. No wait. Bobbyology."

In the bedroom doorway, Althea rolled her glowing eyes.

"No votes for Bobbyology? Sheesh, everybody's a critic these days." He flashed a gleaming smile at Harmony and Jessie as a wave of static rippled through his hologram body. "Okay, fine, I'll cut to the good stuff. I'm sure you already know I was a big investor in ProcGen. You know, before you ruined my life, froze my assets, and sent me on the run as a wanted fugitive."

"And in Praeda Electronics," Harmony said. "The heart of the octopus."

He lifted an eyebrow, mildly surprised.

"You know about Praeda? Kudos, I really didn't expect you to dig that deep. Do you know who *runs* Praeda?"

"As it stands," she said, "signs point to either Muffy St. John or Charles Stepford."

"Yeah, well, signs also pointed to me being dead as a dodo, yet here we are. Anyway, moot point. I got in tight with Muffy — not like that, mind out of the gutter — and she took me aside and showed me what ProcGen and their pals are *really* working on. I had to get in on it. Cost me everything I had left, every dollar I could scrape together from the reserves that you, the feds, and the IRS couldn't lock down, but it was worth it."

"Considering we're at the Phoenix Clinic..." Harmony said, putting the last pieces together, "you're talking about the Treatment."

"That's the public-facing name, sure, but behind the scenes we call it Project Soul. Not to be confused with Muffy's self-help book. I mean, have you read that thing? Absolute garbage, but I digress. What you see before you, ladies, is more than just a stunningly handsome and brilliant hunk of a man. I am the future incarnate."

He did a twirl, holding out his arms, trailing stardust in the beam of the hologram projector. His gaze flashed with the glow of a dozen tiny television screens reflected in his eyes, feeds from all over the world beaming from his irises.

"I," he said, "am the world's first digitized human consciousness. Project Soul mapped my neurons into an unprecedented quantum-computing interface. I'm told it takes the resources of an entire coastal power plant to keep me online. Honestly, small price to pay for immortality. I have been freed from the bonds of the flesh. I think, I am, and I *live*."

He leaned closer, his eyes broadcasting one of his own commercials as his grin grew wide.

"There's the answer to your riddle, Agent Black. There's no clone, no trick, you were correct the entire time. That *is* my corpse. I didn't need it anymore once the upload was complete, and what better way to lure my worst enemies into a trap than using my own discarded flesh?"

Harmony flashed back to April's autopsy report. Bobby had been killed by lethal injection, potassium chloride and pancuronium bromide combining to deadly effect. The parallels to a state execution had led her the wrong way, made her think it was vigilante justice. Now the real reason was clear.

Even before he spoke the words, Harmony flashed back to her phone call with Nadine, and the demon's impossible question: "*Who could get close enough to Bobby to stab him in the back, and then use the bloody knife to lure you in?*"

"There it is," he said. "The last murder mystery you'll ever solve. Who killed Bobby Diehl? *Bobby did.* It was me all along."

"Well," Victoria said, "to be fair, I administered the injections after Muffy and Charles performed the upload procedure. Then I implanted Roman's electronic gadget, and Althea orchestrated the entire dark web exchange between Mercury Blaise and Herbert West, knowing all the little verbal triggers that would draw her daughter's immediate attention."

"You're so easy to read," Althea said, staring across the room at Jessie.

"Have to give Ben Crohn his fair share of kudos," Bobby added. "It was his plan, really. For a guy who got pulled out of an abyss of endless screaming torment, he seriously has a chip on his shoulder."

It all came together.

Except...it didn't.

Harmony was silent, poleaxed, not because of the grand revelation...but because it was wrong. She had already put her board back on its feet, scooped up the glowing notes and thread, reconfigured the clues with all she'd just learned. And it didn't work.

Someone in this room is lying, she thought. And for once, she didn't think it was Bobby. His confidence wasn't his usual bluster and bravado. He believed every word of it, though she saw a glaring hole in the story. For the moment, she kept it to herself. It was one tiny, desperate card, and it needed to stay up her sleeve until the right moment.

"You see the beauty of it all?" Bobby said, spreading his shimmering hands to take the room in. "What does Vigilant have? A witch, a wolf, a hacker, and a strategist. What do I have? Let's see. A witch...a wolf...a hacker...and a strategist.

I couldn't beat you alone, so I put together my very own team. And if I do say so myself, I made the right draft picks. The same skills you've got, the same powers, just a whole lot less in the way of moral compunction."

"So you're...an AI?" Harmony asked.

He waved a hand and puffed out his cheeks.

"Please. As if. I'm not some pale imitation of a human being, Agent Black. I am the man himself, reforged. All my memories, all my neurons, everything that makes me, *me*. I've been reborn in the light of Muffy St. John."

"Muffy St. John," Jessie said. "The nutritionist? The talk show therapist? You're telling me that *she* invented a way to put human brains into a computer? I'm calling bullshit on that."

"Well, not by herself. *Duh*. She's just the public face of the program. Believe me, you ladies have no idea what's coming. Praeda Electronics is going to transform the nature of humanity itself. Eternal life, eternal youth, for everyone. Well, everyone who can afford it. The peons will have to keep working endless hours, suffering in squalor, and dying in poverty like usual. Somebody's gotta do the physical labor, after all, and every king needs his serfs."

He paused, catching something, and turned to Victoria.

"Doctor Carnes? You look like you have something to add."

"I'm wondering if you're going to say it."

Bobby squinted. "Say what?"

She raised a hand sheathed in a snow-white surgical glove and gestured at Harmony and Jessie.

"You went to all this trouble for the big reveal."

"I did, and...?"

"The line," Victoria said.

"What—"

She took a deep breath. "'But it's too bad...'"

"Oh, shit, right!"

Bobby snapped, his hologram fingers rubbing together without making a sound.

"But it's too bad you won't live to see it," he said.

Althea punched her beefy palm into her fist and took a step forward. Opposite her, firefly sparks danced around Victoria's gloved fingertips.

***

The plan, back on the *Imperator*, came together with one last triumphant click of a button.

At the drone controls, April looked over and gave Kevin a grim thumbs up. The signal blocker crumbled under one last push, freeing their encrypted frequency. Bobby's last words drifted in, muffled, over the comms: "—won't live to see it."

"Harmony, Jessie," Kevin said. "Don't react to this. Roman still thinks you're blocked, and I don't want to give him a chance to get the jammer back online. We've got a distraction inbound. Brace for it, and on my signal, get ready to move. Wait for me to give the go sign."

***

"Now, then—" Bobby started to say.

A knock sounded at the door.

He blinked, his eyes flickering with irritated static. His hands fell to his sides.

"Are you...are you kidding me right now? I get all warmed up for the big victory speech and...Althea? Please? I'd get it, but, you know. No hands."

She grunted, marching across the living room. She twisted the lock and hauled the door open. A small pack of orderlies in white scrubs stood outside, flanking a cart laden with mops, brooms, and cleaning supplies.

"We're here for the room, ma'am," one chirped.

"Excuse me?" she replied.

"The room. We got the email from Doctor Stepford."

"What email?"

"Yeah." Bobby leaned out behind her, staring. "*What* email?"

Nervous now, the orderly held up his phone.

"Uh, the all-hands emergency email? He said that the occupant of the Royal Suite—"

"Who is me," Bobby said.

"—uh, yes, yes sir. Well, Doctor Stepford said you'd actually left earlier this afternoon. He said that another priority client was arriving by helicopter within the hour and had reserved this suite, so he wanted us to clean it from top to bottom right away."

Even Victoria had turned her porcelain half-mask toward the open door, drawn by the unexpected confusion. Harmony's fingertips brushed soft against Jessie's, and she signaled the opportunity with a subtle nod.

"Now," Kevin said in their ears. "*Duck.*"

Harmony and Jessie hit the floor as the glass wall exploded, the drone blasting through on screaming rotors and flying over their heads. It careened wildly, making Victoria dive for cover behind the bathroom door before cutting through Bobby's projection, scattering stardust, and sending Althea lurching into the cleaning cart to avoid getting hit, knocking it over and scattering orderlies like bowling pins.

Jessie grabbed Harmony's hand and they bolted for the shattered window and the deck beyond. Jessie scooped Harmony up mid-run, holding her tight in her arms as her pace became a canine lope.

"Cover your face," she growled in Harmony's ear.

Jessie hit the ruined window with her shoulder, blowing aside chunks of razored glass, charging onto the deck. The cold forest wind whistled in their ears as she leaped over the railing and into the dark.

Chapter Thirty-Five

"I t's not my fault!" Roman squealed, hammering his keyboard.

"You said they were isolated, cut off from contact with the rest of their team," Bobby seethed in his ear. "So *explain that shit*. And explain it to my complete and total satisfaction, or I'm sending Althea to hold a termination conference. It'll be a meeting between you, her, and her extensive knife collection."

"I can," he stammered, lying through his teeth. "I can explain everything."

"Good. Oh hey, you know I collect snuff movies, right? Kind of a hobby. Just bear that in mind before you choose your next words."

Roman was trying to connect with the signal jammer, to get it back online and figure out how it had failed in the first place. Maybe he could paper this all over, paint it as a random glitch, blame it on the long-distance connection and the fact that he was sitting in an office in California two thousand miles from the fight. All he had to do was reestablish control, save the day, and all would be forgiven.

He reestablished the link, clicked *connect*, and...

His screen erupted in a field of pixel stars. Instead of his custom-built interface, he stared at an image of an animated cat, streaming rainbows as it sailed across a videogame void. At the bottom of the screen, a message unfurled letter by letter.

Hey, Roman. Just letting you know that you suck. Love, Kevin. BTW, you just downloaded a whole suite of my favorite malware, so have fun disinfecting your hard drive.

"Oh no," he breathed.

"Those," Bobby said, "were not the words I wanted to hear."

***

Jessie landed in a crouch in the forest loam, light and chaos at her back as her burning eyes instantly adjusted to the darkness. She set Harmony down in one smooth motion, placing her gently on her feet and grabbing her hand again. Then she took the lead as they ran together, sprinting away from the Phoenix Clinic into the woods, angling toward one particular spot on her mental map.

Harmony had a computer's memory. Jessie just had a nose for leather and gun oil.

She dropped to her knees next to a fallen log, reached into a pile of dead leaves, and dug like a dog, sending sod flying as her fingers gouged ragged rents in the black dirt.

***

Furious, her teeth clenched and bared, Althea drew her .357. The drone was still spinning around the living room, forcing Victoria back into the bathroom as it drunkenly bobbed and weaved. It came for Althea again, rotors whining as it zipped toward her like a giant hornet. She stood her ground, calmly raised her gun, and squeezed off a shot without bothering to aim.

It hit, dead center mass, and blew the drone into a twisted pile of scrap. The wreckage bounced and rolled across the sanded planks, trailing broken chunks of metal and plastic in its wake.

The orderlies in the hall were ducking for cover and running. A pair of security guards struggled the other way, fighting through the pack, converging on the sound of trouble with their sidearms ready. Althea grabbed the closest one by the collar, swung him around and shoved him up against the wall, leaning nose to nose with him.

"Rally the security team," she told him. "I want a skeleton crew working the forest cameras and calling out anything they spot. Everyone else, and I mean everyone else, needs to be armed, out in those trees, and hunting for big game. We have two targets on foot, industrial spies posing as patients, attempting to escape with stolen Clinic property. If they make it back to civilization in one piece, consider yourself a dead man walking. *Go.*"

***

Jessie's fingernails scraped against the rough fabric of a duffel bag. She unearthed her prize as Harmony kept watch, tugging it from the roots and brittle leaves and dusting it off.

"Harmony?" she said, glancing over her shoulder. "You with me?"

Harmony snapped back to the present. She'd been lost for a moment, still trying to reconfigure the facts in evidence, to make the web of string hang in perfect symmetry. It refused her, drawing a frame around a missing space for a missing clue.

"It doesn't make sense," she said.

"What doesn't? Digitizing somebody's brain and uploading it to a computer? I mean, yeah, it's far-fetched, but considering our last mission involved recovering a literal Roswell alien—"

"Not that part. That's hard to swallow, but you're right, we've seen weirder, especially once you throw magic into the mix." Harmony looked over her shoulder, back to the distant lights of the forest lodge, and shook her head. "That *can't* be what the Treatment is. Carlton Grassley got the Treatment this morning. It took twenty years off his face and hands."

"Sure," Jessie said, tugging the duffel's zipper back. "I did think it's weird that Bobby didn't look any different. Less coked up, maybe, and he fixed his hair situation, but otherwise you wouldn't be able to tell the difference."

"Right, but more to the point...I shook his hand, Jessie. I *touched* Carlton. Then I watched him walk out of the lodge, right through the lobby doors. A hologram can't do any of that. Also, Bobby said Muffy and Charles performed the operation to upload him, right? Well, they're not here. We saw Carlton on the gurney, and *Victoria* was the one performing his surgery."

"Like they got sold two different products," Jessie said.

"We haven't seen the whole story yet. And I don't think Bobby could tell us, even if we cornered him somehow, because I don't think he knows."

Jessie pulled the flaps of the duffel back, exposing matte-black steel. In the distance, a shout went up. Maglite beams strobed between the trees, hunting for movement.

"Think later, fight now. Catch."

The Wilson Combat SFX9, locked and loaded with rounds designed to shred a human body like cheap paper, sailed toward Harmony. She snatched the pistol, spun it in her grip, checked the mag, and snapped the safety to the *off* position. Jessie hoisted the Zastava, leaning it against her shoulder as she rose to her full height.

"Kev, April, still with us?" she said.

"Right here," Kevin said. "Drone's down. Also, your mom is pissed."

"Good work, both of you. We're on foot, being hunted, and we have definitely overstayed our welcome with the locals. Need an evac pronto."

Aselia joined the call, hopping onto a free headset.

"We're wheels up in five, ladies, and headed your way. Only problem is, need a clearing big enough to set this bird down in. There's a good spot about two klicks south of your position. Stick to the woods but run parallel to the old logging road 'bout as close as you dare to get, and you'll find it."

Two klicks was a little over a mile, maybe ten minutes on foot if they hustled and kept to the forest, depending on how rough the terrain was between here and there. Faster if they broke cover and took the logging road, but then they'd be totally exposed, sitting ducks for the guards' hunting rifles.

The woods were slower, and the fastest they could move was a brisk but careful jog — with this many brambles, roots, and fallen branches underfoot, every misstep risked a turned ankle or worse. Their only advantage was that the hunters faced the same risks and had to pace themselves the same way.

Except Althea can see in the dark, Harmony thought.

Maglite beams flashed at their backs, cresting a rise as Harmony and Jessie half-ran, half-slid down the wet and muddy embankment, hands out to catch themselves at the bottom.

"There! Down there!"

Suddenly they were framed in a dazzling oval of light. Much too big to be a flashlight: had to be some kind of battery-powered spotlight. It tracked them as bullets whined and thwipped into the mud around their feet. Harmony spun, jogging backwards, raising her pistol and squinting for targets. There were two, now three figures cresting the rise, silhouetted in the flashlight beams at their backs. One held the sun in his hands. She squeezed off a shot. The man on the crest let out a yelp like an injured dog and tumbled back, and the sun went down.

The other silhouettes faded back. Ears perked as they broke into a run again, Harmony listened for distant voices, the squawk of radios, the pounding of boots through the underbrush. Her breath was growing ragged. Running a kilometer was no big deal, and jogging one was light morning exercise. Doing it in the dark, though, in the thorns and brambles with a pack of killers on your heels, was an entirely different proposition.

"This way," she gasped, pointing.

Jessie followed her lead but side-eyed her. "Gonna take longer to reach exfil, and that's a little close to the logging road for comfort."

"They're not dumb, they won't try coming at us from the rise again. They'll circle around. We go this way, angle southeast, it'll take the hunters on foot longer to find us again."

Not the ones on wheels, though. As Harmony and Jessie ran along the edge of the rough muddy road, keeping to the trees and ditches, they heard distant shouts and the growl of engines closing in from behind. The night took on a chaotic nightmare haze, every glimmer of moonlight through the skeletal trees resembling the glint off a sniper's scope, every rustle of branches and loping creature of the forests becoming a killer on the prowl.

A rifle cracked and blew away a chunk of bark just to Harmony's left, spraying her with splinters and moss. She went for cover, pulling Jessie with her, putting a stout tree between her and the sound of the shooter. She chanced a peek out. Couldn't see anything.

"He's wearing night vision goggles," Jessie said, taking a knee on the other side of the tree trunk. Her turquoise eyes glittered in the dark. "All by his lonesome, but that shot's going to bring his buddies and it looks like he's on the radio. He's behind cover, not sure I can hit him from here."

Harmony took a second to catch her breath, her heart hammering from the run, her back and arms caked in cold sweat.

"I'll flush him out," she said.

Jessie lifted an eyebrow. "You sure?"

"Just don't miss."

Every second they stayed pinned would just bring more heat, more bullets, more doom raining down. She had to risk it. Harmony took one last breath, got into a sprinter's stance, and broke from cover.

Chapter Thirty-Six

Harmony ran for the logging road, loud and reckless on purpose, making herself a plum target for the shooter with the night vision goggles. If Jessie missed, if he landed his next shot, she'd never see it coming. Just lights out from behind, and that would be the end of everything.

Jessie didn't miss.

She had the Zastava ready, her lupine eyes locked on target. The sniper knelt up, took aim at Harmony's back, and she pulled the trigger. He went down, pitching backward off his heels, his heart-blood a spray of oil in the moonlight.

Harmony reached the logging road only to be framed in a single headlight, an ATV lurching off a bump in the mud into the air before slamming down, the rider holding on with one hand and bringing up a pistol with the other. Harmony didn't hesitate, raising her pistol in a two-hand grip and firing a pair of HST rounds. The first shot went wide. She dialed in for the second. The expanding bullet punched into the rider and threw him from the saddle, not much left of his chest but bloody hamburger meat and a crater the size of a fist. The ATV flipped and rolled, crashing into a ditch on the far side of the trail.

A second rider was right on his heels, and he angled his machine straight toward Harmony, blinding her with the high-beams as he gunned the engine and poured on speed.

Jessie exploded from the treeline like a cannonball, rifle slung over her shoulder, hands out and fingers curled like claws. She hit the rider from the side and hauled him off the ATV, bones cracking as he hit the dirt with her knees against his ribcage. Harmony threw herself out of the speeding four wheeler's path, hitting the mud on her shoulder and rolling, the machine fishtailing before it sputtered to a stop.

Her eyes were still adjusting, no longer dazzled by the headlight. She made out the dark silhouette of the rider thrashing as Jessie's head descended on his exposed throat. She bit, ripped, and tore, arching her back and tossing her mane as his hot arterial blood sprayed into the night air like a fountain.

Harmony pushed herself back to her feet as Jessie trotted up, wiping the back of her hand across her mouth. Her eyes were bright, glittering in the shadows, her face was a ghoulish mask of blood spatter, and she grinned like a jackal.

"What?" Jessie said, catching the look on Harmony's face.

"Are you...you?"

"I'm always me," she said, showing her wet, scarlet teeth. "Never felt better. C'mon, they gave us a ride, let's take it. I'll drive, you've got shotgun. Well...pistol. Whatever."

She hopped onto the second ATV and Harmony got into the smooth leather saddle behind her, holding Jessie's hips tight. Shouts rose in the distance, a flood of a half-dozen Maglite beams breaking through the trees their way. Shots rang out as Jessie revved the throttle.

She plowed her way down the logging trail, every bump sending them lurching off the road before thumping hard back down, a brutal bone-jolting bull ride. A second engine roared from behind, another rider trying to catch up. Harmony held Jessie's waist with one hand and turned as far as she could, one eye shut as she lined up the iron sights. She squeezed the trigger three times, tight and fast, and the ATV's headlight and its driver died one second apart.

"Hang on," Jessie shouted over the roar of the wind. "Almost to the clearing, gotta off-road this thing!"

The ATV was built for the rigors of the forest, but their mortal bodies weren't, not at this speed, and they both leaned low as branches whipped and whistled over their heads and the wheels jolted along the rough sod. Jessie curved their approach, easing off on the throttle as the clearing came into view. It was the size of a postage stamp. Harmony cast a dubious look at the empty night sky above, a canopy of cold stars glittering down.

"Can the plane even land here?" she asked, swinging a leg over the saddle as Jessie pulled to a jolting stop.

"Any other pilot," Jessie said, "maybe, maybe not. Aselia practices this shit on her days off just for fun."

She tapped her earpiece.

"We're at the extraction point. Tell me you're close, because we've got company inbound."

"Seeing is believing," Aselia said in their ears.

The sky roared as the *Imperator* swooped down, blotting out the moon, its four propellers thundering as a storm of wind whipped the trees into a shuddering frenzy. The hunters were closing in, one pack of flashlight beams approaching from the northwest and another, a little more distant, closing in from the east. Harmony and Jessie kept behind cover in the trees, counting the seconds as the cargo door in the belly of the plane slowly descended and the plane thumped to the earth and churned to a stop.

Gunfire whistled past Harmony's ears as she sprinted from the treeline, making for the electric light ahead. She fired blind, emptied her pistol, loaded a fresh mag on the move and emptied that one too, throwing lead just to keep the hunters' heads down. Jessie was right behind her, rattling off three-round bursts from the Zastava and chopping the underbrush into explosions of shattered branches and dead leaves.

Aselia wasn't waiting. The *Imperator* started to move the second Harmony's foot hit the cargo ramp, the door slowly grinding shut as the plane spun on a dime, lining up for takeoff. Gunshots peppered the hull, sparking and ricocheting off the armored plates. Jessie clung to one of the door's hydraulic pistons, hooking an arm around it and bracing her rifle with the other, and raked the trees with blind suppression fire. Harmony scampered up the ramp, turned and got on her belly, and joined the muzzle-flash chorus as she spent the last of her bullets keeping their attackers pinned.

"Suggest y'all hit the jumpseats and strap in," Aselia said over the plane's intercom. "Bumpy is gonna be an understatement."

They ran for the seats, strapping in next to April and Kevin as the cargo plane poured on a sudden burst of speed and lifted off at a neck-breaking angle, fighting a war against physics and gunfire as it powered toward the moon. They saw the forest slip away through the last open sliver of the cargo door before it ratcheted shut, and then they were gone, airborne and flying fast, fleeing the scene of the crime.

***

A steady train of livery cars and helicopters had been coming and going from the Phoenix Clinic like clockwork for three hours now, an emergency evacuation in the middle of the night. The harried staff played the gunshots off as a random tragic incident: some desperate men, the ginned-up story went, robbed the only bank in Grahamsville and went on the run through the forest, pursued by county and state police. The situation ended in a shootout, and while — they were instructed to stress — the Clinic's clients were perfectly safe, they were evacuating the lodge to err on the side of safety.

All of the patients and most of the staff were gone now, save for the few who knew anything about the Treatment. Victoria was taking care of her nurses now, giving them their severance packages.

Althea hummed to herself as she walked backwards along a hallway, trailing pungent gasoline from a cherry-red jug and painting a long line across the carpet. Humming kept her nerves in check and her rage, always simmering and aching to boil over, under control. At least until she could get back to San Francisco and wring Roman Steranko's fucking neck.

One of the nurses sprinted up the hallway in a blind panic, arms flailing.

"Help! Doctor Carnes has gone crazy, she's killing—"

Althea barely looked up. She drew her .357, shot the nurse in the face, and holstered the gun in one smooth motion, then went back to her work.

Three more cans and she'd painted a grid of gasoline along the forest-green runners, the Lodge a match ready to be lit. Victoria joined her. The masked sorceress wore white scrubs spattered with so much blood that they looked from a distance like they'd been dyed an artful scarlet.

"One got away, did you—"

"No she didn't," Althea said, nodding back over her shoulder. "You're welcome."

"Thank you. Did you hear from Bobby?"

Althea tilted her head, lips pursed in a frown. "If Bobby is smart, he won't talk to me until I cool down. And I don't see myself cooling down anytime soon."

"If he had just let us off the leash, we would have *had* them."

"Yeah, well, he had to monologue first." Althea emptied the last drops of gasoline from her can and tossed it aside. It clattered along the runner. "Real sick of these rich assholes playing Bond villain and making us clean up the mess when everything goes sideways."

"Are you tired of the game," Victoria asked, "or are you just tired of the henchman role?"

Althea turned her way, a faint curious smile playing at the corners of her mouth.

"What are you thinking, doc?"

Victoria sauntered toward her, slow, a graceful prowl. She stared up at Althea, almost toe to toe.

"Ben Crohn is utterly obsessed with revenge against April Cassidy. We can use that, then discard him. That's the only reason Bobby conjured him back from hell in the first place. He's not exactly easy to look at, or much of a conversationalist with those hooks in his face."

"Keep talking," Althea said.

"Roman's a liability. And a lecherous little shitweasel, but I repeat myself. The nice thing about hackers is, they're replaceable."

Victoria reached up. Her surgical glove, still glistening with blood, traced a feather-light path along Althea's shoulder.

"I'm thinking," she purred, "that a couple of enterprising women like ourselves could do some real damage if we assembled our *own* team. No more answering to a halfwit for a boss. Our plans, our profits."

Althea nodded slowly.

"I like it," she said. "But going against Praeda is a bad idea. You know what those people are capable of."

"So we finish the job. I mean, not like I'm going to let Harmony live after what she did to my face, and you and your daughter have an overdue reunion ahead. Then we take our money and...invest in our future together."

Althea's phone started to buzz against her hip. She tugged it out, holding up a finger for silence.

"I like it. We'll talk. Soon." She put the phone to her ear. "Speak."

"Muffy here. How goes the cleanup?"

"We're about to make s'mores around the campfire, want some?"

"I want you and Victoria on a plane immediately. This entire situation has gone south and our masters at Praeda are asking sharply pointed questions."

Your masters, Althea wanted to say. *I'm a free wolf, not a fucking slave like you.* But she knew better, so she gritted her teeth and forced a smile.

"Yes, ma'am. Anything you say, ma'am."

"I'm noting elevated stress levels in your voice."

"Well, *ma'am*, Vicky and I had this situation locked down before Bobby had to grandstand and Roman screwed the pooch, so I might be a tiny bit aggravated at the moment. Ma'am."

Muffy's sigh gusted through the phone.

"It might be time for some...contract renegotiations. I'd like to speak to you and Doctor Carnes privately upon your return. Please don't mention this to anyone. Especially not Bobby. He's a bit fragile at the moment."

"Noted."

"Oh, and please remember to take plenty of Vitamin C before you get on the plane," Muffy added. "That pressurized cabin air is terrible for your health, and I want you both to stay healthy and safe."

Althea hung up. She turned to Victoria.

"From crisis, opportunity. That's my motto. Anyway, light this shit up."

They emerged from the burning lodge side by side, leaving the wreckage at their backs.

Chapter Thirty-Seven

T he plan was to head straight for San Francisco. The team had one lead left, and it was right back where they'd started: ProcGen. Either Muffy was there, or someone would know where she was. With Charles Stepford completely off the grid, she was the last known tie to the conspiracy. Harmony wanted her. Badly.

They had to put down at a desolate airstrip outside Kalamazoo for refueling and repairs. While most of the small-caliber fire hadn't done much more than scratch the *Imperator*'s armored hull, Aselia reported from the cockpit that one of her engine lights was flickering amber and it needed a full diagnostic for safety's sake before they could take flight again. While she and Marco got to work, the rest of the team gathered around the strategy table.

"We've received reports that the Phoenix Clinic has burned to the ground," April said, "with an as yet undermined number of corpses found in the rubble. My guess is cutting loose ends: anyone who had inside knowledge of their real operations but wasn't deemed valuable enough to keep around."

"Stepford was already in the wind," Jessie said. "I have to imagine he's smart enough to keep his head down until the ashes settle. We won't find him, not without a serious stroke of luck."

April pushed her bifocals up on her nose, nodding in agreement.

"And we never count on luck. That leaves us Muffy St. John and the ProcGen offices."

"Harmony's instincts were right as usual," Kevin said, looking her way. "You nailed it. That delay in Bobby's responses? Check this out."

He set a tablet on the stainless-steel table and spun it around, pulling up a graph with the flick of a fingertip. It showed a sudden, sharp spike of data, along with a trail of IP addresses.

"He — I mean, you know, the thing he is now — was never at the Clinic. He was broadcasting remotely. Now, I can't track it to a specific IP or location because it was cycling like crazy, probably a security measure, but what I *could* do was measure the difference in time between the broadcast and its origin point and calculate what that lag means in terms of real-world distances."

"Let me guess," Jessie said, "it'd line up perfectly if he was somewhere near, say, the ProcGen corporate campus?"

Kevin held up a finger. "I need to be clear and say it's just a measurement of distance, no direction included. He could be in northern Canada or South America or on an oil rig somewhere in the middle of the ocean for all I know. We know he had an offshore lair at one point and we never did find the place. But, yeah, the data holds."

"Something struck me when Roman appeared on that screen via webcam," Harmony added. "The background. He was sitting in a corporate office. Clean, pristine...that's not his style at all. Like he was borrowing it."

Kevin snapped his fingers. "Mercury. Look, now we know that Roman was Mercury's secret partner. They worked together to develop tougher security systems for ProcGen, Phoenix, probably the whole Praeda octopus."

"And Mercury Blaise," Jessie said, "in her cover role as 'Molly Millions, Director of Network Security,' has a private office at the ProcGen campus. How much you want to bet he's camping out at her desk? Look, right now, the bad guys know we're onto them. We slipped *both* of their traps and they've got to be running on fumes. I wouldn't be surprised if Muffy goes underground, takes her schemes with her, and leaves us mopping up her leftovers. We need to hit these people and squeeze them for every bit of intel we can before she gets the chance to cut any more loose ends."

"I would strongly advise against going in blind," April said. "Especially now that we know their 'strategist' is Benjamin Crohn. Remember the dog whistle and the flasher that were clearly built to target you, Jessie? Exactly the sort of thing Ben would come up with, and we have no idea what else he's been cooking up. For all we know, this is a failsafe in motion, and he *wants* you to raid the ProcGen offices because he has something suitably nasty cooked and ready just for you and Harmony."

Jessie cocked her head to one side. "Because that's how you'd play it, right?"

"If I was trying to kill you both?" April folded her wrinkled hands in her lap. "Yes. I would absolutely feign falling back to lick my wounds while luring you into an ambush. And I would save my best tricks for last, for when I needed them most. We were partners for a long time, remember. I know how he thinks, and he knows how I think. While I have absolutely no respect for the corrupt clout-chaser he became, much less…whatever he is now, now that hell's had its way with him, I would never pretend he's anything less than brilliant."

"We need an insider," Kevin said. "And it's not like anybody on Team Evil is going to flip—"

"We're not calling them that," Jessie said.

"I'm just saying, Bobby not only put together a team with people capable of mirroring everything we can do, every single one of 'em hates our guts."

Harmony drummed her short-cropped fingernails on the steel table. She offered up a tiny smile.

"But not everyone working for Bobby — or for Praeda — is part of Team Evil. In fact, one person in particular never got an invitation."

Jessie broke into a toothy smile. "Mercury."

"I saw her emails," Kevin said. "She *loathes* Roman. I mean, more than most people. The only reason she was involved in Chicago, kicking this whole mess off, was because he shoved her into the line of fire. Someone did that to me, I'd be looking for a change of scenery."

"Perhaps we can force her hand," April mused. "The initial contact between Mercury and Herbert West was carried out over a dark web trading site. We know how to reach her there, presumably out of her bosses' sight. Kevin, is there any way you could commandeer West's account?"

Kevin grimaced. "Not easily, not fast. Whole point of using the dark web is that it's leagues more secure than your average website. If I had a week to work on it, maybe, but I feel like this is an 'hours' deadline, not a 'days' deadline, right?"

"Correct. Well, then. I suggest we try the direct approach. I'm going to dictate a private message for you to send. Please write it down word for word. If this works, she'll respond exactly the way we want. Just not the way she *thinks* we want."

***

Mercury Blaise was having a shit day, on top of her shit week, the capstone on a shit month. The whole situation at the Phoenix Clinic had gone fubar and now everyone was running around like chickens with their heads cut off. None of that was her problem, *her* security work was tight as a steel drum like always, but the feudal samurai of old had a saying: piss rolls downhill.

This wasn't the first time she'd found herself surrounded by chaos and people looking for someone, anyone, to blame for it. And while she hoped Muffy would protect her from Praeda's weird-ass freak parade, her boss was more and more scarce of late, sending her Gaia AI double to meet her behalf. Considering Gaia had the digital brain of a squirrel who had been repeatedly hit by a car, that didn't bode well for anyone's future.

Now she was staring at her custom-built laptop, safe and snug behind seven proxies, and staring at a private message for her eyes only.

There are times when a person takes the wrong step, opens the wrong door, and finds themselves in a world they were not prepared to face. A world they didn't even know was real.

We are Vigilant. Our job is to save those people. But we are not here to save you.

We know that before working for Muffy St. John, you had no interest in, probably no belief in, the occult. By now you've seen enough to know better, but you're still not the kind of game we hunt. We are coming for your employer. She will not survive. Neither will you, if you're there when we arrive.

Here is your one and only chance to escape: surrender to the civilian authorities. Hand yourself over and confess to your past crimes. You'll do hard time, but there's a good chance you'll beat most of the charges. Stick around, and you'll face our brand of justice. There will be no court of appeals.

The choice is yours, but decide today. Tomorrow is too late.

Mercury sagged in her chair, tilting her head back and staring up at the heavens.

"*Fuck me*," she groaned. "Okay, okay, okay, I can salvage this. This...this is a good thing, really. I've got safe houses, I've got money caches, I can go underground and outlast all of these jerks. Yeah. Just gotta make a graceful exit stage left. If they're focused on Muffy, they won't be looking for me."

She grabbed her phone and called Santiago.

"I hate saying you were right not to get mixed up in this business," she told him, "but you were right. Book us on the first flight out of SFO. How about we hit up that beach resort you like down in Cabo? We can coast on our savings for a year, soak up some sun, and get back to work when the cash runs low."

He liked that idea. Done deal.

***

They had a layover in Atlanta.

Mercury and Santiago walked side by side, silent, through teeming halls filled with swirls of tourists and travelers. They blended in, dressed in civilian disguises that made them look like a pair of bohemian day trippers with cheap hats and plastic sunglasses.

She had slipped out of the ProcGen offices without a word to anyone and burned everything she couldn't take with her in a trash can behind her condo, ready to put this nightmare behind her. The prospect of a few months on a beach, frosty drink in hand, felt real good right about now. Real good.

"Gotta take a piss," Santiago grunted in Spanish.

"You need me to hold it for you?" she said. "G'head, I'll meet you over at the bar."

***

Santiago was bellied up to a urinal, air thick with the stench of piss and industrial disinfectant, when his senses twigged to a threat. A minute ago, the bathroom had been filled with fellow travelers doing their business, but suddenly the sound of the sinks had stopped dead and he wasn't hearing any flushes, either. He was alone at the row of urinals except for one man, cop build, cop shoes, who was taking his time getting his fly open.

They made fleeting eye contact, just for a second.

Santiago's hands moved like lightning, slapping his hips to draw a pair of ceramic daggers. Two men jumped him from behind, TSA agents, trying to wrestle him to the ground. He rammed his elbow into one man's nose, shattered it in a spray of blood, got loose, and tried to slash at the other's throat, but the agent jumped back and the blade sliced stale air.

A heel rammed into the back of his knee, driving him to the floor, and a hand clamped on one wrist with eye-watering pressure. He twisted his hip and stabbed with the other blade. Jessie grappled his left wrist and twisted it until he dropped the weapon, but he was still in the fight, trying to gut her with the right as they wrestled for control over the knife.

She punched him in the solar plexus twice, sucking the wind out of his sails. Then she spun him around and bounced his head against the urinal. He dropped like a rock to the piss-spattered tile floor, clutching his skull and groaning. Jessie brandished a pair of zip ties and trussed him up like a prize hog.

***

Santiago had been gone too long.

Mercury was at the airport bar waiting for her cocktail, but she hadn't stayed in the game this long without developing a sixth sense for danger. She had a contingency, as always. *Forget the connecting flight. Walk out, grab a cab to anywhere, hole up in a hotel room and wait for Santiago to make contact.*

She was about to execute the plan, tossing a crumpled twenty onto the bar, when a familiar woman sat down beside her.

"Leaving without your drink?" Harmony asked.

Mercury froze. She had a ceramic blade strapped to her ankle, easy enough to reach from her perch on the bar stool, and the bitch was in the perfect spot to get her throat slashed.

"You're thinking," Harmony said, her tone soft and conversational, "about murdering me. But you know you can't do it without making a massive scene. You're inside Atlanta International Airport, on the wrong side of the security gate for a quick escape. You have to pass through a TSA checkpoint to get out, not to mention a tram ride and about a quarter mile of terminal walkway. Even if you manage it, by the time you reach the exits every cop in Atlanta will be outside with guns drawn and ready. Now, with that in mind, please calmly look behind you."

Mercury slowly turned. She couldn't miss the obvious: while the crowded bar was mostly innocuous, travelers grabbing a quick drink before their flights just like her, she easily picked out three or four faces looking her way and waiting for her to make a move. Civilian clothes, but with bulges under their jackets.

"You're fast," Harmony said. "Pretty sure you can kill me if you want. But you'll hit the floor right behind me. So you have to ask yourself...do you really want to die today? Or would you like a chance to make your connecting flight?"

"Make my..." Mercury's voice trailed off. She blinked at Harmony, confused now.

"Hear me out," Harmony said. "And we'll see what happens. It's all up to you."

Chapter Thirty-Eight

"You played me," Mercury said.

She sat across from Harmony and Jessie at a little metalwork table in the back corner of the airport bar. Uncuffed for now, but she'd agreed to keep her hands on the table for the sake of courtesy. Besides, Jessie had plucked her ankle knife from its sheath upon her arrival, and she didn't have much left to fight with unless she felt like throwing her plastic margarita glass in someone's face.

"We did," Harmony said, amiable. "We knew there was no chance of you turning yourself in. The point of the message was to convince you to run, to get out from under Muffy's protection. We already had a list of your past aliases thanks to your old heists, and we figured that on short notice, no time to prepare a fresh identity, you'd reuse one."

"From there," Jessie added, "it was just a matter of coordinating with the FBI and the TSA. We had you clocked the second you walked into the airport in San Fran. We waited until you landed just to make sure you had to walk through security first. Figured you wouldn't risk carrying a gun on the plane, given that you didn't think anyone would be looking for you."

Mercury sipped her margarita and shrugged.

"There can't be more than a thimble of booze in this thing," she muttered. "Anyway, fair play. You got me, and I'm not happy about it, but credit where credit's due. Where's my boy?"

"Sitting in a holding cell and waiting for Interpol," Harmony said. "You may or may not be joining him, depending on how helpful you can be. I'm guessing, that when Muffy recruited you, you didn't realize what she was really into."

Muffy snorted. "Hell no. Wouldn't have gotten anywhere near this weird crap if I had. She brought me on board to handle security for ProcGen and a few other companies. She knew my whole deal and she was cool with it. That was the arrangement: she gave me a legal job to launder cash with, I had free rein to research new heists while I was off the clock, and all I had to do was make her servers bulletproof. It wasn't until she got her hooks in that I realized I was in over my head. Way over my head. These people aren't human. Well, I mean, Muffy is, but have you seen—"

She stopped suddenly, staring intently at Jessie's dark glasses.

"She's got eyes just like yours, you know that?"

"Althea," Jessie said.

"Yeah. You two related or something?"

"Something like that."

"So you know. My first week there, I was already thinking about backing out. Then some contractor working on Project Soul got cold feet first and tried to run."

Mercury leaned closer to the table, lowering her voice.

"Althea fucking *ate* him. And I swear, I think she picked the parts he didn't need first, to keep him alive and screaming as long as she could. She got off on it."

"Fear," Jessie said, her tone flat, "marinates the meat. Tell us about Project Soul."

"Assuming you already know most of it, considering the news out of the Phoenix Clinic. You met Bobby, right?"

Harmony nodded. "Is it true? He's been...uploaded?"

"Oh, it's true all right, at least as far as I know. The world's first sentient digital entity. Now, that said, I was *not* an insider. I never even got to look at his code, as bad as I wanted to, and I wasn't gonna risk getting invited to dinner with

Althea for poking around where I shouldn't. Muffy actually offered it to me, you know."

"The Treatment?" Harmony asked.

"Yeah. She thought I'd really be down for it, considering I'm kind of a sci-fi buff. And I liked the idea in principle, but...nah. See, humor me. Do you believe in the human soul?"

"I can tell you," Harmony said, "that the human soul absolutely, unequivocally exists."

"See? I knew it. I've read a lot about theories of consciousness, too — McGilchrist, Jung, Huxley, Blackmore, you name it. So Muffy claims that it's not just a neural upload, it's *spiritual*. Like, literally transferring you, the whole you, soul and all, into the machine."

"And you didn't buy it?" Jessie asked.

"Sounds like a hell of a risk. You ever watch *Star Trek*?"

"Sure."

"Who's your favorite captain?"

"Janeway," Jessie said.

"All right. Respect. I'm guessing your partner here is more of a Picard chick. Anyway, you know the whole thing about transporters, right? Roddenberry made it clear how they work. They literally disintegrate you — kill you — and rebuild your molecules on other side. So you've got the classic Trekkie debate: if that's how it works, then is the person who comes out on the other end of the transport beam really you? Or do you die, dead for good, and the person on the other end is just...a soulless carbon copy? The people around you will never know, because you talk the same, act the same, but *you* would sure as hell know."

Mercury tossed back a swig from her margarita glass, shook her head, and winced as she swallowed.

"I don't need to ride the cutting edge that badly. Anyway, Muffy reports to her bosses at Praeda Electronics. I don't know their deal, and I don't want to, because everything I've seen out of that place is scary as hell. But I do know they've been using the Phoenix Clinic to give the Treatment to rich weirdos and probably raking in hundreds of millions, cash money. Here's the weird thing:

you'd need a metric ton of data storage for that project, right? But only one patient is stored at ProcGen's HQ. Bobby Diehl. I have no idea what happens to the others."

"Help me with that," Harmony said. "I met one of the recipients of the Treatment after his procedure. He wasn't a hologram. We shook hands, and I watched him leave the lodge."

Mercury squinted. "Nah. You couldn't have. The upload process is...I don't know the medical jargon or anything, but it's destructive. A big chunk of brain tissue literally gets seared away as it's translated into data. Nothing's left but root functions, a vegetable, then they give 'em a lethal injection to put the body down. There wouldn't be anything left to walk around *with*."

"Is it possible," Harmony said, following her hunch, "that what they're calling the Treatment is actually two different procedures? Some customers get one, some get the other?"

She shrugged. "Anything's possible with this crowd. I mean, look, at the risk of being cynical, 'you don't get what you pay for' is kinda Silicon Valley's whole thing these days. Have you meet Gaia?"

"Unfortunately," Jessie said.

"However bad you think that piece of crap is, trust me, it's worse. Last week I asked it for a healthy lunch suggestion. She told me to glue rocks to a carrot to get my daily requirement of minerals. That thing is in no way, shape, or form ready for prime time."

She glanced off to the side, furtive for a moment.

"Tell you what is, though. That whole spiel about data security? Total BS. Once 'Wellness 2.0' goes live, every word spoken in listening distance of a Gaia-connected app gets piped straight to ProcGen. People are gonna dox themselves left and right without even knowing it. That's the real product they're selling. Their own customers' private data."

Harmony took that in. They'd suspected exactly as much, but it was good to have confirmation. More to the point, it sounded like Mercury was ready to play ball.

"We're getting ready to stage a raid on ProcGen's offices," she said. "We want you to help us."

Mercury leaned back in her chair. "Now's the part where I ask what I get in return. And no, 'we'll put in a good word with the DA' isn't going to cut it, so don't waste my time."

"Queen for a day," Jessie said.

Mercury blinked.

"You tell us everything we want to know and hold nothing back. In return, you walk. We never caught you, we never met, we never had this conversation. One hour from now, you're back on your trip to Cabo."

"Me and Santiago," she countered.

"No." Jessie placed her hands on the table, her voice firm. "He's got civilian blood on his hands, gallons of it, and we couldn't save him if we wanted to. Which I don't. He's going down, but you don't have to. We know you don't like violence, you try to do the whole 'in and out without a trace' cat burglar routine, and that's the only reason you're getting this offer. Doesn't mean you're not a criminal, but you do industrial heists. We're Vigilant. We don't cover that. Your life outside the occult underworld is between you and the feds. Keep your nose out of our sphere, and you never have to meet us again."

They gave her a second to think it over, while she drank down the dregs from her plastic margarita glass.

"Eh, he'll land on his feet," Mercury said as she set the glass down. "Let's do business. First things first, if you mean 'help you' by physically getting you into the building, no can do. I burned my access card and employee IDs on the way out of town, and they change the secure-area keycodes on the regular. I can give you mine, but I guarantee they won't work."

"That's fine," Harmony said. "We can handle the doors, we're more interested in what we'll be up against once we get inside. That, and any vectors for a digital attack. Our hacker managed to get into ProcGen's network but ran into a...I believe he called it a 'dungeon?'"

Mercury quirked a smile. "Nice. My setup got pen tested by the glowies, and my setup won. Might sound petty, but the way my day is going I really needed the ego boost. All right, let's start with that. I can give you my backdoors, handshake protocols, everything you need to make the local servers stand up and dance. All that shit is mine in case of a rainy day, so there's no chance they've found 'em yet, let alone plugged the holes. They forced me to work with Roman, and I didn't trust that little dick not to stab me in the back so I installed the backdoor just in case he ever tried to lock me out. One catch: it only works via direct access, not remotely, so your console cowboy's gonna need to be physically onsite to say 'open sesame.' Can she handle that?"

"He can," Jessie said.

"Ooh. 'He.' You know, it's impressive that he even got to the dungeon. Not a lot of people can hang in my weight class. He cute?"

"He's too young for you."

"Oh come *on*," Kevin's voice crackled through her earpiece. "Damn it, I'm never going to get a goth girlfriend. Never."

"*Que será, será*," Mercury said with a twirl of her black-painted fingernails. "On the physical front, anticipate traps. I'm sure you already figured out that a lot of that business back in Chicago — the dog whistle, the LED flasher — was a test run to see how you'd react."

"I'm guessing that was Ben Crohn's brainchild," Jessie said.

Mercury laughed. "Oh, hell yeah. He is *terrified* of you. I'd say piss-scared, but I think they ripped off his...well. I mean, they told me you sent the guy to hell. It left a certain indelible psychological mark. He came up with the designs and tested them on Althea first. She was so pissed off she almost unplugged him on the spot. Bobby had to talk her down."

"Unplugged him?" Harmony asked.

"Okay, so this is secondhand info. I don't understand this magic shit and I don't want to. After everything I've seen these last few months, I'm gonna need to invest most of my heist money in a good therapist. Allegedly, just before Bobby relinquished his mortal coil, he figured out a way to conjure Crohn back from the Bad Place. It's this...techno-magic thing, a big round stone slab engraved with occult shit and packed with circuitry."

Harmony nodded. She had seen it on the camera feed back at the lodge, a conjuring pentacle with a modern-day twist. Very much up Bobby Diehl's alley.

"He wouldn't tell anyone how he built it, only that if the generator powering the thing ever went offline — poof, Crohn's going straight downtown, no return ticket. Anyway, I don't know the details, but Muffy had contractors come in for an overnight and installed his anti-freak gadgets in strategic spots. Not everywhere, and they don't go off on their own—"

"Because Althea is just as vulnerable as I am," Jessie said.

Mercury pointed a finger gun at her. "Bingo. Muffy's got a remote control to operate the things just in case of emergency. Grab her remote, you're safe."

"Did he build anything to deal with me?" Harmony asked.

"That's Victoria's job. He said you've got a whole bag of tricks, but your batteries run out fast. Victoria's only got the one trick, but she can do it all day long, like a fire hose...that...spews fire. Okay, shitty analogy, but you get my meaning. He said that pound for pound, she can bring you down with brute force."

Harmony contemplated the road that had brought her here. All the life changes, the mutation of her magic, the way her alien biology had taken Nadine's curse and planted it like a seed in the bed of her own heart. Crohn had last squared off against the old Harmony, the one who could manage a single burst of powerful magic before collapsing in a pile of jelly.

The old Harmony was gone, and she wasn't coming back.

That didn't change the facts at hand. He was right about one thing: Victoria Carnes was a powerhouse, a pyrokinetic witch fueled by rage. Harmony wouldn't win in a fair, level, toe-to-toe fight. Her job, then, was simple: don't give her one.

"Back on our tour of ProcGen," Jessie said, "we got into the server room. I'm assuming that's not the real deal."

Mercury shook her head. "I mean, sort of? That's where we keep all the stuff the government is allowed to see. Employee records, payroll, basic R&D files. If you want the juicy stuff you have to go up to the second floor. That's not just the C-suite offices; there's a secure clean room where all the Project Soul data is stored, along with the bits and bytes that make up Bobby Diehl. Bobby's not on the normal servers; they've got a special tandem rig set up for him, custom-built, with tech I've never seen before. Quantum stuff, with some kinda cutting-edge coolant that moves with a mind of its own. Trust me, you'll know it when you see it."

"If they know there's trouble coming," Harmony asked, "is there any failsafe in place? Any plan to transfer that data elsewhere?"

"There is, but it has to be manually triggered from either my office PC or Muffy's. Well, Roman's office now, and he's welcome to it. The bad news is, unless you've got some serious ninja shit up your sleeve, they're going to see you coming. Ben Crohn's got access to every camera on the corporate campus, and considering he can't leave that stone circle he's got nothing to do but watch for trouble. He doesn't sleep either, so going in at night won't help any. After dark, you've also got double the armed security to deal with."

Mercury held up a finger.

"But there's a little good news. That only applies to basic proprietary data. Tech specs, internal emails, payroll, that kind of thing. You're asking about Bobby, right? You want to know if there's a dozen more copies of him sitting around out there somewhere."

"The thought crossed my mind," Harmony said.

"Nope. Not yet, anyway. You know that custom rig I mentioned? Had to be built from the ground up to accommodate him. When somebody gets digitized, it doesn't just suck up ungodly amounts of memory and power, you need a whole carefully built framework to keep the lab rat from going—" Mercury twirled a finger around her ear and whistled. "Muffy said they tried to make a copy of Bobby once, to see what would happen. Then she went pale, paler than usual, and said 'he came back wrong.' Whatever they got, it was enough to stop them from trying that again. There's just the one and only Bobby Diehl. You take out the rig, you take out the man."

Jessie grabbed a cocktail napkin and set a pen on top of it, sliding it across the table.

"We're going to need you to draw us a map."

Mercury took up the pen and gave it a click.

"I'll throw in a bonus," she said as she began to sketch the floor plan. "You know that prototype LED flasher I used on you back in Chicago?"

"Hard to forget."

"Want it? My car's parked in the garage back at SFO. Flasher's in the glove compartment. If you get a chance to use it on Althea, give that creepy cannibal bitch my regards."

Chapter Thirty-Nine

"What do you mean, Linder isn't back yet?" Jessie demanded.

The *Imperator* sat in a secure hangar at the edge of San Francisco International, bullet-pocked wings casting a hawkish shadow across the oil-stained concrete. Jessie paced under their shroud, phone to her ear, a secure line open to headquarters.

"He's been incommunicado since he left on that undisclosed mission, ma'am. Though I did find out something...odd."

"Hit me."

"According to his admin, he left after getting a call on one of the *old* lines. The black phones."

There were three black phones, vintage Bakelite models straight out of the 1950s, lined up on a shelf in Linder's office at Vigilant headquarters. They had been his constant companions since long before Jessie met him, following him from job to job, office to office, and in all the time she'd known him, she had never heard one ring.

She had checked once, sneaking a look when he was out. They weren't connected to anything. Dead cords, nestled against a wall without a landline jack.

"Thanks," she said. "If you hear anything from him, anything at all, call me back."

She couldn't worry about this right now. Bigger fish to fry.

In the belly of the plane, Kevin had commandeered the strategy table, putting the finishing touches on a new drone to replace the one they'd lost at the clinic.

Not entirely from scratch — he usually had four or five builds in progress at any given time, his hobby as much as it was his job, and tooling up the new one just meant building in a special little surprise.

The new drone was a quadrotor about the size of a pizza box, matte black, with a forward-facing camera and a sleek, fat curve in its belly studded with LED diodes. The size and shape of the onboard weapon made Jessie think of a claymore mine. *Front toward enemy*, she thought as she strolled up the cargo ramp, pocketing her phone.

"Kev, how we looking?"

He wore a magnifying visor over his eyes, which he flipped up with the tip of his screwdriver as he raised his head.

"One hour, boss. That includes flight checks. That's a real estimate, not an engineer estimate, so please don't tell me to do it in half that time."

"An hour you can have. Harmony? Wexler come through with the good stuff?"

Over by the console, the mouth of a cheap canvas backpack yawned open next to a small pile of C4 bricks, each plastic explosive the size of a stick of butter. Harmony carefully inserted the prongs of a remote detonator into one brick, then put it in the pack to join the rest.

"Enough to level the building," she said. "Also, the courier from headquarters just arrived with a shipment of DOVE shells, fresh from the armory."

They had stolen their latest technological edge straight from the Ardentis weapon labs. DOVE rounds — the name was an acronym for Directed Overload Voltage Emitter — were shotgun slugs with a recessed spiral channel along their length, strung with copper wire. They were designed to be less than lethal, packing a brutal punch and an electric onslaught in every blast.

"Good deal. Aunt April?"

April gave her wheels a shove, rolling her chair over to the table. She glanced down at a tablet on her lap.

"Just confirmed. The equipment Kevin needs for his social engineering gambit should arrive within the hour. That's the last of the gear."

Jessie leaned closer, pitching her voice a bit softer.

"You ready for this?"

April arched an eyebrow. "You mean, am I ready to go mind to mind against Benjamin Crohn, the man I once shared a reputation and a bed with?"

"I wasn't going to put it quite that way, but yeah."

Behind her bifocals, April's eyes were cold, blue-tinged and iron hard.

"In the name of wealth and power, Benjamin betrayed his badge, his country, and humanity itself. He falsified evidence, sent innocent people to prison, and that's not even getting into what he did on behalf of the demonic courts. I won't lie, I was shocked to see him back from the grave." She pushed her glasses up on her nose. "But please believe me when I tell you this: I will send him back to hell with *great* gusto."

"All right." Jessie clapped her hands together. "Huddle up, team. We all agree on the basics: at this point, Muffy and company know the jig is up. We survived everything they could throw at us, and ProcGen is obviously our next target. They're going to be expecting us. In fact, under normal circumstances, I — and this is me talking, the queen of reckless choices — wouldn't touch that place with a ten-foot pole. But that clean room on the second floor is, for now, the home of what's left of Bobby Diehl."

She paced the steel floor, her bootheels clicking.

"Diehl is the worst enemy we've ever faced. He's been directly responsible for the abduction, torture, and murder of multiple Vigilant agents. He unleashed a bioweapon attack on Harmony's hometown, deliberately targeting civilians. He builds monsters and sets them loose for fun. In short, this fucker needs to *go*. Data or flesh, he dies today. And so does his entire crew. We could almost thank Muffy, in a way. She just handed us a golden opportunity to take all our old foes off the board with one big play."

"Benjamin knows how we operate," April said. "More to the point, he knows how I operate. He'll be anticipating a nighttime infiltration, maximum stealth. Mercury's disclosure about how he's wired into the surveillance grid, plus the custom traps he built, lays his counterstrategy bare. Slip in under the cover of darkness and you'll find a remarkably easy path ahead of you, funneling you straight into a kill box."

"They don't know that we flipped Mercury and got the inside scoop," Jessie added. "For once, we've got the information advantage. To exploit that advantage, we're going off script and pulling something Bobby and company won't see coming. Kevin, you got everything you need?"

"As soon as the rest of the gear arrives," he said. "Thanks to the handshake protocols Mercury gave us, all you need to do is get me into that clean room and I can shut Bobby down for good."

"You okay with this? Going back into the field?"

He looked up from his work again, meeting her gaze. He nodded, firm.

"That's the job," he said.

"Good man. Harmony? You ready?"

Harmony held up a butter stick of C4, tiny detonator pinned into it like a jeweled brooch.

"I'm still concerned about all the unanswered questions," she replied, "but one fact is self-evident. The only reason Praeda Electronics and its people launched an attack on Vigilant is because they want — they *need* — us out of the way for whatever they're planning next. This is a golden opportunity to stop or at least delay their plans. We can't let it slip away."

April nodded grimly.

"There are times when investigation must take a back seat, in favor of direct action and the judicious use of violence. As for me...it's funny. I keep thinking about the last time I met Benjamin face to face. He mocked me, quite cruelly, for being 'confined' to this wheelchair."

Her gaze slid to the table, and to the sleek new drone, awaiting flight.

"Now he's bound to a summoning circle." A faint bitter smile rose to April's lips. "And as for me? I don't feel confined in the slightest. Let's go pay our old enemies a surprise visit."

***

As a young man, a blue flamer rising like lightning through the ranks of the FBI, Ben Crohn had scoffed at the notion of hell.

"The human mind is resilient," he was fond of saying, "and can get used to anything. Over time, after a century, even a lake of fire would hold no terror, because you wouldn't remember what it didn't feel like to burn."

Then he got dragged down into the pit, a plaything in the hands of the demons he'd oppressed and consumed to steal their power, and realized it was so much worse than a lake of fire. He had forgotten the essential ingredient of a truly horrifying hell: *creativity*. And his captors were very creative.

Now he was a ragged, ghostly shell of what he'd been, a stretched, torn ghost dangling from hooks in a neon-lit pentacle, surrounded by security monitors on tripods in a dark tiled side room just off Muffy's private office. Still in agony — every move, every breath a fresh burning ordeal. And a slave. Bobby had made it clear that if he even thought of disobeying or if he slipped one inch out of line, the generator would shut off and he'd go straight back to his eager and waiting torturers.

When he decided to steal power by exploiting captive demons, he had made a terrible mistake. He had done the worst thing you could do to a demon, committed the unforgivable sin: he had insulted them. And they had all eternity to punish him for it.

But now he was safely in the land of the living, on the right side of the veil, and not only did he have a second chance, he had happy work to occupy his time. Soon Vigilant would make their move. Maybe even tonight, under cover of darkness, slipping in like thieves intent on plunder. They would find no succor here, only death. And with Temple and Black neutralized in his perfect trap, April would be so deliciously vulnerable, a prize ready to be plucked and savored at his leisure.

He had so much pain to share.

Ben cast a casual glance over the monitors, then paused. Something was wrong.

Two cars were lined up at the security booth on the outer perimeter, waiting to get into the campus parking lot. No surprise there: it was early afternoon, they were probably coming back from a late lunch. But instead of a guard with a clipboard checking IDs and working the gate, the security hut stood empty.

He cycled the feed, checking the parking lot cameras, and froze.

Harmony and Jessie marched toward the office building in broad day-light, swaggering across the parking lot like they owned it. Harmony carried a heavy-looking pack over one shoulder, a tactical shotgun slung across her chest on a nylon harness. Jessie cradled a second shotgun in her grip. Kevin was at their side, wearing a heavy mountaineering backpack and a Kevlar vest, a bulky pistol on his hip. A black quadrotor drone hovered in the air at his shoulder, keeping pace.

Jessie reached up, took hold of her sunglasses, and whipped them off, tossing them across the asphalt. She gazed up at the security camera with her glowing, radioactive eyes, and raised her middle finger.

"Muffy," Ben called out, his voice rising to a panicked squeak. *"We have a problem!"*

Chapter Forty

The office doors thundered open and the team strode into the lobby. Harmony rushed over and yanked the closest fire alarm. A klaxon sounded, alternating with an electronic voice that calmly instructed employees to walk, not run, to the nearest emergency exit.

One of the receptionists jumped up and ran. The other reached for the desk phone, but her hand froze mid-grab as Jessie leveled the shotgun at her.

"*Leave,*" Jessie said. "*Now.*"

The scene in the Great Hall was a polite stampede, one that became markedly less polite when the churning crowd of employees got a look at the guns. Someone screamed. That set it off: people stampeded in all directions. The drone, with April at the helm, fired straight upward to the rafters for a bird's-eye view of the swirling chaos.

"Heads up," April said in their ears. "North-facing door. Althea and Muffy."

***

Althea spotted them through the panicked crowd, three targets standing stone-still like rocks in a whitewater river. Her hand slapped the grip of the Magnum at her side.

Muffy grabbed her wrist. "Are you nuts? You don't have a clear shot! You'll hit my employees."

Althea turned her head slowly, glowering down at her.

"You can get new ones."

"I like my employees," Muffy snapped. "And they're expensive."

Althea jerked her hand away, breaking Muffy's cold grip.

"You don't ever want to touch me like that again."

"Just wait for the crowd to clear out. We'll have the whole building to play cat and mouse."

Althea watched, her eyes burning, as the team split up. Harmony went west, bulky backpack bouncing on her shoulder, while Jessie and Kevin headed east through the employee cafeteria.

"Pardon me," she told Muffy, stepping past her. "I see a couple of those mice right now. Haven't had lunch yet and I am *famished*."

***

"As expected," April said, watching the drone cam feed from the plane, "Althea can't resist the bait. Jessie and Kevin, she's on your heels. Harmony, you're clear for the moment. Make it count."

Jessie clasped Kevin's shoulder as they came to a three-way junction. Proc-Gen employees ran the other way, pounding footsteps muffled under the constant electronic drone of the fire alarm.

"Okay, I'm gonna hang here and make sure Althea follows me on a fun little goose chase. You know what to do."

He flipped a quick salute. "On it, boss."

They had all committed Mercury's cocktail-napkin map to memory. He followed the ragged lines of black ink to the left and then right, making his way to the second-floor stairs. Just shy of his destination, he ducked into an alcove and dropped his heavy backpack on the tile floor, yanking the zipper back.

Inside nestled an SFFD firefighter's hat along with a dark, heavy coat, black and lined with yellow visibility strips. He changed fast and was already moving again as he pulled on the finishing touch, a neck lanyard attached to a completely bogus ID card.

"Fire department, coming through!" he shouted as he climbed the stairs, fighting against the stream of bodies. "Keep it calm and orderly, people! Just make your way to the nearest exit, no pushing, no running in the halls. We've got this under control."

At the top of the stairs, an engineer in a plastic clean suit came out of the server room and started to seal the door. He was tugging his helmet off, catching his breath, when Kevin cornered him.

"You. Get this door open right now. Orders of the San Francisco Fire Department."

He blinked. "Uh, I'm really not supposed to, um—"

"Do I look like I'm screwing around?" Kevin barked at him. He shoved his badge into the man's sweaty face and yanked it away fast. "Does this badge say I'm the firefighter in charge of playing games with idiots? Listen pal, we're looking at a class three which is precisely seventy-two seconds from turning into a class *five*, and you know who's gonna be held responsible for that? *You*. In fact, this needs to go into the official report. What's your name, so we can call your family and tell 'em you won't be home for the next twenty years due to your ass being in *prison*?"

"Uh, let me just..."

He keyed in his code. The secure door opened with a hydraulic hiss and a whiff of machine oil. He had never seen a server room with security like this. Meant he was in the right place, at least.

"Thank you for your service, citizen. You're free to go."

Kevin walked into the abandoned clean room, listening to the door whisk shut at his back, peeling off the heavy coat and tossing his hat into the corner. Then he stopped dead in his tracks.

The room was pristine, museum-cold, with floor tiles cast in soft blue and walls of faintly luminous white plastic. Immaculate server racks stood in regimented rows, pulsing in unison beneath four round ceiling lights, like a quartet of vast moons. But that was nothing compared to the discovery waiting at the far end of the room.

Two bulky custom rigs loomed there, like tanks made of gleaming brushed steel mounted upon white plastic plinths. Exposed coolant tubes ran along their sides, pulsing with viscous black oil.

Not oil. He stared at the transparent tubes, watching the way the liquid bubbled and slurped, sparking an eerie memory. He tapped his earpiece.

"Uh, I'm in, but this is beyond weird. They've got some tech in here I've never seen before, a couple of massive rigs, custom-built for certain, and here's the kicker: I'm pretty sure they're using Ink as coolant."

Harmony's voice crackled in his ear: "Say again?"

"It's Ink," he repeated. "I mean, we'd have to get a sample back to the lab to verify, but...it's got a distinctive way of moving."

Ink had been a brainchild of the interdimensional mob known as the Network, a party drug designed to turn its addicts into psychic antennae. Since its debut, more and more forces in the occult underground had fought to get their hands on the recipe, going far beyond the original factory design. Ink, it turned out, had an unintended side effect: it was naturally attuned to the energies of the multiverse itself.

And Muffy was using it to keep her computers cool. He couldn't even begin to speculate why, not until he got under the hood.

"Can you handle it?" Jessie asked.

Kevin grabbed his laptop, flipped open the clamshell, jacked a USB cable into its side and circled the two alien machines, hunting for an open port.

"Count on me," he said.

***

Kicking back in Mercury's office with a cold Pepsi, his dirty gym shoes propped on the desk, Roman lazily watched a steady stream of data scroll along his monitor. The fire alarms were still whining, muffled by the closed office door, but Muffy had gotten in touch quick and told him the score. Hostiles on site, so stay put, keep the door locked, and get ready to rumble.

And here it was. Not the way he expected. He shot bolt upright, swinging his legs down, as internet ports began to flick from *open* to *closed* one by one.

ProcGen security was bulletproof. He knew that because he'd built it especially with that little shit Kevin in mind. Kevin was a coward. He didn't go on missions in person. He'd try to hack in from outside and fail, utterly, lost in the dungeon.

But here was a warning alarm just for Roman, telling him that somebody was here, physically in the clean room, directly attacking the network through a backdoor that only could have been created by a single person.

"Mercury," he growled, "you traitorous bitch."

No time to think about it. He sprang into action, tossing back a swig of soda before he spun up a counterattack.

"You want a duel, Kevvie? Yeah, okay, fine. Let's duel."

***

Kevin had modified the new drone for stealth. While it was hardly invisible, it flitted through the high hallways of ProcGen's office complex, humming above the heads of the evacuating employees, barely noticed in the chaos. April still considered herself an amateur pilot at best, but she kept her hands steady on the controls and flew by remote camera, navigating the maze.

She wanted to get eyes on Muffy's office. On her way, just shy of the polished double doors, a side passage whispered open. A steel-clad security door swung wide of its own volition.

An invitation to the dance if I've ever seen one, she thought, her eyes narrowing behind her glasses. *All right. You've enticed me.*

Beyond the door, the drone dipped into a dark, dismal room floored in dark tile, plastic sheeting tacked up over bare concrete walls. Dim light glowed from a cluster of security monitors but the overhead lights were cold and dead. All it needed was a drain in the floor to look like a butcher's perfect abattoir.

Dangling from his splintered cross and fishhook chains, Ben Crohn raised his spectral head. His lips, what was left of them, twisted in an approximation of a grin.

"April. That is you, isn't it?"

Kevin had built a small speaker into the belly of the drone. April adjusted her headset, her fingertip hovering over the *talk* button. She almost didn't touch it. Her throat felt bone dry. She hesitated, just for a moment, then pressed it down.

"Hello, Ben."

"Come to revel in my downfall?" He raised one arm, flayed flesh drooping like a cloak. "I'm not as handsome as I once was."

"You were ugly long before you went to hell, Ben," April said. "A strong jawline doesn't do much to make up for moral rot."

"And yet you seem drawn to me. I'll give you this, you really did surprise me, April. A brazen daylight assault? Not your style. But you always were good at thinking outside the box, even if you were too much of a coward to turn that genius intellect into profit and power like me."

"And look where that got you," April said.

He gestured to the monitors all around him, inviting her to take a look. She saw her team scattered, on the move, carrying out the plan. Harmony ducked out of an empty office, backpack riding on her shoulder. Jessie roved up a hallway, Althea's shadow looming at her heels. Kevin sat cross-legged on the clean room floor, laptop hooked to one of the strange custom servers, typing up a storm.

"I prepared for this," Ben said. "All of this. I didn't just join Bobby's 'team,' I trained its members. Day in, day out, drilling them on the best ways to neutralize their counterparts. You surprised me today, but this changes nothing. All you had to do was set foot on the battlefield, and you instantly lost the war. Stay with me for old times' sake, will you? We can watch your friends die together."

Chapter Forty-One

The doors to Muffy's office swung wide and Jessie marched in, shotgun braced against her shoulder, ready to fire. She took the whole room in at once. Glass desk, glass chandelier, a wall of bookshelves lined with pristine, never-opened covers, a monitor on the wall offering a view of Crohn's prison down the hall. Muffy sat in her high-backed executive chair, primped and coiffed and regal, with Victoria Carnes standing at her shoulder.

Before Jessie could pull the trigger, Muffy brandished a slender television remote and clicked a button.

A pair of tall Bose speakers on tripods, strategically spaced to the left and right of the office doorway, erupted to life. Jessie dropped to her knees, the shotgun slipping from her grip and clattering to the floor. She clutched her ears as ultrasonic sound bombarded her like a barrage of punches from a heavyweight boxer. The noise was all-consuming, devouring her thoughts, driving out all reason and replacing it with raw electric pain.

The assault ended as soon as it began, leaving her senses reeling, her muscles too stunned and shaky to move.

"Don't kill her yet," Muffy said as Althea loomed in the doorway. "She's good bait. Just get her weapon."

Althea paused. "Put the remote down first."

Muffy rolled her eyes, held up the remote, and set it down on her desk. Only then did Althea enter the crossfire, scooping up the shotgun and moving around the desk to flank Muffy's chair.

"I'll stay on *this* side of the office," she said, "just to be clear."

***

Kevin was halfway done when Roman swept in like a digital grim reaper, answering the call to battle.

Roman launched a denial-of-service attack, aiming to overload Kevin's laptop with traffic until it slowed to molasses. He countered by throwing up a pair of firewalls and hopping to a different branch of the network like a train jumping rails. That worked for a second, until Roman anticipated his next move and met him with an injection of code that hit his hard drive like a pool of spreading acid.

Their digital duel had turned physical. Roman was attacking Kevin's rig directly now, spiking the CPU heat to the point that the chips would literally start to fry one by one if he didn't do something fast. Roman was aiming to stop the hack by reducing his gear to a barbecued hunk of worthless plastic.

Kevin's fingers flew as he worked harder, faster, digging deep to pull out every dirty trick he ever learned. It was a losing battle, but he still had to try.

***

Watching through the drone cam, April hovered near Ben's pentacle. Together, on his security monitors, they saw Jessie go down. She was alone, incapacitated and disarmed, outnumbered three to one.

"And this is how your family dies," Ben said. "The only family you've ever had, anyway. Does it hurt? Knowing that you're responsible for this? Just admit it: I outsmarted you. I beat you."

Sitting back in her wheelchair on the *Imperator*, April allowed herself a tiny, thin smile.

"Harmony," she said over the private comms, "Jessie is down. The trap is exactly where we anticipated, and the remote control is on Muffy's desk. She's got Victoria and Althea with her. Initiate phase two."

In the dank, gloomy containment chamber, Ben appeared to take her sudden silence as regret.

"What? Nothing to say?" he gloated. "Too proud to admit when you've been bested by a superior mind?"

"Actually," she told him over the drone's tinny speaker, "we just needed the lay of the land. We knew about the sonic trap, just not the specifics. We had to nail it down before we could make our next move."

His one remaining eyelid blinked. "Excuse me?"

"It's called 'taking one for the team,' Benjamin. A concept that you know precious little about."

***

Jessie was still weak, pushing herself up to her shaky knees, when Harmony stormed into the office. She had her shotgun slung over her shoulder, one hand holding her backpack high.

The other held a detonator, with her thumb on the trigger.

"I've got enough C4 to level this building and I *will* set it off," Harmony said. "Stand down. Hands open and visible, keep them where I can see them. Any sudden moves, and we all die together."

"Bullshit," Althea said, taking one stomping step toward her.

Muffy held her back with her arm, eyes wide. "Wait. Wait a second."

She turned to the monitor on the wall.

"Ben? You walked us through twenty possible assault scenarios, and this was *not* one of them. Could really use some guidance right about now."

On the screen, his mutilated face twitched, his bluster flickering and fading.

"Well, that's, I mean...that's a difficult question to answer—"

"Tell them the truth." Harmony turned, facing the screen. "Think back. You read my Vigilant file, back when you were running the show. You know my history, the things I've done. You know how many times I've thrown myself into the meat grinder without hesitation to save one civilian life."

She paused, taking a breath.

"And now I'm standing in the belly of the beast, surrounded by some of the most evil people I've ever known, people who are going to wreak untold havoc if I drop the ball today. So tell me something, *former* Director Crohn, master profiler, behavioral science pioneer. Look in my eyes and tell me...am I the kind of woman who would commit suicide to get the job done? Would I kill myself, without hesitation, to end this right here and now?"

His flayed throat worked as he swallowed, hard.

"She means it," he rasped. "She'll do it. Don't go near her. Stand down."

"You three," she said, nodding across the glass desk. "Turn around, face the wall, and place your hands behind your heads."

A steel tube, mounted high in the corner of the office, whirred to life. A beam of light shot down, and Bobby Diehl joined the party.

"Hey folks, Bobby Diehl here! Now, does that include me too?" He waved his arms together and through each other, making them sparkle and break into dust before reforming once more. "Because I'm a little hard to cuff. No wrists."

Jessie winced as she pushed up from one knee, still wobbly from the sonic attack. "We've got somebody taking care of your ass right now, don't you worry about that."

"Mm, oops, bad news. Status update!" He leaned over Muffy's desk. "Roman's beating the kid like a rented mule. You can go ahead and thank me now, for pulling this five-star team together."

Muffy stared at his hologram. Something shifted behind the woman's eyes. The bubbly talk show host persona, her cheerleader spunk, vanished. What replaced it was cold. Reptilian.

"I told you to stay in your server until I called for you."

"Yeah, well, I'm not good at taking orders from chicks, unless I'm telling them how I want my sandwich made."

Dead silence. He looked around the office, from Victoria, to Muffy, to Althea, to Harmony and Jessie. He winced.

"Oof, yeah, sorry, forgot I was dealing with the estrogen brigade over here. I tell ya, that joke kills in the boardroom."

Muffy inhaled through gritted teeth.

"I brought you here," she said, "for one purpose. To eliminate Vigilant Lock. And did you succeed? No. You failed at every possible turn. Now I'm sitting in my personal office, my private sanctum, staring at a madwoman with a pack of explosives and a detonator. You are rapidly outliving your usefulness, which was limited to begin with."

"You have to break a few eggs to make an omelet, you know? I'm working on it."

Muffy ignored him, turning to Harmony instead.

"Did you know that Bobby had stomach cancer? When he came to me, he wasn't just a disgraced, coked-out exile, he was looking at the prospect of spending the last agonizing months of his life handcuffed to a bed in a prison hospital. I offered him an alternative."

"The Treatment," Harmony said.

"No. I offered him something I *claimed* was the Treatment."

Bobby blinked, his body rippling with static. "Excuse me?"

"He had caches of money all over the world, goods to trade, favors to call in. I milked him like a cow." Muffy wore a nasty little smirk now. "He was afraid of dying. Even more afraid of what would happen after that. His one chance of escaping hell lay with the Network, but they don't like losers and had already abandoned him. His only salvation...was me. And when a man is desperate for salvation, he'll believe anything you tell him."

Bobby waved a hand in front of her. "Hello? Hey, pay attention to me, please? Why are you talking about me like I'm not here?"

Muffy put her hands flat on the glass desk.

"Because you're not Bobby Diehl," she said. "You're an iPhone app with delusions of grandeur."

Althea slowly turned to stare at Muffy, eyes wide. Victoria looked placid, and Harmony knew why. She had been the head of surgery at the Phoenix Clinic, standing in for Charles Stepford, the clinic's mouthpiece and frontman. Whatever the Treatment really was, she knew all the inside dirt. She'd just been keeping it to herself until now.

"I mean, Harmony—" Muffy paused. "Can I call you Harmony? You're a professional witch. I'm guessing, given how far you made it today and her conspicuous absence, that you managed to interrogate Mercury Blaise and wring her dry. When you learned about the Treatment — well, the Treatment as she knew it, since I never let her into the inner circle — how did you react?"

"It seemed..." Harmony chose the next word carefully. "...improbable."

Muffy laughed, slapping her hand on the desk.

"That's a very diplomatic way to say 'complete nonsense.' It's absurd! Digitizing a human soul? Come on, don't be ridiculous. Nobody can do that."

Bobby took a silent step back, his hologram shivering, flickering with a wash of static.

"But...but you said...you promised..."

She fixed him with a serpentine glare.

"Grow up, you whiny little worm. You've been ripping people off your entire life. A little too late to cry 'unfair' now that it finally happened to you." She turned back to Harmony. "Nobody falls for a con quite like an overconfident con artist. Anyway, we really do have a radically advanced AI prototype — leagues better than Gaia, not for public consumption considering it eats electricity like candy and there's no way to make it profitable. And we really have been working on advanced methods of brain scanning, so Bobby...Bobby was our lab rat. We created an imprint of his neural network, slapped it onto a large language model, and programmed it to think it was the real person."

Bobby stared at her, gaping in horror. "But if I'm not...I mean, then Bobby..."

Muffy shrugged. "I shot him up with a lethal cocktail of drugs and watched his EKG flatline, so my best guess is he's in hell right now answering to a whole bunch of angry former victims and people he screwed over. Sucks to be him. Oh, well! Now go back to your room."

She snapped her fingers and the hologram died, winking out of existence.

Harmony still brandished the detonator, her thumb on the trigger. "This changes nothing. Turn and face the wall, hands behind your heads."

Althea looked from Muffy, to her, and back again.

"Do you trust me?" Althea asked, her voice low.

Muffy smiled. "You and Victoria are the only members of this operation who haven't bitterly disappointed me. You have my absolute trust. Do as you will."

Without warning, Althea charged across the office in a wild burst of homicidal fury. She shoulder-checked Jessie, throwing her to the carpet, blindingly fast. One more step and she punched Harmony across the jaw with her bare knuckles, a spine-jolting blow that sent Harmony sprawling to her knees with blood gushing from a cut lip, and snatched the backpack out of her hands as she fell.

"She was bluffing, and Crohn should have known it," Althea growled as she unzipped the backpack. She turned it upside down and gave it a shake. Books on business, management, and accounting, hardcovers for weight and bulk, pelted the carpet around her combat boots. "He was only half right, the wrong half."

Muffy leaned forward, propping her elbows on the glass desk and cupping her chin in her hands, beaming. "Do tell."

"Some profiler — can't see past his own goddamn nose. Of course she would die for the mission, like the good little soldier she is. But you know what else I know?" Althea stood over Harmony, imperious. Harmony reached for the shotgun, but Althea brought her heel down, pinning Harmony's hand to the floor, slowly crushing her knuckles with cruel pressure. "This bitch is in love with my daughter. I can smell it on her. She'll kill herself, but she won't kill Jessie."

Harmony grimaced against the pain, her bones threatening to fracture under Althea's weight. She still had the detonator in her other hand.

"Half right," she croaked.

Althea squinted at her.

"Look at those books. They won't be familiar to you, but Muffy should recognize them. She bought them."

Muffy pushed her chair back, craning her neck.

"Are those from...the executive lounge downstairs?"

"I planted the bombs before I came up here," Harmony said. "You were half right, Althea. Wrong half."

She clicked the detonator's trigger.

"Boom."

Chapter Forty-Two

A ll they needed was time. Time for the fire alarm to do its job, time for the civilians to clear out and leave the ProcGen campus an empty battlefield. The Bobby AI had, unwittingly, given it to them.

Now, as one, the butter sticks of C4 — planted all over the facility, under desks and behind support pillars and tossed down the mail room delivery chute — ignited as one. The building rocked as earsplitting eruptions went off in a chain of fireworks, blasting offices into debris and flooding the halls with flame and billowing smoke.

"Basic rule of warfare," Harmony told Muffy. "If you can't capture an asset...deny it to the enemy."

Althea bared her teeth and raised her other boot high to bring it down on Harmony's head, when Jessie hit her from behind. She clung to Althea's back, one arm squeezing tight around her throat, struggling to choke her out. Althea staggered back and swung her around the room.

Muffy clutched at the remote control for the sonic trap, but Victoria slapped her hand out of the way. "No! You'll hurt Althea!"

Harmony grabbed her shotgun, but Victoria was faster on the draw. She had a split second to let go of the gun, raise both palms, and conjure a shield of hardened air as Victoria unleashed a plume of searing furnace-fire at her. Harmony was a hero with only a shield to protect her, facing down a dragon's breath as the blistering, howling torrent shoved her backward along the carpet, scorching the wall behind her black and igniting the furniture.

Althea rammed her elbow into Jessie's ribs and threw her, slamming her flat onto her back on the office floor. She stomped her foot down. Jessie rolled out of the way just in time, only to catch a fist to the back of her head when she tried to get back on her feet. She grunted, hitting the wall, dazed and brutalized as Althea eagerly grabbed her neck with one hand and her belt with the other, hoisting Jessie's limp body high above her head.

***

Ensconced in the clean room, Kevin heard the bombs go off, felt the building shake, but he couldn't lose focus. Roman had outflanked him at every turn, a lightning-fast chess match of feints and attacks, and Kevin knew he was all but finished. His laptop was literally melting, every meter in the red, the fan screaming like a jet engine. He had less than five minutes to pull a miracle out of his backpack.

He was all out of miracles.

***

"For what it's worth," Ben said, watching the chaos unfold on his bank of security monitors, "you put up a better fight than I expected. But in the end, it just wasn't good enough, was it? Admit it, April. Give me this much. Admit that I beat you. You owe me that."

Back on the *Imperator*, April stared at the drone feed, but she wasn't really there. She was deep inside herself, nestled in a steel trap, weighing every angle, every last clue, looking for a glimmer of hope.

On the feeds, Althea was beating Jessie within an inch of her life. She couldn't tell how things were going on Kevin's end, but his body language on the security camera reeked of despair. Harmony was holding her own, pitting her magical shield against Victoria's conjured flames, but Ben's profile was right: she

CRAIG SCHAEFER

couldn't win like that. Her strength would fail before Victoria's did, and then she would die screaming.

His profile, she thought.

Don't think about the enemies they're fighting. Think about the one I'm fighting.

Ben's greatest weakness is the sin of sloth. As an agent, he cut corners, took the easy way out every time. Never put in the hard work. What did he say when I first arrived?

"I didn't just join Bobby's 'team,' I trained its members. Day in, day out, drilling them on the best ways to neutralize their counterparts."

That was it.

She jumped onto the private channel, heart pounding.

"Team, listen to me! Ben only trained his people in how to beat their *exact counterparts*. Switch targets!"

She hauled on the yoke, her drone spinning away from Ben's room and firing up the hallway toward Muffy's office.

"Harmony, take Althea. Jessie, neutralize Roman. Kevin, take Ben."

***

Good advice, but Harmony didn't know how. She was flagging, her body caked in burning sweat, her shield of conjured air beginning to fracture and fail as Victoria's endless onslaught beat her down with raw fury.

The drone whipped through the open doorway, launched over the steady pillar of rippling, all-consuming fire, and dropped directly in front of Victoria's face.

April triggered the flashers.

The LED lights erupted in a blinding storm, sending Victoria staggering backwards, stunned, her spell broken. Before Althea could hurl her daughter onto Muffy's table, aiming to break her back, Harmony lunged and grabbed her ankle.

She *pulled*. Toxic magic flooded Harmony's veins, her pupils dilating as she mainlined wolf-blood. It was like a shot of adrenaline straight to her heart. Althea sagged, her strength stolen, collapsing to one knee. Jessie slipped from her grip and tumbled, rolling onto her shoulder as she hit the floor, then popped up on all fours and launched herself out the office door to lope up the hall.

Harmony and Muffy both dove for the remote control. Harmony was faster, using her stolen speed, and triggered the sonic trap. Althea howled and went fetal as the weapon designed for Jessie hit her instead, pinning her between the two rigged speakers. Victoria was still recovering from the light blast, hands over her eyes, so Harmony went for Muffy first. She clamped her hand on the side of Muffy's neck, pulled, and—

Nothing.

No magic. No power to steal. Nothing there at all but a sense of a deep, empty winter's night and a howling, hungry wind. Muffy tilted her head and smiled.

"Sorry, sweetie," she said. "That doesn't work on me."

She lashed out and backhanded Harmony hard enough to send her tumbling over the desk and onto the carpet on the other side. She blacked out for a second, seeing stars, as Victoria's conjured flames licked up the office walls and threatened to swallow the entire room in choking black smoke.

***

Ben looked to the doorway of his containment room.

Kevin stood there, a fire axe in his sweaty grip.

"You know," he said, "normally I'm all about high-tech solutions, but in some cases...in some cases, you've really got to do things caveman style."

"What are you...*no!*"

Kevin charged, axe high, and brought it down on the cables running from the base of the containment pentacle. One split, sparks flying and flashing, the rest hanging on by a thread.

"Tell me something," Kevin asked, raising the axe one more time. "Did you plan for this?"

He didn't wait for an answer. The blade whistled down, chopping the last cable in half, beheading the snake. The neon glow of the containment pentacle flickered and died as a whirlwind erupted at Ben Crohn's feet, spreading, growing, howling as open-jawed skulls and desiccated bones whirled within the foul tornado. Clawed and skeletal hands latched onto his spectral form and dragged him down. He had time for one last scream as the whirlwind engulfed him.

Then it receded, sucked into the base of the rock, and took him with it.

Nothing remained but silence.

***

Roman was congratulating himself on a job well done when the office door blasted open under the heel of Jessie's boot.

"Hold on," he said, kicking his chair back and holding up his open hands, "we can talk about this—"

Those were Roman Steranko's last words. She leaped across the room, teeth bared, fingers hooked into murderous claws. There was too much work left, and Jessie didn't have time to play with her food.

***

Muffy turned off the sonics as Victoria ran to Althea and put an arm around her shoulders, helping her up. Harmony was still down, moving a little but stunned senseless, and the room was filling with billowing, strangling clouds of jet-black smoke. Victoria shot a look at her nemesis, prone on the floor, and hesitated.

"Leave her," Muffy snapped. She yanked the spine of a hardcover on the shelf behind her. The bookcase to the left swung open, revealing a private stairwell washed in the glow of pale amber emergency lights. "Let's go!"

The bookcase swung shut behind them, sealing off their escape route.

***

Kevin met up with Jessie as she emerged from the office, wiping fresh blood from her lips. She was drenched in it. He looked past her, through the open doorway, and suddenly wished he hadn't.

"Let's go," she said, not breaking her stride. "You get Crohn?"

"Confirmed kill," Kevin said. "I mean, sort of. He was already dead. Considering Bobby was the only one who knew how that pentacle worked, hopefully he'll stay that way for good."

The floor rumbled underneath them as the overhead lights flickered and died. The air smelled like a chemical burn, foul and wrong, the odor of a mortal wound.

Jessie tapped her earpiece. "Harmony. What's your status? This building's coming down, we need to evac *now*."

"On the move. Kevin, were you able to handle Bobby?"

"Started a format process running before I left the server room. It's gonna take at least twenty minutes, considering how much data needs to be wiped, but it'll get done without us. He's good as gone."

Harmony's voice was sharp. "Data can be reconstructed, yes? As long as those hard drives are physically intact, there's a chance someone could bring Bobby back."

"I mean, under normal circumstances, sure, but these aren't really—"

"I'll meet you both outside," she said.

***

One last thing to do.

Harmony headed for the clean room with murder in her eyes and a tactical shotgun in her hands.

"I'll meet you in the parking lot," she said.

Kevin had wedged the door for her. She marched between the server racks and up to the two Ink-cooled custom rigs. Then she racked the shotgun.

"Hey folks," she said to the empty room, "Harmony Black here."

A hologram projector hummed to life. The Bobby-thing stared at her, wide-eyed with horror.

"Look — listen — you don't have to do this. I can be useful! I didn't give Muffy everything, you know? I've got resources, assets! What do you want? Money? I've got money. Power? I can *get* you power. Anything you want, just name it!"

Harmony shook her head. Then she raised the shotgun and braced it against her shoulder.

"No deals, Bobby. You're dead. Let's keep it that way."

An electric slug hit the first server, punching through the brushed steel shell and setting off an eruption of sparks and licking flames. She blasted the second server, then the first again, racking the slide and firing round after round until there was nothing left but molten, sparking slag and a spreading puddle of Ink spewing from ragged rubber hoses.

She had enough left in her to conjure a single spark of magic. She let it fly, gliding like an ember to the clean room floor, where it gracefully alit in the puddle of Ink.

It went up like a bonfire. She turned her back, leaving the wreckage without a second glance, and headed for the fire escape.

✳✳✳

A rooftop door whistled open. Muffy stormed out, Althea and Victoria right behind her, muffling coughs from the smoke. A Bell helicopter, beige with the ProcGen logo on its tail, waited on the helipad with its rotors spinning. The rooftop shook, harder this time, nearly knocking them off their feet.

"We gotta go!" the pilot shouted, leaning from the open door. "No time, this whole place is coming down!"

Muffy ducked under the rotors and hauled open the back door of the helicopter, the wash nearly stealing her voice as she turned to the others.

"Ladies. You've acquitted yourselves nicely, today's setback notwithstanding. You need gainful employment, and I need skilled hands. I had to keep you at arm's length during that whole regrettable enterprise, but things have changed. I'd be pleased to bring you into the inner circle, and I know my employers will happily agree. How about it?"

Althea and Victoria shared a glance. Althea looked back at her.

"We'll need some concessions."

"We can discuss it in the air. Now, if you please..." Muffy extended her cold hand with a flourish, inviting them into the chopper. "Join me. And welcome to Praeda."

Chapter Forty-Three

The *Imperator* sailed through skies of glass, smooth and steady above a blanket of fluffy white clouds.

Harmony sat in a jumpseat, alone, holding a bag of ice against her swollen lip and getting lost in her own head.

"Sorry, sweetie. That doesn't work on me."

Muffy had ignored her magical attack. Not defended herself, not powered through it, she'd *ignored* it, like it didn't exist.

Or like she didn't, Harmony thought. *Like she was just an illusion.*

Then she had lashed out with the back of her hand, and the petite, perky TV therapist hit Harmony with the force of a sledgehammer. Her jaw was still throbbing. There was no questioning the fact that Muffy was made of flesh and bone. No hologram, no trick. And yet, on a magical level she simply *was not there.*

Jessie dropped into the seat beside Harmony, nursing a long-necked bottle of beer. "Penny for your thoughts."

"I'm still sorting those out," Harmony admitted.

"I hear you. Lot of questions, a few unsolved mysteries. So you know what we gotta do, right?"

She reached over, and patted Harmony's thigh.

"Let's go get those answers."

"I keep looking back, second-guessing everything, every choice we made—"

"And that is why you need to start drinking beer when the mission's done. Come on, I want to show you something."

She took Harmony's hand, pulled her up, and pulled her over to the strategy table.

"Kevin," Jessie said, "pull up the scoreboard."

With a click, the main wall display lit up with a string of candid photographs, profile pictures, each ringed in green neon light. Santiago's mugshot had bars across it. Others were blotted out with big green *X*'s.

"Ladies and gentlemen," Jessie said, "here's where we stand. Mercury Blaise earned a walk, but we're keeping an eye on her. Probably won't venture over to our corner of the underworld again, but if she does, we're ready to come down on her like the hammer of God. Her partner, meanwhile, is sitting snug as a cockroach in custody. Last report is three different countries are arguing over who gets to put him on trial first."

She swept her arm out to take in the rest.

"Bobby Diehl is dead, and so is his AI clone. He will not be missed. Ben Crohn is back in hell where he belongs, and this time, without Bobby's tech and know-how to conjure him, he's gonna stay there. Roman Steranko had bad taste all his life, and I can confirm that he also tasted bad in death."

Kevin winced. "Too soon."

"That leaves four targets on the board," Jessie said. "Muffy St. John, Victoria Carnes, Althea Temple-Sinclair, and Doctor Charles Stepford. Stepford is a wild card. He might be a harmless mouthpiece and a patsy, or he could be directly involved in Praeda's operations. We'll find out once he resurfaces."

April shoved her wheels, rolling up to sit alongside Jessie.

"Make no mistake," she said. "Praeda Electronics is at the heart of the octopus, and Ms. St. John is their emissary. They chose to attack us, unprovoked and without warning, to clear the decks for whatever they're planning. As of now, Vigilant's top priority is to learn their true objectives, identify their leadership, and stop them in their tracks."

Jessie nodded. "This was a win today, people. And we didn't just come home with a few trophy heads. Odds are, the Treatment — the real one, not the bogus one they sold to Bobby — is key to understanding Praeda's goals. And they handed us one hell of a clue. Kevin?"

He tapped his mouse, adding a new photograph to the board.

"Carlton Grassley the Third. We met him at the Phoenix Clinic and confirmed that he's a Treatment recipient. He's currently convalescing at his cattle ranch outside Houston. I suggest we go look him up and have a polite chat."

Harmony was getting the wind back in her sails. She stared up at the board, burning every face into her mind's eye. They had earned a brief window. A window to breathe, to lick their wounds, to regroup before heading right back into the fray. She raised a hand.

"If I may?"

"You have the floor," Jessie said.

Harmony took a breath. Looking at her teammates, her family, the people who had walked through hellfire at her side time and time again.

"This isn't like any enemy we've ever faced," she said. "Normally we move in stealth. So do our targets. Espionage is a game of shadows. But Praeda isn't interested in that. They're coming at us with guns blazing, and they aimed to wipe us out before we even knew they existed. They failed, and now, at least for the moment, the momentum is ours."

Harmony put her hands on her hips and gazed back up at the target board, locking eyes with the smiling image of Muffy St. John.

"They want an all-out war," she said. "So let's give them one."

Afterword

I f you want to amuse the gods, tell them your plans. Some years back I had just put the finishing touches on *Cold Spectrum*, Harmony and Jessie's fourth adventure, and set up the plot seed for Bobby Diehl and Team Evil (we're not calling them that) only for my then-publisher to abruptly end the series. With the rights back in my hands I finally had the ability to overhaul and very softly reboot the series to look more like my original vision, but part of that meant putting a few things on the back burner for a bit.

Still, I play a long game (even if that means shuffling my plans around and altering the outlines for two years' worth of planned stories), so I knew that plot thread would return as soon as I had an opening. Muffy gave me one (she and Praeda have been in the works for a very long time, and the seeds of their ongoing scheme can be found in the events of Never Send Roses), along with a very unpleasant chat I had on social media one afternoon. This random dude wanted to crow at me about how soon I would be homeless and begging for spare change in the streets, because generative AI was within months of making artists and authors obsolete forever and that was a good thing because…reasons, I think? He was sure that he was somehow going to become rich as a result of this mass joblessness and the death of art, though he couldn't articulate how or why that would work.

I thought, "My, what a deeply shitty person with a deeply shitty worldview. Huh. You know, I think there's a story in this. Come to think of it, Bobby would definitely be investing in this junk…"

Just goes to show: inspiration is everywhere. Even when you feel like chewing your arm off to escape a conversation you didn't want to have in the first place.

Thanks as always to my team: to Jay Ben Markson (my awesome editor), to Damonza for cover design duties, and to Susannah Jones for her always-excellent audio narration.

And thank you for spending some time with us! I hope you enjoyed the ride; Harmony and Jessie will be back again soon in their next adventure, along with a whole bunch of problems. Praeda is about to unleash their long-simmering plans upon the world, and let's just say it's going to get messy.

Made in the USA
Columbia, SC
07 January 2025

51380698R00176